Beyond This Point There Be Dragons
(The Chronicles of the Rainbow Travellers)

Beyond This Point There Be Dragons

(The Chronicles of the Rainbow Travellers)

By Julie Burgess Wells

Illustrations by Jill Ogilvy

RAINBOW PATH PUBLISHING OF KENT

An imprint of Upfront Publishing,
Peterborough.

Beyond This Point There Be Dragons
(The Chronicles of the Rainbow Travellers)
Copyright © Julie Burgess Wells 2006

LIMITED FIRST EDITION

First published 2006 by
RAINBOW PATH PUBLISHING OF KENT

An imprint of Upfront Publishing,
Peterborough.

Printed by Copytech UK Ltd.

Chapter 1

Yellow Zone - Elver

*T*here is, as humans will tell you, an Earth myth that speaks of a pot of gold at the end of the rainbow. We other beings in the Universes know the ancient truth behind the story, and clearly at one time the Old Ones of that planet must also have known. Perhaps this truth is too amazing for the human to accept; I cannot be sure because I'm not very familiar with the species. It seems sad that one race should have lost this knowledge, but perhaps their Wise Ones judged them not to be ready. The reality is quite simple. The rainbow is no brief ethereal arc, but a strong constant doorway that floats in the sky. A doorway which leads to many places in the universes.

Although beings in other dimensions are aware of this cosmic opening, only the race known as the Elverine holds its secrets. The

1

Elverine, unmistakable, incredibly beautiful even by universal standards, the Keepers of the Rainbow, Guardians of the Seven Doorways, I could go on, but all this you will gather for yourselves! Suffice to say they are trusted and honest mediators. Their traditions, folklore, and Honoured Ones go back to the beginning of time. It is the story of one of the Honoured Ones that I am about to relate; a great adventure, a quest, which I was proud to be part of. (Who am I? Ah, later, my friends.) You must bear in mind that although to the Elverine this is now ancient history, to some it is reasonably modern, for not all the lands and dimensions which lead from the rainbow are of the same age or time span ...

The day started innocently enough, it certainly did *not* have the ring of one wherein events would have repercussions throughout the universes. The air crackled with anticipation, but just the drink and be merry kind! Peolis, King of Elver (situated in the Yellow Zone for those unfamiliar with dimensional geography) had ordered a feast day to celebrate the betrothal of his son the Lord Loriscus to Silbeamia daughter of the great Lord Manuit. Peolis was known for throwing a particularly good party, so the people converged eagerly on The Place of Rejoicing.

In accordance with tradition the Wise Trees which encircled The Place of Rejoicing had intertwined their branches to create a soaring protective canopy over this sacred space; each burnished trunk forming a unique column of strength. Violet-hued leaves fluttered delicately beneath a ceiling of silver bark, shot through with sunlight from the sky beyond. A few branches had even managed to enthusiastically burst forth an occasional unseasonable blossom. Gleaming roots pushed up through the freshly mown grass to form living tables for the revellers, each twisting and curving thickly to settle into carved solid shapes, fine tendrils interlacing to give the impression of a delicate cloth thrown over the whole. Earth music thrummed from every root, trunk, branch and leaf, adding its own deep vibration to the pipes and harps of the musicians. The Elverine poured excitedly through the welcoming arches and into the newly-formed banqueting hall.

King Peolis sat on his magnificent jewel-encrusted throne that had been placed on a raised marble dais. A rainbow dazzled over and around him. There by magical invitation, it was the symbol of his power, the key to inter-dimensional travel. The Elverine alone knew the incantations for each colour, thus opening portals to every place in the universes. This secret had brought many riches to Elver, not least amongst them the gift of harmony. This peace had lasted for so long that the Elverine thought of themselves as untouchable by dark forces. Complacency is always a mistake.

A child, chest swelling with importance, climbed the dais steps carefully carrying a goblet from which the delicate aroma of spiced nectar drifted temptingly into the air. She relinquished it with obvious relief at not having spilled a drop, Peolis smiled kindly at her as she scuttled away. He sat back comfortably and watched the people dance. His wandering gaze picked out a happily grinning young man weaving his way through the masses towards the throne. The youth's long pale hair hung in the single plait of manhood. He had thrown back his dark blue cloak to reveal a simple green tunic cinched at the waist by a jewelled belt from which hung a silver engraved scabbard containing his ray shooter. As a matter of courtesy this was switched to light rather than stun, the Elverine had moved aeons beyond killing. The King raised his goblet in greeting. In response to Peolis's recognition the man clenched his hand to his chest and managed to bow whilst still pushing his way determinedly forward. Fortunately he was tall, 225 centimetres in his bare feet, and as the people saw him they nudged each other and let him pass. At last he was able to leap up lightly and stand before his monarch.

"Greetings father," his voice, attempting nonchalance, barely suppressed his excitement.

"Loriscus," Peolis nodded, lifting his goblet to his lips to hide an amused smile. Loriscus leant casually on the throne as he and the King watched the moving tapestry below them. They chatted in a desultory fashion, each pausing occasionally to acknowledge friends as they danced past. All the while Loriscus's feet moved restlessly, betraying his underlying impatience. Finally an Elverine dressed in the uniform of the King's guard approached and bent to speak in low tones to Peolis. Loriscus stood tall as the soldier drew a pipe from his belt and blew a long clear note. The music ceased instantly and the dancers stopped mid-step before surging towards the dais. Children pushed forward hurriedly, not wanting to miss anything. In contrast Peolis rose slowly to his feet and lifted his hand. The buzz of their chatter drifted into respectful silence.

"Welcome my friends," his face softened as he looked down on them. "Thank you for joining us on this special day, and many thanks especially to Virena, our trusted Weather Mage, for arranging such a beautiful day. I would also like to express our gratitude to the Wise Trees for their work in preparing the canopy and feasting tables, the Hummers for their hard work in harvesting the nectar from the celebration blossoms, not forgetting the Water Nymphs for collecting the Crystals of Tranquillity from the Magic Waterfall. As you can all see they have been crafted into magnificent feasting platters." As with all speeches the people murmured their appreciation in the right places, desperate for Peolis to get to the point. "Now we reach the reason for today's celebration," Peolis took a deep breath and looked rather emotional. "It gives me great joy to announce the betrothal between my son Loriscus and

Silbeamia, daughter of Lord Manuit." The crowd applauded tumultuously whilst the piper blew another clear note. All heads turned as Lord Manuit stepped onto the dais leading his shyly smiling daughter by the hand. There was a concerted gasp at the sight of her. She was incredibly beautiful.

Silbeamia's hair was the colour of a tender sunbeam breaking through the early morning mist; it fell like a glistening waterfall all the way to her knees. It was intricately woven and decorated with iridescent flowers, crowned by crystallised raindrops that flashed the reflected glory of the rainbow encompassing them. Her tall elegant figure was enhanced by a simple blue dress, which fitted to her hips before flowing to the floor. It perfectly matched her shining eyes.

Lord Manuit gave Silbeamia's hand to Loriscus who took it reverently before turning to grin triumphantly at his friends who were grouped languidly near the dais steps. They roared their approval, the heady scent of nectar on many a breath. A slight cloud caused a few to shiver unexpectedly, but only Virena turned her face up in puzzlement, knowing she had magicked a perfect day. Certainly no one even glanced at an Elverine woman who was emptying her goblet with an angry gesture. With her plaited golden hair and smouldering green eyes she would have been lovely had it not been for the brooding expression on her angelic face. She grabbed another jug of nectar, refilled the chalice, and gulped a hasty mouthful.

Elsewhere the Watcher tuned into her jealousy and chuckled. It was almost time.

The drummers began a rhythmical beat, the pipes joined in as the King and Lord Manuit stepped back. Loriscus and Silbeamia began the Dance of Betrothal, their commitment for the world to see.

The Watcher, eyes fixed on the scrying pool, began a dark incantation.

The Elveriness thumped down her goblet, causing a pained creak of protest from the table. She shook her head as if there was an unbearable din within, and then began to move in a trance-like fashion towards the dancing couple. Some called out as she passed "Hello Joalla," but she didn't react. Their eyes were sympathetic. Word had been that it should have been her standing up there beside Loriscus … but that was before Lord Manuit had brought his daughter to the city. Distantly she could feel their pity reaching out, yet it only served to increase the overwhelming rage that overtook her. Somewhere deep inside her Elverine nature began to war with these unnatural feelings.

The Watcher felt her waiver and strengthened the enchantment.

Peolis announced the blessing. The betrothed couple stood hand in hand before the rainbow as the people filed past to wish them joy. Loriscus could see Joalla's violet gown out of the corner of his eye, aware that it was coming closer as the procession drifted past. He suppressed a guilty pang.

The Watcher's hand clenched as it gathered the dark magic.

Joalla came at last before Silbeamia's happy face.

The unseen hand pointed.

The floating sensation left Joalla as the hissing evil sounds in her head reached a crescendo, followed by complete blackness. Then, as if it came from another place a shrill shriek erupted from her lips, her arms lifted of their own accord, and she pushed her rival with such force that Silbeamia flew backwards. The violence of the action was almost unknown in that place. Strange words streamed from Joalla, causing the King to start with shock. Galvanised into action he strode rapidly towards the two Elveriness.

Too late. What happened next became a tableau of unimaginable horror, etched in everyone's mind, but over in a second.

The portal to the Indigo Realm opened to reveal the monstrous form of Gordagn, Lord of Zorgia. Zorgia, realm of darkness from which there was no return. Silbeamia, still falling backwards, suddenly felt the vortex sucking her in. As she wrenched her head around, her amazed expression became a mask of terror. She struggled in vain as she saw the twisted hands reaching out to catch her. Peolis, already in motion, only had time to desperately grasp his son as he frantically attempted to jump in after her. Loriscus gave out a despairing cry as the portal faded. The last picture they had was of Silbeamia's now inert figure held in triumph above Gordagn's head, her hair covering her like a shroud.

Momentarily everything stood still, as if time itself were in shock. Then pandemonium erupted. Over the sound of the screaming and shouting Loriscus turned in murderous fury on the perpetrator of the crime, just as the Lord Manuit converged on her from the other direction. Joalla had fallen to her knees with the force of her violence. She rubbed her face as when awakening from a dream; her eyes were distant and misty. The fog cleared as Loriscus jerked her to her feet, snarling wordlessly. Lord Manuit was yelling loudly, an edge of hysteria to his voice. A sick sensation hit her solar plexus and she doubled over, retching soundlessly.

Meanwhile Peolis pulled the sounding pipe from the soldier's belt and blew loudly. The babble of confusion died away as all eyes looked to him for direction. At a signal from his father Loriscus released Joalla disdainfully. She fell to the floor again. Those around her drew back in disgust. Peolis however put out his hand to the Elveriness and gently raised her from the ground. She rocked unsteadily, her face bewildered. Peolis spoke to her quietly as to a lost child. His actions calmed everyone. Then he spoke aloud so that all could hear.

"What happened Joalla?"

"Happened?" Joalla sounded genuinely puzzled. She glanced nervously at Loriscus who was growling under his breath.

Peolis raised his voice further, so there could be no mistake about his next words, "Joalla did not do this, it is not possible."

Loriscus's eyes snapped to his father. "Have you gone mad?" he exclaimed in astonishment. "Of course she did this evil thing, we all saw it!" The people murmured angrily in agreement.

Peolis shook his head "It is not possible," he repeated firmly. The noise from the crowd began to rise, but once again he silenced them. "Joalla, how did you know the correct incantation to open the portal?"

"What incantation?" she asked tremulously.

Loriscus looked sceptical and exasperated, but Peolis nodded to himself. "This woman cannot have known the magic spell to open the Indigo Doorway. Think all of you. It is a secret so well guarded that only I as King and Nasturtia the Colour Mage share it." His son looked stunned, words eluded him, others gasped in realisation. Peolis continued "It is well known that the Zorgian do not acknowledge us as the Keepers, it is thus a dangerous and unused doorway. Clearly some powerful force has manipulated Joalla as an instrument to create this situation." He paused. "The question is *why*?"

"Father, whatever the reason, Silbeamia must be rescued," Loriscus was pale with reaction.

The King nodded, "My son, truly I feel for you, but we must be careful not to set the wrong chain of events in motion, we may cause your betrothed more harm."

The young prince gazed blindly at the rainbow for a moment, his shoulders slumped. He was the son of the King, and although not spoiled, used to everything falling at his feet, but now for the first time in his life he did not know what to do. Then taking a deep quavering breath he addressed the Elverine. "Who amongst you has the smallest inkling, perhaps a tale related in family lore, of any way in which the Indigo Gateway has been safely breached?" There was ominous silence. Loriscus lifted a shaking hand to shade his eyes as despair encompassed him. Then like a beam of light an unknown voice spoke up.

"Breached, yes. Safely, well that might be asking too much my Lord," it mused. There was a concerted gasp as all swivelled to its source. An old Elverine with waist-length white hair and the tunic of a traveller sat at a table, a cup of nectar before him. Loriscus strode over, hoping the ancient spoke from knowledge rather than an excess of potent liquid.

"Thank the Stars," he thought as a clear, intelligent gaze met his. The younger automatically touched his chest and bowed his head in respect for the elder. "Speak," he said aloud, noting the sympathetic gleam within the glacier blue stare.

"I am Crysgar," the stranger said simply.

"Tell me Crysgar, how may I rescue Silbeamia?"

"I cannot tell you that my Lord."

"But you said ..." frustration grated in Loriscus's voice.

"It is true that another has passed through and returned from Zorgia, although the experience changed him forever, but I am not the one to tell you of this. I can only guide you to One who knows all. It will be for you to request her aid in your quest." Crysgar looked grave.

"Who?" Loriscus was desperate.

"The Amorga," the words hung in the air. Even Peolis was amazed.

"The Amorga," Loriscus repeated doubtfully, "but does she still exist? I thought her to be part of past legend!"

"She is immortal," Crysgar stated, somewhat saddened at his ignorance.

"Why do you know of her and not us? Where is this immortal?" Loriscus demanded.

I can guide you to her," Crysgar said, then he hesitated, "Well to the lands in which she lives at least. Whether she will see you or not, or if she is willing to help you, is beyond my power to know."

"How will I know whether she will meet me?" Loriscus asked, not noticing that Crysgar had avoided the first part of his question.

"You will know," the mysterious stranger replied.

"It is a beginning and I thank you for it," hope lightened the young prince's features. "When can we start?"

"Tonight we must prepare for the journey. We do not know what the Amorga will tell us, but it is most likely only the very beginning of your quest," Crysgar said gently.

"Loriscus," a familiar voice called from the listening crowd, "let me go with you." Loriscus saw his good friend Poldant standing among the Elverine. Large, muscular, although perhaps something of a dandy with every piece of clothing matched with finicky attention to detail, he was an awesome example of a Peace Warrior, a universal traveller and negotiator in harmony. He was used to plenty of female interest, but that was the last thing on his mind. "Let me go with you," he repeated, "you may need me."

"Thank you," Loriscus nodded grimly. "I would be grateful for your company. But," he cautioned, "should the Amorga demand I travel on alone then you must return to Elver with Crysgar." Poldant nodded in curt agreement.

Meanwhile Virena and another magnificent Elveriness approached Joalla and led her to a seat, which happened to be the throne. Virena exuded power, but her companion dwarfed her into insignificance. This was Nasturtia, Colour Mage, and possessor of the Rainbow's deepest secrets. Her rich robes and haughty bearing underlined her exalted position. She nodded a brief greeting then launched into questioning the hapless Joalla without ceremony.

"Are you aware that you have spoken aloud a dark spell thought to be known to only myself and Peolis?"

"Well, I am now," Joalla pointed out with some irritation, teeth gritted. As her normally fiery spirit began to re-assert itself she was beginning to feel much misused. Virena's lips twitched, but Nasturtia's eyes flashed at such disrespect.

Virena intervened hastily "Tell us what happened inside your *head*."

Joalla's irritation disappeared instantly as the guilt came flooding in. "I don't really know ..." she tried to think, running her hands distractedly through her hair and loosening wild golden tendrils as she did so.

"Then tell us how you were *feeling*," Nasturtia prompted, her voice uncompromising.

"I was angry ... and jealous," Joalla's cheeks flamed. "Loriscus and I, you see, before Silbeamia ..." words tumbled out.

"Ah," the Colour Mage glanced pointedly at Virena who was still looking puzzled. "Someone or something knows how to enter the emotional vibration."

Virena's face cleared. "By the Stars!" she exclaimed. "To turn and use emotions ... what power!"

"Yes but the incantation? How did this being project it through Joalla and more important still, where did such knowledge come from? Not even you my friend have heard the spell before." They fell into silent reflection for a moment, while Joalla's gaze shifted anxiously from one to the other.

Peolis and Loriscus approached. Joalla automatically rose to her feet. The younger male acted as if she wasn't there but Peolis, courteous as ever, flipped his embroidered ceremonial cloak behind his shoulder and greeted all three Elveriness with a bow before addressing Nasturtia.

"Well?" he questioned briefly.

"Some power tuned into Joalla's dark side and projected the spell," Nasturtia paused, "but why is still a mystery. We must ensure in seeking the answer we do not fall into a trap."

Joalla's head shot up. "I am the key to this plot - whatever it is. I must be involved in the resolution, it is only fair! Surely I should accompany Loriscus on his journey?"

Loriscus looked furious. "What?" he almost shouted.

"You will go nowhere until we have thought this through," Nasturtia said coldly.

"Father, we shall leave at first light, whether you have an answer or not," Loriscus said determinedly. "But not you!" He pointed rudely at Joalla before marching over to Poldant and Crysgar.

Joalla's jaw set stubbornly. These people obviously didn't know her very well.

The Watcher chuckled.

Chapter 2

The gentle light of dawn found Loriscus waiting as patiently as he could for his companions in The Place of Rejoicing. The only sounds came from the occasional creak of roots being retracted back within the earth as the Wise Trees returned to normality after the feast, and the gossiping leaves which whispered of the previous night's events. Starlight, a unicorn steed, stood quietly by the Elverine he had chosen to serve. No being in its right mind would attempt to force a unicorn into anything, magical and unpredictable creatures that they are.

"They are late," Loriscus muttered, his thick, soft cloak wrapped around him against the early morning chill, shadowing eyes already dark from lack of sleep.

"No, not late, you were just very early," Starlight replied, lifting and turning his noble white head. His ears twitched, a wickedly sharp horn thrust from between them arcing sparks of magic, which hung in the air filling the space where his head had been. Even as he spoke the drumming of hooves could be heard. Loriscus's half smile of greeting wavered into puzzlement.

"Surely I can hear three riders approaching," he cocked his head to one side and listened with renewed concentration. Starlight nodded. Crysgar and Poldant rode into sight from behind some ancient gnarled trees; Poldant raised his hand in greeting. Before they could speak a third rider was seen to approach from another direction. Loriscus's bemused expression became one of flashing anger when he recognised Joalla. She sat straight and determined, her legs straddling the bare back of her unicorn, refusing to be cowed by his fury. "What do you want?" he demanded coldly, noting with some incredulity that she was dressed in travelling tunic and leggings, her feet protected by soft knee-high riding boots.

"I wish to come on the quest so that I may right the wrong I have done," she answered quietly. All three Elverine males looked taken aback for a moment.

"How dare you?"... "You must be mad!" Loriscus and Poldant spoke simultaneously.

"Hold fast my friends," Crysgar said firmly, speaking over their outrage. "By our own lore, any Elverine is entitled to have the opportunity to right a wrong that may have been committed. Do we have the authority to deny Joalla?" Joalla cast him a grateful look and then turned pleading eyes upon Loriscus and Poldant.

"Do you not see that I must try? Would not you if our roles were reversed?" she asked. Grudging respect momentarily gleamed in Loriscus's eyes. Poldant glanced questioningly at the young lord, and cocked a quizzical brow. Loriscus looked furious. However resentful of this female's presence, he was unable to prevent her joining them. Crysgar was right, damn the Dark Places, by lore she had rights. The shadow of Silbeamia tormented and alone, knifed into his mind momentarily, causing his face to set against the pain of loss. Finally, heaving a great sigh, Loriscus acceded.

"You may come as far as the Amorga. Then, as with my other companions, all depends on what I am bid." He looked Joalla coldly in the face and continued, "You must swear to return *uncomplaining* with Crysgar if it should be necessary." Joalla returned the straight look.

"I swear my lord, as does my unicorn friend Crest," she gave her pledge proudly and simply, her steed nodded in mutual agreement. Loriscus's eyes raked her disdainfully, taking in the tightly wound hair and the neat travelling pack held in place by Crest's own magical will, and then he turned his face to Poldant and Crysgar.

"Come my friends, it is time to be off, for the sun is rising fast!" The unicorns wheeled and trotted in single file behind Crysgar, their unknown guide.

Through the beautiful countryside of Elver they travelled receiving much hospitality from the good people. Willingly doors of shining cylindrical homes were thrown open to give them succour. Most knew of their quest and wished them good fortune. Joalla suffered a great deal in silence when she heard the conversations and discussions of those people. Few recognised her as the perpetrator of such treachery. She was embarrassed to receive warmth and admiration from them under the circumstances and dreaded to see the scorn in their eyes should they discover the truth. Her companions were too honourable to betray her to strangers, but although she knew this, it did not prevent the constant torture caused by her sense of guilt. At night she would awake suddenly in a sweat of horror, terrified screams echoing through her mind. By day she had to bear with Loriscus's ill-hid resentment at her presence, which he displayed by pointedly ignoring her. She knew that he also slept restlessly and muttered all the while.

Despite all this, for the first ten days the travelling was pleasant and could have been fun if it were not for the serious nature of their mission. They passed through tall forests of beautiful purple and orange leafed trees, suffused with the knowledge of more generations and history than even the Elverine could possibly tell. Carpets of flowers, brilliant in their full array of colours, surrounded them. The odour of peace and tranquillity floated on the warm breeze. The companions rode with the usual awareness of their kind. They were careful to harm no living thing, for the balance of She Who Creates must be kept. Thus the abundant life sources wandered freely around them, knowing themselves to be safe.

On the eleventh day, the terrain began to change. It became bleaker and stranger. Soon only Crysgar knew where he was. The ground was rockier and less fertile, fewer and fewer trees or animals were to be seen. The rocks became hills, and the hills rose to become mountains. The following day they reached a mountain pass, which was slippery and narrow. Grim silence prevailed, all knew that one dangerous mistake on the twisting track could cost the life of one of the Elverine or unicorns. In several places there was a sheer drop onto the rocks below and it took all the skill of their mounts to keep their precarious footing.

Suddenly, when the path was at its narrowest, Starlight pricked his ears, sniffed the air and stood stock-still. He called a low warning to his kind, and they also stopped and sniffed the air. Loriscus leant forward to murmur in Starlight's ear, "What is it?"

"I don't know," Starlight whispered, "it may be nothing but there is a scent I don't recognise." Loriscus drew his stun ray and the other Elverine did likewise. Cautiously the unicorns advanced, their ears pricked and turning for the slightest sound. Even so, none were quite prepared when they rounded a huge boulder and came face to face with a strange-looking being standing with legs astride, blocking their pathway. It gave the impression of being quite tall and broad, yet slightly translucent. Colour, mainly hues of blue, vibrated in waves from the massive head down to feet, which seemed to meld into the very soil itself. A huge green truncheon rested over its shoulder. It was difficult to see quite where its body ended, because it pulsed with barely contained energy, however the creature appeared to be powerful in shape and form, with eyes that flashed darkly.

Three stun rays were instantly pointed at the creature. It did not move or blink. Slowly it raised one hand in greeting and Loriscus cautiously followed suit. The companions relaxed back slightly in their saddles, but kept their weapons at the ready.

"Greetings to you Lord Loriscus," the creature spoke in the universal language. Loriscus started slightly at the use of his name.

"You have an advantage over me friend. How is it that you know my name? I do not recognise which dimension you come from," he responded courteously.

A deep chuckle sounded from within its barrel-like chest. "I am Camelion, of the Tribe of Changelings. I choose to be seen by you." There were gasps of comprehension and wonder as Camelion spoke. Loriscus dismounted and bowed with his hand to his chest.

"I am most honoured Camelion. We are aware it is rare for one of your tribe to choose to be seen by others. May I ask again how it is you know my name?"

"I have been walking beside you for the past three days Elverine, and therefore have come to know you and your companions well enough," he answered simply and as if such a feat was of no great account.

"It is not possible!" Starlight expostulated, insulted that any creature would claim to go undetected by him. Once again Camelion laughed.

"I made sure I flew or ran constantly down wind of you, O great unicorn. As for any other way, why, can you see me now?" He suddenly disappeared from their vision, and it was only because they were watching intently that they noticed a tiny brown creature scuttle from view. Confusion and consternation reigned for a few seconds as the unicorns restlessly stamped their hooves, and the Elverine called to one another in astonishment. Suddenly Camelion reappeared on the opposite side of the group. He walked soundlessly back to Loriscus, who bowed in acknowledgement of the trick.

"The skills of your kind are not exaggerated Camelion, you are a true shapeshifter," Loriscus stated with admiration. "What is it you want of me?" His admiration turned to puzzlement.

"Lord Loriscus," Camelion's face became serious, "I have heard of your quest and wish to accompany you." Loriscus looked surprised.

"Why?" he asked bluntly.

"I cannot yet tell of my reasons, but you know that my race is true to their sworn word. I offer my services and loyalty to this quest." Having made his oath, the changeling stood quietly, arms staunchly folded, while Loriscus pondered his words. He knew this to be too strange to be a coincidence; clearly some other hand was involved. However …

Suddenly the Elverine smiled broadly, "I would be pleased to gain your presence and skill in our company," he raised his eyebrows, "but I must tell you the same as the others. All depends on what the Amorga tells me, it may be necessary that I travel on alone."

Camelion nodded eagerly, "You will never have cause to regret your trust," he swore. The shapeshifter went forward and reached a hand in greeting to each of the rest of the companions. Joalla, Crysgar and Poldant introduced themselves and their unicorns formally even though they knew that the newcomer had already acquainted himself with them.

For the rest of the day Camelion marched seemingly tireless, and amused everyone with a display of his skill. It appeared that he had a great sense of humour. When he wasn't making them incredulous with admiration at his abilities, he had them laughing constantly at his font of jokes. Often he would metamorphose into the form of a large blue bird that flew ahead, returning to rest on

Crysgar's shoulder. Clearly his reports made the old Elverine guide smile.

The countryside became slightly more hospitable, and when they rode into a reasonably flat clearing protected to some extent by the surrounding rocks, Crysgar called out, "This is a most likely place to camp for the night. We may have to travel many leagues further before we find anything so convenient." There was general relief at the chance to stop earlier than usual. A fire was soon lit with some provisions boiling in a pot which hung over it, seemingly suspended in mid-air. Later, replete and content, they all sat sipping hot cups of nectar and telling tall stories in the warmth and light of the flickering flames. "Well," Loriscus sighed eventually, "I suppose we should turn in, who will take first watch?" Poldant opened his mouth to offer, but before he could say anything, Camelion stood up.

"Let me have the honour of the first guard duty my friend," he requested. As no one else particularly considered guard duty to be much of an honour Loriscus agreed willingly and without more ado Camelion melted into the background before their very eyes.

"I don't think I'll ever quite get used to that." Poldant looked a little disconcerted. Joalla laughed properly for the first time since the day of the feast, causing the others to look over in surprise. A slight flush spread over her cheeks.

"I'm glad he is with us and not against us," she explained. The others nodded and grinned back at her, exchanging amused looks, even Loriscus softened for the first time. No one wanted to say too much, because after all, the changeling could be standing in their midst listening. One would be a fool to make an enemy of him.

Joalla lay down by the fire more content than in many a day. The others had laughed with her, and for the first time she had felt herself to be one of them. Only Camelion was aware of Loriscus sitting gazing into the dark, his face a mask of melancholy despair.

During the night a biting wind blew up, from which they were somewhat protected by the surrounding rocks. Once they had left their shelter at daybreak however, the wind howled and tore at their cloaks causing even the mighty Starlight to walk with his head bowed in an effort to make headway. Joalla struggled on with clenched teeth. She would not for the world admit that this first real test had her secretly longing for the golden warmth of home. Crest, aware of her friend's difficulties, sought to comfort Joalla by creating warm energy within her aura. Her presence and gentle encouragement had made the early lonely days more bearable for Joalla.

By lunchtime the weather had improved and a tremulous sun lightly warmed their faces. The talk and laughter rose with their spirits and Joalla sighed with secret relief that no weak words had passed her lips. She felt moved to sing an ancient Elverine song, looking and sounding so unconsciously beautiful that her companions gradually fell silent in appreciation. Thus they were less attentive than usual and so unprepared when it happened.

Loriscus, who was walking ahead in order to stretch his legs, fell into its dark mouth with a startled cry. The path had unexpectedly dropped away into nothingness. His companions rushed forward in consternation, fearing the worst. Poldant peered anxiously over the edge of the hole. "Loriscus are you there? Are you hurt?" he shouted.

"Yes I'm uninjured," Loriscus's voice sounded surprisingly close. "Hold fast, I'll set my stun ray to give light." They heard sounds of fumbling and eventually could see an eerie light glowing as Loriscus explored his surroundings. "It's an underground cave," he called excitedly, "but I cannot see how far back it goes."

"Wait!" Poldant demanded, "Do not go on alone."

He conferred hastily with his companions and then ran to get a coil of rope from his travel pack. Tying one end around a large boulder, he threw the other end into the hole. Giving the rope a mighty tug to test its security, he nodded to Crysgar, nimbly swung over the side and climbed down to join Loriscus. Camelion sat stoically near to the edge of the cavern ready to respond immediately to any cries of alarm. Once the unicorns had gently allowed their burdens to float to the ground aided by Crysgar and Joalla, they came swiftly to join him. They talked but little, for all were afraid that they would not hear a cry of distress.

Then, Crysgar started to look around thoughtfully. He became restless and began to pace around the edges of the dark hole, every now and then kneeling and peering more closely at particular stones. When he was on about his fourth circuit, his face took on an expression of suppressed excitement.

"What are you doing?" Joalla finally demanded in exasperation.

"Look can you see ..." he pointed at the stones, but was interrupted by a deep yell emitted from below.

Is all well my friends?" Camelion's voice bounced around in the cavern.

"Yes, yes," Poldant's voice bounced back eerily, "but come and see what we have found." Joalla and Camelion leapt forward instantly, the shapeshifter taking on the form of a night bird in a blur of a split second and was about to plunge into the blackness when Crysgar halted him.

"Hold a moment," he said urgently, "I must think."

"What about?" Camelion demanded irritably, forgetting to be respectful in his hurry.

Crysgar stared quellingly at Camelion. "You see here and over there, and there again, look closely – I can see an ancient writing carved into the rock, although worn and faded through many aeons of weathering."

"Yes, very interesting, but what does it matter at this moment?" Camelion held onto his patience with difficulty. "Loriscus and Poldant may need us, we must go to them," he urged, looking to Joalla for agreement, but she stood unsure. Part of her wanted to go to the aid of Loriscus and Poldant, but her mind heeded the caution in Crysgar's words.

"What do you suggest?" she enquired of the old Elverine.

Crysgar relaxed slightly. "I think we should call them back until I have deciphered the meaning of the writing. It could be a warning, or dark magic, or some other important sign." By now Camelion stood back on solid land.

"Your words make sense." He sighed grudgingly and glanced at Joalla, who nodded firmly in agreement. It occurred to her that the changeling had been rather looking forward to a fight of some sort!

"Let Crysgar find the meaning in these stones," she said, pushing the thought to the back of her mind.

The changeling knelt down, cupped his great hands, and shouted. His voice echoed away into silence, a silence that seemed to go on forever as their ears strained for an answering sound. They looked at one another anxiously as the silence continued.

"Shall we go down?" Joalla suggested, her stomach clenching anxiously as she unclasped her ray shooter. "We may not have time after all to heed these writings."

"I'll go," Camelion said briefly before metamorphosing once again into an owl-like bird.

Fortunately, just then, much to their relief, Loriscus's cross face reappeared from out of the darkness, and Camelion rematerialised just as effortlessly.

"By the Great Star, what have you called us back for?" Loriscus demanded. Joalla remembered that he had always a slight tendency to be peremptory.

"Is Poldant with you, my Lord?" Crysgar asked urgently.

"Yes of course he is, we thought you might be in trouble and returned ready to fight." Loriscus unclenched his fist to show his weapon at the ready, it having been reset from light ray to stun. Camelion grasped the young lord's arm and swung him up easily, repeating the process for Poldant who was close behind. A startled expression flickered across Poldant's eyes as his plait pendulumed wildly, he was no lightweight, yet the changeling had lifted him like a baby.

"It is possible that you were in danger," Crysgar informed them.

"What has occurred?" Poldant asked, realising that their faces were seriously troubled.

"You see, while we were waiting for you, an old memory flittered through my mind, but was gone before I could quite grasp it." Crysgar held up his hand as Loriscus shifted impatiently. "So I walked around and examined the outer edges of the hole, and I found this and several more like it." His hand moved again, this time to indicate the faded writing on one of the rocks.

Loriscus dropped to one knee. His brow wrinkled with curiosity. "What does it mean? I have never seen this language before."

"I'm not certain," Crysgar replied hesitantly, "but obviously this is no ordinary cave, a door possibly, or an opening perhaps?" The others gazed at him expectantly, waiting for the rest of his explanation. Crysgar laughed reluctantly, "I cannot say more until I have deciphered these ancient words."

"I think my talents have been forgotten," a voice spoke from behind the group. They swung around to see Starlight standing there, tossing his noble head, and trying not to look hurt.

"By the Maker of the Universes!" Loriscus exclaimed, slapping his forehead as realisation struck him. The

Elverine grinned at one another, as the same thought rippled through them. Only Camelion stood perplexed and unsure.

"What then?" The words almost exploded out of him when it became obvious that no one was about to share their knowledge with him.

Starlight tossed his white mane again, "I see that perhaps you do not know all about me after all," he sounded rather pleased with himself, betraying how the meeting with the changeling had rankled. Handle the temperament of a unicorn with care! Camelion's face darkened angrily. Poldant stepped forward hastily, and placed a placatory hand on the newcomer's shoulder.

"We apologise for our rudeness Camelion, sometimes we forget that you are new to our ways." He smiled his golden smile; he was not a Peace Warrior for nothing. Camelion's face literally lightened – into a radiant blue. "Let me enlighten you. Starlight is a noble among unicorns, and therefore holds particular powers and knowledge."

"I am none the wiser." Camelion's hand shifted restlessly on his truncheon.

"Just a moment, I will show you," Starlight said. He trotted elegantly over to the rock that Crysgar had indicated. Bowing his beautiful head the unicorn delicately touched his horn to the worn scratchings on the rock surface. For a second or so nothing happened, causing Camelion to glance questioningly at the Elverine who were standing in a semi-circle to the side and slightly behind Starlight. The expectant look on their faces did not lessen, so his eyes returned to the rock just in time to see the magic beginning to work. The words began to glow. The glow became stronger and brighter. Initially the ancient letters showed more clearly, but as they all stared intently the form of the words shifted until they were translated into the universal language. Poldant leant forward to peer more closely at it, muttering the translation under his breath in an effort to commit it to memory. The words faded back into normality as the unicorn's power faded.

Joalla, as the one standing behind Starlight, had suffered a slightly obscured view. "I couldn't quite see all of it, what did it say Poldant?" she asked.

"Well, I'm not positive," he looked perplexed. "I could read the words but whether they mean anything is a different matter."

"Let us write them down and examine them," Loriscus suggested. "Good work, O noble friend, you have saved us a great deal of time and trouble," he remembered to add hastily, but Starlight grinned to show his good humour had returned

"We hope," Camelion muttered under his breath.

"Please tell me the words!" Joalla was almost dancing with curiosity by now.

Crysgar, whose view had also been clear, busily scribbled on a piece of paper before reading out aloud:

"For those who dare

to find the One

risk light, dark, and stair

to brave the lair ... '

It appears incomplete," Crysgar commented.

"Is that it? It doesn't make sense." Joalla was dismayed.

"I can't help that." Starlight swished his silvery tail, "I am only able to translate what is there."

"Oh no, I'm not blaming you," the young Elveriness hurriedly assured him. Turning she continued, "Crysgar, does this perhaps have more meaning for you?"

"Not yet," Crysgar replied, causing them all to look hopefully at him, "it is well known that in times past, the Wise Ones delighted in writing in poetry and riddles. It was a test of ability ... for fun you know."

"I don't think it is much fun," Camelion said grumpily. "It is likely to take an age to understand the meaning behind this riddle or whatever it is; even then it isn't complete as you said yourself." They all stood with brows wrinkled in thought.

"Hold on!" Crysgar stated suddenly, "we are missing an obvious point."

"Which is?" Poldant prompted.

"Well, there is more than one stone, so there may be more than one message," Crysgar said.

"Oh yes," Joalla started to become excited again, "so if we put them all together...."

"It might make more sense!" Camelion finished.

"By all the Honoured Ones, of course!" Loriscus thumped his fist into the palm of his other hand. The companions turned to look at Starlight who had been standing quietly by listening to their discussion. He twitched his ears, gazing around at the other unicorns in some silent communication. They appeared to give him the answer he was looking for. "Of course I will translate the other stones, but my power will weaken with use and therefore my friends here have agreed to share their own power with me. Crysgar do you have quill and parchment at the ready?" He led the way around the cave mouth to the next stone, which Crysgar had discovered. As previously they stood in a semi-circle around the unicorn whilst Crest, Uraj and Glore focused a violet beam of light onto Starlight. Once again he touched his horn to the ancient writing. As the magic worked there was a general cry of excitement. The words *were* different! Crysgar scribbled busily, whilst the others mouthed the words to themselves. This happened three times until all the translation was down on paper. No one said a word on completion, apart from the odd murmur of "well done Starlight," and "good work." The Elverine and the changeling gathered to stare perplexedly at the paper. Starlight and the other three unicorns moved off to replenish his spent energy.

"I don't wish to sound stupid," Camelion said finally, "but it still doesn't mean a thing to me."

Joalla sighed and shook her head, "Nor to me either." One by one Crysgar, Poldant and Loriscus also admitted defeat. "Very well, come on everyone, I think a nice warm brew of nectar will help us to think more clearly." Joalla moved briskly towards the pack which Crest had removed from her own force field before gently allowing it to float to the ground. The others trailed behind her and started to sort out their own provisions. Once the group were sitting comfortably with the nectar warming their hands and stomachs quite deliciously, the mood relaxed.

Loriscus sighed, "I believe that this discovery may be important to our quest. I don't quite know why, or how to express it, but I do not feel we should go on until some sense has been made of these words." Joalla noted his fatigued expression and remembered with a pang the jaunty, carefree Elverine whom she had previously known.

"I agree," Crysgar said. The other three nodded their assent.

"Good, let us set up camp and then set to work," Loriscus commanded. There was a brief frantic period of activity before they came back together, yet another cup of magical nectar in their hands. The unicorns stood among them, waiting to add their own wisdom. Loriscus said, "Now, please read out all of the translations Crysgar, and we will attempt to puzzle them out piece by piece."

"Obviously I'm not reading them out in any particular order," Crysgar explained "bear that in mind and keep your thoughts open. So the first one again …

For those who dare
to find the One
risk light, dark and stair

to brave the lair …

Any views on that one yet?" He looked around the silent group as they stared back blankly. "So, here we go with the remaining translations …

Beware ye all
who have faint heart,
or do not quest for good
Only the pure of thought and deed
should surely enter here
One who knows
One who cares that
few alone shall dare
or live beyond the lair."

Crysgar paused to lift his eyes enquiringly. The silence was deafening. Several minutes ticked by and the silence became gloomy. Another cup of nectar disappeared. Still nothing. Eventually Poldant said, "Perhaps each of us should take a turn actually reading and looking at the words. Sometimes things become clearer when seen by the eye as well as the ear."

Crysgar handed the paper to Camelion. The parchment floated above his blue hands as he perused it perplexedly. "The bit about the pure of heart entering seems reasonably clear, but who or where or why is still a mystery to me," he commented.

Joalla took the paper from him. She willed her mind clear of all but the mystical words. Then …"Crysgar," she asked quietly, "why did you write 'One' like that?"

"Like what?"

"Well it seems to be written about *a* being, not beings in general. *One* important being. Could it be … ?"

"The Amorga," Loriscus finished excitedly. "That's it! So the lair must be her dwelling. Let me have another look." He virtually snatched the paper from Joalla, who only smiled to see his delight. Crysgar took time to note the love undisguised for a moment on her face before joining in the general chatter of ideas which were suddenly being brought up and thrown around.

"Either my memory is faulty or this is a different entrance to the one I was seeking," Crysgar said reflectively. "However if this is so then it will save us several days' ride."

"I do not think it is a coincidence that this has crossed our path now," Loriscus considered. "Let us continue to unravel the riddle." In unspoken assent, they bent their heads over the scroll once more.

"What do you think 'few alone shall dare' means in relation to the Amorga and her lair?" Camelion questioned.

"I believe it must be connected with 'pure of thought and deed'," Crysgar answered as he busily wrote down all suggestions as they were called out.

"Possibly the part about 'faint heart' and 'questing for good' means that the visitor should be brave and his mission true and not for personal gain," Poldant almost shouted to be heard above the babble.

"Yes, yes." Crysgar wrote furiously.

"Then there must be some danger in the getting there before we even see her," Camelion pointed out, "because the first translation says 'risk light, dark and stair'. We must have to pass through some sort of trial to reach the Amorga." The companions grew silent at this. The realisation came that they had possibly reached the next stage of the venture, and with it came the need to make decisions. Excitement faded as a more grave discussion ensued. Starlight pointed out that he and his kind would be unable to follow into the cave, and Crest, Uraj and Glore agreed. The danger of breaking a limb in a sudden fall in the dark would be disastrous, possibly fatal, even for light-footed creatures such as they. Crysgar suggested that one of the companions should remain behind also, as a back up and they all became heated again whilst trying to decide who this should be. No one wanted to miss out on what lay ahead. Eventually, because he was the least agile Crysgar reluctantly volunteered, and besides, if dangers threatened and help were needed, he was the most likely to know where to find it.

The camp was a restless place that night. Even when all plans had been made, sleep proved elusive. Loriscus was heard pacing around well into the early hours. Being that much closer to saving his beloved Silbeamia made it all seem so much harder to bear. It was only after Crysgar pointed out that he would not be at his best to face the morrow that he could be induced to rest.

Daylight broke and the sun cast gentle shadows among the rocks. Only the occasional twitter of birdsong or the stamp of a unicorn hoof floated on the air. Joalla opened her eyes and remembered instantly that this was to be an important day. She hoped she had enough strength and courage to face whatever test lay ahead. She had determined to beg the Amorga, if necessary, to allow her to accompany Loriscus on his quest. Her heart was constantly heavy with the knowledge of her deed, and she so wanted to put things right.

Breakfast was a silent affair as each mentally prepared for whatever may come. Equipment and supplies were checked and re-checked. Those venturing into the cave were to explore for two days, and then to return if nothing of note occurred. All were intensely aware that failure at this point could possibly lead to their return to Elver emptyhanded, with Silbeamia left to her fate. For every day that passed increased the risk of her golden sunbeam body absorbing the pervasive evil of the Land of Zorgia. Loriscus looked grim yet excited all at the same time; his mood was reflected on every face.

An hour after dawn found them sliding down a stout rope into the black mouth of the cave. Poldant first, followed by Camelion, Joalla and then Loriscus.

"Poldant, if you set your ray shooter at light to help guide the way, Joalla and I will set ours at stun to cover any eventuality," Loriscus ordered.

"'Eventuality' meant danger of course," Joalla thought with a shiver and Camelion defensively hoisted his great club onto his shoulder. As Poldant shone his light around to seek the most obvious direction, Joalla and the changeling took in the first impression of their surroundings. They were in a hole which on one side opened into a large rocky cavern. Every movement echoed and reverberated like claps of thunder, which gradually whispered away as if an unseen audience had grown silent at their appearance. Joalla resisted the impulse to clutch at Poldant's cloak and Camelion tightened his grip on the club. The remaining Elverine, although knowing what to expect, were momentarily held rigid with renewed awe.

Shaking off his reaction, Loriscus said, "Poldant, lead the way to the place we reached before. You two walk in the middle and I'll take up a rear position to help you along." Obediently Poldant walked carefully ahead of the group, his wavering light throwing weird patterns and shadows upon the unwelcoming stones. After a while they were brought up short by a steep and seemingly uncompromising wall of rock.

The four debated their options until eventually Camelion said, "It does not make sense that this should be a dead end, I can only think that the stairs mentioned on the rocks above must be hereabouts."

"That's it!"

"Yes of course."

"Well done!" They all chorused. Immediately the three Elverine started casting their beams of light up and down the unrelenting wall, clambering here and there for a better view. Camelion meanwhile changed his shape and became as of rock himself, deeming it wise that one of them should keep watch.

A good half an hour later Poldant sat down wearily. "We must be wrong, I can see nothing even slightly resembling a stairway," he said gloomily. The rock next to him suddenly metamorphosed back into Camelion, causing Poldant to jump virtually two metres into the air with fright. "Don't do that!" he shouted crossly. The other two started to laugh and Camelion grinned infectiously at the discomforted Elverine. Reluctantly an answering smile appeared. The high ceiling of the cave rang with mirth, an unknown sound in this hidden place. The laughter eased the tension and the companions resumed their search with renewed vigour. Nobody noticed two glowing red eyes appear and then disappear during those few unguarded moments.

Happily unaware that something in the deep dark depths had been disturbed, Joalla pulled herself upward over a jutting outcrop of rock. The creature watched unmoving as she approached ever closer. Suddenly an excited, ear-splitting yell resounded around them. Joalla turned and hastened in the direction of Loriscus who was almost hopping with glee.

"Look here, I think I have found something," he pointed to a disappointingly ordinary boulder.

"That is certainly an exceptionally interesting piece of stone," Poldant retorted sarcastically as he tried to catch his breath. Joalla stifled a giggle behind her hand.

"Stop being clever and look properly," Loriscus snapped back. Obediently, slightly doubtfully, the others peered more closely, running their hands and lights over it.

"I suppose it is sort of door shaped," Camelion commented eventually.

"And?" Loriscus prompted.

"It shouldn't be able to balance at that angle," Joalla realised.

"Yes," Loriscus clapped her on the shoulder delightedly, "that's what I thought." The boulder was top heavy and appeared to be resting on a slender point, rather like a dancer on tiptoe.

"You could be right," Poldant said, "but if it is a doorway, how do we open it?"

They tried rolling the boulder on its side, pushing down from the top, and even at forcing it inwards. Nothing happened. A perplexed silence grew as they ran out of ideas.

"I must be wrong," Loriscus sighed. He leaned dispiritedly on the rock - and immediately disappeared.

"What!" Poldant leapt forward in dismay.

"Oh no!" Joalla exclaimed.

Camelion set his jaw and heaved and pulled at the place where Loriscus had vanished. The two Elverine joined him and there was a minute of frantic, panic-stricken activity, which got them nowhere.

"Stop, this is senseless," Poldant commanded, being the first to calm down. Camelion and Joalla took hold of themselves and stood worriedly but quietly next to Poldant. "Let us think this through step by step," he continued. "Where precisely was Loriscus when he vanished?"

"Just here," Joalla answered demonstrating an area on the left side of the rock.

"If you are right then I suggest we stay very close together in case the magic works again," Camelion stated. The Elverine sheathed their ray shooters, plunging them into instant blackness, and as one they linked arms and stepped onto the spot they had last seen their friend. In anticipation they waited a moment. Nothing happened.

"That can't be it," Poldant said. "What else did Loriscus do?"

"He leant on this part of the rock," Joalla replied forgetting for a moment that they couldn't see her. Poldant flicked his beam on briefly so that they could all see where Joalla was pointing to. Carefully, still holding onto one another, the companions stretched forward and pressed their free hands to the hard surface. Instantly the rock pivoted on its narrow axis and spun them into an even deeper darkness.

Catching her balance as well as her breath, Joalla spotted the only glimmering of light in that gloomy place. A shout of glee went up. There sat Loriscus, calmly watching and waiting. As his friends rushed towards him he grinned and called, "I was certain you would work it out in the end." Joalla only just managed to stop herself from throwing her arms around his neck with relief.

"You had more faith in us than we did in ourselves then," Poldant admitted as they delightedly crowded around him.

Eventually Camelion went back and examined the rock interestedly. "It is a very clever devise," he said admiringly. The mechanism for pivoting the huge door was more obvious from this side. Then a thought struck him quite forcibly. How did the thing work in order to get out?

"I've had a quick look at our surroundings," Loriscus drew their attention. "There is a stairway cut into the floor going downwards over there," he pointed towards a particularly menacing and unwelcoming corner. "We don't appear to have any choice but to find out where it leads," he looked questioningly at his companions. The air of relief and joy fell away as realisation of their predicament hit them.

"We'll walk in the same order as before," Loriscus said. More than one drew a steadying breath as they approached the chasm of the stairway. Eerie echoes percolated up to fuel their foreboding. Joalla's mind fluttered briefly to her comfortable home in golden Elver, before she firmly quashed the memory and plunged downwards, staying as close as possible to Camelion's large form. The whispering noises grew more threatening and the descending travellers drew into an ever-tighter knot. They seemed to be going down to the very centre of the earth. Poldant had just begun to point out rather uneasily that the whole thing was a waste of time, when Loriscus stopped short, causing a catapult effect behind him.

"Ow!" yelped Camelion, as his arm melded momentarily with cold stone. "What did you do that for?"

"Give us a bit of warning, for the Universes' sake," grumbled Poldant.

"Sorry, but I didn't really have a lot of choice," Loriscus snapped. The companions peered over his shoulder and instantly saw his dilemma. Firstly the main source of the whispering echoes became clear. There was running water everywhere. Secondly the stairway ended in a steep drop before them, which was filled with a rushing, raging torrent. Water fell from enormous cracks and crevices crashing onto the rocks below. A thin, wobbly-looking bridge without a handrail arched into the darkness.

"Do you think that perhaps we ought to go back?" Joalla let her fear show for the first time. That bridge looked perilous, not to mention scary.

"Er, she may have a point you know." Poldant, generally so brave and in control, hated fast moving water, and this was certainly moving fast.

"What for?" Camelion demanded. "To return will mean we have achieved nothing. Besides we aren't even sure if we can get out if we return. I say we go on."

"This must be the bit about faint heart," Loriscus said. "I don't want to give up now."

"I think we should vote on it," Poldant said stubbornly, fear momentarily overcoming friendship, "and I vote for going back."

"I am with Loriscus," Camelion said staunchly watching Poldant with a piercing glare.

Three pairs of eyes bored into Joalla awaiting her decision. Finally she said, "If this is the part to do with faint heart, then it is a test the Amorga has set. In turning back now we may never find her. We are here because of my actions. I request the right to go first. Anyway, I am the lightest and least likely to fall," she concluded bravely. Her companions reacted with a mixture of admiration, horror and embarrassment, the latter being Poldant's response as he recognised the sense of what the young Elveriness said. Making a decision, he turned and nodded at Loriscus, setting his lips into a firm line. If Joalla could do it, then so could he.

"It is agreed then." Loriscus blew out his breath in a relieved sigh.

"I am not happy about Joalla going first," Camelion said. "It may be even worse than we anticipate; besides I could probably fly across."

"Probably?" Poldant questioned.

"Well it may not be easy to hold the form of a winged creature under these circumstances," Camelion admitted.

"Surely then, it would be dangerous for whoever makes the first attempt," Joalla looked baffled.

Loriscus understood the changeling better. He placed a comforting hand on Camelion's shoulder, "In Elver all are merited according to their abilities. We do not think to disallow simply because one is male or female. Joalla has shown herself capable of achieving this, it probably is best that she goes first." Camelion still looked uncertain.

"At least let us tie a rope around Joalla's waist so that we may pull her to safety if the bridge should crumble," he begged.

"Certainly," Poldant replied. "It would be foolhardy to take unnecessary risks." He unclipped a length of rope from his belt and tied one end around Joalla's slender waist. She in turn tucked her cloak into the rope at the back so it would not billow or distract her at the wrong moment. Holding the light steadily, her beautiful face set with determination, she nodded firmly to indicate she was ready. The other three grasped the free end of the rope and braced themselves against a possible fall.

"Tie the rope at the other end if possible," Loriscus instructed grimly.

Joalla nodded curtly and stepped into the abyss. The bridge was perilously slippery from the spray of foaming water, causing Joalla to step very cautiously indeed. Once out of the protection of the tunnel, the noise was incredible, making communication impossible. The faint beam from her ray shooter was pathetically small as it wavered across the great echoing cavern, until eventually she was swallowed up in the darkness. No one spoke or even moved. The waiting stretched on, rather like the rope which was unravelling to an alarming degree. Suddenly when there was virtually no rope left, its movement stopped. All three held their breath anxiously. Then far away a pinprick of light flashed to signal all was well. They let go of their breath in unison, unaware until that moment that they had stopped breathing altogether.

"It is well done!" Camelion exclaimed, as he tested the taut rope that now served as a handrail. Poldant and Loriscus grinned at him.

"Well done indeed!" they yelled in an upsoaring of spirits. Initial celebrations over, the three companions formed a plan on the way in which they would proceed.

After much deliberation, it was eventually decided that Camelion was to go next, followed by Poldant and lastly Loriscus.

"What about the safety rope?" Camelion asked. "Should we leave it tied here? The problem is that we may need it again."

"That's a point," Poldant said, annoyed that he hadn't seen this flaw in the plan himself.

Loriscus went quiet momentarily. "No, obviously we must bring the rope with us," he said.

"Well?" Poldant said.

"Loriscus must simply tie his end around himself, we will reel him in like a fish," Camelion said gleefully.

"A fish!" exclaimed Loriscus in horror, he had never killed anything in his life. "That sounds as if it will work," he added hastily as Camelion's face suffused with colour.

Meanwhile Joalla sat alone and frightened in the emptiness of the other side. Her light beam was turned low to preserve power, and every wavering shadow seemed to hold an evil threat. The worst thing was not knowing how the others were faring. Had they begun another crossing? What if they couldn't make it? And, worst realisation of all, she would have to return and face the treacherous darkness again should their attempt prove abortive.

Taking deep breaths; Joalla forced herself to remain calm. She began to hum a popular tune to keep herself company, but that caused the echoes to sound even worse, as if an army was growling in the background. She leaned forward and was immediately assailed by the noise of rushing angry water. Momentarily Joalla became intrigued with the observation that when she leaned backwards again the sound at once became very distant by comparison. "How strange," she thought. Running her beam around the tunnel entrance, she tried to work out what was causing the sound barrier.

Joalla succeeded in becoming so mentally engrossed that she almost jumped out of her skin when the friendly form of Camelion loomed from out of the darkness. "Camelion!" Joalla threw herself at him joyously. "Thank the Keeper of the Universes."

Camelion patted her shoulder awkwardly, only then realising the enormity of her long vigil alone. His admiration at her courage increased. Gently he disentangled her arms from his waist. "I must signal to the others," he told her. Immediately Joalla pulled herself together standing erect and self-contained once more.

The wait for Poldant was very different. They sat side by side, aware of what was happening across the dark void, aware also that if Poldant did not manage to conquer his fear of the fast moving water, his panic would lead to almost certain death. To distract her companion, Joalla explained her discovery regarding the strange sound barrier. They were exchanging ideas and exploring the rocks with their hands when Poldant's breathless voice came from the blackness.

"Your concerned welcome overwhelms me," he commented dryly. Eager hands reached out to pull him to final safety. The large Elverine was almost as wet and slippery as the treacherous bridge. His heart was still beating rapidly despite his wry humour; his dampness was more due to a sweat of terror than water spray. Poldant's face reflected huge elation, he had successfully conquered one of his worst nightmares, and he had passed a personal test beyond that set by the Amorga.

Loriscus had been suffering the same lonely pangs experienced by Joalla, only yet more terrifying, the roaring had taken on the sound of Silbeamia's desperate last screams. When the all clear signal winked through the blackness he almost ripped the rope from the rock and attached it around his waist. Thankfully the young Elverine scrambled onto the narrow bridge, desperate to rejoin his friends. The shrieking volume of the water deafened him, striking his body like a physical blow. Only the thought of Silbeamia forced him into taking the next step. Fear rose like bile in his throat, causing him to speed up subconsciously. Suddenly the inevitable happened. One carelessly placed foot slipped from under him and Loriscus tumbled off the bridge towards a watery death.

Poldant, who still had his hands on the rope, found himself being catapulted backwards. His surprised yell warned Camelion and Joalla. With the speed of light the shapeshifter turned into an octopus like creature and grabbed the Elverine just before he plummeted over the edge. Sticky tentacles clung both to the rocks and to the petrified Poldant.

"Loriscus must have fallen," the octopus shouted in alarm as it metamorphosed back into Camelion. "Quickly, pull in the rope!"

Poldant scrambled to his feet. With grim urgency they fought and pulled at the straining rope. After a couple of minutes Joalla began to feel panic overtake her. She knew that Loriscus could not survive in the freezing water for much longer. Nobody could see or had any way of knowing how their friend was doing, nor how much further they had to pull him to reach safety.

Loriscus could have told them he was not doing very well at all. The shock of the icy torrent had initially nearly stunned him into unconsciousness, only the gallons of water trying to force its way into his lungs brought him to. Choking and spluttering Loriscus struggled to keep his head above water, scrabbling and clutching with torn and bleeding hands at prominent rocks in a bid to prevent himself from being swept away. He realised he would have to get the bulk of his body out of the water if the other three were to stand any chance of helping him. The force of the water pulling and sucking at him was such that he feared even their great strength would eventually be overcome. As he held onto a sharp, jagged piece of stone, he looked around with desperation. His eye alighted on a flatter rock a small distance away. Bravely he released his grip and launched himself towards it and was thrown against the rock with a chest-crushing thump as a great surge of water took hold of him. Loriscus summoned all his power and heaved himself half onto the cold slippery surface. His legs still dangled in the water, which tore evilly at them in an attempt to recover its prey, blood ran from numerous cuts amongst the bruises, but the ploy seemed to be succeeding. Gradually Loriscus became aware that he was lifting off his precarious haven. He started bumping up the side of the crevice and briefly attempted to help pull himself up, but his strength was gone, his hands numb. The best he could do was to prevent wickedly sharp stone teeth from tasting more of his blood as he bounced painfully against them. Then a jagged boulder struck his head with such impact that he knew no more.

Chapter 3

L oriscus drifted into consciousness dimly aware of wonderful warmth, light, peace and best of all, caring voices. The companions had stripped the wet clothing from his frozen limbs. Magical Elverine cloaks were securely wrapped around him, pulsing a healing energy into his torn body. On noticing slight movement, kind hands lifted his head and a cup of nectar was put to his lips. Invigorating warmth coursed through his veins and the mist in his brain lifted briefly. Now he could see three worried faces peering down on him.

"Thank you my guardians," he murmured with a faint smile, before a healing, regenerating sleep overcame him.

Joalla, Camelion and Poldant decided to sleep encircling Loriscus in order to increase the heat surrounding him. They slept heavily, their strength exhausted. So deeply, in fact, that no one felt the creature with red eyes gently alight amongst them, nor observed its nod of satisfaction with what it saw. There it sat watching and waiting until the first stirring of wakefulness caused it to flit gently out of sight.

Loriscus awoke filled with a great sense of well-being. By the Stars it was good to be alive! He stretched luxuriously. "Ouch!" Every muscle in his body still ached unbearably. Despite magical intervention it was as if every limb had been torn asunder and stuck together by someone ignorant of Elverine biology! Loriscus wasn't even sure that anything worked any more.

Joalla sat up hastily. "What is it?" she asked with concern.

Poldant opened one laconic eye. "Stiff, O great leader?" he jested. Loriscus groaned pitifully in reply whilst Joalla's worried frown became a mischievous, impish grin.

"Poor Loriscus," she sympathised sweetly.

Camelion chortled quietly, quickly straightening his face when Loriscus's jaundiced eye swung in his direction. Suddenly they were all laughing uproariously in happy reaction to the terror and despair of the previous night.

Joalla sobered first. "I suggest we move on quickly," she said, "because firstly we don't know how far we have yet to travel, and secondly we must be running out of time before Crysgar starts to worry and sends for help." Camelion smiled to himself as she unwittingly asserted herself on them for the first time. Her act of courage had obviously given back some of her self-respect.

"By the Maker of the Universes I had forgotten about that," Poldant said. "You are right Joalla, we must make haste." Loriscus nodded and hobbled around painfully attempting to dress in dry clothes as they rewound ropes, packed supplies, slung their cloaks around their necks and left quite precipitately.

The creature blinked and flew behind them at a safe distance, those strange red eyes able to see perfectly well in the inky blackness. The passageway narrowed quite drastically, until the companions had to walk carefully in order to avoid scraping their skin on the rocky walls either side. Camelion became a snake the easier to slide along, but Poldant kept stepping on his tail in the dark, so he gave up and became himself again.

Several hours later Loriscus felt impelled to call back, "Is all well with you?" Joalla and Camelion answered, but Poldant didn't respond at all. Camelion turned his head.

"Didn't you hear..." His voice trailed away in horror. There was no one there. "Poldant is missing," he bellowed in alarm. Loriscus and Joalla stopped short and peered blankly at the empty space where the big Elverine should be.

"Perhaps he fell," Joalla said.

"I should have felt it if he had," Camelion said worriedly. "We shall have to go back and find him. Joalla, give me your light because we will have to walk in reverse order. Can you manage the weight of my club?" He handed the club back leaving one hand free to feel for unexpected apertures in the tunnel wall. Joalla automatically grasped it, too anxious to answer.

"Be careful," Loriscus warned, "just in case he didn't fall but has run into some other trouble."

Camelion led them for approximately ten paces when he came across the next problem. "We can't go back, there is something blocking the way!"

"Impossible! What do you mean?" Loriscus, who was now at the back, sounded impatient and frightened at the same time.

"Just that," Camelion replied. "I cannot see anything, but there seems to be a sort of invisible wall preventing me from moving any further." They were momentarily stunned into silence.

"You mean we are being prevented from going back to find Poldant," Joalla finally stated the obvious.

"Yes."

"Then our only hope is to go on and find out whether the Amorga can help us." Loriscus's voice held sadness and pain for the feared loss of his best friend. Once again there was a horrified silence at the enormity of such a decision.

"Do not despair," Joalla said tremulously and put out a comforting hand to him, "it is written that everything happens for a reason. You are right we must proceed and ask the Amorga for her guidance." She swapped weapons with Camelion once again and they swung about in the direction that they had been travelling a few moments before.

"I think we must hold onto one another to prevent this from happening again," Loriscus suggested. Joalla grasped a great handful of his Elverine cloak feeling more secure in doing so.

"Hold on to me Camelion," she said. He did not answer. The two Elverine were almost afraid to look.

"He has disappeared too," Joalla's voice wobbled.

"May the Maker protect them," Loriscus prayed. "I think this is the next part of the test Joalla," he said, "try not to be apprehensive."

"Try not to be apprehensive!" Joalla thought crossly. "Just like a male to say something so ridiculous!" She found herself chattering nervously, feeling somehow that if she could just keep talking then everything would be all right. It wasn't. At first she thought her light ray was fading and gave it a little shake in the hope of a power surge. Then she realised with dread that it wasn't the light that was fading, it was her!

Loriscus and the tunnel vanished. Joalla began to experience a floating sensation. Initially this was quite pleasant, but then a bright blinding light shone around her, and with the light came voices. Some were dulcet and tender, others menacing, threatening, urgent. The voices tore her inner self apart, there was nowhere to hide. She saw her jealousy and temper for what it was, not liking that side of the person that was Joalla at all. At the same time she saw her kindness, courage and love fighting and vying with her bad side to dominate. The most dreadful and yet comforting insight was of her minuscule size and unimportance in relation to the universes, and yet the wonderful knowledge that she was at one with it. Eventually she could stand no more.

"Please, enough! I will try, I promise," she cried out, not knowing if anyone or anything was out there to help her. As soon as the words left her lips, it ceased. The bright light dimmed and the young Elveriness found herself in a hitherto unseen cave. It was comparatively large to the rest of the underground network. Best of all, there in the corner sat Poldant and Camelion.

They turned in her direction and stretched welcoming arms to her. Joalla ran to their friendly embrace and looked into familiar faces that were yet different. Each held a remnant of the glow that some secret knowledge had wrought, a new serenity, and so they were slightly changed forever.

As they held one another with delight, Loriscus appeared beside them. He was white, shaken, and very, very relieved to see them. Explanations were unnecessary. No one felt it to be important to share what each had learned, some things were only significant to oneself.

They sat quietly to rest and recover, then natural curiosity and a need to move on shook them into activity. It was time to explore the new cave.

"The trouble is," Poldant commented, "that we don't actually know where we are. We won't know which direction to take even if we find an exit."

"Well we can't stay here," Loriscus said. "That will achieve nothing."

"Perhaps I can be of some assistance," a strange deep voice spoke politely from the darkness. They turned in unison, grabbing at stun rays in panic. Their light shone upon a large outcrop of rock on which sat a tiny creature who was, to say the very least, strange in form. It was something of a cross between a monkey and an owl, with big staring red eyes, feathered wings, and a furry body and limbs.

"Gremlic is my name," the peculiar red eyes blinked at them.

Loriscus, as leader, politely introduced himself and his companions, at the same time discreetly keeping a hold of his weapon. Poldant and Camelion murmured politely in response, their eyes occasionally darting around the cave. Joalla quietly studied the interloper. Gremlic was tiny but great power emanated from his being.

"I believe," Gremlic pointedly ignored the weapon, "that you seek an audience with the Amorga."

If he hadn't had their complete attention before, he certainly had it now! Joalla gasped in astonishment. Camelion spoke rapidly, "If you are able to lead us to the Amorga, we will be forever in your debt." The little creature didn't move or speak for a few seconds. He looked at their faces and seemed to consider deeply. "Yes," he decided aloud, "I think the Amorga will be pleased with you."

Exhilaration gripped the company. At last they were almost there!

"Thank you," Loriscus's face lit up. The three Elverine put their fists to their chests and bowed as a mark of respect. Camelion held out his hand in the universal sign of peace.

"To be frank, we were at our wits end as to which direction to take," Joalla told Gremlic confidingly.

A weird little smile flicked across his face. "Young and most courageous female, you and your noble companions would have found the Amorga whichever path you took so long as you quest for good." In his quaint way Gremlic had explained a further part of the mystic writings.

"You mean all paths lead to the Amorga," Camelion looked amazed. "How is this possible?"

"There is a long climb in front of you before you understand so much, O changeling," Gremlic said gently. "So far you have taken only the first step." Spreading his wings the little creature flew over their heads to the far side of the cave.

As they trooped behind him Poldant whispered to Loriscus, "What if he isn't as he appears? Supposing he has been sent from Zorgia?" Loriscus glanced at his friend with trepidation, but before he could think of anything to say Gremlic answered Poldant himself, much to that young Elverine's consternation.

"Those from the Land of Zorgia cannot enter here. They would fail at the first test. The raging water could confirm many an attempt." Loriscus shuddered at the unpleasant memory. Gremlic flew towards an apparently impassable wall of rock. He chanted a few magical passwords and an invisible door slid open before him.

They were hit by a blast of energy that forced them back a pace or two. "Courage," Loriscus whispered. They stepped through the doorway and were met by a sight which struck wonder and reverence into their hearts. It was like looking into a many-faceted prism. Although they were aware that they stood in the presence of the Amorga, it was not possible to tell exactly where she stood. There was an overall image of a being of unimaginable, indescribable beauty, but the image projected and shimmered in so many places at once that their minds became confused. The cavern appeared to have no walls; nothing was prominent except a sense of omnipotence.

Gremlic knelt down and with bowed head spoke to the Amorga. "These travellers have passed the tests well, O Great One. I have watched and listened ever since they entered the hallowed doorway. It is well." The Amorga, as had her servant before her, looked into each of the faces turned up to her.

"Bring them to me," she ordered. Her voice sent chimes and shivers down their spines like a shock wave. Gremlic beckoned, and led them unerringly to the real Amorga. As they reached her their images immediately became reflected with all of hers.

"What a peculiar sensation," Joalla thought. Then she felt the eyes of the Amorga upon her; her own eyes lifted and all conscious thought ended. The entire joy and sorrow of the Universes was in that gaze, to the extent that Joalla felt crushed by their burden. The colours of the rainbow alternated like glittering rain through the whole body of the Magnificent One. Camelion, Loriscus, Poldant and Joalla felt impelled to fall to their knees in obeisance. Delicate yet strong hands touched each head in turn, and they knew themselves to be blessed.

"You wish to venture into Zorgia," the Amorga stated. Nobody experienced surprise at her comment, omnipotence did not need an explanation.

Loriscus cleared his throat nervously. "We need your advice on how to enter and leave in safety, if you please O Amorga."

"There is a way, but it is a long and often dangerous journey," the deity warned.

"I am willing to try," Loriscus said eagerly. "I just want the chance to rescue Silbeamia before it is too late." The note of desperation in his voice was clear for all to hear.

"And do the rest of you stand behind your leader, or do you wish to return to Elver?" she asked.

"We stand with Loriscus," Camelion confirmed firmly whilst the other two nodded their support.

"I think then that you had better sit down while I explain the process," she said gently, her smile was like a welcome sunbeam breaking through a cloudy sky. Joalla looked around just as a table and chairs appeared magically beside them. On the table were a jug and four goblets together with a plate of particularly succulent looking delicacies. "Please sit," she urged as they stood around uncertainly. They were very soon occupied by their feast whilst the

Amorga serenely waited for them to finish. Eventually even Camelion and Poldant had had enough.

"By the Maker, that was delicious," Camelion patted his stomach which had distended hugely to encompass the food. Renewed energy began to pulse through his form. The empty utensils dematerialised to be replaced by an enormous map unlike any they had ever seen before.

The Amorga leant over the map and pointed with one long exquisite finger. "Each colour leads to a new universe and dimension," she explained. The Elverine nodded, this knowledge being part of their heritage. "You will have to travel through many of the dimensions to find artefacts or beings necessary to aid your cause. Of paramount importance is a red dragon from Jalmar in the Red Zone, because all the while you are in its vicinity it can repel the colour vibration of indigo and prevent it from being absorbed into your bodies." Across the Red Zone was printed in bold black letters BEYOND THIS POINT THERE BE DRAGONS. "You will need to persuade a good dragon to join you of its own free will. Not easy, most dragons dislike adventure or travel intensely. They have had some very unpleasant experiences in other dimensions." She paused a moment.

"Through the Green Zone you must go to the planet its inhabitants call Earth. I suggest you visit this place before Jalmar, no dragon will accompany you there for the reasons I have just mentioned. Earth was the worst. There in a deeply forested place you will find a particular tree that gives a magical gum only known by a chosen few. The Tree of Knowledge is well secured; you will need to represent your case well to its guardians. The gum will be needed to hold the oxygenated ingredients necessary to enable you to breathe in the water-filled world of Kephlopodia, which is accessible through the Orange Zone. It is the only doorway through which Gordagn will not be expecting you. The magical oxygenated ingredients to put in the gum must be obtained from the beings of Chjimmer which exists in the Violet Zone, for they are the Shimmering People Yet to Be who are waiting to be born into different dimensions. Those who are born into Kephlopodia are given the magic antidote to enable them to breathe and exist there." The Amorga paused again to give them time to assimilate the information. "When travelling to each of these Zones you will have to take the chance of using little known doorways through the Rainbow, because the followers of the Lord of Zorgia will be waiting for you at the established ones. This means that wherever the rainbow happens to be floating at your time of entrance is where you will end up; you will be unable to use the usual controls." She looked pointedly at the Elverine. "It is risky, but not as dangerous as allowing the Evil Ones to know your whereabouts." She glanced up to find the adventurers engrossed in her explanation and poring over the map in an attempt to memorise it. "Under these circumstances are you still willing to go ahead?" she asked again.

Excitement reflected in the eyes of the companions. They were young enough to relish the unknown, despite the underlying seriousness of their quest.

"We never expected it to be easy," Poldant said, knowing he spoke for all of them.

The plan was explained in greater detail, with the Amorga patiently reiterating anything they were unsure of. Gremlic laid some fascinating extra equipment on the table, a gift to aid them when travelling in other dimensions. Principle amongst these was individual teleporters that strapped to the wrist. These enabled them to transport instantly to co-ordinates set into the control panel; a necessary correction device for anyone who travelled through unpredictable doorways. Camelion was very intrigued by a rather handy little gadget called a translator, which sat inside the ear making it possible for the user to understand all forms of language. Gremlic explained that these would work automatically, the only thing they had to control was the volume, which could be adjusted by thought.

Once the Amorga was certain that they were all clear on every point, she took Loriscus aside for a private conversation. He returned to the others looking grave, but declined to explain.

Finally there was no more to be said or done. "It is time to join Crysgar on the surface," the Amorga commanded. Joalla looked apprehensive, she had no particular desire to cross the narrow bridge again. Loriscus, struck by the same thought, had turned pale.

Gremlic understood and laughed heartily. "This will be your first use of the teleporter, young Elveriness," he chuckled. Joalla's face cleared, Loriscus resumed his nonchalant stance.

"Ah! By the Stars! What a good chance to practise!" Camelion exclaimed.

Each of them knelt before the beautiful deity. The Elverine laid their hands on their chests while Camelion simply bowed his head. "Many thanks for allowing us into this blessed place," Loriscus as usual spoke for the group. "My own eternal gratitude is yours for showing me a way to rescue Silbeamia. Whatever the result, we honour you."

The Amorga stood with Gremlic perched on her shoulder, and as she smiled her indescribable smile her words floated around them, "May the Power of Goodness protect you."

They pressed their buttons and instantly found themselves standing next to an extremely startled Crysgar. But most incredible of all, Gremlic sat calmly upon the shoulder of Loriscus.

Chapter 4
Green Zone - Earth

A rainbow shone magnificently in the skies over glistening, freshly-washed forest lands which grew on an island the inhabitants called Britain, planet Earth. A group of beings materialised from a faint green mist. The companions had arrived.

Starlight snorted and trotted over to sample the greenery. "Very good, very good indeed," he called to Crest and the other unicorns. Eagerly they joined him and were soon munching away contentedly. Loriscus and his friends watched in amused silence for a few moments before having a good look around at this place hitherto unvisited by any of them.

"It is a place of great beauty," Joalla exclaimed, "although the air is not as sweet as that on Elver."

"Ah," Crysgar shook his head sadly "this was once the jewel of the universes, of such wonder that it was called Paradise."

"What happened to it?" Camelion questioned, horrified.

"The most evolved inhabitants, humans they are called, have no respect and little understanding of the living thing that provides their every need. They pollute the waters, poison the lands with chemicals, and cut down millions of trees causing the air to thin and sour."

There was a concerted gasp from the other beings. "Cut down the wise, life-giving trees!" "Poison!" "Pollute!"

"What manner of creatures are these humans?" Loriscus framed the question in all of their minds.

"Ah, who knows? Once they were fully part of the Universes and many dimensional travellers passed through here. Now all such knowledge is lost, very few visit this place. Humans do not welcome the unusual."

"What happened?" Poldant asked.

Crysgar shrugged. "A Great War which wiped out their Wise Ones. Those who survived had to start again. Our ancestors withdrew then hoping that this time it would be different."

"Apparently not," Camelion said dryly.

Just then a small furry creature darted past them and shot down a hole in the ground.

"What was that?" Joalla squeaked with fright.

Camelion laughed "It looked perfectly harmless, do you think it could be a human, shall I go down to make contact?"

"It can't be a human," Joalla said crossly, "It isn't advanced enough to cause all the trouble Crysgar was telling us about. Anyway surely you cannot wish to follow it down that muddy hole." As she spoke an even larger furry animal bounded into view, making an incredible amount of noise that was indecipherable to any of them.

"Quick, adjust your translators," Loriscus ordered. Obediently the others communicated a little uncertainly with their new gadgets. "Gremlic, I cannot quite remember how to do this," Loriscus called up to the little servant of the Amorga who had been sitting far up in the branches of a tree, making some calculations of his own.

"You do not need to do anything, the translators will automatically track and adjust to the new language," Gremlic reminded him. "Anyway, not to worry about this noisy one, it is those that follow who are human." There came a crashing through the undergrowth and more voices. These, although in a different language, were of a kind their ears understood. Gremlic flitted down to Loriscus's shoulder.

"Rufus, you stupid dog," a voice yelled, followed closely by a human form not dissimilar to that of the Elverine, although not nearly as tall. A young male burst into the clearing and stopped short at the sight of the cavalcade, his jaw dropping open in silent astonishment. A female human who was running just behind bumped into him abruptly, still laughing madly until she also spotted what had brought him up short. Her reaction was much the same except her eyes continued to dance in anticipation.

Loriscus stepped forward and put his hand to his chest. "We greet you people of Earth," he said. As he spoke Loriscus started slightly because he was *thinking* the words in Elverine, but they left his mouth in a strange language. The translators obviously worked with both hearing *and* speaking. Two enormous pairs of eyes took in his giant form before becoming glued to the sight of Gremlic, who was still perched on Loriscus's shoulder. The girl's hands clutched at the boy's sleeve. He opened and closed his mouth, but nothing came out. "Perhaps the translators are not working properly," Loriscus said to Gremlic. Everyone looked perplexed. The boy finally managed to find his voice.

"Who or what the hell are you?" he exclaimed bravely, jerkily pushing the girl behind him as he spotted Camelion, whom was pulsating in blue and purple waves and doing his best to look friendly. Camelion held up his hand in the Universal sign of peace, but the boy did not relax. Sadly this sign was clearly unknown here. No wonder the dragons had such trouble!

"Er," Loriscus looked puzzled. "We are travellers from Elver, which is situated in the Yellow Zone; we are on a quest. There is no intention to cause harm."

"Yeah, right!" The boy gulped. The girl seemed to make a decision, stepped away from him, and awkwardly attempted to put her hand to her chest and bow in the way that this golden being had done. "What are you doing you idiot, get ready to run!" he growled out of the side of his mouth. She shrugged off his restraining hand, throwing him a speaking look. Then she turned back to Loriscus with a rather wavering smile.

"Hello," she said hesitantly, and then added as a brilliant afterthought, "welcome!" Her jaw tightened at a further growl from her companion and she glared back at him, her expression a mixture of beseeching and warning.

The boy held his silence momentarily but darted his eyes back and forth, tense and ready for trouble, his lips in a grim line. Once again he stepped in front of the girl protectively, his hands bunched into fists. "Deanna! Stop it! These are weirdoes from outer space or something, have you lost your mind?" he whispered urgently.

The girl shrugged slightly and continued to beam in a falsely bright way at the strangers. "Well it's not as if we are going to have time to run is it, so shut up!" she gritted through her smile. The boy looked the strange band up and down once again and gulped shakily.

Loriscus was trying to follow their conversation, but was completely baffled. Gremlic leant forward and murmured into his ear. Loriscus lifted his eyebrows quizzically at his companions and beckoned them forward. "These are my friends and guardians," Loriscus explained slowly as he endeavoured to save the situation. "Poldant, Joalla, and Crysgar are all Elverine. Camelion is a member of the Tribe of Changelings who exist in the Blue Zone. Gremlic is servant to the Amorga, the All Knowing. These are the unicorns that choose to travel with us, Starlight, Crest, Uraj, and Glore." As each name was called out the one referred to responded in whichever way was his or her custom. When Starlight murmured, "Greetings human," the children looked even more startled.

"Oh, real unicorns, and they can talk," the girl gasped with delight, relaxing a little.

"Blimey! I'm going to wake up in a minute," the boy murmured. His face lightened momentarily, "Of course! That's it! I'm dreaming," he told himself hopefully. The girl soon disabused him of the thought by jamming him hard in the ribs with her elbow.

"Do the unicorns here on earth not speak then?" Starlight was aghast.

"I'm afraid there are no such things as unicorns here, excepting in stories," the girl said regretfully.

"This is just too weird," the boy muttered. He unclenched his fists but remained in fighting stance.

"We are called Douglas and Deanna, we are twins," the girl introduced them, frantically trying to cover up her brother's aggression and lack of manners.

"Ah, twins," Gremlic said knowledgeably, "two beings born from their mother's womb at the same time."

"How extraordinary," Joalla said. "What a convenient way of producing young." She stepped toward the two humans smiling so angelically that even the boy began to visibly relax. Everyone became aware that the two humans were very similar, both having dark brown curly hair (although the girl's was shoulder length), long-lashed hazel eyes, and very slender figures. Douglas had a squarer, more stubborn jaw than his sister.

"Our mother probably would not agree with you," Douglas said ruefully. The faces of the two humans saddened at the mention of their mother and the travellers sensed the shift in their emotions.

"Your mother ..." Joalla prompted gently, her clear green eyes seemed to look straight into his soul.

"Our parents died last year," Douglas said, not sure why he was explaining this to a complete stranger.

"Ah! It is always sad when a loved one goes to join the Maker of the Universes," Poldant empathised. Everyone went quiet for a moment.

"Please, will you not join us in a cup of nectar?" Loriscus offered jovially, hoping that they had breached the boy's barriers.

"Yes, thank you," Douglas accepted cautiously. OK, he thought, we're never going to outrun the weirdoes so I suppose we'd better act friendly until I can work out what to do. "Stick close to me," he muttered to Deanna as they moved further into the clearing.

The twins watched with stupefaction as small brown pellets were produced from a travel bag, which when placed on the ground burst into flame. They marvelled as a metal pot filled with golden liquid hung over the heat without support. The gorgeous smell it gave off filled them with anticipation despite their caution. Thick blankets of a material unencountered on Earth were thrown onto the grass to constitute comfortable bivouacs. Douglas and

Deanna were invited to sit down and taste the nectar. Douglas noted with relief that at least his sister had the sense to watch Loriscus take a sip first before trying her own.

Once the first drop had passed his lips Douglas found himself gulping all the contents of his cup down as if his life depended on it. "Fantastic!" he exclaimed enthusiastically, relaxing fully for the first time.

"Mmmm, delicious," Deanna agreed sipping the nectar in a ladylike way. She became aware of a wonderful warm comforting glow and with a sigh lay back and dreamily watched the unicorns as they continued to munch tender grass. Unicorns ate a lot.

It was obvious that the beverage had the same effect on Douglas because all his antagonism melted away, but instead of going quiet as she had done he didn't seem to be able to stop talking. In fact it was the most animated she had seen him since the deaths of their mum and dad. He had been so withdrawn and defensive since then, and yet here he was chatting away to complete strangers with all his old enthusiasm.

"We have come here to live with our Gran." Douglas explained, "Oh, I mean our grandmother. She is … was … the mother of our father," he added, realising he had lost them. "It was a bit strange at first because she's … well … different, you see."

"Different?" Joalla encouraged.

"Gran prefers trees and plants to people. She always has, as long as I can remember. Dad used to say there was nothing she didn't know about them. Sometimes people come for her advice because she can cure sickness just by adding hot water to the right leaf or something. Dad said she could do more to sort someone out than any doctor. Gran thinks doctors are rubbish anyway."

"Do you like living with her?" Joalla cocked an interested brow.

"It's OK I suppose," he paused, "at least she's not on our backs all the time. I mean we can go off all day without her worrying. She says she would know if we were in trouble – the trees would tell her. That's the kind of weird thing she believes you see. Anyway Gran thinks that 13 is plenty old enough to be independent, and she's right, we can take care of ourselves. She even lets us camp out overnight on our own, mum would have freaked wouldn't she Dee?" He glanced at his sister for confirmation and she nodded a little sadly, rumpling her dark curly hair to hide her eyes. It was time to change the subject.

"Please, please tell us about yourselves. What are you and why are you here? Where are you going?" Deanna's questions tumbled out. She drew breath to continue but Loriscus held up his hand laughing as he tried to keep up with her.

"Hold human female ... sorry ... Deanna, one question at a time. Indeed it is our turn to tell our tale. It began on one beautiful day in Elver ..." As he told the twins of their adventures it was his turn to look sad. The twins gasped at the terrible tale of Silbeamia and yet at the same time his melodious voice painted pictures of incredible, unimagined places, amazing beings. The other Elverine and Camelion joined in, eager to add their part. Douglas and Deanna sat entranced as the visitors talked, hardly able to believe all that they heard. Other races of beings, the possibility of travel through different dimensions, space and even time zones, surely these were science fiction stories!

"If you weren't sitting here in front of me I would never have believed it." Douglas stared around at the strange cavalcade with awe. "We have always thought that there must be other forms of life - particularly Deanna," Douglas added hastily at her indignant glare. "Actually, I didn't believe in anything at all particularly since our parents were killed," he admitted, his lips in a straight line.

"All that I have discovered is that adults are afraid to talk about death so they kind of go embarrassed and sidle away when I ask them stuff. At least Gran is pretty straightforward about it, but I think she finds it too hard to discuss dad or mum just yet." Her face reflected her bewilderment and frustration. Douglas flushed and looked away.

"I wish we could go with you and see those cool places that you've been talking about," he murmured wistfully. He was struck by an incredible thought and could see that Deanna had had the same notion; they looked at one another wide-eyed with hopeful anticipation. "Would you … could you … possibly consider taking us with you?" Douglas stammered in a rush, before he lost his nerve.

Loriscus and Poldant looked rather taken aback, to them the twins were the size of very young children back home (they were actually both above average height for humans). Joalla hid an appreciative grin at the consternation in Loriscus's eyes.

"Gran isn't expecting us back until tomorrow because we're camping, and anyway you said that you can do the time thing, so we could be brought back to today and no-one will miss us," Deanna interposed hurriedly, "please, please let us come with you."

All eyes turned to Loriscus whose verdict this had to be, and he gazed back gravely.

"This is no light decision young humans, for I am not sure that your world is ready for this knowledge as yet," he said.

"Then we will swear not to tell anyone," Deanna urged. "We never break our word."

Douglas nodded in affirmation. "No-one would believe us anyway," he muttered under his breath.

"It cannot be a coincidence that these … er, twins should be here at this moment. Have they perhaps been put on our pathway for a special reason? I think they are supposed to join us," Joalla stated, earning a grateful glance from Deanna.

"The humans are right, they have much to learn, especially about this their own planet," Crysgar said meaningfully. "Perhaps the Amorga desires that we should teach them," he hesitated as another thought struck him, "but equally it is possible that the test is to refuse this request."

"Thank you my friend, I'm afraid that is no help at all," Loriscus said dryly looking to the others for their thoughts.

"What is your opinion Gremlic? Do you feel the Amorga has put these two in our way for a purpose?" Poldant asked.

Gremlic was crouched comfortably on a blanket with a cup of nectar clutched pleasingly between his claws. The companions became aware that none but Loriscus knew of the reason for the presence of the small being. He was however well liked and respected, also his company made them feel closer to his mistress, which was very comforting. The silence grew while Gremlic pondered.

Finally he spoke, "I do not think that anyone can decide whether a being is in one place for a purpose except for the being himself. However I do think it is important that these humans are available at this moment to make such a choice, it is part of their life path."

"What do you mean?" Deanna looked puzzled, but at the same time felt that here at last was someone who might start to answer all the questions buzzing in her head.

"Do you not know that no one can tell you the answer to life, because one's questions are different? The paths I choose are not the paths you choose. My answer comes from my experience, my questions, and my choices. I can only tell you that every decision you make, big or small, affects your future and that you must choose after careful consideration of what is right, not necessarily easy. Above all let love, compassion, integrity and an open mind be your guide. Then at least you will rarely have reason to be ashamed of your path in life. In this way eventually you will have your own answer."

Deanna sat engrossed in the wisdom of Gremlic's words, drawing them inside to ponder later. Douglas however had taken on a glazed blank expression, it was all he could do not to roll his eyes at his sister's rapt face. Deanna ignored him pointedly and then heaved a sigh from the very depths of her soul. "I see," she said, "so first we must find and understand the question before we seek the answer." Her brother did a double take, his jaw dropped, this was all way above his head! He shifted restlessly looking from one to the other.

Meanwhile the sagacious little creature smiled beautifully into her face. "You have now taken the first step, O young and perceptive human."

"Is the answer yes or no?" Douglas asked trying not to look confused.

"Yes," Gremlic and Loriscus said together.

The twins leapt to their feet and whooped with joy only to be stopped in their tracks by the dry voice of Camelion. "What about this Rufus, does he wish to go?"

"Of course he must come," Douglas sounded indignant.

"But Douglas, you have chosen to come into possible danger with us, perhaps Rufus does not wish it," Camelion said.

"Whatever do you mean?" Deanna was astonished.

Joalla knelt down by the shaggy coated mongrel and tucked something into his ear. "Rufus, do you wish to travel the Universes with us?" she asked gravely. The twins giggled behind their hands. The dog gave a couple of short barks and wagged his short curly tail. Douglas's broad grin froze as a strange, deep voice emitted from their pet.

"Yes, I would like to come, thank you," Rufus said politely. Douglas's jaw dropped yet again and Deanna squeaked with surprise.

"Was that really Rufus speaking?" Deanna cried out in wonderment.

"Of course it was," Joalla answered somewhat taken aback. "All creatures communicate; it is just a matter of translation." She ran long slender fingers through the dog's shiny coat. "You are welcome Rufus." Rufus licked her hand and panted happily while the ever-larger group of companions laughed with delight.

The evening was well drawn in before the discussions and plans were complete. It was decided to camp for the remainder of the night and then to set the co-ordinates into their teleporters ready for the rain forests of the Americas in the morning. The twins were beside themselves with elation, until eventually Loriscus supplied them with some more of the magical nectar after which they both fell into a deep dreamless sleep.

In the early morning mist Deanna slowly drifted into tranquil awareness. It was very early, with the pink rosy fingers of the rising sun sweetly touching the lightening sky. Why did she feel so wonderful? It had been a long time since she had woken with that feeling of happiness and anticipation. The distant snort and stamp of one of the unicorns instantly brought back memories of the previous incredible day. "Please let it be true," she prayed before she risked opening one brown eye. The first thing her sight alighted on was Gremlic who was lying on his stomach in fascinated contemplation of a tiny perfect daisy. Her slight movement distracted him and he smiled gently. "Enchanting," he said indicating the flower with his claw-like hand. Deanna beamed with relief, it hadn't been a dream, it had all really happened. Energetically she sat up and said, "Thank you," very politely, although she was not really quite sure what she was thanking him for.

"Your planet is very beautiful, it is a great heritage," his eyes were telling her more than the words, but she could not quite decipher the message.

"Is Elver lovely too?" she asked with interest.

"Yes Elver is a place of exquisite beauty. The Elverine value and guard it in order to keep the balance of nature, it is a joyous duty." Deanna began to understand. Seeing her brow wrinkle in a worried frown he went on more brusquely, "Now it is time to wake these sleepy beings, for we must prepare to teleport to the other side of your world." Deanna's stomach lurched with excitement, her eyes sparkled and she grinned happily at Gremlic. With a lingering look at the glorious dawn they both turned and began to rouse the others.

Douglas, never a particularly charming prospect first thing in the morning, groaned crossly when Deanna shook his shoulder. "Go away," his voice was muffled beneath the blanket. She shrugged and went to join her new friends for breakfast and then helped to pack up the camp. Douglas slept throughout. Eventually Poldant decided to take matters into his own hands, turning his ray shooter up to full light he triggered a quick beam at the boy's backside. Douglas yelped crossly as the ray stung him into consciousness, muttering rude words under his breath as he came to.

"It is time to go my friend," Poldant said amusedly.

Douglas shot up to find his sister and the others circling him with huge grins on their faces. He turned rather red, but embarrassment was not a natural state for him, and a sunny smile broke through almost immediately. Anyway, who could be in a mood under these circumstances?

"Sorry," he said, and then continued expectantly, "Is there any breakfast left?"

Joalla came forward with some biscuit-like substance that they had saved for him. It was a travelling meal, containing all nutrients in one convenient package, that the Elverine carried on journeys. Douglas wolfed it down with more haste than manners, "Terrific, right I'm ready to go now," he said complacently, hastily cramming his belongings into his rucksack.

Starlight and his kind wandered back through the trees from the sheltered grove they had chosen for overnight and greeted everyone before magically floating the packed travel bags onto their backs. Deanna and Douglas approached the mystical creatures with awe. Crest, in keeping with her gentle nature, allowed them to examine her razor sharp horn and to touch her translucent white mane. Her beautiful dark eyes looked deeply into those of the human girl, and they became friends. Deanna knew this had happened without being able to explain it, but she felt more honoured by the gift than anything else that had ever happened to her.

"Rufus, Rufus, where are you?" Douglas suddenly yelled. "Oh, that stupid dog has wandered off again."

"Probably chasing imaginary rabbits," Deanna said dreamily, still enchanted by the unicorns.

"No, I'm not," a dignified voice came from behind a tree, "I'm just having a last drink of morning dew before we leave."

The twins goggled, disconcerted, "I don't think I'll ever quite get used to that," Douglas remarked. "If you are quite ready Rufus," he continued far more courteously.

"Certainly," Rufus said as he walked over to join the group.

"I never realised he was quite so dignified," Deanna giggled to Joalla from behind her hand.

"Right, if we are all present, then I suggest we set our teleporters. Oh, here is one each for you twins, you will have to take turns in holding Rufus I'm afraid," Loriscus said. "Also place these little translators in your ears, you will need them before long." The twins excitedly took the devices with shaking hands and attached them trying to act as if this were a completely normal thing to do. The translators fitted perfectly, but the teleporters were much more complicated. They strapped to the wrist simply enough, looking like high tech watches, but the buttons and displays meant nothing, so when Loriscus called out co-ordinates they stared blankly at the digital controls. Poldant smilingly stepped close and helped Deanna who had to resist the temptation to touch his waist-length plait, while Camelion did the same for Douglas.

Just as the companions stood together, teleporters finally set to exact co-ordinates, an eerie cry rang through the treetops. Gremlic and Crysgar froze, their expressions enough to hold the others still. Gremlic's little head turned from side to side as he listened attentively.

Loriscus whispered, "What in the name of the Universes was that?"

"Bathawk," Crysgar stated grimly. All but the humans looked appalled.

"I've never heard of one before," Douglas felt apprehensive without knowing why.

"They are not of your world Douglas. Bathawks are the searchers - the eyes - of the Lord of Zorgia. He must have found a way of sending them through the rainbow," Joalla explained worriedly, her voice rose at another ear-piercing shriek. "They are almost onto us!"

"I don't quite understand," Deanna protested, fear prickling her skin.

"Earth girl, operate your teleporter, there is no time," Poldant whispered urgently, his hand grasped the silvery mane of his unicorn.

There was a slight scuffle, and then in an instant, nothing in the clearing but a slight shimmering of disturbed air. The bathawks circled and screamed with frustration, sensing that their prey had fled.

Chapter 5

he companions re-materialised ten seconds later. Hot, heavy air hit their bodies.

"What a weird sensation!" Douglas exclaimed to Deanna, who blinked rapidly in an effort to regain her equilibrium,

"Are we here?" Camelion sounded querulous; he hated teleporting, preferring to control his own energies.

"Whew! If the heat is anything to go by, then I would imagine so." Joalla wiped an already damp brow.

"More to the point are we alone or did the bathawks lock in and follow us?" Loriscus, always the leader, remained alert.

They instantly stopped talking and scanned the area. "All is well," Gremlic smiled gently "I do not feel their evil presence." There was a general sigh of relief. "But," Gremlic added a warning, "if the bathawks are now aware of which world we are travelling on, then we must make haste, it is only a matter of time before they find us." The relief shifted to a sense of urgency, slightly soothed by the beauty that shone on all sides.

The trees surrounding them were thick, tall and magnificent. Giant cedars stretched luxurious green fingers towards a clear blue sky. Birdcall and other less identifiable sounds seethed from all directions.

"Is anyone missing?" Loriscus glanced around authoritatively. "No?" Thank the Stars." He had been secretly concerned about possible mishaps with such a large group teleporting. The unicorns scented the air, nervously adjusting to new aromas, their ears twitched back and forth as they took in this new environment.

"Wait here," Gremlic commanded as he flew into the treetops, the better to ascertain where they were.

"What exactly are we looking for?" Deanna whispered to Crysgar, not wishing to make a fool of herself.

The stately Elverine bent down and whispered back, "The pure liquid of a magical tree, the properties of which will enable us to travel through the world of Kephlopodia."

"Oh," said Deanna, not really feeling any the wiser. Before she could say more, their conversation was interrupted as Gremlic rejoined them. "Yes, very good," he looked pleased, "this is the place to start looking." There was a momentary stunned silence.

"Don't you know which one is the magical tree!" Poldant expostulated. Varying degrees of horror and amazement passed over every face.

"No, why should I?" Gremlic was complacent, "I have never visited this place before"

"But we thought you were here to guide us!" Camelion exclaimed.

"Then you were wrong O Son of the Tribe of Changelings," Gremlic said gravely, elucidating no further, but adding, "I suggest you take on the shape of the human, we do not know what manner of people inhabit this place." They digested this during another pregnant silence.

"Ah well, mayhap we had best drink a cup of nectar whilst we decide what to do next," Joalla said calmly, coming up with her usual remedy in a crisis.

The confounded group sat in a circle thoughtfully drinking cold nectar. Meanwhile Camelion sat and studied the energy patterns of the two humans before attempting to shape shift. After a few minutes he suddenly transformed into a mirror image of Douglas, but the youngster was so disconcerted that he rippled through many changes before he became satisfied. The twins were glued to this incredible sight, but the others were too engrossed in current events to take much notice.

Loriscus had just begun to voice an inkling of an idea when he froze mid-sentence. "Do not move," he ordered with soft urgency.

An ominously silent wall of natives dressed in ornate loincloths surrounded them. The sun gleamed onto their long dark hair, bedecked with mirrors and feathers, red and black body paint decorated their supple brown skin.

"They don't look very friendly," Douglas muttered stating the obvious to Deanna who cast him a scared but scornful look in response.

"Have your teleporters ready in case of need," Loriscus said calmly as he slowly stood and faced the warriors who murmured fearfully at the size of the blond giant. Douglas hoped fervently that it wouldn't come to that, because he hadn't quite got the hang of his teleporter and knew he could end up anywhere! Loriscus put his fist to his chest and bowed politely. "Greetings," he said. A particularly ornate man stepped forward and spoke fiercely in an unintelligible tongue. Loriscus waited a moment allowing his translator to adjust and tried again. "Greetings," he repeated. The man jumped back in amazement.

"Who are you? What do you want here?" the warrior demanded grimly, quite obviously gathering his courage so that he would not lose face.

"We are travellers," Loriscus replied briefly, not wanting to give away too much until he had sized up the newcomers. Suspicion flared in the face of the warrior leader. He gestured to his men who instantly closed in on the companions and forced them to their feet. There was instant consternation at the height of the other Elverine, Poldant being even larger than Loriscus, and the majority of the spears swung in their direction. A couple of men cautiously approached the unicorns, only to cry out at the sight of their horned foreheads. The travellers glanced at each other as they realised they had made a big mistake in not disguising their mounts. They tensed in readiness for the next wave of reaction. It came.

"What manner of creatures are these?" one was heard to ask another.

"I like it not," came the reply, "there is bad omen in these strangers." The words 'bad omen' swept through the ranks of natives, leaving fear and unease in their wake. Fear bred aggression.

"Shall we teleport?" Poldant murmured under his breath to Loriscus.

"No, they would cut us down before we reach the unicorns, besides, let us see what happens first. If we can convince these people of our harmlessness, they may become willing to help us to find the tree," Loriscus hissed without moving his lips.

"I do not like this," Camelion grumbled, aggressively feeling the weight of his mighty truncheon. Meanwhile, Crysgar the serene glanced around casually. "Is your translator turned off from their frequency Loriscus?" Loriscus mentally made the correction and then nodded. "Gremlic is not here," he continued. Joalla felt her heart lighten at this, while Deanna clutched Rufus and prayed hard. At the same time she noticed that her brother's reaction was the strangest. He was staring in a thoughtful rather than scared manner at their captors as if a startling idea had occurred to him. The warriors nudged their captives on, forcing them to walk for what seemed like hours into ever-denser jungle. Starlight whinnied with irritation when yet more undergrowth snagged in his silvery tail. Crest nuzzled him comfortingly and he gratefully touched his nostrils to hers. The heightened senses of the unicorns and Elverine were aware of Gremlic flitting through the treetops far above their heads.

Unexpectedly the cavalcade broke into a clearing. Douglas gasped at the sight that confirmed his secret beliefs. A settlement lay before them. Dwellings surrounded one huge building that stretched towards the sky. The smaller houses were apsidal with thatched roofs and decoratively painted walls. Larger houses were made of stone, sculptured and also elegantly painted. The centrepiece, the tall building, had the appearance of a pyramid with a house on top. Hundreds of steps led up to it, all carved in stone. Columns decorated with serpents' heads supported the building at the top of the stairway. At each corner was a dwarfed image holding real feathers.

Other members of the tribe began to notice the strange prisoners being led towards the steps of the pyramid. Women came out of their houses, their dresses were beautifully woven chemise-type robes, from behind which the large round eyes of tiny children peeped. Older children danced around the strangers excitedly, some daring to tentatively reach out to touch Joalla's golden hair, then leaping back making a huge amount of noise. There was an even greater outcry when the four unicorns trotted out of the trees. Men crowded around examining them with awe. Their prodding and chattering ceased abruptly and an eerie silence fell when a figure appeared in the doorway between the pillars at the top of the pyramid.

Slowly the regal figure descended, his eyes never leaving the travellers. He beckoned the warrior leader towards him. The man approached and fell to one knee, then he straightened himself and they held a low-voiced conversation with many sidelong looks and gesticulations towards their captives.

Douglas appeared transfixed by the sights of the civilisation around him. Finally he muttered below his breath, "This isn't possible, I must be mistaken."

Camelion who was standing closest looked puzzled. "What?" he asked.

"These people no longer exist." Douglas's comment dropped like a stone into the centre of a pool causing ripples of reaction. Camelion grunted in surprise, the heads of Crysgar, Loriscus and Poldant whipped around, and Joalla drew in a swift breath of astonishment.

"Don't be ridiculous," Deanna said crossly to her brother, highly unimpressed.

"I'm not," Douglas replied earnestly. "Look, you know anthropology was dad's thing and he often chatted to me about stuff. Well I'm sure these people bear a great resemblance to the ancient Mayan civilisation. Besides, we know that no-one on earth lives quite like this any more," his hand indicated the pyramid. "This is a place of worship and sacrifice."

"What do they worship?" Loriscus asked curiously.

"The sun, I think," Douglas wrinkled his brow in an effort to remember.

Before he could go on Crysgar interrupted grimly. "More to the point, what do they sacrifice?"

There was a horrified pause, all eyes were on Douglas. "Mainly animals, but occasionally people," he admitted.

"I told you I did not like it," Camelion commented with ghoulish satisfaction.

All further discussion was brought to an end when the warrior chief turned from the other man and strode purposefully back to his captives.

"This way," he said briefly, and pointed them towards a highly decorated hut with a woven strip of cloth hanging in place of a door. The companions began to enter obediently but were stopped in their tracks by the angry voice of

Starlight protesting as some men attempted to force him and the other unicorns towards an animal enclosure. Loriscus knew it would be impossible to teleport without them. Bravely he attempted to stand between Starlight and the spears.

"No," Loriscus said firmly, hoping fervently that his trepidation did not show on his face. Violence erupted immediately; rough hands jerked the Elverine away and thrust him at the doorway. Starlight reared furiously, his lethal hooves flailing in the air. The other unicorns enjoined him in battle and the companions surged forward to aid Loriscus. Joalla clenched her teeth and aimed her stun ray at the nearest Mayan. He dropped to the ground heavily causing a wail of terror from those around him. Crysgar and Poldant used their weapons to great effect, whilst Camelion swung ferociously around himself with his club. As their cohorts fell unconscious for no apparent reason, consternation and panic spread amongst the battling Mayans. The noise brought men and women running from every direction, and soon any means of retreat was cut off. Rufus barked hysterically at anyone who got too near to Deanna; she, being weaponless, shouted advice and warnings to anyone who would listen.

"What now?" Douglas gasped breathlessly as he swung furiously with a stick to keep a warrior at bay. Everyone was too busy staying alive to say anything particularly comforting.

Meanwhile the women had gathered into a force and began pelting stones rather indiscriminately in the direction of the battle. As one young woman raised a stone above her head, she glanced up and then cried out in awe. A ball of light hovered above the heads of the companions. Gradually all fighting ceased as one after another the Mayans became aware of it and fell on their faces in obeisance and terror.

From within the glowing light came a beautiful voice. "Enough! Who dares to threaten those who travel in My name?" Deanna started slightly only to be nudged into silence by a warning elbow from Douglas.

"Lord of the Sun, we did not know," one of the braver men quavered, "forgive us!"

"Send for the priest," the voice commanded, and at once one of the prostrated men squirmed backwards and then leapt up and ran towards the temple.

The priest came hurriedly, not nearly so majestic now. He fell before the phenomenon in a position of devotion. "What is your wish Lord?" he asked simply.

"These beings are my servants. They have my protection and guidance. Do not harm them." The voice was beautiful and gentle, but powerful.

"No Lord, as you wish," the priest had regained his dignity. He gestured wordlessly to his people who fell back respectfully from the strangers. Starlight tossed his mane haughtily and trotted to Loriscus's side. Crest, Uraj and Glore followed close behind. Joalla touched Crest's silky mane in relieved appreciation, knowing now that they were back in control of the situation.

"I thank you wise priest," the beautiful voice said, "and now, my servants require a place to rest and food to eat before they go on their way. Please take us where I may consult privately with them."

The warrior leader stepped forward and spoke bravely, "Forgive us Lord of the Sun if we have offended you, we sought only to protect our people. If you wish for retribution I am responsible." Loriscus's eyes lit with admiration; here was a true soldier willing to die to save his men.

"Come here Anjan," the voice gently ordered. The man stepped before him unsurprised that the Great One knew him by name. A low moan broke from the lips of a young woman in the crowd, and Joalla knew instantly that this must be Anjan's beloved. His eyes closed as if in pain for an instant, but otherwise he did not flinch. "It is an honour to have a brave heart such as yours working in the name of light, there is no debt to be paid," the golden ball shimmered and some magical sparks touched the face of the Mayan, whose eyes glowed with pride at these words. His men lifted their spears and gave a shout of joy, and the mood of the people swung from fear to exhilaration. The Sun God was here!

Chapter 6

A jovial crowd followed at a respectful distance whilst a very upright Anjan led his erstwhile prisoners to a large stone dwelling. The 'Sun God' floated effortlessly above their heads, shimmering with crystal-like beams. When the Mayan lifted the decorated cloth that hung in the doorway, the companions stood to one side simultaneously to allow the deity to pass. Once inside the cool dimness, Loriscus turned to Anjan and bowed with his fist to his chest. "We thank you for your courtesy and request not to be disturbed." To his delight, Anjan imitated his gesture with a smile before silently withdrawing.

As soon as he had gone the light sank to the floor and became the familiar form of Gremlic.

"By the Heavenly Stars, that was a good trick," Camelion exclaimed in admiration, "even the best of the Tribe are unable to transform in such a way."

Gremlic smiled at his large friend, "It was no trick Camelion," he replied simply.

Crysgar nodded in understanding, but everyone else looked blank. Douglas was totally confused, and said so. The deep laugh of the Amorga's assistant rang against the stone walls causing those outside to lift their heads and listen with pleasure, "Not to worry young human, the mists of uncertainty will lift sooner or later, no doubt." And so they were left to their own thoughts, for neither Gremlic nor Crysgar chose to elucidate further. Crysgar would only say, "When the time is right for each of you, enlightenment will come."

The companions sat in a comfortable circle, and were in deep discussion as to their next step, when there was a slight shuffling from the other side of the woven curtain. Poldant put his finger to his lips and crept across the room. Camelion and Joalla continued talking as naturally as possible while their friends quietly stood in readiness for possible attack. Deanna's heart was in her mouth, but her lips were set in a determined line. Her hand calmed Rufus whose ears were pricked, his eyes glued to the doorway. Poldant whipped back the curtain, raising his ray shooter simultaneously, only to find himself staring into the affronted eyes of the priest. "Ooops!" he muttered. There was a moment of embarrassed silence. Crysgar quickly came forward using his elegant mixture of dignity and charm to full effect.

"We beg your pardon for our crass manners O great priest! Much travelling in strange places has made us wary, we do not doubt your good intentions for one moment." An appreciative fleeting grin on the face of the man behind the priest (Anjan as it happened) showed that the Elverine had struck the right chord. The priest nodded with great dignity and walked past Crysgar towards Loriscus.

"You are the leader of the servants of the Sun God?" His dark eyes flickered over the golden mane of hair belonging to the strangely pale being before him. Loriscus inclined his head slightly and gestured politely for the visitors to sit down. A small cool cup of nectar was handed to each of them. The priest's brows shot up at his first taste of a drink from another world, his entourage reacted similarly. Anjan's normally impassive face became infused with thoughtful pleasure and Loriscus recognised that this man's curiosity would drive him to continue further contact with them. He might prove useful to the quest. The Elverine was still unprepared for Anjan's question however.

"Has the Sun God returned to the sky?" Anjan asked as he looked around the room curiously. Gremlic! No one had given him a thought! The other Mayans also looked around the room with interest.

"Ah, of course," Loriscus glanced around casually, playing for time, "one as great and … er … busy as the Sun God …"

"The Golden One has left to attend to others who work in his name," Joalla's voice came serenely from behind him, "he pays respect to his brother the Moon and has gone to make way for night."

"Has he indeed! I mean, indeed he has," Loriscus said admiringly.

"Yes," Joalla said firmly, quelling the laughter in his eyes with a firm look. The priest was obviously disappointed. A mutter of dismay rippled through the entourage.

"Is there perhaps something we can do for you?" Poldant asked pointedly.

"Indeed, on the contrary," the priest replied blandly.

Poldant looked confused for a moment, "I don't understand, Priest."

"We were wondering, O servant of the Sun God, what it is you seek," he glanced sideways at Douglas's subdued chuckle. "This world of trees is well known to us, it is our protector and our provider, there is nothing we do not know about it," he leant forward in his eagerness. It was all Loriscus could do not to breathe an audible sigh of relief.

"Thank you for your generosity, you are a good man." The Mayans looked delighted; in pleasing his servants, surely they pleased the Sun God himself! Loriscus waited for the words to take effect before he went on, "There is a special tree with magical properties somewhere near the place in which you found us. In this tree is a wondrous elixir which the Great One has told us to fetch in order to travel through another world very different from this." Awe and superstitious fear touched the faces of the men.

They rose to their feet. "It will be an honour to help you; tomorrow Anjan will lead you back to that place. Meanwhile, tonight we hold a feast of celebration. The people will rejoice." The words were helpful, but the expression on the priest's face was unreadable. Crysgar's eyes narrowed slightly.

"I'll bet they will, whether they like it or not!" Douglas thought irreverently, he came to the conclusion that he didn't like the priest.

Loriscus and the other Elverine bowed respectfully, as was their custom. For the first time Camelion and the twins did likewise. They were as one.

"Whew!" Camelion wiped his brow as the last Mayan left and dropped the curtain back into place. Crysgar, ever vigilant, touched his arm warningly before he could go on. Camelion looked puzzled until the older being pointed at their translators. Immediately the companions adjusted the volume to low. "I make many mistakes," Camelion looked mortified.

Crysgar laughed and turned his touch to a pat of comfort. "My good friend, everyone makes mistakes. It is only a subject of sorrow when they continue to commit the same errors, which you do not." Camelion cast him a grateful look.

"Anyway," Deanna said, "where on earth did Gremlic go?"

"Why, I never left you," mysteriously Gremlic's voice seemed to be coming from Joalla who stood with a mischievous grin on her lovely face.

"How on earth!" Douglas came to stand beside his sister. He wondered whether they were about to learn more about these magical beings. His illusion was shattered instantly by the sight of Gremlic's little face peeping up at them all somewhat incongruously from under the folds of Joalla's gown. A great peel of mirth shattered the air as the companions fell about clutching their sides.

"It is just as well that one of you had the forethought to hide me," Gremlic stood before them, the picture of injured dignity.

"Oh, I am sorry Gremlic, I don't mean to offend you, it is just that you looked so ... so ..." Douglas gasped and wiped his eyes in an attempt to contain himself, only to break down again at the sight of Camelion lying on his back with his legs in the air. The huge changeling was shaking with great gusts of laughter to the point that his legs had given way. Wise old Gremlic's eyes gleamed; he understood that this was the way many reacted to a difficult situation, bringing relief to an over-stressed mind.

"By all the Stars, I feel better for that," Poldant grinned as a new sense of ease and well-being pervaded the stone hut.

Loriscus agreed. "However, my friends, be warned that now is no time to relax. We must be vigilant during this feast tonight that we do not betray ourselves nor allow any of our equipment to fall into the wrong hands. Those who work for the Lord of Zorgia may soon be upon us and they have many ways and means of gaining co-operation."

"Perhaps it would be a good idea to set out tonight, straight after the feast," Crysgar suggested. There were a few groans, but a general buzz of agreement.

"In that case you must all try to rest now, whilst you can," Gremlic said.

"What about you then?" Deanna questioned, having noticed that his comment did not include himself.

"Ah, you are observant, young human," Gremlic smiled. "No, I need very little sleep or rest. I will use this time to reconnoitre. I am not wholly convinced that this tribe's intentions towards us are true."

"I think I will come and help you," Rufus said in his strange gravelly voice. Douglas started slightly.

"It is still so strange to hear you speak Rufus. Why is it that now we understand you, you speak very seldom?" he asked

Rufus cocked his head, "I've always just listened I suppose. It will probably take me quite a while to get used to having my opinion considered." Deanna felt rather criminal.

"It is a good idea for Rufus to come with me," Gremlic said. "He will go unregarded by the tribesmen, for it will certainly never have occurred to them that a dog can communicate with us."

Rufus slipped outside and gave a short sharp bark to signal that it was safe for Gremlic to flit quickly up onto the roof. Then he sauntered up to the unicorns that were in a type of corral attached to the hut.

"Oh, I see that someone has remembered us!" said Starlight sniffily. "What is going on? What was all the hilarity about?"

"There's a feast tonight. We plan on leaving straight after," Rufus, not having much time or inclination to pamper lordly unicorns, was to the point.

"Tell Joalla that they must keep us with them when the feast begins," Crest said urgently.

"Why?" Rufus looked as surprised as it was possible for a dog to look.

"I do not really know," she replied hesitantly. "The people here have been crowding around us until a few moments ago, and then one of the priest's guards came and said something which sent them hurrying away. Something does not feel right."

Starlight dropped his injured act instantly. He lifted his head and scented the air. Uraj and Glore trotted over and did likewise.

"Crest is right, there is too much tension in the air," Uraj agreed.

"Gremlic and I are going for a bit of a scout around," Rufus said, "I'll pass your message on to Joalla and the others when I get back."

"As you will O furry one," Starlight said absently, he was busy trying to focus his powers towards the temple to see what energy waves he could pick up.

"O furry one indeed!" Rufus growled to himself as he padded silently away. People pointed and called to one another as he passed, but no one attempted to bar his way.

Without quite knowing why, Rufus found himself at the base of the temple. As he craned his neck back he realised that Gremlic had had the same idea. The little creature was right up on the roof of the temple, and on seeing the dog had observed him, beckoned almost frantically. Rufus lolloped swiftly up the hundreds of steps, and although fit, he was panting so hard on reaching the top that his tongue almost touched the ground. Gremlic briefly put his bony claw-like finger to his lips to indicate that there were humans nearby. It occurred to Rufus that he was so out of breath that he couldn't have made a noise even if he had wanted to!

From inside the building, voices could be heard murmuring. Gremlic and Rufus listened intently. The priest was definitely one of those involved in the discussion, but it was the other two voices that had caused the grim expression on Gremlic's face. Instinctively Rufus reacted with a low growl in his throat, but Gremlic shook his head vehemently in warning, causing the dog to subside in unquestioning obedience. There was something that Rufus couldn't quite put his paw on, but his hackles were rising as if danger were nearby.

"You have done well," one of the unseen said, and the air echoed with the sound of evil. "Are the travellers unaware?"

"They have no inkling of your presence," the priest said obsequiously, "the people hold a feast in their honour tonight. When all is quieter in the early stillness of the morning, you will be free to make your move."

"It is good," the second voice replied in tones that caused Rufus to take a fighting stance. It was only Gremlic's soothing claw that prevented him from revealing himself. "You will be rewarded with great power, as much as your heart desires," it went on sibilantly.

A slight movement from the opposite corner caught Gremlic's attention. He lightly flitted upwards to enable himself to observe more widely. There, flattened against the stone, was Anjan. The emotions pictured on his face told their own story. He had not seen the other listeners, and they had no intention that he should. Gremlic suddenly turned his head and looked down into the compound that held Starlight. The unicorn was looking straight up at Gremlic, his incredible sight untroubled by the great distance between them. Then Rufus observed an amazing spectacle. Starlight's horn began to glow, as did Gremlic's eyes in response. The dog realised they were communicating without sound, and that Starlight had been made fully aware of the danger they were in. Within seconds Gremlic signalled for Rufus to silently slip away.

In the few minutes it took Rufus to run back to the stone hut, the companions had already been fully informed by Starlight who had called Loriscus to him with the special signal known only to rider and unicorn. Reactions varied from dismay (Deanna) to rumbling fury (Camelion). Poldant stood stalwartly on guard near the door, whilst Loriscus and Crysgar discussed the new turn of events.

"The bathawks must have found us," Loriscus said worriedly. It was only then that the identity of the hidden creatures became clear to Rufus.

"Yes, they were quicker than anticipated," Crysgar answered, his brow creased anxiously. "Do you think we should leave now, or play them along until we can escape unobserved?"

Loriscus shook his head, "If we try to leave now we shall have to fight our way out of here."

Douglas, who had been quietly listening to this interchange, cleared his throat. "There is still more to this than I understand," he said, "we have yet to explain how these people came to be here in the first place."

Deanna exclaimed, "You said something about that when we arrived at the village. Why should these Mayans not exist?" Douglas turned his head towards her, "The Mayan civilisation as we are seeing it in this place died out hundreds of years ago. These people should not exist in this form unless ..." his voice trailed off.

"We have gone back in time!" Joalla exclaimed.

There was an appalled silence. If they had gone back in time, did anyone know how to get them back to where and when they should be?

"No that cannot be right," Poldant said, "I do not doubt your knowledge young friend," he glanced apologetically at Douglas, "but our teleporters from the Amorga would surely have to be set for time travel. If it happened that one of them was faulty, then maybe such a thing is possible, but they could not all be defective together."

Loriscus gave a relieved sigh, "I agree with you Poldant, but that being the case, who are these people?"

"We are the Hidden Tribe," someone said from the doorway. The companions whirled around in shocked horror. Poldant, shame-faced at not only being distracted from his guard duty, but guilty of having left his translator turned up, raised his stun-ray towards the intruder. Anjan, for it was he, hurriedly raised his hands in supplication. "Do not attack me Golden One; I am not your enemy." He walked carefully towards Loriscus and fell to one knee as he had done with the priest. "Traveller, some evil has entered our village and those who bring it have turned the mind of Jarin, our priest."

Loriscus relaxed slightly. Anjan had no way of knowing that they already knew this information, and so in bringing it he was offering his services. This proud warrior was on their side. Bright blue eyes locked deeply with dark brown orbs, and their searching regard was steadily returned. Finally Loriscus nodded. Smilingly he put out his hand and raised Anjan to his feet. Then in turn he showed respect to the Mayan by bowing and touching his chest. "We accept your friendship," Loriscus said simply. A smile lit Anjan's face as welcoming hands drew him into their circle.

Douglas moved forward eagerly. "What do you mean, why do you call yourselves The Hidden Tribe?" he questioned.

"Long ago, the leaders of our tribe found to their dismay that our civilisation was destroying itself through greed and lack of discipline. The old ways were being lost, but they were not being replaced with traditions that enabled the people to survive with honour and dignity. The elderly were becoming disrespected and the poor and sick were unprovided for by those who should by right have eased their suffering." The Elverine and Camelion looked shocked, but the twins sadly shook their heads, they knew this world. "A meeting was held, and the people agreed that the only answer was to go deep into the jungle and disappear. In this way they could bring up their young in the correct way without having to fight the corruption of others. We rarely glimpse other humans in the jungle, and we make sure that they are totally unaware of our existence." Anjan's forehead creased, "Now all we have tried to do is under threat. Strange beings full of evil power are at this very moment in the temple and I fear they bode ill for my tribe."

"Your people must have so much knowledge to offer the world of anthropology," Douglas muttered. Deanna looked annoyed as only a sister can.

"Is that all you can think of at a time like this?" she demanded. "Anyway, even if you could go and reveal this place to all and sundry, surely your conscience must tell you how wrong it would be. It would destroy these people more certainly than the bathawks."

Douglas's initial reaction of anger quickly became apologetic. "She's right," he said briefly to Anjan. Deanna looked amazed. Douglas never usually gave in so easily, he seemed to have grown somehow.

"Well done young humans, you progress," Crysgar smiled at them. Deanna flushed with pleasure, but Douglas's face was closed.

"Does Crysgar's praise offend you Douglas?" Camelion enquired.

"No, of course not!" Douglas looked startled. "It is just that all of a sudden I have a sense of ... a feeling that ... somehow the world, the universes, everything I have taken for granted, is completely different, that I have to start again ... Oh! I can't explain what I mean!"

"That is why you progress Douglas. It is because you are willing to look and understand without preconception. Look for the truth and do not always put yourself forward, I mean, do not always consider how a situation will affect you. In this way you will find the right path," Crysgar said.

"Yes, I see," Douglas said slowly. He recognised that this adventure he had taken part in so light-heartedly was going to change the person he was, or would have been, forever.

Anjan coughed slightly impatiently. "Ah, yes of course, we digress," Crysgar said. "Er, does anybody have a plan?"

The door curtain fluttered slightly, and Gremlic appeared. Anjan leapt a metre into the air with fright, and it was all that Loriscus could do to prevent him rushing from the hut in noisy terror.

"There is nothing to fear Anjan. This is Gremlic, he is a friend," he said urgently.

"What manner of creature is this?" Anjan's breath came in short gasps as if he had run too far too fast. Gremlic settled calmly on the floor and fixed his deep red eyes on the Mayan. He seemed to emanate waves of tranquillity that gradually took effect on the warrior. Anjan glanced around and noted the deference with which these other beings held the weird creature, and decided to withhold judgement. He did however rather cautiously keep Loriscus between himself and Gremlic.

"It is good to have a man such as you on our side," Gremlic smiled gently. Anjan's doubts abated rapidly as the beautiful voice had its usual efficacious result. The others hid their appreciation as their little comrade charmed the human into the palm of his tiny hand. Once he was sure of Anjan's feelings, Gremlic turned his attention to the whole group. "You are aware of the danger we are in?" Several nodded. "We must leave during the feast whilst everyone is distracted. Hopefully, with Anjan's help, it will give us a head start. Jarin has told them of what we seek, fortunately the exact place of the tree is unknown to this tribe, only the area. With luck we will gain enough time to find it in the morning light before we pass through the Rainbow."

"If I do this for you, how will it help my people? This evil pervades our home because of you. Will they not seek revenge when they find you have fled?" Anjan retorted. His absolute loyalty lay with his own kind.

"But do you not see, if we are gone the bathawks will follow. They will have no further use for this planet," Joalla said. Anjan's face lightened. "You will however need to ensure that there are no lasting effects on Jarin. Awakening a lust for power in any being is a perilous thing," Crysgar warned.

Attention was then turned to the matter of escape. Gremlic kept the unicorns informed through telepathic messages with Starlight, but only Rufus seemed to be totally aware of this. The dog realised that for some reason Gremlic had decided to keep his marvellous ability to himself. "I wonder who else he can communicate with," he pondered privately. "And no wonder the unicorn seemed to be so all knowing!"

Douglas whistled tunelessly under his breath as he and Camelion wandered, apparently aimlessly, around the village. Their attitude was belied by a certain tension in their stance and eyes that betrayed wariness to the trained watcher. Fortunately most of their entourage were a motley group of giggling children, the adults being mainly preoccupied with the coming feast.

Suddenly the glowing ball of light appeared near the steps of the temple. The children lost interest in the two friends and ran shrieking with excitement informing all and sundry of the return of the Sun God. People streamed from every direction, and for a valuable few minutes all attention was distracted from the travellers.

Douglas glanced around. "Now," he said quietly. Camelion metamorphosed into a small tree. Meanwhile Loriscus and Crysgar stood in stately silence before the Sun God, and all eyes were transfixed on them. Douglas walked swiftly back to where the remaining companions were waiting to see if phase one of the plan had been successful.

"It is a great pity that we are unable to use our teleporters to find the magical tree," Poldant was saying as Douglas strolled in.

"I know," Deanna said consolingly, "but if Gremlic is right in suspecting that to transport over such a small distance will enable the bathawks senses to lock in on us, then it just is not worth the risk."

"Besides," Joalla added, "how would Anjan explain the co-ordinates to us?"

"I am afraid you are going to have to walk through the night Poldant," Douglas said. His friends whirled at the sound of his voice. Douglas put his thumb up, "So far, so good," he grinned.

Outside the people sighed aloud as the Sun God drifted over the treetops and out of sight. Loriscus and Crysgar turned purposefully back towards their hut, giving the impression that some important information had been imparted to them. From the periphery of the crowd Anjan watched Jarin, who stood at the entrance of the temple. The man's impassive face gave nothing away, but he may suspect. It was as well to keep a constant vigilance.

As the gentle dusk of evening fell, the air was filled with a combination of gorgeous wafting smells and a growing sense of excitement. The twins sniffed expectantly. "I hope we stay long enough to enjoy some of the feast," Deanna said wistfully.

"Mmm, yup, me too!" Douglas exclaimed. There was nothing like a lovely bit of roast. "Come to think of it, do the others eat meat?" he queried.

"Oh, I can't say I have really thought about it," Deanna answered. Her brow wrinkled, "None of their own food tastes like meat does it?"

"Well, that doesn't mean much," Douglas said, "I don't recognise anything we eat anyway." Behind them, unseen, Joalla laughed silently to herself. She did like these two humans.

Rufus had had a wonderful couple of hours trotting around scrounging scraps from accommodating housewives. "Shame we have to leave them so soon," he thought as he contentedly cocked a leg against a convenient tree.

"Don't you dare, furry one," Camelion hissed. Poor Rufus somersaulted into the air and yelped with shock.

"What the hell ... ! Why hadn't anyone warned him?" He growled and grumbled under his breath all the way back to the hut.

Douglas saw him sitting crossly in the corner of the hut dejectedly watching them as they quietly packed their possessions into various bags and rucksacks. "Poor old Rufus, what's the matter boy?" he asked in the soothing way that one talks to an irate dog, quite forgetting that Rufus was perfectly able to communicate without any of that condescending claptrap thank you very much!

"For a start I'm neither old nor a boy," Rufus growled.

Douglas straightened and caught Deanna's eye. "Right!" he said rather faintly. Then gathering himself together manfully he tried again. "What seems to be bothering you old ... er ... I mean ... Rufus?"

"No-one tells me anything," Rufus launched into a catalogue of miseries without further bidding. "I go out on a spying mission for you all, and very exhausting it was too..." he exaggerated, not thinking it necessary to add the enjoyable bits, like the interesting scraps of food, "and then, finding it necessary to do what a dog has to do, I'm scared half to death by a talking tree who isn't a tree. What are you laughing at?" he demanded.

"Sorry friend," Joalla apologised. "We were only picturing Camelion's reaction to ... to ..." she giggled again. Rufus looked less dejected, his tail wagged slightly as he began to enjoy the joke.

"Come, let's get on," Loriscus said quietly. The companions sobered instantly. Crysgar laid several bags end to end and threw a blanket over them, the rest of their belongings were piled neatly at the back of the hut. Then they sat down to wait.

The sun lowered and darkness fell with an eerie suddenness. "Not long now," Camelion murmured as Anjan's voice was heard from outside. Douglas lifted the door curtain just as the Mayan reached it with his warriors, their skin was covered with intricate painted patterns, and they looked frightening and awe-inspiring at the same time. Deanna could hear her heart thumping so loudly that she was surprised that no one looked over at her.

"We are to escort you in honour to the feast," Anjan said formally, but his eyes spoke volumes. Loriscus walked out of the hut and bowed politely. "We are honoured indeed," he replied, "but our friend is not well and will join us in a little while," he indicated what looked like a sleeping form under the blanket. Anjan, knowing well what was planned, nodded in a concerned way. He allowed the travellers to reassure him so that his men would not suspect his part in this. The escort formed lines on either side of the guests and marched them towards the temple. As they neared the steps of the little pyramid they saw the crowds of excited people, dressed in their best, craning to catch sight of the servants of the Sun God. The buzz of excitement ceased as the cavalcade reached Jarin, who sat upon a throne in a clearing. There was a line of chairs on either side of him and each companion was led to one by a warrior who then stood behind it. Loriscus managed to look interested and happy whilst his mind darted about frantically at this unexpected turn of events, Anjan had not forewarned them that they would be guarded in this way. The priest was cleverer than anticipated. Jarin and Anjan were meanwhile having a low-voiced conversation regarding the missing Camelion. Jarin was quite obviously not happy at all about the situation and Loriscus gathered by his gestures and angry expression that he was insisting the missing guest should be fetched. Anjan bravely volunteered to take up the duty himself. He nodded almost imperceptibly to Loriscus as he marched past. Loriscus hoped that it meant Anjan had taken account of the priest's attempt to foil any escape; they could only wait and see.

As Anjan walked swiftly to the hut in which Camelion was supposedly resting, a horrible, creeping cold sensation caused the hairs on the back of his neck to lift. Even though it was night, it suddenly felt darker still. He was afraid, but didn't know why. His steps slowed and his eyes slid from side to side as the sense of terror grew. It became harder to walk with purpose as waves of pure evil made him feel he was wading through icy water. He staggered and leaned against a tree, only to yelp with terror as a branch curled around his shoulders.

"Shhh," hissed Camelion, "try to clear your mind, there is a bathawk in that tree over there." After one confirming glance at the ugly hunched shadow, Anjan shuddered and closed his eyes. The bathawks' power must be growing he realised, because he hadn't felt this bad when he had spied on them at the temple. The branch brought him closer to the trunk and Camelion shared his energy with the Mayan. Strength began to flow into his body, the dark fog cleared from his brain as he felt rather than saw the bathawk lift its bony body to soar away, its evil eyes piercing the dark in search of prey.

Camelion metamorphosed back into the human shape he had adopted, his usually cheerful face set in grim lines. He beckoned wordlessly to Anjan before changing into a tiny bird. Anjan felt as though he were in a weird dream. The changeling flew warily just above Anjan's head as they approached the hut, settling gently on the doorpost as the warrior slipped inside. At his chirruped signal the unicorns floated over the fence of the corral, their magical hooves soundless as they landed back on solid earth. When Anjan staggered out under the load of bedrolls and bags, they stood ready to receive them. One by one they disappeared into the dark shadows of the trees. A small owl-like creature flitted down onto Starlight's back; Gremlic telepathically gave directions to the meeting place. A small sigh of relief escaped Anjan's lips as phase one of the plans went without a hitch.

Camelion landed, reformed with a brief grin before metamorphosing into a rather mangy looking cat. The odd pair padded back in the direction of the feast. They stood for a moment, away from the light of blazing fires, watching as children approached the guests to do their ceremonial dance. Rufus, sitting between the twin's chairs, spotted them and tensed in readiness. Douglas, who had been automatically stroking his pet's head, felt the reaction and coughed dryly. The companions shifted slightly in their seats. The crowd moved closer to watch the children who were beaming with concentrated pride. At that moment the cat shot through their legs causing instant chaos and straight past Rufus. Rufus barked excitedly and charged after him into the complex of huts. Deanna and Douglas leapt to their feet and shouting anxiously ran after their dog. Pandemonium broke out as excited children started scuttling in every direction, some after Rufus, and others looking for a sane adult. The remaining companions split in different directions, all of them yelling loudly that they could see Rufus in this direction. Jarin looked murderous and signalled for his men to follow the travellers, but by now this was a difficult command to obey, the Mayan men did not see them as enemies but as honoured guests and were therefore bewildered at this reaction. They mistook the signal and began searching for the missing dog rather than watching their charges. The companions quietly evaporated into the trees in ones and twos as each saw their chance, time was of the essence, the chaos and hysteria would not last long.

As Deanna and Douglas approached the meeting place cautiously, Deanna felt something cold and wet touch her leg. She leapt 15 centimetres into the air, but somehow managed not to scream out loud. Douglas whirled ready to fight, but found to his relief a panting Rufus with lolling tongue alongside them. He smiled slightly at Deanna as she tutted crossly and tossed her hair back with an air of bravado, then his eyes narrowed in concentration as he watched for the others. He nudged his sister and pointed as Poldant closely followed by Loriscus ran towards them. Joalla and Crysgar appeared from another direction. Anjan and Rufus lolloped up last. The second Rufus reformed into Camelion, who doubled over panting heavily, having hared all over the compound to add to the confusion. Loriscus raised his thumb to congratulate his friend, but Camelion was too out of breath to respond.

Anjan beckoned anxiously and led them further into the trees for several minutes until they came upon the unicorns that stood alert and ready to fly. Gremlic sat placidly on Starlight's back, for the entire world as if they were about to go on a pleasant outing. Waves of peace emanated from him as he fluttered to Loriscus's shoulder. The moon began to disappear behind a cloud as they all turned to Anjan and silently shook his hand in thanks, Loriscus then bowed and his friends followed suit. The Mayan warrior smiled sadly and was gone.

The companions travelled through the night, unable to use magical instruments or any other energy that would bring them to the attention of the bathawks. They hesitated at unusual shadows and cringed at the odd shrieking cry, but dawn found them still free and as the sun rose so did their spirits.

Douglas became aware of a slight roaring sound in the distance, and when he glanced around he saw that others had noticed it too. Gremlic indicated that they should move towards it and they obeyed, still silent, all aware that whispering sounds carried above trees to the ever-sharp ears of the evil circling and searching above. The roaring turned out to be a small waterfall, and to their amazement, Gremlic flew straight through it and disappeared. Crysgar glanced at them from over his shoulder, shrugged and stepped forward. No one was surprised when he disappeared too. Each walked into the roaring torrent trustingly and found themselves in an amazing cave; the water-carved walls twinkled with strange white crystals that threw out a mellow light.

"Rest my friends," Gremlic spoke aloud for the first time since they had made their escape. They dropped with obedient exhaustion onto the dry soil of the cave floor and slept.

A few refreshing hours later the smell of nectar bubbling in a pot suspended in mid-air tickled their senses and caused them to stir. Gremlic sat clasping a small goblet, his face broken into a great grin. "Ah, good," he said as Crysgar sat up groggily, "drink this quickly, it is time."

"Oh no! What now?" Deanna exclaimed irritably, rolling over to bury her face in her arms.

"It is time for the mind-link," he replied calmly.

Deanna sat up hastily. "The mind-what?" she exclaimed.

"Oh come on!" Douglas said at the same time, he really felt things were going a little too far.

"You don't mind-link on this planet?" Joalla looked astonished, but not nearly as astonished as the twins.

"The mind-link, of course!" Loriscus interrupted, "Why did you not mention this before Gremlic? It would have saved a great deal of trouble."

Gremlic looked at him. "There was no time," he pointed out gently.

"Well never mind now," Poldant said soothingly, "will the humans be able to link with us?" His question was directed at Gremlic.

"Not this time," he replied, "they have not acquired the skill as yet, they will learn more by observing."

The companions had by now finished the nectar, and began to form into a circle. Upon Douglas's hesitant request for breakfast he was informed that the process was best operated on an empty stomach. This didn't impress him much. The twins stood aside as everyone else including the unicorns stood in silence and closed their eyes. At first nothing happened, but as they watched a light white mist appeared in the centre of the circle. The mist began to form into a shape, then several shapes, and the shapes took on colour. Suddenly they realised they were looking at a panoramic view of the forest and then the picture zoomed in to focus on one area. There stood the old tree in a clearing. It was unlike anything the twins had ever seen before, with ancient gnarled branches that stretched into the sky, but also along the ground. It was part of yet obviously beyond the bounds of this world. Deanna noticed that Crysgar reached down and pressed a button on his teleporter, and with that the picture faded.

"We shall certainly know the tree when we come across it," Camelion remarked as they all blinked and refocused. The twins were too awe-struck to speak, they could not believe the power their companions commanded as a matter of normality.

"Did you all see the direction?" Loriscus asked brusquely.

"Better than that," Crysgar grinned, "I locked in on the co-ordinates with my teleporter."

"Oh, by the Stars, that was clever," Joalla said admiringly, "we shall not have to sense the direction now!"

"Yes, it was well done," Gremlic said. "Now we must go there whilst it is still dawn, and the shadows are dark on the ground. In a few hours it will be harder to hide." The friends prepared to leave hastily and within minutes were standing ready to walk one by one back through the waterfall. Douglas noticed something that had escaped him in his tiredness a few hours earlier; the water didn't seem to make any of them wet! Deanna, who was one of the last to leave, bent to scoop one of the pretty crystals into her pocket, hoping to have a chance to examine it later.

The cavalcade, led by Crysgar with Gremlic on his shoulder, walked quietly in single file. The old Elverine checked his instruments now and then and accordingly adjusted their direction. Then, as the sun was becoming a little too high for comfort, they walked into the clearing and saw the magnificent magical tree that had such presence that it appeared to be a planet within itself. Large monkeys ran along its branches and beautiful brightly coloured birds flew in and out of the foliage. More than one of the travellers drew in their breath in reverence at the incredible size of it.

As they stepped towards it, however, the monkeys stopped playing and began to gather in a threatening knot at the base of the trunk. They bared their teeth alarmingly, and the companions stepped back hastily. "So near and yet so far," Douglas groaned.

"Do not despair young human," Gremlic said. He turned to Loriscus who was watching the scene perplexedly, "Adjust the volume on your translator," he ordered.

"Of course!" Loriscus's brow cleared as he hastened to comply.

"I'm getting quite good at this," Deanna thought smugly as her own instrument gave a tiny bleep when it had tuned itself in. Her smugness faded when the monkey leader's words became clear, he was ordering his troop to be ready to attack.

"Hold, we are no threat," Loriscus stepped forward again. The monkeys froze in mid-chatter, and a smaller one fell off its branch in fright. The monkey leader found himself standing alone as the others seemed to miraculously dissolve into the protective branches. He was obviously made of sterner stuff, because he bravely stood his ground.

"Return now!" he barked angrily, and several large, rather shamefaced monkeys slipped back down to the ground with large thick sticks held before them. Once again their teeth were bared in a frightening display.

Loriscus knelt and opened his hands in supplication. "We are no threat," he repeated calmly. "Stand still and hold your hands open," he commanded in a soft aside to his friends, "do not react unless told." The monkeys ran towards them, weapons raised, stopping only a centimetre or two short of the travellers. Although some flinched slightly, there was no other movement. The monkeys regrouped and chattered quietly.

"Come forward and state your business," the leader instructed. The companions gazed warily as Loriscus obeyed.

"We request the right to fill this vessel with some of the sap of the magical tree," Loriscus took the small golden container from the pouch in his belt.

"Ah, you ask much yet I see you are aware that only the golden metal can hold the liquid," the monkey looked taken aback. "Who told you of this?"

"The Amorga sent us"

The whole attitude of the troop changed in a millisecond. "Why didn't you say so? Please come with us and be welcome," the monkey looked as aghast as it is possible for one of his kind to look.

Deanna sighed with relief, and only then realised that she had been holding her breath. She dutifully followed behind her brother into what appeared to be a living cavern formed by the branches and foliage of the tree itself. As they walked into it the branches closed behind them creating a secluded place that glowed in a radiant green light created as the sun filtered through the leaves. Deanna just knew that these leaves contained healing power, as she gazed around, she saw Crysgar watching her thoughtfully. He smiled slightly on catching her eye, and then she was distracted by the discussion between Loriscus and the monkey, who had introduced himself as Chole. "Please sit and be comfortable," he bid his guests and they sank gratefully onto soft piles of leave.

"Is it permitted to eat the leaves?" Starlight questioned hesitantly.

"You may eat those on the ground and to the level of your chest, but higher than that may prove too much for you," Chole answered mysteriously. Loriscus and Poldant exchanged quizzical looks. Deanna, who felt more alive and safe than she could ever remember, was aware of every little nuance; that was why she saw a private signal pass between Crysgar and Gremlic. She felt compelled to pick a small leaf and chew it, instantly the colours around her appeared even brighter, and her senses of hearing and smell heightened to the point that she had the impression that some great hand had delicately retuned her onto a better channel. She nudged Douglas and whispered to him, and he rather doubtfully picked a leaf and did the same. The expression on his face would have been laughable if the whole experience had not been so beyond human understanding. As the twins looked at one another they realised each was different, nothing would ever be the same again. The enlightened glow of their faces told the others what had happened without words, there was no need to speak of it.

Chole asked them to sit in a semicircle behind him as he spoke to the tree. Ten minutes ago the twins would have found this a great joke, but now they could see wisps of energy rising from it and they could hear a whispering sound which was obviously a language clear only to Chole and his troop.

"Wise One, these beings travel in the name of the Amorga, your sister. It is requested that some of your precious life-giving sap be gathered for their journey into Zorgia." Chole sat back stoically and waited for the answer. The whispering increased, and the monkeys appeared to go into a state of trance, as did Gremlic and the Elverine. Camelion glanced over at the twins and shrugged slightly to show that he, like them, did not understand what was being said, but pointed to his eyes and made a great show of shutting them. The twins hastily followed suit and found that the whispering became clearer, but not clear enough, yet they could feel ancient knowledge and warm dark earth in the sound. Deanna opened her eyes at a slight movement and saw Chole approach the great trunk with the golden container. She watched in astonishment as a delicate branch took it from the monkey and held it to a small dark hole in the bark. Beautiful translucent drops of liquid silently wept into the vessel and immediately gelled into something more solid.

Chole gave thanks and turned, holding up the container for all to see the gift. The trance state was broken and the air became noisy with excited chatter. Many of the monkeys had never seen the life-sap of the great tree, the honour was rarely given. The vessel was passed from claw to hand as each looked upon its contents, yet none attempted to touch it or even smell it as one would expect. The monkeys were treating it as a sacred object.

As Loriscus talked to Chole he discovered that he and others were quite ancient. "It is one of the advantages of being guardians of the Wise One," Chole told him mysteriously. Loriscus suspected that it may be the pure atmosphere causing this phenomenon, but he had no real answer. There was no time to enquire more deeply because Chole was discussing with his band all that the Tree had told him. Obviously some were more tuned in to its language than others Loriscus realised. Chole turned to the travellers and said, "The Tree suggests you move very fast now, the bathawks are close on your trail." The silence was immediate and tense. Deanna realised that the safety of this place was transient, because they could not stay, they had to continue.

Loriscus and Gremlic led the debate as to how best to act with speed. "Before we can make any decision we have to locate the nearest rainbow," Joalla pointed out practically.

"That is true," Poldant admitted, "so let us look now and find out."

"How are you going to do that?" Douglas asked curiously.

"Watch," Loriscus said simply. "Come Crysgar, if we enjoin we will see more quickly."

"I will save my energy for the journey my friend, the three of you will be sufficient," Crysgar answered. The others accepted this but Deanna watched the old Elverine with aroused curiosity, she was beginning to think that all was not as it seemed, yet there was nothing she could actually put her finger on. Now was not the time though.

What the twins saw next almost caused them to run in panic. Deanna could feel a wail of terror building in her throat that she only regained control over when Camelion put a firm hand on her shoulder. "Unknown things are often frightening," he whispered reassuringly. Douglas actually grasped Deanna's hand, so she knew he was feeling pretty thrown himself. He made a small throat-clearing sound, a nervous habit from when he was much smaller.

As they calmed down Douglas's analytical mind took over. To see their friends close their blue eyes only for each to have a large round purple one open in the middle of their foreheads was incredible. The three enormous eyes appeared to peer around in a constantly circular motion, until Joalla's suddenly stopped revolving and fixed on some distant object.

"I have one," she said delightedly. The other two orbs turned in her direction.

"Ah yes," Loriscus said.

"I have it too," Poldant agreed.

The purple organs vanished. "You … you always seemed so normal to me," Deanna gasped, then she slapped her own forehead, "What am I saying! I'm halfway across the world in the middle of a living tree, talking to monkeys with creatures from another dimension. I must be mad!"

There was a pregnant pause followed by a shout of laughter.

"What's normal anyway?" Camelion unwittingly repeated an old earth joke.

"Do you have time to make the journey?" Chole asked uncertainly, humour was obviously lost on him. "No," Loriscus became serious instantly. "The arc is hours away on foot, we will have to teleport."

"But … I thought … What about the bathawks?" Douglas stammered.

"We will have to teleport and create the opening within moments. It is risky, but the only way."

"Oh by the Stars!" Joalla exclaimed "Risky indeed! You know much depends on the strength of the rainbow. If it is faint it may take time to open a doorway."

"Well we don't have time," Crysgar said brusquely, "So we will have to be ready to fight."

"Oh no, not again," Joalla and Deanna moaned.

The companions appeared in a thicket of ferns, and it was drizzling. A faint luminescent rainbow shimmered above them. They did not speak as the three younger Elverine reacted with speed. Once again the purple orbs opened, but this time a golden beam radiated from each. The beams joined into one powerful light, which directed itself at the rainbow. The red colour became stronger and seemed to move towards them. The sound of a magical incantation filled the air as the Elverine controlled this power with ancient knowledge. The very air around all of them became like a red mist, just as the now dreaded sound of screeching was heard in the trees just above them. Another beam of light, this time pink, shot from amongst them and appeared to hold the bathawk in suspended animation for a moment. "Quickly," Starlight groaned, "I cannot hold it for long." Deanna glanced sideways and saw the light shining from the tip of his horn, but hastily looked forwards again as a red door opened before them.

"Run!" Gremlic ordered. They needed no second bidding and sprinted. Starlight backed through last, the pink beam still projecting, but weakening rapidly. Camelion slammed the door shut and Loriscus gave a sharp command. It disappeared, as did the rainbow. Only as they caught their breath and gazed around did the two humans realise the enormity of what had happened. They were in a different dimension and didn't know the way back!

Chapter 7
Red Zone - Jalmar

*T*he twins didn't have much time to go into shock, because the next thing that hit them was a heat wave so solid that it literally sent them reeling.

"Oh my God, it's so hot!" Deanna gasped.

"Whew! That's an understatement," her brother replied wiping the back of his hand across his forehead.

If their reaction was strong, it was nothing to that of the Elverine. Joalla literally wilted before their eyes, whilst Loriscus and Poldant were busily stripping off their cloaks and anything else they could decently remove; their movements were slow and unco-ordinated.

"I can see steam rising from the rocks," Joalla wailed. Rocks of every shape and colour surrounded them. It became obvious that very little could grow and survive here.

Before despondency could set in, the most amazing phenomenon occurred. The sky clouded over without warning and rain fell, hitting the earth with hissing, steaming, splashing sounds. Instantaneously tiny green spike-like plants sprung up in the steam, causing an even more spectacular reaction. Within seconds, little rocks began to roll aside and from behind them ran gnome-like creatures (only smaller), their heads protected by woven hats from under which poked tufts of brown hair. Tiny hands plucked the plants hastily as if their very lives depended on it, and as the last piece of greenery was grabbed, they disappeared as suddenly as they had appeared. The rocks steamed lazily in the heat as if nothing had happened, the whole thing had taken less than two minutes.

Deanna blinked rapidly, not sure if she was hallucinating in the heat, and then glanced sideways at her friends to see if anyone else had noticed anything unusual! From the stunned expressions on their faces they obviously had.

"What … what … or who were they?" Camelion stuttered.

"Those were the Igrul People, one of the life forms on this planet," Gremlic replied. "Very difficult to get to know, and not altogether pleasant I believe," he went on as if nothing out of the ordinary had occurred.

"How do you know?" Loriscus sounded bewildered, although at that moment he was more interested in sipping liquid from the flask normally attached to his belt.

"I have been to this world before," Gremlic replied nonchalantly.

"You jest!" Camelion exclaimed.

"No, this is probably not the best time for humour," Gremlic said wryly.

"So," Camelion drew a deep breath, "which way do you suggest we go then?" He peered around uncertainly at the magnificent display of rocks that spread as far as the eye could see in every direction.

"Also," Crest was concerned, "what do you suggest we unicorns eat?" It was rare for her to speak to anyone but Joalla, so she was obviously worried.

Douglas realised that they had barely eaten for 24 hours and that his stomach was objecting noisily!

"Ah, indeed, I meant to mention that," Gremlic sounded apologetic. Starlight snorted noisily and the other unicorns started to complain, but Gremlic held up his hand for attention, "What I meant to say was that I have taken the problem into account." He pointed to a bag on Uraj's back, which on closer inspection proved to be stuffed with succulent leaves.

"I'm surprised you did not smell it," Loriscus said gleefully. It wasn't often that anyone got anything over on a unicorn. All four unicorns pretended to go deaf.

"Now," Gremlic continued as if no-one had interrupted. "Hold a moment whilst I get my bearings," and he flew up onto a high outcrop.

"You know, this is an amazing place," Douglas commented. The Elverine watched enviously as he coped easily with the heat. He was down on his knees examining the stones scattered around their feet. He held one of them up to the sun to watch it sparkle with deep green lights, but instead of being enthralled he gasped in astonishment.

"What can you see?" Deanna was craning her neck over his shoulder.

"Those," he pointed past the green rock into the sky. Two things struck Deanna at once. Firstly there were three small suns (which accounted for the heat), and secondly there was what appeared to be a flock of dragons flying towards them. They were getting bigger by the second!

Gremlic landed on Loriscus's shoulder with more haste than dignity. "Those are the Dragon Sentries, they will have been told that there is unknown movement in this area," he said mysteriously. No one had a chance to ask why, because the Sentries were upon them. Seven enormous dragons landed causing the earth to judder with a mini shock wave. The companions steadied themselves and tried to look friendly rather than frightened, which was quite hard because the largest, a beautiful emerald green dragon, opened its mouth and a deep rumbling noise followed by a brief flicker of fire emitted.

"I hope that was dragon talk for welcome," Loriscus muttered out of the side of his mouth to Gremlic and Poldant. They all stood like frozen statues, trying not to breathe in case they gave out the wrong signals. By the Stars those dragons were big!

Crysgar recovered first and attempted a few welcoming words. The resultant noise made his translator sound like it was about to blow up.

"Eh! What's that? Stop whispering!" the dragon roared. Crysgar cleared his throat nervously and tried again. "Can't you speak up?" came the reply.

"I am!" Crysgar shouted.

"What are you whispering for?" it bellowed.

"Turn up the volume Crysgar," Douglas recommended pointedly.

Crysgar mentally adjusted his translator to loud. "We come in peace," he shouted lustily.

"Well, Great Heavens, no need to shout!" the dragon exclaimed. "Funny, squeaky little things aren't they?" he commented to the rest of his squadron. There was a general rumble of agreement as several gigantic faces moved in for a closer look.

"What shall we do with them?" asked the blue dragon. His following comment made Deanna's toes curl, "They don't smell very edible." His great snout sniffed gustily at Camelion causing him to lift off his feet in the updraft.

"Um," Crysgar sounded decidedly shaken by now, "we have come to talk to the King."

"Right, good idea," the red dragon brightened up. "Let's take them to King Rialstus." The companions drew a heartfelt sigh of relief.

"I suppose we had better carry them on our backs," a vast golden brown dragon commented.

"Are you sure?" Deanna said in a very small voice, knowing that objections were pointless. Camelion shrugged his mighty shoulders and climbed up with much huffing and puffing. The others followed suit, but no amount of thought could work out how to carry the unicorns; so it was decided that they would have to walk, much to their relief.

"How are they going to find their way may I ask?" Loriscus enquired politely.

The red sentry looked crestfallen for a moment. "We will use an igrul," he exclaimed. "There's bound to be one of the little insects around here. Come out insect or we'll blast the surface," he shouted happily.

"Oh no," Joalla spoke for the first time, "how cruel!" Poldant nudged her warningly as the great black eyes turned on her, and she gulped hastily. Then to her surprise one eyelid dropped in a cheeky wink. "We wouldn't incinerate the insects really you know, we need them to keep the planet surface clean," he said in what he obviously imagined to be a whisper.

"Oh," Joalla said again. At that moment a rock the size of a football rolled back and a really angry-looking igrul marched out. A pair of brown wings unfolded from the centre of his back and he fearlessly flew straight up onto the green monster's nose. He shouted a good deal and even stamped a minute foot, but this was obviously going too far because the dragon, who had been looking quite amused until now, started to rumble dangerously. The little igrul hastily fluttered down and, to Starlight's annoyance, landed right on his head and leant insolently against the unicorn's horn.

"Right, that's arranged then," said the blue dragon jovially, "let's go." At which point the seven colossi soared into the air as their cargo clung on for dear life. A blessed warm breeze lifted their damp hair.

The scenery below flashed past, but enough could be seen to gain an impression of harsh grandeur. There was no greenery and no obvious life forms. Douglas realised that it must all live below ground, away from the searing heat. If they had not come across the igrul it would have seemed to him that the dragons were alone on this planet. He decided to keep his mind and eyes open; this was such a different world that none of his previous concepts or knowledge was valid here. He began to appreciate the beauty of the place without the hindrance of expectation. The craggy surface was littered with huge boulders that twinkled with veins of crystals in every conceivable colour. There was the odd trickle of water bubbling up, but these quite clearly turned into steam within minutes of reaching the surface; obviously the source of the tiny rainstorm they had witnessed. Over all of these strange sights drifted a red heat haze, which treacherously sucked away their energy.

The dragons began to drift into a downward spiral that ended as they landed before the dark mouths of enormous caverns. The sound of roaring with intermittent clanging noises floated up from within the unseen depths. The travellers clambered off gratefully, and Loriscus attempted to look in control and not as if his knees were shaking. "Thank you that was really er ... fun," he lied to the sentries.

"Would you like another quick spin?" The green dragon seemed pleased.

"No!" Loriscus exclaimed. "Many thanks," he added hastily. "It would probably not be a good idea to keep the King waiting," he babbled. The twins actually giggled and the Elverine looked annoyed.

"Sorry, earth humour," Douglas whispered apologetically as he jabbed his elbow into his sister's side.

"Ouch!"

"Are you in charge?" asked the blue dragon who had been watching with interest. "Because if you are then you don't seem to have much control over your squadron? I'd give them a bit of an orocrump if I were you."

"Orocrump?" said Deanna faintly.

"Yes, you know, blow a bit of fire at the old toes," he explained.

"Ah, that sounds like a good idea to me," Loriscus grinned mischievously at the humans who suddenly stopped smiling.

"I'll do it for you if you like," the dragon offered in a friendly way.

"Oh there's no need," Loriscus's eyes grew as round as the twins.

"Would you tell King Rialstus that Gremlic is here," Gremlic said, managing to distract them from an increasingly worrying situation.

"Knows you does he?" the red sentry enquired. "Well, don't depend on that, he's been in a foul mood for a month," he said discouragingly.

"Shooting Stars! The day just gets better," Camelion commented with unaccustomed sarcasm. Fortunately sarcasm was lost on the dragons, which seemed to take the words as a compliment.

"Come," commanded the red sentry as he turned and led the way into the darkness.

The companions clung together as closely as possible, the size of the tunnel increased with each step, dwarfing them by comparison. It was extremely gloomy after the brightness of outside, but very slightly cooler.

"Would you mind if we use some light?" Loriscus asked, trying not to sound irritable, when he stumbled for the sixth time on an unseen rock.

"What! Can't you see?" exclaimed a dragon voice, he wasn't sure which, but realised that their hosts must have exceedingly good eyes to make up for their lack of hearing. "How are you going to do that anyway?" the same voice asked curiously. Several of the Elverine switched their ray shooters to light, immediately causing weird shadows to be thrown in every direction.

"Bless the Crystals. That is a good trick!" one exclaimed.

"Odd little creatures, must be slightly blind," another one said as if they weren't there.

"Could we go on now?" Loriscus asked patiently.

They moved on into an increasingly complex system of tunnels, which opened out now and then into an adjoining hollow. The travellers knew they would never find their way back to the surface without help. Suddenly the troop stopped before the biggest cavern yet.

"Right," said the red dragon, sounding uneasy, "we are here, I will take you in and introduce you, but after that you are on your own."

"Thank you," said Gremlic calmly. Douglas wondered at the little creature's courage, his own throat was so dry he couldn't have made a sound if you paid him! The sentries shuffled around for a moment, as if surreptitiously trying not to stand too near the front of the group. The next moment they were marching across the gritty floor to the most awe-inspiring dragon they had yet seen. It made its own kind look small! There was smoke drifting from its nostrils and a very dejected yellow dragon was clutching its toes whilst half a dozen others scurried out of range.

"Obviously been orocrumped," Deanna thought with dismay.

"What do you want?" the King roared angrily as he spotted the sentries walking towards him. Then he noticed the other beings with them and sat up, his irritable expression changing in an instant to one of interest. "Well, well, if it isn't my old friend Gremlic! Have you brought me a solution to our problem?" He stretched out a great claw.

Gremlic flew onto it trustingly, causing Joalla to grip Poldant's arm anxiously. "I am afraid we have no knowledge of your problem, but we would be happy to help if possible," he said.

"So what do you want then," the King demanded, charm obviously not being his best point. The travellers waited, stepping from foot to foot as their little friend explained their mission. "I cannot see how this can be done," Rialstus said thoughtfully. "None of my people have left Jalmar for a very long time, not since adventurers of old had some very unfortunate experiences, particularly in the Green dimension." The twins shifted uncomfortably and tried very hard to stay out of his eye line. "Things have changed; we don't wish to explore further. Anyway our ancestors found it very uncomfortable in other dimensions, cold and wet I am led to understand. Also generally we hate adventures."

"Er'nest doesn't," the yellow dragon ventured with trepidation, "and he's red."

"Er'nest?" Gremlic said hopefully.

"My youngest son," Rialstus sighed. "His name is actually Rialstusis, but he got lost so often as a dragonet that he for ever had to be directed back to his mother." Even Gremlic looked confused at this explanation.

"When you have said 'from her nest over there' often enough, it tends to be shortened to 'er-nest' and a quick point of the claw," the yellow dragon continued the explanation.

"Ah," light dawned on Gremlic's face, "quite so," he added trying not to react to the chuckles of his companions behind him. The King luckily couldn't hear them.

"Anyway," Rialstus said craftily, "he only gets my permission if you help us out first."

"Tell us of your difficulty," Gremlic answered. Rialstus's voice rumbled on and the companions tried not to look dejected as their hearts sank.

"May we rest and eat while we discuss this amongst ourselves," Gremlic requested much to Douglas's relief. They were led into a smaller cave and at last broke out the nectar and travelling biscuits. It was no feast, but tasted heavenly all the same.

"So," Poldant sat back with a satisfied sigh, "who are the Igrimig?"

"The Igrimig are a form of igrul, but have developed tails and gills, they are water dwellers," Gremlic stated.

"Like mermaids or something?" Deanna squeaked excitedly.

"Mer-what?" Camelion looked confused.

"Water dwellers," Loriscus and Poldant said at the same time. "What water?"

"I saw water when we were being brought here," Douglas looked thoughtful.

"There are underground pools which have funnel-like openings onto the surface. The consequence of blocking off these funnels will be a total disaster," Gremlic looked worried.

"But why? As far as I can see the dragons don't drink liquid at all," Douglas remarked.

"Not the dragons you twit!" Deanna exclaimed suddenly. "The igrul, they will be wiped out! That's right, isn't it?" she looked enquiringly at Gremlic.

"You're right, I am being a twit!" Douglas slapped his forehead. "Gremlic, their whole eco-system would eventually fall apart, an entire race of beings would be wiped out. In fact once the igrul are gone the dragons may die out too!"

"Would someone mind explaining to me, because I have not understood anything at all," Camelion complained. He looked apologetically at Crysgar who patted his shoulder comfortingly.

"The Igrimig have declared war on Rialstus, for reasons as yet unknown, and to keep their race safe they have started to block the water funnels. If no water reaches the surface, there will be no rain. No rain, no spike plants, therefore no igrul. Without the igrul there are no creatures keeping the surface clean. There will be disease and disaster," Crysgar said sadly.

"Oh," Camelion said blankly. "That's terrible," he added resisting the temptation to enquire why it mattered to them.

"The next question is how to speak to, or even find, an Igrimig," Loriscus mused.

"I would suggest the use of an igrul," a voice rumbled behind them. The companions leapt to their feet and swung around. There was a large red dragon sitting just alongside them. Two enormous black eyes stared at the disconcerted group with great interest. They stared back. How on earth had something so gigantic slipped in so quietly? Although the dragon was by no means the biggest they had seen, he was certainly big enough. His tail alone must have been two metres long! Yet despite his size and the upright tuft of spiky scales between his ears that should have made him look ferocious, the wide mouth somehow gave the appearance of a permanent grin. "Sorry, didn't mean to startle you," it said apologetically. "I heard you were here and couldn't resist joining in the fun," he sounded hopeful.

"Er'nest I presume," Loriscus guessed.

"However did you know that?" Er'nest's voice rose in astonishment. Joalla who was nearest clapped her hands over her ears.

"We have been trying to persuade the King to allow you to come with us," Loriscus told him slyly.

"By the Crystals! Really? I would like that above all things!" Er'nest bellowed excitedly.

"Good, we are pleased to have you," Loriscus rubbed his ears ruefully, "only we have to help solve the Igrimig problem first."

At that moment there was a further disruption as the unicorns trotted in with the igrul sitting smugly on Starlight's head. There was a happy scene as the friends were reunited, until Starlight, as practical as ever brought the proceedings to a halt.

"Tell us what is going on and then we must eat and drink, even we cannot live for ever without sustenance," he said dryly.

"Of course, of course," Loriscus said jovially, "but first let us introduce Er'nest who will be coming with us if we are successful."

Starlight came forward to greet the dragon, which appeared to be so fascinated that he forgot to speak. In the middle of politely introducing himself Starlight broke off and looked suspicious. "What do you mean... if we are successful?" he asked. So the whole situation was discussed again for the benefit of the newcomers.

"What a coincidence, we just happen to have an igrul with us." Starlight looked wryly at the tiny creature who was now poking around the cave in cautious investigation. "It's not particularly nice though, I'm not sure it would help us."

"Not even to save its own race?" Joalla was shocked.

"The igrul live mainly for themselves, they are incredibly selfish and would take a lot of convincing about a distant disaster. They are only insects after all, they have no imagination or vision," Er'nest said. Deanna wished he wouldn't refer to the igrul as an insect, it didn't sound right somehow.

"We will eat and talk at the same time," Crest said firmly. "I for one am too hungry to think." The bag of leaves was taken down from Uraj's back and some of its contents emptied onto the cave floor. Unexpectedly the igrul went into an absolute frenzy of excitement; it threw itself into the air and turned somersaults whilst squeaking with delight. They watched in some puzzlement until the light dawned on Camelion.

"Of course! We have more food here than the little thing will have seen in a year," Camelion realised. "My friends, I think we have the answer."

"At the risk of sounding thick," Deanna said hesitantly, "why exactly do we need the igrul in the first place?"

"Yes, well you are being thick Dee," her brother said crossly. "We obviously need it because … um … actually I don't think that bit has been mentioned yet." He went slightly red and muttered, "sorry." Everyone turned and looked at Er'nest enquiringly.

Er'nest looked pleased at being the centre of attention. "The igrul and Igrimig are related and still stay in touch with one another. I wouldn't say they trust each other exactly, but in hard times the Igrimig have allowed the igrul to join them in their water dwellings." Everyone continued to look at the dragon. "Therefore," he went on, "the igrul will be able to take you to the Igrimig leader without days of searching."

"Oh, right," said Douglas, "only, if they already communicate, why can't they sort out the water situation between themselves?"

"That's true," Joalla stated. "So where do we come in?"

"There is obviously something else which King Rialstus has chosen to keep from us," Poldant mused. "Any idea what?" He cocked an eyebrow at Er'nest.

"Well, *I think* it may be to do with Allamang," he answered cautiously.

Crysgar sighed impatiently, "*I think* that you had better tell us the full story, starting with Allamang and what or who that might be."

Er'nest looked worried. "I only know a little of the story and I may be wrong about what is going on."

"Just tell us as much as possible," said Gremlic hastily as Camelion's hand tightened angrily around his truncheon.

"Allamang is a dragon who has started a rising against the King; he wishes to set himself up in opposition. He is trying to draw the young dragons away to join him, but he thinks only of his own glory and does not care in the least about the other creatures. He does not understand that the King and his counsel are responsible for more than just their own kind. King Rialstus suspects that Allamang is behind the actions of the Igrimig and he needs someone trustworthy to liaise. He needs to know what is planned and he will not get the information from an igrul, who will only help itself. I suspect he knows that he can trust you to do the best you can and that your consciences will not allow the wiping out of a complete race of beings." Er'nest looked directly at Gremlic.

"So the King will use our consciences to help him fight his battle," Loriscus said bitterly.

"Yes, but whatever his ultimate reason, he does care about the insects and other wildlife on our planet," Er'nest said loyally. He was after all the King's youngest son. "Also," he added loftily, "you appear to be able to understand the little things, which we find astonishing as they make no sound." The travellers looked at Er'nest in amazement and then at the somersaulting igrul who was making a tremendous racket as far as they were concerned. The dragon's hearing had to be poor indeed! "Besides, unless the Igrimig come to a surface pool, we have no way of going down those tiny tunnels," Er'nest finished.

"It seems that the problem is one of basic communication," Loriscus folded his arms. "Apart from that, your war situation is nothing to do with us. Agreed?"

The dragon nodded fervently. "I will go and speak to my father immediately," and he hurried off.

"That sounds easy," Deanna said doubtfully.

"Hmm, we will see," Loriscus sounded grim.

The negotiations began in earnest with the igrul, who munched greedily throughout. Its language was basic and interspersed with clicks and snarls, which made it really difficult to understand, even with the translators. In the end it was Joalla who befriended the little creature whose name sounded something like Rackap. She managed to stop him chewing long enough to strike a bargain that he seemed to think promised incredible riches! Apparently half the sack of leaves would push him way up the social scale within his clan. By the time the Elveriness had finished with him, Rackap had a beatific smile on his face, a couple of leaves tucked into his belt as a down payment, and one in his hand which he waved about happily as they all discussed the first steps towards contact with the Igrimig.

"We will have to move quickly as you have given away half our food supply," Starlight pointed out.

"Food good," Rackap clicked happily.

"So pleased for you," Starlight stressed sarcastically, which was luckily quite lost on the igrul.

Er'nest swept back into the cave looking agitated.

"What's up?" Douglas asked tersely.

"The King agrees to your condition, but asks you to hurry it along please because Allamang has been spotted at the Emerald Caves inciting rebellion. It looks like war!" His nostrils blew out small clouds of smoke, which they came to recognise as his worry signals.

"Add a little pressure, why don't you?" Douglas muttered.

"I take it the insect has agreed to help." Er'nest stared at the igrul who was lying with his head on Rufus's back and clicking a happy little tune to himself. "Um, could I point out that you appear to have got it drunk," he added worriedly.

"Drunk! Of course not, Rackap's only had a couple of leaves, nothing to drink at all," Loriscus exclaimed indignantly.

"Are they very *sappy* leaves?" Er'nest enquired delicately.

"Certainly they are, that seemed to be the whole point," Loriscus said irritably. Then light dawned on his face. "Oh no! You are joking!" he moaned, not knowing whether to laugh or cry. Joalla started to giggle and couldn't stop even when Loriscus glared at her. He struggled with his emotions for a moment and then gave in and roared with laughter. Only Rackap, who leapt behind Rufus with fright, and Er'nest, who just looked puzzled, didn't join in.

"What do you suggest we do now?" Camelion asked the dragon, trying not to grin as the igrul tottered away from Rufus and fell behind a rock.

"I don't know," Er'nest said crossly. "I have never got an insect drunk before."

"Well he doesn't have time to sleep it off," Deanna said anxiously.

"I think I may be able to sort this out," Gremlic said, calm as ever. He walked behind the rock that hid the igrul, who could be heard happily clicking again. As they watched curiously a ball of light grew and whirled around the two strange little beings. Gremlic pointed and the light sank and enveloped the igrul's body. Rackap sat up suddenly, straightened his hat, and walked purposefully towards Loriscus.

"Ready foreigner?" he asked for all the world as if *they* had kept *him* waiting.

Ready." Loriscus nodded, not trusting himself to say more. Rackap jumped onto Rufus's back, and directed them onwards into the darkness. Rufus actually looked rather pleased as he led the cavalcade.

The tunnels became steeper and narrower, causing them to slow their pace considerably.

Eventually Er'nest said sadly, "I'll have to wait here for you, I will get stuck if I come any further." They bid him goodbye and walked on with his voice roaring "Good luck," behind them.

Their small beams of light revealed nooks and crannies that had never been out of darkness before. In one place the walls shone with a green radiance. Douglas, the ever-curious, stopped for a closer inspection. "These crystals look rather like emeralds," he said jokingly.

"Emeralds good. Young dragons must eat greens," Rackap responded pragmatically.

"You are kidding! Do you mean that all the crystals and jewels are the dragon *food*?" Douglas gasped.

"Yes, no good for anything else," Rackap replied disinterestedly.

"In our world they are very valuable," Douglas explained.

"Why?" the igrul asked. Douglas opened his mouth to explain, but couldn't think of an answer that would make any sense to the little creature, so closed it again.

At last, as their legs ached with weariness, a narrow tunnel opened into a small water-filled cavern, beyond which they could just see a much bigger pool. The larger pool was dappled with diffused light, which appeared to be coming from several small holes in the cave roof.

Loriscus and Poldant ran their own light beams over the calm water and around the edges in an effort to find a pathway. Rackap was not fazed at all by the water barrier, instead walking straight along the left-hand side of it, close to the cave wall. It was no more than ankle deep.

"Do not wander from this path, water dangerous," he whispered tensely. The others clung as closely as they could, but the path turned out to be a narrow ledge which was broad enough for a tiny igrul, but a difficult balancing act for them. The unicorns, with four hooves to control, had a terrible time. Crest's hind hoof slipped and trailed momentarily into the pool. Instantly the water began to boil and frightening clicking sounds echoed around them. Rackap gave a shriek of terror and bolted for the larger cavern. Great pincers began to appear all over the water surface, followed by beady black eyes on stalks. Loriscus automatically turned his beam onto the creatures, just as Gremlic frantically called for them to stand still and turn off their lights. It was too late; the beam brought the creatures straight to them clacking greedily as they closed off all avenues of retreat.

"Switch to stun," Loriscus ordered trying not to sound scared. The Elverine shot their stun beams hurriedly at anything that moved, but although the clacking lessened here and there, the giant forms drew ever closer. Deanna felt pincers enclose her leg and screamed with horror, she clutched desperately at her brother as the creature began to force her into deeper water. Douglas yelled and kicked at her captor's gruesome maw, holding onto Deanna with all his strength. Their shouts brought Gremlic to their side, and a ball of light flew from his fingertip and batted the monster away from the terrified girl. The other creatures became more menacing still and seemed to increase their efforts.

"I don't think we can hold them," Crysgar called despairingly, as Camelion's great truncheon crashed onto the hard shell-like head of one of the attackers. Just as all seemed lost, the water boiled again.

"Oh no!" Joalla screamed hopelessly. "There are more of them."

As the words left her lips, the attack stopped as quickly as it had begun. The monsters simply sank beneath the water and disappeared.

"What happened?" Poldant's great chest heaved as he gasped for breath. The sudden silence was eerie and almost as scary. He had his answer as Rackap waded towards them, a huge grin splitting his face.

"Rackap get help, still get good food?" he asked hopefully.

"Many thanks Rackap, yes you have earned every leaf," Loriscus assured him gratefully. There was a movement and a splash in the pool, causing them all to swing around anxiously.

"Not to be frightened," Rackap piped, "I bring Igrimig friends." At that, many little heads popped up from the water's surface. They were similar to the igrul, but each had a shock of deep green hair, which looked like floating pondweed, and a vicious little spear held high. The spears were pointing at them!

"Rackap," Gremlic said, his eyes never leaving the little beings, "they are not acting like friends to us."

"Oh no," the igrul said happily, "not your friends! No, Rackap's friends, they not like you."

"Great," Douglas sighed, "so what happens now?"

The Igrimig parted as a large version of them approached, his hair was bound with small white crystals, and his face was grim. "The Boss," Rackap looked excited, "wearing salt crystals, very important time." They realised on closer inspection that his hair decorations were indeed salt pieces wrapped in a clear filmy substance.

The Boss lifted his spear and started to speak in angry clicks and snarls. Rackap's face fell ludicrously, "He says foreigners not welcome - are prisoners now." The companions had hastily tuned in their translators to add this sound frequency.

"We have come to help you and to prevent the war," Gremlic started to say soothingly.

"Ah, you speak Igrimig language foreigner," The Boss said admiringly. "I will talk to you but these ugly creatures must stay here," he gestured towards the others.

"My friends all speak your language The Boss, we all wish to help," Gremlic said placatingly.

"We also thank you for rescuing us from the water monsters," Joalla added. The Igrimig started to make a weird squeaking sound and Rackap joined in.

"Very funny foreigner," Rackap wiped his eyes and began to squeak again.

"Are you laughing?" Deanna asked as she realised that this wasn't some odd ceremony.

"Of course! You foreigner very stupid," Rackap said sunnily, "calling Igrimig pets monsters!"

"Pets!" Camelion exclaimed, ruefully rubbing his arm which ached from constantly wielding his truncheon.

"I can't see the joke myself," Poldant muttered out of the side of his mouth to Joalla who rolled her eyes in agreement.

"Why were they attacking us then?" Loriscus asked The Boss.

"Guard pets hungry," The Boss said.

"Oh!" Loriscus gulped "So they were going to eat us?"

"Not all, only one or two," The Boss explained kindly.

"That's all right then," Douglas said faintly, feeling quite sick.

"Told The Boss you make pets ill," Rackap whispered slyly.

"Thank you," Loriscus replied, and he meant it.

The conversation seemed to have the effect of restoring The Boss's humour. "All ugly foreigners may come," he said magnanimously. Rackap jumped up and down with glee and turned to lead the way towards the larger pool.

The pool was alive with Igrimig who had come to see the visitors. Tiny young ones cavorted with excitement and pointed out how odd-looking and ugly they were. Some of them had red hair that floated behind them in the water, and now and then their fish-like tails could be seen flicking above the surface.

"Oh, aren't they sweet?" Deanna cooed.

"No, they aren't!" her brother exclaimed crossly. "We were almost lobster bait back there!" Deanna flushed slightly and tossed her head, but wisely kept her own counsel.

They were led to a dry rock shelf that was a metre wide, allowing even the unicorn to relax and rest. "You and you come," The Boss pointed peremptorily to Gremlic and Loriscus, who obediently followed him and his entourage. Once they had gone, the travellers sat down for a bite to eat, having learnt by now that they had to do this at any opportune moment. Joalla had her work cut out trying to stop Rackap getting drunk again, much to the amusement of the others. Thus it was that Loriscus and Gremlic found quite a merry group when they returned. The humour disappeared rapidly at the sight of their faces.

"What's happened?" Poldant asked for all of them.

"It is very bad," Gremlic shook his little head sadly. "We are the cause of this war, we cannot avoid the fight."

"How can that be?" Crysgar voiced their bewilderment.

"Allamang is indeed behind the Igrimig's declaring war, but …" Gremlic paused.

"The Boss has described the creatures colluding with him, and I'm afraid it sounds like he is in the clutch of the bathawks," Loriscus finished.

"How is that possible?" Douglas questioned. "We have only just got here ourselves."

"We are not ruled by human time my friend, Gordagn's seer must have worked out that this is where we would be heading, some of the bathawks have been here for days," Loriscus replied.

"But the sentries said King Rialstus has had a problem for longer than that," Douglas reasoned.

"Yes, Allamang was already inciting rebellion, but nothing may have come of it if the bathawks had not found such a ready-made accomplice and situation to exploit. It is their evil power which threatens to topple this world," Gremlic said.

"Surely, in that case, when we move on the bathawks will follow and the situation will be over," Deanna pointed out.

"I wish it were that easy young human," Gremlic answered. "Sadly, the rebellion will not now simply disappear; some of the young dragons have already been persuaded that Rialstus should be toppled. Allamang has also convinced The Boss that the Council has a nuisance policy for exterminating insects."

"Its madness, they can't believe that!" Poldant exclaimed. "The Igrimig have a valuable place in the planet's eco-system, they care for the water and keep it clean!"

"All war is madness, Elverine," Crysgar said. "It feeds on fear and there is no place for logic."

"Besides, if we do not sort this out to the King's satisfaction, then he will not allow Er'nest to come with us and the quest will be over anyway," Loriscus's face was white with anxiety.

"All is not lost as yet," Gremlic said soothingly. He turned to the companions, "We have managed to persuade The Boss to stop the work on blocking the funnels for now. We tried to explain how this act would alter the weather systems on the planet and therefore bring irreversible change, but he did not seem able to think that anything he did could cause such a consequence. He sees only his short-term responsibility, to protect his people now. He did agree however that if King Rialstus has sent us to liaise with him, then it is safe to halt the work briefly. The Boss has given us time to prove ourselves, and therefore Rialstus, through an act of faith."

"What does he want us to do?" Joalla asked, she felt increasingly concerned about the constant hold ups in reaching Silbeamia.

"And why does he not trust King Rialstus in the first place? He doesn't appear to have done them any harm," Douglas puzzled.

"Allamang is apparently charming and charismatic; Rialstus sadly is not. He can be high handed which does not make him popular," Loriscus replied.

"Perhaps Allamang has promised the Igrimig something besides telling them their safety is threatened," Gremlic pondered. His eye alighted on Rackap who was slyly nibbling a leaf whilst Joalla's attention was distracted. "Come my friend, there is work for you to do," he beckoned the igrul over. Rackap sighed despondently and trailed over on unwilling feet.

"What now foreigner?" he demanded irritably, he was beginning to think that making his fortune required rather too much effort. Camelion cleverly pulled some leaves out of the bag and nonchalantly fed them to Crest, who made a great show of enjoying them. The igrul's face changed rapidly, he forced a little sharp-toothed smile, all the while keeping an anxious eye on the scene. "Rackap ready to help," he claimed.

Gremlic sent the little creature off to find out whether his Igrimig friends knew of any gossip to relate regarding the war. He went willingly enough when a few juicy leaves were handed over as bribes!

"Do not give him enough to get drunk again," Joalla said, "or he will never get back with the information." They all grinned as Rackap looked affronted and marched away determinedly. Joalla had forgotten that he could understand everything she said.

"It's funny, but you used to act as if I were deaf too," Rufus commented to the twins.

"Sorry, but we are *learning* to be more considerate aren't we?" Deanna apologised as she ran her fingers through the dog's fur.

"I should not have said such a thing," Joalla was now mortified, realising she may have hurt the igrul's feelings.

"There is no point in worrying about it now," Poldant assured her, "I'm sure that once he and his friends sit down around a nice couple of leaves, your words will soon be forgotten."

"I'm not so sure that would be a good thing," Loriscus murmured wryly.

Once again they played the waiting game whilst their small ally was gone. There was very little sound as each sat engrossed in their private thoughts. So much had happened and yet they were aware that the most dangerous part of the quest lay ahead of them, but any further progress depended on a creature which this world considered to be an insect!

Several hours later the 'insect' could be heard returning long before he could be seen. There was a strange high-pitched caterwauling sound that quickly brought the companions to their feet. Deanna, by now used to the idea that she may have to fight her way to freedom, grasped a small rock in readiness. They stood together and prepared to face the foe as it emerged from out of the dark tunnel mouth. Rackap swayed out of the darkness towards them, the awful noise coming from his wide-open mouth. He stopped abruptly at the sight of the aggressive group, and closed his lips with a snap, cutting the next wail off mid flow. "Greetings foreigners," he lifted his hat, the effort causing him to rock backwards slightly.

"Drunk again!" Starlight snorted in disgust as everyone groaned with dismay.

"I bring friends to talk to you," Rackap said grandly, loftily ignoring their reaction, and pointed to the water lapping at the side of the rock shelf. They saw several Igrimig weaving towards them, each smiling beatifically; one appeared to be doing a form of backstroke.

"How helpful," Starlight commented sarcastically.

"Yes indeed," Joalla said hastily, seeing Rackap's brows starting to lower with temper. "You have been so clever." The igrul's smile returned as he walked over to Loriscus with exaggerated care.

"Friends have information you desire, have promised them reward," he explained grandly, then he hastily put his hand up to his mouth and whispered, "only one leaf each, yes?"

"Information first," Loriscus declared firmly, reaching into the sack and grasping a handful of leaves which he held just out of their reach.

"The Boss want save Igrimig from extermination," one said, his greedy eyes never leaving the bribe.

"We know that," Loriscus replied patiently. "What else has Allamang offered to convince The Boss that he is on the side of your people?"

"Precious salt-crystals," another replied reverently, as if that were all the explanation needed.

"What on Earth does that mean?" Douglas looked puzzled.

"Indeed, what does it mean on any planet let alone Earth?" Camelion added, looking equally puzzled.

"Salt crystals great treasure," Rackap looked shocked at their ignorance, "very rare, only The Boss allowed to own some."

"Why only The Boss?" Loriscus asked, feeling as if they were getting somewhere.

"Salt crystals make him The Boss, give him power," Rackap said simply. "More crystals, more power."

"Where do they come from then?" Deanna asked curiously. "Don't they just form wherever the water and sun meet? And why do they give The Boss power?"

The igrul and his friends looked at her in amazement. "Big but stupid," one commented as he shook his head sadly.

"Water pure, not have salt," Rackap explained kindly. "Salt crystals only on High Mountain called Aidem, very dangerous place, only dragons have strength to fly there and survive."

"I see, but why do they give power?" Deanna asked again.

"Crystals have healing energy," Rackap replied, patting her hand benevolently.

"So if we bring the salt crystals instead of Allamang, then it will prove Rialstus's loyalty to the Igrimig," Loriscus stated excitedly.

Rackap's eyes grew enormous in his head. "Very dangerous, big fire inside Aidem, too hot, not go, no no!" The words tumbled out of his mouth. "Allamang and the creatures will fight you," he added for good measure.

"Big fire," Gremlic mused thoughtfully, "Ah! I believe we are speaking of a volcano!" he exclaimed as the information took shape in his mind. There was a mixed reaction from his friends, mainly groans of dismay, but Douglas at least was delighted.

"I've always wanted to visit a volcano," he explained to no-one in particular.

"Why?" Deanna sounded exasperated and scared all at once.

"Why not?" Douglas replied simply with a shrug of his shoulder.

They found Er'nest sitting where they had left him, almost beside himself with impatience. "Hello there," he bellowed happily as their wavering beams of light caught his eye. Rackap jumped and rubbed his aching head crossly, snarling what sounded like rude words under his breath. "So what's happening now?" Er'nest asked. "Are we on for an adventure?" His great skip of joy at the affirmative that Gremlic gave him crashed heavily in mid-step when he heard where they were going next. "Aidem! Are you quite mad? Only very experienced soldier dragons ever go there and not many of them." He went quiet for a while as they continued to plod through the tunnels. "Actually, that is not true; there is one other whose name has been whispered with awe for many centuries. The hermit dragon who is said to hold the wisdom of the ages within himself, he is a dragon of peace, yet he has been."

"What is the name of this dragon?" Gremlic asked with interest.

"Taerg," Er'nest said reverently, and the very walls of the tunnel seemed to murmur with admiration.

"Take us to this Taerg," Loriscus demanded curtly, time was running short.

"Taerg is a recluse, he speaks to no-one," Er'nest sounded anxious.

"He will see us," Gremlic promised quietly, and they all knew that it would be so.

On returning to the cave in which they had set up camp, Gremlic advised them to try to sleep whilst they could, then he flew away into the darkness.

"I wonder how he can see where he's going," Deanna thought as she drifted into a pleasant doze. Joalla shaking her gently on the shoulder waked her.

"Come little Deanna," she said softly, "Gremlic has returned." Deanna sat up and rubbed her eyes sleepily, finding that her vision had adjusted to the darkness. She peered around the cave still rubbing her face. Her hands stopped mid-action as she looked over to her companions. There was a blue glow around the Amorga's servant that disappeared almost as soon as she registered the fact. She blinked twice and came to the conclusion that she was imagining things as she stumbled sleepily to join the others.

Gremlic looked around at his friends with luminescent eyes. "Taerg has agreed to talk to us," he said with a smile. Loriscus's head went back as a sigh of relief exploded from him. Poldant clapped Loriscus on the back with delight as an excited murmur rippled around the cave.

"How did you manage this?" Er'nest's voice boomed with astonishment. Gremlic smiled, but did not answer.

"It matters not!" Loriscus exclaimed delightedly. "When can we go?" His question was directed at Gremlic.

"Now," was the answer.

Chapter 8

The companions blinked and covered their eyes as the sunlight hit them with the effect of a thousand flashlights going off at once. Then a second wave hit them, the heat! Rackap spread his wings with delight, and Douglas realised that the little being had not attempted to fly in the tunnels. The wings grew and changed colour slightly as the sunrays were absorbed into them. "They are like solar panels," he thought with wonderment, "they only work in sunlight." The sight of the Sentry Dragons flying rapidly towards them distracted his observations. The ground shook as they landed and the yellow dragon called, "Hello there," in a happy rumble. Er'nest greeted them like the old friends that they were, and then Gremlic explained where they needed to be carried next. There was a stunned silence. "Did you say Taerg?" the red sentry asked hesitantly. Gremlic and Loriscus nodded. "By the Three Suns," the great creature muttered almost under his breath, "and this has been agreed?" He looked enquiringly at them. They nodded again. Respect dawned in his eyes "It would be an honour," he said.

"Hold on," Starlight said as they began to clamber onto the Sentries' backs. "What about us? You can't mean to leave us behind again."

"No indeed," Gremlic agreed. He pointed a long claw like finger at the four unicorns and chanted a few words. Instantly they levitated into the air and hovered with their hooves suspended just above the scaly back of the brown sentry. "Our dragon friend's energy will hold you magnetised for the duration of the trip," he told them.

"Thank you," Starlight sounded rather uncertain. "Er … why didn't you do this before, you know, when we first arrived?"

"I knew we needed to bring the igrul with us," Gremlic answered. There was no time for further explanation as they took off.

"By the Universes, this is wonderful," Uraj said excitedly.

"Mmm," Crest agreed faintly. Glore stood staring straight ahead, as if afraid that any movement would cause an undignified fall. As they rose into the air Rackap waved merrily from the ground, a small sack of leaves tied to his back with a tail hair of a unicorn (Starlight's).

Once again they flew high above rocky terrain with the suns catching different outcrops of crystals in occasional magnificent flashes of colour. The heat pulsated and caused the air to shimmer; if it were not for the wind of flight blowing through their hair, it would have been almost unbearable.

Deanna was sitting just behind Gremlic, who sat for all the world as if he were in peaceful meditation, he was making no effort to hold on and was as at ease as if he were on firm ground. She hesitated for a second and then gently touched the little creature's shoulder. Gremlic opened his eyes and smiled gently at her, "Yes my friend?" he said.

"Why is everyone so worried about going to Aidem?" she enquired.

"Aidem is a place of myth and legend, very few have seen it, and so the superstition has grown," Gremlic replied.

"Oh," Deanna said, "but *is* it a scary place?"

"Sometimes one thinks there is reason to fear," Gremlic answered somewhat mystifyingly.

"Oh," Deanna said again, not sure whether she was any the wiser. Poldant, who was clinging on for dear life, nudged her and nodded his head towards Douglas who was just ahead on the blue dragon. They all laughed at the sight of the human boy who sat with his arms held wide as he whooped and yelled ecstatically, urging his mount to go faster and higher!

A mound of green rocks appeared on the horizon, and the Sentry Dragons started to spiral down towards it. They landed in front of a black cavern as high as a three-storey house, just as the rain phenomenon occurred again. From all around the cave mouth small boulders rolled aside as a tribe of igrul rushed out to pick the crop as it magically appeared. These igrul were slightly different in that their wings were more golden and their faces were far pleasanter in expression.

"I wonder why they are different," Douglas the curious asked aloud.

"The Great Taerg is an ecologist," Gremlic said unexpectedly.

"What do you mean?" Douglas asked, confused.

"Well, this is a rare breed of igrul which Taerg helps to keep alive by creating the right environment for them," the yellow dragon said, "not sure why myself, but there you are."

"Cool," Douglas muttered faintly.

The companions followed their guides into the darkness, having waited patiently for the dragons to argue out who was going in (they all wanted to see the Great Taerg). In the end, as none of them would back down, everyone went. The first thing that struck them with blessed relief was how much cooler it was within, the second was the pleasant sound of running water.

"What *is* that noise?" one dragon asked uneasily.

Loriscus strained his eared "I can hear nothing but the sound of running water," he answered.

"Running water!" another dragon exclaimed, "Running where, what do you mean?"

Douglas realised the enormity of the question. These dragons, which had never been able to get down to the rock pools of the Igrimig, had no concept of water beyond the tiny brief cloud bursts which they had witnessed above ground. The rich diversity of life that existed on his own planet Earth depended on this substance which he had always taken for granted.

"Not to worry," Gremlic said cheerily, "Taerg will doubtless explain." The dragons seemed willing to accept that.

They followed the sound of the water until they reached its source. The sight that met their eyes was incredible. A very large dragon, which gleamed wetly with a myriad of sparkling droplets, was busily working at the base of a small waterfall. Around him ran many igrul, all deeply intent on some task, while several Igrimig darted around in the pool of water. All were chattering loudly apart from Taerg himself who was so absorbed that his visitors went unnoticed.

"By the Three Suns!" exclaimed Er'nest, whilst the Seven Sentries seemed dumbfounded. Taerg turned quickly at the sound, and bustled forward with his front claws extended in welcome. Taerg appeared unperturbed by the various beings that had appeared in his cave; in fact he seemed to be rather delighted considering his reputation.

"Ah! My guests! Come, I have been expecting you," he roared happily.

Loriscus stepped forward with Gremlic on his shoulder. "It is kind of you to meet with us good Taerg," he said.

"Nonsense, always charmed to meet the new and unexplained," Taerg answered rather bafflingly. "Would you Other World creatures care for a drink of liquid, I believe it is very necessary for your survival." The great black eyes took in the Companions rather wilted condition.

"Thank you," Loriscus said gratefully, "this planet is very hot."

Taerg beckoned an igrul forward. The creature carried a tray containing tiny red goblets, each filled to the brim with a clear fluid. Gremlic took his cup first and gingerly sampled a minuscule sip. His odd little face became wreathed in smiles. "It is fresh water," he confirmed happily. The others surged forward eagerly, and quickly downed the contents of their own goblets, protocol forgotten for the moment. Meanwhile, Taerg watched with great interest and even began making notes on a scroll lying on a flat rock. "Fascinating, fascinating," he kept murmuring as he scribbled.

Er'nest and the other dragons became even more bewildered. "What are you doing?" the red sentry asked almost plaintively. Douglas realised that along with never having seen running water before, the dragons had never seen anyone drink either! He opened his mouth to explain, but Taerg's booming voice over-rode his.

"The Other World beings need liquid or they will die," he explained enthusiastically. "That is right is it not?" He turned questioning eyes to Loriscus, who nodded in a bemused fashion. Taerg slapped his scaly tail against the rock floor. "I thought my conclusions were correct," he exclaimed excitedly, "and tell me, is it not also correct that in your world, water falls from the sky continuously and lies all over the ground in pools? And that there are several great pools, so large that the eye cannot see across them, in which creatures similar to the Igrimig live?" His words tumbled out.

"Not quite continuously," Loriscus started to explain.

"Really? Come, all of you, I have waited many a year to meet some of your kind, let us sit down comfortably and you can tell me everything!" He glanced at the Seven Sentries. "You may go and be refreshed by my insect friends," he pointed peremptorily to another cave.

"All except Er'nest, if you please," Gremlic said firmly. "He is one of us." Gremlic's thoughtfulness was rewarded by the red dragon's grateful glance. Er'nest brought up the rear of the party with a very definite swagger.

The companions told their story well, each adding their own personal part to it. It was indeed the first time that Camelion and the twins had heard of the earlier adventures in such detail. Taerg listened intently whilst the insects continued to work undirected. He turned his eyes onto Joalla and then Deanna. "You are both females of your species are you not?" he enquired looking fascinated.

"Er … yes," Joalla responded, feeling rather like a new scientific discovery.

"Well, I will help you," Taerg nodded "but on one condition." Their hearts sank. Not another condition! "Er'nest must promise to collect information and samples of these other worlds and bring it to me on his return."

Er'nest looked pleased and enthusiastic. "Of course, of course," he nodded feeling rather important. He realised that there was no point in saying much because Taerg had only interest in the unusual and to him Er'nest was quite ordinary.

"Why have you never travelled the other dimensions to see for yourself?" Douglas asked.

"That is not my path," Taerg answered simply.

"Ah," Douglas said trying not to look more confused than ever.

"In the history of the Dragons there were those who ventured to other dimensions, but they were not well received. Their shape and form is too unusual for any civilisation that may be in the early stages of development. Their presence created fear and that often resulted in violent reaction. Many stalwart dragons were lost to the ignorance of others," Crysgar explained. Douglas nodded, trying not to look guilty, but Deanna became aware of how seldom the old Elverine voiced anything aloud. In fact sometimes he appeared more of an observer than anything. Her train of thought was interrupted by a commotion at the cave entrance. An igrul flew in hastily, calling out and scattering the other igrul in all directions. From Taerg's reaction this was not a common event. He snapped from the easy manner in which he had been plying his scientific questions to one of intense awareness.

"What is it?" Gremlic questioned urgently.

"Allamang must have scouts out, they are approaching fast." The old dragon sounded amazingly calm considering the import of what he was saying. The seven sentries marched in, their bearing grim and ready for battle. There was no sign of their gentle good humour now.

"Stay here," the green dragon ordered. "We shall go out and head them off." Smoke puffed aggressively from his nostrils.

"Wait a moment young warrior that may not be necessary," Taerg's tail twitched momentarily. "I have created a weapon which I have long desired an opportunity to try out." With these words his tail virtually danced with suppressed excitement.

"He's actually pleased," Deanna realised with astonishment.

The old dragon barked out some curt commands, which caused a momentary stunned silence from the suddenly still igrul, followed by frenzied rushing about. Taerg drew himself up to his full magnificence and marched towards the entrance of his cave. "Do not show yourselves under any circumstances," he called over his shoulder. "Any of you," he added as he spotted the Sentry Dragons forming into a fighting unit. "I am sure he knows what he is doing," Loriscus shouted up to them, aware that all genial buffoonery had disappeared from the Seven. They had converted in seconds into terrifying fighting machines.

Meanwhile the golden igrul were excitedly pulling and pushing at levers which seemed to operate great metal chains. As these groaned and creaked into life a huge barrier rose up to block the waterfall, and the water stopped flowing. An unnatural silence hung in the air, all eyes and ears straining to follow what was happening at the cave mouth.

Taerg stood alone and unafraid, ready to greet his unwelcome visitors. Three warrior dragons landed heavily some little distance from him, the ground shaking in response to their weight. He waited for them to speak, retaining control of the situation. An enormous dark green dragon cleared his throat and spoke in what he clearly hoped was a cool arrogant voice, but actually sounded slightly nervous and awestruck.

"So you are the Great Taerg."

Taerg neither moved nor acknowledged the comment, but continued to stare them down.

The three looked rather perplexed; they were used to a somewhat different reaction. "We understand that you have some strangers here and have come to take them off your hands," the green dragon became peremptory in his puzzlement.

"Indeed," Taerg murmured at last, and then "strangers," he said rolling the word around his mouth as if it were an interesting snack. A little puff of steam rose lazily from his nostrils, at which warning sign the intruders stepped back hastily.

"We know of your reputation old dragon," one called angrily, "but you are no match for us."

"Ah." Taerg's voice remained quiet and yet dangerous, "Was that a challenge?"

"Er … no, well yes," the green dragon became slightly tongue-tied. "Look," he shouted, suddenly losing his temper as he felt that he had begun to lose face in front of his friends, "do you have them or not?"

"You are not welcome here," Taerg stated calmly, refusing to answer the question. "Please leave or I shall be obliged to force you to do so."

The warrior dragons gaped back at him in astonishment. It was true that the ancient had an awe-inspiring reputation, but after all he was old and alone. How could he possibly repudiate them? The leading dragon gave an order and they formed into a threatening knot, ready to surge forward. Instantly Taerg signalled the waiting igrul with a flick of his tail. Willingly many hands rushed to pull another great lever, and for one dreadful moment it appeared that nothing happened. Then the companions heard a terrifying rushing sound followed by incredulous shouts of alarm that faded as the unwelcome visitors rapidly retreated. Taerg virtually danced back into his cave. "It worked, IT WORKED! By all that is Mighty. What a wonderful opportunity to try out my invention," he crowed with delight. The others all gazed at him perplexedly. He clearly wasn't fazed at all by the threats of the warrior dragons.

"What happened?" Loriscus shouted when he finally got the old scientist's attention.

"Come and see," was the gleeful answer.

Cautiously they moved outside, first ensuring that no warrior dragons were circling above Taerg's sanctuary.

"All clear," Taerg pronounced, peering around. Douglas noticed that he even looked straight up beyond the mountain tip. The renowned eyesight of a dragon would go both ways he realised. Then he saw the comparatively abundant greenery that had sprung up a little distance from the cave. An ecstatic crowd of igrul rushed past him and began to gather in the harvest at great speed. Already some of the spiky tips were turning brown in the heat.

"What happened?" Loriscus asked again.

Taerg pointed to a smallish opening above the cave mouth. Protruding from it was something that appeared to be the circular end of a large pipe. "My invention involves building water pressure and then releasing it in a controlled direction," he explained happily.

"A water cannon!" Douglas realised with awe. Such an unknown thing would have been terrifying for the attacking dragons.

"Ah, so this concept is known on your world?" Taerg's interested eye swung in the boy's direction. Douglas nodded and began to excitedly discuss the weapon with him, but Joalla interrupted them

"So you didn't hurt them?" She sounded relieved.

"For God's sake Joalla, they were going to hurt *us*!" Even Deanna felt that the Elveriness was going too far.

"If we inflict injury on purpose, then we are no better than the bathawks," Joalla replied.

"Not if it is self-defence," Deanna argued defiantly.

"But look, we did win without harming them," Joalla pointed out gently.

"Not for long," Taerg interrupted this burgeoning disagreement. "They will return with reinforcements quite soon, so let us get on quickly."

They hurried back into Taerg's stronghold and were refreshed with more goblets of water as the old dragon dug about in his huge pile of scrolls, muttering to himself. "Aha!" he exclaimed at last. "Here it is." He pulled out a rather battered specimen, which he proceeded to study thoughtfully. His great claw appeared to be following a path as he read intently. "Yes, this should do it," he announced, satisfied.

The travellers had stood all this while, patiently waiting for Taerg to include them in this little episode. He turned and espied them, and yet for a moment looked through his visitors, his mind clearly full of far off memories. Then he shook himself and became all purposeful and business-like again.

"This is an old map that I created when I made the journey to Aidem myself. Of course, there may have been the odd rock fall or some such thing; it was after all at least a century since I drew this. Be aware my friends that the path is pitted with magical obstacles which will be far harder to overcome than the physical ones. I have tried to note where these danger spots are, but of course the Guardians may have changed some of them."

"Guardians?" Loriscus's eyebrows rose slightly.

"Aidem guards many treasures beside those which you seek Traveller, you must win the right to gain the crystals." Taerg replied.

"Of course," Loriscus sighed. "Nothing has been easy so far, why should this be?"

"Exactly!" Taerg boomed jovially, completely missing the note of exasperation in his guest's voice. They gathered round so that Taerg could point out the path he knew, meanwhile reiterating the danger spots.

"Why can't we fly to the top on Er'nest's back?" Loriscus asked reasonably.

"Because there is a magical magnetic field that will pull you to your death," Taerg rumbled casually, ignoring their stricken faces. "It occurs to me," he concluded, "that perhaps the little furry one had better stay with me for now." He pointed at Rufus who was swimming, sublimely content and cool at last, in the rock pool.

"No!" Both twins cried at once.

"But think young humans, he does not have the thought process to cope with this situation, he could unwittingly betray you." They all stared at Rufus and then at the twins.

"The quest cannot be jeopardised, your dog will be safe here, the same cannot be said for Silbeamia." Loriscus looked at them pleadingly.

"I'll go and talk to him," Douglas sighed.

"Me too," Deanna strode after her brother.

They sat together for some minutes deep in conversation. Eventually Rufus wagged his tail, licked their hands, and jumped back into the water. They returned, Deanna's eyes brimming with tears. "We will come back for him you promise?" she gulped at Loriscus.

"I promise," he said, knowing guiltily that it may not be possible.

"Your little friend will be safe with me and that is more than you can offer him right now," Taerg soothed. "He will greet you when you return to the King." No one questioned his statement.

The adventurers quickly donned their packs and prepared to climb aboard the dragons' backs. Each thanked Taerg personally, but as Douglas followed suit their host presented him with a gold and silver encrusted flagon, rubies and diamonds winked in the bright sunlight. He was overwhelmed with the gift, but even more so when the old explorer explained, "This is a magical flagon which I came across on one of my youthful adventures, it refills with water whenever it has been emptied. I feel you may need it more than me. Also I suspect that you are a scientist at heart and one day I would be delighted if you could return so that we may compare knowledge." Douglas stammered his thanks and was touched that the few simple questions he had been able to ask had brought him so great an acknowledgement.

"I would love to come back," he told Taerg realising at the same time how bizarre it was for him to promise inter-dimensional visitations as if he did it all the time! As they soared up into the sky he knew that he would keep his promise one day, survival permitting.

The dragons flew up and onwards, undaunted by the searing heat, until they came in sight of Aidem. Even without Gremlic pointing it out, the mountain was unmistakable. It rose steeply from the smaller peaks around it and was made of dark rock that belched red jets of fire and grey plumes of smoke which hung ominously in the air, obliterating the very tip. The companions drew ever closer in silence, the enormity of their task dawning on even the most optimistic.

The Seven Sentries landed in a valley about a quarter of the way up their adversary. "This is about as far as we dare go," the golden dragon said apologetically. "I wish we could come with you, but we have been ordered to wait here for your return. May the Light of the Three Suns bless you on your journey." The dragons lined up to form a guard of honour watching unblinking as the cavalcade wound away until the rocks obliterated them from view.

Douglas held on tightly around Poldant's waist, even the wonder of riding on the back of a unicorn was unable to curb his anxiety. He glanced over to check that Deanna was still sitting behind Loriscus. He knew she would be of course, but this frightening place was making the hair lift at the back of his neck. His sister grinned weakly at him, trying to be reassuring but not quite succeeding. She had never felt so scared in all her life, but knew there was worse to come. After all at the moment nothing had really happened, they were just riding up the side of a mountain, so far unhindered. Yet the grim words of warning uttered by Gremlic echoed around her head. "Silence, caution, no sudden moves, no-one is to move anywhere without my permission."

The path abruptly veered off at a right angle, and Gremlic, who was sitting up before Crysgar, raised his claw to signal a halt. Obediently they waited whilst he consulted the map. Gently he fluttered to the ground and picked up a small rock that he threw onto the path ahead just at the point where the right angle was created. Instantly there was a tremendous rumble, the earth shook, and then the enormous rocks on each side of it slapped together like two huge hands. The reverberations rumbled off into silence as the companions sat frozen with horror at what might have been.

Once again Gremlic warned wordlessly that they were to keep calm and not react. He seemed to be waiting for something. The very air was loaded with foreboding. As they watched, the space between the two vicious rocks filled with a deep red energy. "Now!" Gremlic urged (later the twins were to realise that the word had formed straight into their minds), and the unicorns galloped with all the might their great strength allowed. Deanna held on for dear life, her eyes tight shut, so she didn't see the fissure opening darkly on the other side of the energy field. Nor did she see Gremlic pointing at it, directing them within, the bulk of Er'nest only just scraping through. When she opened her eyes it was so dark that she was momentarily disorientated. Loriscus reassuringly patted the arms clenched in a death-like grip around his waist, then he switched his light ray on to low beam.

Within that black space even such a small radiance made a huge difference. Strangely they felt slightly safer. "If only to see what is coming," Douglas thought grimly. As his eyes adjusted he realised with a jolt that the beam seemed lost within a never-ending gloom. Loriscus, who together with Gremlic had ascertained their direction, interrupted his thoughts. "Remember, no magic, no sudden movement, as little noise as possible, nothing that will unnecessarily disturb the Guardians. This way!"

Douglas swallowed dryly and squared his shoulders. "What the hell am I doing here?" he thought before pushing it to the back of his mind. Well they had no choice now, the only way for him and Deanna to get back home was to complete the quest.

They marched slowly but steadily for at least an hour until Joalla prodded Poldant to get his attention and he in turn poked Loriscus who halted and looked around enquiringly. "Something is travelling with us," she breathed. Instinctively the companions gathered closer. They listened intently. Nothing. Loriscus shrugged perplexedly at Joalla as he signalled for them to continue. Starlight didn't move, nor did the other unicorns. Their silky ears were still twitching in every direction. Loriscus immediately settled back in his saddle and waited. Unicorns have excellent hearing.

Not however as excellent as the sight of a dragon. Er'nest quietly moved from the back of the group. "We are in great danger," he whispered to Gremlic. They all jumped at the volume, dragons aren't good at whispering. Deanna realised that this could be their saving grace. If the Guardians were dragons then they wouldn't be attuned to their comparatively small sounds. Meanwhile Gremlic signalled urgently to Er'nest to be quiet. He flew up to the dragon's head and began a telepathic conversation that caused such a reaction from the huge beast that it would have been funny had the situation not been so serious. To everyone's amazement they could all hear every word as if it had been spoken to them personally.

"Er'nest do not speak out loud, just think your thoughts and I will think mine back to you as I am now." Er'nest literally looked over his shoulder in consternation even though he knew the voice belonged to Gremlic.

"Isn't this magic?" Er'nest responded fearfully. "We aren't supposed to use magic."

"No, this is energy transference, not magic. Calm down. Tell me about the danger."

"There are creatures the like of which I have never seen before slithering all along the rock face beside us." The companions were almost palpably thrown into silent panic.

"Oh hell and damnation!" Douglas forgot that everyone was tuned in to him.

"Could be," Poldant answered as he drew his own ray shooter.

"No Poldant, be still!" Loriscus was stern with the need to control them. They subsided obediently but maintained their fighting stance. "Did Taerg mention this Gremlic?"

"Er, not exactly. He did tell of cave dwellers unique to this place, probably created by a fusion of magic, but I'm not sure that he had any trouble from them. It was more than a century ago, they must have multiplied. I can see them now."

"Hell and damnation!" Douglas thought again. "What now?"

"I am reading their vibrations," Camelion said unexpectedly. "They have some similarity to the igrul, but less substantial. I am going to try to shift into a similar pattern, perhaps they will communicate with me."

"Do you think that is a good idea?" Joalla said anxiously.

"What else do you suggest? If we find they are working for the Guardians then it will make little difference anyway." He melted away, everyone else held their breath and strained to see what was happening.

Minutes passed. A unicorn stamped restlessly. Then just as the companions were coming to the awful conclusion that a rescue mission was going to be needed, they found themselves faced with two of the strangest creatures they had yet seen. Completely white, scaly, with the head and tail of a lizard, the body similar in shape to an igrul, but much bigger (about a metre tall) they stood carefully just within the perimeter of Loriscus's light beam, red eyes blinking at this unusual light source. One of the creatures made a sound between a croak and a hiss. It made Deanna's hair lift at the nape of her neck.

"Adjust the translators," Gremlic reminded them telepathically.

The creature spoke to them again, but this time they were in a position to understand.

"Intruders are not welcome here."

Undaunted Loriscus held up his hand in the universal sign of peace. Unfortunately it was not recognised and there was a scary scuttling sound from all around them as others started to close in. "Er ... we come in peace," Loriscus said as calmly as he could, aware that his heart was in his mouth. As ever the experience of hearing their language from that of a total stranger had its usual effect. The threatening movements stopped instantly and the speaker froze before them. "Just like a lizard back home," Deanna thought.

"That's true," Douglas replied.

Deanna started slightly. "This telepathy thing is a bit weird!"

"Stop chatting," Loriscus interrupted.

"Well I didn't mean to!" Deanna said crossly.

"Shhh," Gremlic took over. "And don't be rude," he warned her as she started to automatically think the sort of things that people do when they've been told off.

"Oops!" was her final comment.

"We have not come to bring harm to this place," Loriscus said aloud and tried not to sound nervous.

"No-one comes here without purpose," the lizard thing said.

"Well, why would they?" Douglas thought irreverently, but caught hold of himself at a warning growl from Crysgar, a faint accusation of pointlessly bubbling human minds reaching him.

"Indeed my friend, you are right," Loriscus said aloud, and then added in a more decisive voice, "we have come here to find something that we need to help us fulfil the quest we are sworn to."

"Ah," it said, "and what would that be?"

"Salt crystals," Loriscus replied bluntly. Well these creatures were either going to help them or not, might as well get on with it.

The thing bowed its head a second and then disappeared out of the circle of light. The second lizard stayed. It looked directly at Loriscus and, to his astonishment, winked. They stared at each other momentarily until light dawned in the Elverine's mind. "Camelion?" he whispered. It winked again. "By all the Stars be careful!" Loriscus breathed anxiously. Camelion nodded and then faded away.

Er'nest and Gremlic continued to scan the darkness beyond.

Suddenly the silence was broken by the sound of Camelion's frantic voice. "Run, for the love of the Universes run. Take the right-hand cave and stop for nought, I will find you!" There was a horrible crunching noise, then nothing. The troop galvanised into action and the unicorns galloped forward, the incredible speed of their kind taking the enemy unawares. Loriscus and Poldant shone their light beams ahead, switching them to dual action so that they could see and stun at the same time. In the increased light they could all see the terrifying creatures running up the cave walls preparing to surround them. Crysgar aimed and fired between Glore's ears as he leant forward into the gallop. Er'nest threw spouts of flame to either side hearing shrieks of pain as he lumbered swiftly in the wake of his new friends. The two younger Elverine swathed a path clear in front of them, Poldant proving to be a crack shot as they prevented the attacking horde from blocking their way. The twins held on for dear life, not for the first time Douglas wished he had a weapon of his own.

They had been riding fast for half an hour when Gremlic called a halt. Stillness replaced chaos, for the moment at least they had outrun the host. Starlight and the other unicorns breathed deeply, the sweat of terror and exertion running over their white hides.

"What now?" Poldant voiced what was uppermost in all their minds.

"We keep going," Loriscus replied grimly. "There is no other choice."

"And Camelion?" Crysgar was very upset.

"Camelion told us not to wait, we must honour his request, we cannot go back. He of all of us has the skill to escape if he is able." Loriscus was finding the role of leader held many difficult moments, but he knew he was right. He could not risk them all for the sake of one, nor would Camelion want them to. Heavy-hearted, they moved forward at walking pace, weapons at the ready. Deanna felt tears streaming down her face.

Chapter 9

*D*ouglas reached for the magic flask and took a deep cool draught of water, then he handed it to Deanna so that she could do the same. One by one they quenched their thirst, each giving it to the next in turn. Finally it reached Gremlic who was focusing deeply on the way ahead. He took it almost absently from Loriscus and then became aware of what was going on, his huge red eyes transfixed with horror.

"Have you used this?" he demanded into Loriscus's head.

"Yes, we all have," Loriscus was puzzled.

"But are you not aware that this is a magical artefact? It will act like a beacon to the pursuants." For the first time ever they saw him lose his composure.

"In that case you may as well give me a drink before we have to run for it again," Starlight snapped. Gremlic tipped the water into his mouth.

"We only have to travel in the dark for a little while longer," Gremlic urged, "and then we will be travelling out in the sunlight. Hopefully it will be a little cooler than earlier."

"Right my friends, are you ready?" Starlight asked peremptorily. Once again the beautiful steeds prepared to bear their burdens to safety. They galloped courageously with Gremlic giving them telepathic directions, his red eyes scanning the map in the blackness.

"There it is!" Gremlic exclaimed. "There is the light leading to the outer path, only a few more minutes."

"My heart is going to burst," Crest gasped desperately. Joalla patted her friend's neck anxiously, there were no words. And then they were out in the blessed sunlight even the heat a welcome relief. Er'nest, rearguard and therefore last to exit, keeled over panting great gouts of steam as he tried to get his breath back. Everyone leapt off the backs of their mounts and formed a defensive circle. Starlight, Crest, Uraj and Glore stood with their heads drooped low as they tried to regain their strength.

"Well they know we are here now," Loriscus pointed out the obvious.

"Yes, well done, thank you for that," Douglas said sarcastically.

"What I'm trying to say is that we may as well just go for it now using magic or whatever it takes." They all looked at him.

"You're right," Gremlic said decisively and instantaneously threw an invigorating energy field over them all. The unicorn revived like magic. Deanna was aware of a sense of growing strength flowing through her body. It was wonderful, even her terror floated away! She felt she could face anything. Shoulders straightened, heads went up, and they became an operating fighting unit once again.

"Right, let's go!" Poldant sounded almost exuberant.

They prepared to mount but were halted in their tracks by an unknown voice just above them.

"Go where?" it asked simply.

All ray shooters were swung in its direction and Gremlic was pointing ready to hurl a magical blast. They saw one of the lizard-like creatures standing calmly, all alone. Its white body was covered in a green robe that culminated in a cowl from the protection of which steady red eyes gleamed. A small but wickedly sharp sword hung at its side. Not one of them considered even for an instant that the little warrior was anything but deadly. Yet, what held their fire was not the fact that it was alone, but the unexpectedness of its actions. To their astonishment it held up a claw in the universal sign of peace!

"Hold!" Loriscus ordered. As one the companions obeyed, although all weapons remained at the ready. They stood poised.

"I am Drock the Outcast," it said. "I have been waiting for you."

"Er ... I do not think that is likely," Loriscus said cautiously.

"Indeed I have. Legend foretells of strange and weird beings coming to change the order of the Drock."

"That isn't us," Loriscus said firmly. As if they didn't have enough to do! "Anyway, I thought you said your name is Drock."

"I am Drock the Outcast of the race of Drock," the Drock responded patiently.

"You mean you are all called Drock?" Loriscus was astounded.

"No, because I am called Drock the Outcast."

Loriscus blinked twice. The conversation was surreal! "Right," he said at last. "What can we do for you, er ... my friend?"

"It is what I can do for you stranger. I am waiting to lead you to the crystals."

"Why? And how do you know we seek the crystals?"

"Because in doing so I will meet my fate," Drock The Outcast said calmly. He ignored the second question.

"By The Universes!" Loriscus was now really irritated. "Can't anything be simple?"

"It is simple," Gremlic was amused, "it is just that everything is linked in one way or another whether you like it or not."

"Right, come on then," the elegant Elverine manners were temporarily lacking.

The lizard somersaulted and leapt lightly down to join them. Douglas could have sworn that it was grinning.

"This way and be wary, the others will be waiting to ambush you in The Passage of Death."

"The what?" Loriscus was disconcerted again.

"The Passage of Death," Drock the Outcast said slowly, obviously beginning to suspect that he was dealing with a bunch of morons.

"You do keep things simple don't you?" Loriscus sighed. "Very well, you had better inform us of what this entails whilst we travel. It is not safe to linger here."

"Indeed," Drock the Outcast agreed. "Their outrunners have already gone ahead to warn that we are on the way."

"Great!" Douglas thought.

"God, I know," Deanna thought back. So the telepathy was still working then!

Drock the Outcast joined Loriscus as they wound up the narrow track. His tale was ancient yet one that was clearly little known.

The Race of Drock were not a new species formed by accidental magic as Taerg had supposed. They were in fact the most ancient race on the planet. They had developed underground away from the heat, a tranquil and spiritual people until the Time of Change had begun. Then some young Drock became tired of living in the darkness and asked for permission to try their luck on the surface of the planet. This was given, mainly with the adult expectation that these young would 'soon be back'. The intrepid explorers never returned. In fact they had gone out and populated the planet but had genetically changed according to their chosen environment. Some had become enormous and scaly and eventually taken on the form now recognised as that of the dragon. (Er'nest was amazed at this unknown part of his genetic history but realised that the Drock's head was very similar to his own.) Others had become smaller and had learnt to live off the occasional spurts of greenery, these became known as the igrul, and yet others had taken to the little known waters beneath the caves, the Igrimig. Through the centuries all developed peacefully and in unity, but gradually the dragons saw themselves as the superior race and chose to ignore that the Drock existed. Eventually the knowledge was lost in truth.

The Drock continued their peaceful way of life unperturbed, indeed undisturbed, by the outside world. However, they took the precaution of gathering all their treasures and protecting them at the top of their most easily fortified and guarded mountain – Aidem. They were fully aware that the new race of Dragon had become violent to the extent they had in-built weaponry, the ability to breathe fire!

There came a day (as there always does) that some old dragon came across an ancient manuscript mentioning the Drock. It told of their store of treasures and clearly showed that the Drock were of a far older lineage. This caused outrage! They were the superior race! How dare anything or anyone claim otherwise! And that ludicrous claim of ancestry. Why they had simply been born superior, it was their Universal given right! The best thing to do was obvious, kill the evidence, to deny it was not enough for some.

And so the Dragons marched upon the Race of Drock with the cruel intent of annihilation. Er'nest looked shocked and mortified at this, how could such a thing have been allowed! The Elverine were completely bewildered, never in their own history had such an evil act been known. The twins however, although saddened, had heard of such horror before.

The Drock, being a race of peace, had no weaponry with which to fight and had been obliterated, almost. The few survivors had withdrawn even deeper into the underground caverns and had with time replenished their numbers and strength. Until now it had suited them to let the Dragon think that they were extinct. Any dragon that attempted to gain access to their territory would mysteriously disappear, creating a myth of magic and fear around Aidem that persisted long after the original story was forgotten. The Drock had learnt to defend themselves, the secret of their existence was well kept.

"I wonder how Taerg survived," Douglas thought, but his attention was abruptly brought back to the present when Drock the Outcast urgently signalled a halt. The companions automatically fell into battle stance and waited for instructions as Loriscus and Gremlic listened intently to a whispered warning.

Gremlic spoke to them telepathically. "They await us amongst the boulders of the next twist in the path. It is the presence of Er'nest that will cause the most violent reaction. We must surround him and walk slowly with our hands held in the sign of peace. Sheath your weapons." Even the Elverine stared at him with amazement at this last command.

Er'nest spoke, displaying a courage that they would come to know and respect. "I am willing to wait here and take my chances. It would be wrong to bring further danger to you all." Loriscus hesitated not for even a moment.

"We have sworn to rescue Silbeamia, but I could not look with joy into her eyes knowing that it had been at such a cost. We remain together." They all nodded decisively in agreement and Er'nest lifted his head high with pride.

Each moved quietly to take position around the dragon. The twins looked briefly into each other's eyes knowing that at this moment their childhood was left behind.

Douglas nodded encouragingly at his sister and she tried to smile back bravely. Then they both looked ahead and took up the universal sign of peace. Loriscus glanced around, and then taking a big breath, signalled the cavalcade forward.

As they rounded the bend white shapes cloaked in brown cowls swiftly merged on them with threatening cries. It took every ounce of resolve not to react. Briefly, terrifyingly, all seemed lost, then suddenly the leaders of the ambush halted, causing complete confusion in the ranks behind. Their attention had shifted from the hated dragon to the small figure of Drock the Outcast who stood bravely unmoving with the strangers. There was a moment of impasse.

"Why are you, a Drock, with those who would keep company with an evil one?" a leader asked finally, rage and offence were emitting from every pore of his body.

Loriscus glanced at their new-found friend just as he pushed the green hood back from his face. There was a concerted gasp. "Not all Dragons are evil," the outcast stated calmly.

There was a surge of bodies as the attackers recognised their quarry. His name was murmured like a ripple from one mouth to another.

"How can you utter such filth when you know of their wicked treatment of our people?" the spokesman raged.

"I do not believe that any race is entirely without good. The behaviour of the Dragon to our ancestors was unacceptable, but we cannot assume that they have learnt nothing and we cannot believe that we are superior to them." There was an outcry and Drock the Outcast calmly raised his voice further. "If we do believe this and destroy every dragon that comes our way, surely such a belief and behaviour makes us comparable to the very beings we abhor." As the brave little Drock faced down the entire troop, Deanna noticed that Gremlic was radiating a sort of light coloured energy that was playing its part in having a calming effect on everyone present. It occurred to her that not so long ago she would neither have been aware of the energy cloud nor been able to see it.

An argument broke out within the ranks as the Drock discussed this astonishing concept. They had after all descended from those who had lived by a philosophy of harmony and equality. It is however sadly impossible to change an attitude bred at the mother's knee with one sentence. The Drock were not convinced, yet they did finally decide to take the prisoners to the Council. It did not sit well with them to kill one of their own, outcast or not. The soldiers ranged themselves alongside the intruders and prepared to march forth. Deanna clutched her brother's shirt, determined not to be separated from him.

They walked for an eternity. The suns at least were less searing as all three began to drop toward the horizon. Poldant raised his sleeve to wipe it across his glistening forehead, and in doing so happened to glance upwards. He froze and then leapt into action, almost causing the instant deaths of his companions. "No, no, not me! I am not the danger here, - look! Look in the sky! The bathawks! The bathawks have found us!" he yelled desperately. Some Drock raised their rock-hewn swords to the captives, others automatically peered beyond the Elverine's pointing finger. Even as they did so the mind-numbing cry of the bathawks reached them. Every soldier lost interest in the prisoners and swung to face the new unknown danger.

"What shall we do?" Joalla thought frantically to Loriscus.

"The bathawks are our problem," he responded grimly. "We shall fight."

Then the bathawks were upon them. Ten loathsome monsters swept down, evil poison-tipped talons at the ready. The Drock were caught unawares, they had no concept of what these creatures were, or indeed what they intended. The uncertainty did not last beyond the first ghastly swathe created by the foremost harbinger of death.

Terror-stricken but unbowed, they raised their swords in a hopeless attempt at defence as the second bathawk dropped for the kill. All four Elverine pointed their unsheathed ray-shooters, holding steady until Loriscus deemed it to be in range. He opened his mouth to shout the order but was pre-empted by an enormous spout of flame. Er'nest was no longer their slightly bumbling new recruit, but had become a well-honed fighting machine, roaring with rage and power. The bathawk swerved as the fire blasted it, shrieking horribly as smoke streamed from painfully scorched feathers and flesh.

"By the Stars that was well done!" Poldant was impressed. The Elverine as one shifted their aim to another target and shot it out of the sky, causing it to fall stunned into the ranks of the Drock. Deanna looked away, her stomach turning as the little stone swords finished it off. Her petrified glance spotted two bathawks preparing to throw what appeared to be a darkly glowing net over them.

"Gremlic look out!" she screamed, instinctively knowing that this was for him to deal with.

Gremlic heard her and in one motion aimed and fired an energy beam from the tip of his claw, blasting it into obliteration. "You have good eyes young human, but use telepathy next time, no noise can overcome that," he stated calmly, clearly unruffled by the battle raging around him.

"Right," she gulped.

A bathawk plunged directly at the twins and Deanna found herself thrown to the ground by her brother. He stood over her, weaponless but determined as the monster loomed until it filled his entire vision. The bathawk was equally fixed upon its victim, for neither saw Drock the Outcast until it was too late. The tiny warrior leapt lightly onto the boy's shoulder and swept his sword across and up, slicing a talon cleanly from the attackers body. Black liquid flowed from the wound as the screaming bathawk spiralled unevenly away.

"Thanks," Douglas panted as grateful as he was repulsed. His saviour bowed his head quaintly in acknowledgement and bounded away.

The unicorns meanwhile were causing further havoc. Each galloped around the battlefield giving aid to the Drock by allowing them to jump on and off their backs as they flashed past, creating a much more difficult target. The cries of the bathawks became increasingly frustrated and wary.

Er'nest turned another bathawk into a living furnace bringing a shout of triumph from the beleaguered Drock and then unexpectedly the attack ceased as quickly as it had begun. They all watched suspiciously, waiting for the next impact, but it never came. Gradually it dawned on them that they had won, and the air was rent with cheers.

Joalla's knees buckled from beneath her as the adrenaline ceased to flow. "Oh by the Gods, that was terrible," she sobbed. The other Elverine were white with reaction. To kill was completely against all they had been taught.

I agree," Gremlic said gently. "Yet perhaps there are occasions when one must defend oneself. Evil cannot be allowed to run amok."

"There must be a better way," Joalla sighed, her beautiful hair had come loose cascading around her like a golden shield. She looked as defenceless as she had appeared magnificent only minutes before. Poldant gently raised the Elveriness to her feet. Although more experienced in the way of the universes, he did not have the words or the understanding to help her with this, all he could do was to offer comfort.

Crysgar raised his bowed head, his face full of something more than the recent horror. "What of our friend

Camelion?" the elder of the Elverine brought them abruptly back to the moment. They looked at each other despairingly wondering what to do next. This decision was immediately taken out of their hands as Douglas nudged Loriscus and nodded succinctly toward the Drock. The soldiers had recovered, re-grouped, and quietly surrounded them again.

"You jest!" Loriscus exclaimed as they once more faced the vicious little swords that blocked their every exit. "Look my friends, there is no need to threaten us, we *want* to address your Council. We come willingly." The swords remained raised. Loriscus sighed, so much for the comradeship of battle. Douglas was red with fury. This wasn't supposed to happen. They had saved these creatures lives! Where was their gratitude? Deanna recognised the signs of a fast-approaching explosion and shook her head at him rapidly. Douglas was pretty unpredictable when he lost his temper. Her actions, immediately noticed by their captors, had the effect of bringing her brother to their particular notice. Quite a few swords swung to point at him, which naturally created the immediate effect of being doused in an unexpected ice bath. Douglas blinked rapidly twice and tried to look harmless. He must have convinced the Drock, as their attention became more general. Fortunately they didn't appear to be gifted with telepathy otherwise they may have heard the human promising himself that he was going to lay his hands on a weapon just as soon as possible.

Gremlic, however, was telepathic. "Keep your head Douglas or you may cost us dear," he warned, and then more gently, "there is nothing to fear; we are in control of the situation." The twins glanced at one another in astonishment. It didn't look that way to them!

Drock the Outcast took over. "Who amongst you is Drock the Lieutenant?" he demanded.

"I am," a soldier stepped forward, the sun glinting off the many tiny pebbles which had been interlinked to form an armoured jacket.

"I wonder what happens to his name when he gets promoted," Deanna thought irreverently.

"Your human minds chatter on pointlessly," Crysgar rebuked her. "We need to be discussing our next plan of action, there is only time for productive intent." Deanna tried very hard to control every thought, but ended up having an argument with herself about shutting up. Crysgar sounded unwillingly amused. "Well at least stop shouting at yourself," he said.

Meanwhile Drock the Outcast was engaged in an earnest discussion with Drock the Lieutenant. This had a more successful outcome than Loriscus's earlier request, because at a given order the swords were sheathed in one smooth motion. Joalla and Deanna sighed with relief.

"On to the Council," Drock the Outcast declared, displaying something of a taste for the dramatic. The entire cavalcade marched on as the suns began to sink beneath the horizon. Er'nest, the hated dragon, was doubly guarded; he had proven himself to be a ferocious fighter and so although the weapons were not kept at the ready, the ever watchful eyes of the enemy were constantly upon him.

In the encroaching gloom the travellers began to stumble over the uneven ground, only the four unicorn, Gremlic and Er'nest navigating their way without trouble. The Elverine had not been allowed to remount for fear of an attempted escape. The Drock, despite everything, remained suspicious.

Finally, in desperation, Poldant called out to Drock the Outcast. "Ask the lieutenant whether we can use our light beams, we are not able to see in the dark like you." This information caused some amusement in the ranks. The Drock had never come across a species that was blind at night before. No wonder the stupid great things couldn't keep their balance.

A halt was called whilst the lieutenant and his sergeant gingerly inspected the ray-shooters; they had after all seen them do considerable damage only shortly before. The Elverine showed them how they could flick to light rather than stun and the sudden beam that illuminated the gathering caused immediate and complete consternation. Some Drock threw themselves to the ground, others drew their swords fearfully and closed in on this unknown entity. Hastily the four handed their ray-shooters over and watched as the soldiers experimented with these new toys, becoming ever more confident and even jovial. The companions relaxed slightly and waited for the verdict.

Drock the Lieutenant turned to Loriscus eventually and with what probably passed for a grin announced, "These are interesting oddities. We shall keep them." The decision fell on their ears like a bombshell. Even Gremlic was temporarily bereft of speech.

Drock the Outcast was ready though. Obviously he had suspected this was coming. He jumped in hastily and with great flattery declared the decision to be a wise one. "However," he continued, "perhaps it would be even wiser to claim them at the end of the journey, otherwise it may take twice as long if the strangers cannot see." There was a pregnant pause whilst the lieutenant pondered this.

"And what is to stop the strangers using these things to attack us?" he pointed out reasonably.

"Nothing," Loriscus's answer startled the Drock. "However, we give our word. Besides we could not run through this magical pathway at night, we would be killed within minutes."

The Lieutenant considered this point. Eventually he nodded decisively and his soldiers reluctantly handed their booty back. Douglas blew a silent whistle of relief and

Poldant managed to give their new friend a subtle pat on the back.

Despite weary legs they made good time. Every now and again Drock the Lieutenant paused the march in order to pre-empt a magical obstacle. This took the form of rocks slamming together or dark bottomless pits suddenly yawning where the feet of an unsuspecting traveller might be. Once the air crackled with an electrical charge designed to fry its prey.

Loriscus thought back to the original conversation that he had had with Drock the Outcast. "He was right, it is much safer to be led to our goal despite being captive. It would have been almost impossible to have navigated this abomination alone, especially in the dark."

They all watched as once again the leader struck yet another hidden valve. This time however, instead of the expected nasty result, an immense boulder rolled aside exposing the entrance back into the underworld of the Drock. "Here we go again," Deanna sighed to her brother.

As the very mixed procession traipsed along a complete maze of dark passageways, some narrow and others like vaulted cathedrals, the prisoners quickly realised that it would be something of a challenge to find their way back. In effect they knew they now had no choice but to remain with their captors. At least that is what the majority of them thought until Loriscus spotted Crysgar regularly pressing the buttons of his transporter. The wily old Elverine had kept his wits about him and was plotting their route!

Presently other sounds started to intrude. The slithering scampering noise they had first come across as they entered the lower caves of Aidem became audible. Er'nest transmitted the information that they had company and, almost imperceptibly, the friends drew closer together.

"Oh how I long to feel the gentle sun of Elver on my back, and the lush green grass beneath my feet," Joalla groaned.

"It will be a long time before that happens," Poldant responded dismally.

Drock the Lieutenant called an order and his troop drew their swords. The prisoners tensed momentarily until it became clear that the soldiers were holding their weapons pointing ceremonially upwards. They had arrived and were about to be presented. Drock the Outcast, appearing nervous for the first time, hastily indicated that the ray-shooters were to be turned off. They were plunged into a state of blindness.

The Council was waiting. The place in which it sat was vast, but the prisoners only knew that by using their other senses - the way sound vibrated away into the distance, the feeling of space - because it was pitch black. It was only then that Loriscus and his companions truly realised that this race had infra-red vision and actually operated without any form of light whatsoever. No wonder they all kept their cowls pulled well over their heads if they had to go outside. The sun made them almost as blind as the Elverine and humans were in the dark! It also explained why they had marched at night instead of making camp.

The Elverine and the twins had to rely on Er'nest and Gremlic to keep them telepathically informed as to what was going on. It was a very odd experience.

Initially there was complete silence, but Er'nest told them that twelve Drock were quietly encircling them as they tried to ascertain what the captives were. There was a frightening, hateful hissing as the onlookers took in Er'nest's presence. The dragon was as close to death as he had ever been and yet he continued to keep his friends informed with a cool running commentary.

"They have returned to their seats, some sort of stone throne-like objects, right over the other side of the cave. Now they have summoned Drock the Lieutenant. He is kneeling before them. They must hold great power because he's pretty scared." There was some further scurrying. "Two soldiers have come and taken Drock the Outcast, and now he is kneeling before the Council. He is very brave because they are clearly not pleased to see him. He is talking fast and pointing at us. Now he is pointing at me and the lieutenant appears to be agreeing but without lifting his head. I think they are discussing the battle because our little Drock is making dramatic gestures." He paused. "Right, keep calm, the soldiers are coming to fetch us."

They felt small claw like hands grabbing their arms and forcing them forward. Deanna was breathing fast and loud because she was so terrified and she knew she wasn't the only one. She remembered her dad telling her once that it was OK to be frightened. Brave people were often scared. The point about being courageous was to get on with the job despite the fear. It helped to steady her a little.

"We are before the Council. They want us to kneel," Er'nest's voice intruded into her thoughts. They knelt.

"Where are Starlight and the others?" Poldant asked.

"They have been left standing across the cave. The Drock do not see them as a threat. Something is happening over there … I can't quite see."

"I understand you strangers were brave in battle and saved many Drock lives." The sudden unexpected loudness of the voice made them all jump. There was a brief hesitation. Loriscus was not sure if they were expecting an answer.

"No, just wait," Gremlic instructed him.

"Even the Evil One joined in, although I suspect he was only interested in his own life." The Drock was not willing to believe any good of an enemy. "What were those monsters with whom you battled and why were they after you?"

No one spoke, waiting not for the permission of the Council, but the advice of Gremlic.

"They have a stone rod with a red stone at the tip. I think it has to be pointing at a person before they are allowed to speak. Ahh … yes, now it is pointing at you Loriscus."

Loriscus swallowed. His mouth was so dry he wasn't sure that he was able to force any words out at all. Before he managed to do so Drock the Outcast, unaware of their telepathic abilities, spoke out of turn.

"The strangers are blind in our world, allow them to use their light creators or they will not know what is going on." From the angry reaction this was a pretty unacceptable thing to do, but before the soldiers could pounce on him the sense of his urgent words prevailed on at least one Councillor who gestured for them to halt. There was a lengthy explanation as the ray-shooters were discussed, but eventually permission was given.

The Elverine adjusted their instruments to the lowest most ambient light possible. Even so the result was startling. There were Drock present who had not seen the light of day for aeons and so the tiny gleam had the effect of a flash of lightening. Many had to shade their eyes to protect them.

"This is too much!" one of the Councillors shouted angrily. "It is a trick!" White shapes from all over the chamber began to move forward threateningly.

"Crysgar, Joalla, switch your ray-shooters off – quickly," Gremlic urged. Hastily they obeyed. The Drock calmed down, as the dimmer illumination became more bearable.

Order restored, the Chief Councillor signalled for Loriscus to speak. Loriscus told his story with the mellifluous beauty of his kind. The Drock remained still and listened captivated to the words that painted a picture of a hitherto unimagined universes. When he came to the part which explained how they had come to be risking the dangers of Aidem, it seemed the audience was almost holding its breath. Loriscus's account of the coming war between the factions of Dragon initially amused and even delighted them, until he was able to persuade them to understand how this would affect the whole planet, including their own world. Once again they would be facing their biggest fear, annihilation.

The twelve Councillors sat frozen, stunned into speechlessness at this grim news. Eventually, as if he were dragging himself from a waking nightmare, the Chief Councillor beckoned Drock the Lieutenant forward and instructed that the prisoners be taken away whilst they discussed this new situation. The prisoners were marched out as the Race of Drock decided their future and that of every living being on the planet.

Chapter 10

*T*he subdued group was taken to a steep-sided cave only just big enough to hold them, Er'nest engulfed a third of it all on his own. There were no comforts available, but the floor consisted of soft dry sand. Douglas and Deanna sat down with some relief; they had been running, walking or fighting non-stop for hours and their bodies were incredibly weary.

Loriscus looked around anxiously. "Where are our unicorn friends?" he demanded of the departing soldiers. The others became aware of their absence at these words and roused themselves in an exhausted attempt to join forces with Loriscus. Gremlic called out and interrupted their hoarse questioning. He could sense the unicorns approaching.

" ... and something else," Gremlic swiftly changed to telepathy. Immediately the companions shifted their awareness and held themselves ready for what was coming.

"Oh can't we just rest for a short while?" Deanna felt despairing. "I couldn't move another step." Joalla put a protective arm around the girl's shoulders.

"At least they have left us with our ray-shooters," she observed. "They must have forgotten owing to their fear over the news we bring." The Elverine loosened their instruments within their sheaths. Drock the Outcast, who was not privy to the mental conversation, jumped forward and put his claw on Loriscus's hand.

"Do not make the mistake of fighting here. It will not have been in error that you have been allowed to keep your

171

light creators. You must do nothing to jeopardise this situation."

As the words of warning echoed off the walls of the austere prison, the rock blocking the exit rolled back to reveal the unicorns who trotted into their midst thankfully. They appeared to be alone apart from their escort and Loriscus began to look questioningly at Gremlic, but was stilled by a warning glare from Starlight. The soldier who led the steeds turned to leave, but as he did so winked directly at the puzzled group. Douglas jumped, Deanna squeaked and the Elverine revived miraculously at the sight. Camelion! It could only be him! He had survived and - bless his impudence - had managed to place himself as one of the Drock on guard duty!

As soon as the rock was back in place the travellers gave vent to their jubilation. Everyone talked at once wanting to know how the changeling had made himself known. Had he explained how he had escaped the first attack? What was the plan?

Starlight neighed with laughter. "We have not had the chance to talk. All we know of the situation is that Camelion is a very convincing Drock. He was left as part of the troop in charge of us while you were taken before the Council. He whispered to us when the attentions of the other Drock were upon you. We nearly gave the game away with our reaction. Fortunately he pretended to sternly contain us and the moment passed." Loriscus slapped Starlight delightedly on the back, this was such good news! Camelion was their ace in the hole, literally!

Drock the Outcast had not followed the conversation and appeared somewhat bewildered, they seemed to be over-pleased at the sight of the unicorns. He of course had not met Camelion and knew nothing of him.

"Should we tell him?" Poldant asked of Loriscus.

"Yes, but not yet. Let us see which way the wind lies first."

"Gremlic, can I use the water flagon now," Douglas brought their attention to more urgent matters.

Gremlic probed the cave with his senses. "Yes, the magic will have no adverse effect here."

They quenched their thirst urgently, the wondrous flagon easily keeping up with their demands. Then Joalla pulled out a package of travelling biscuits and it became a feast! Drock the Outcast watched the process in astonishment. He, as with many of the creatures on Jalmar, had no physical need to drink liquid, and the food was a complete anathema to him. Having politely refused their offerings, he took a small curved stone from his belt pouch and proceeded to scrape fine filings off a rock. The resultant gravel was as eagerly relished as had their own meal been. Douglas shook his head to himself as he observed the little Drock's activity. Amazing!

The twins propped themselves against a smooth rock, sitting companionably. "Are you OK, Dee Dee?" Douglas asked, running his fingers through his dishevelled locks. She smiled tiredly at him and nodded, she realised he had gone all protective because he was using her childhood name. "How the hell did we end up in this weird situation?" Douglas continued, talking more to himself than his sister.

"Because we wanted an adventure I think," she grinned at him.

Douglas guffawed. "Well we got that right then," he grinned back. The moment was broken as Joalla handed him the golden flagon with a word of thanks. Douglas slipped it back into the top of his backpack and then turned back to his sister. "What do you …" but he was never destined to finish the sentence because Deanna's head had slipped sideways and she was asleep. Within seconds everyone had followed suit. Soon the only sound was that of deep breathing and an occasional shuffling as someone settled deeper into the sand.

The Council of Drock must have raged with argument for most of the remaining night, because it was some hours later before the prisoners were stirred by the sound of the rock being moved. Groggily they came to their feet as the guards roughly shouted for them to form up and prepare to be brought before the Twelve once again.

As the soldiers of Drock marched them back to the Council, several of the companions sensed that there were far more creatures watching from the darkness. The news had travelled, and many had hurried to the tunnels surrounding the council chamber. Only the soldiers ever normally left the darkness of their home and so the sight of the enormous strangers caused quite a stir. Er'nest received the most attention, because in reality dragons had become things of myth and terror, almost no one had seen his like in living memory.

Revived and clear-headed, Loriscus walked ahead of his friends guiding them with the low beam from his light creator. The Twelve were sitting, silent now, and focused on the prisoners. As they were brought to a halt all sound ceased. The leader of the Council was either not ready or not willing to speak because it was a long minute before he opened his mouth. Loriscus stared straight back at him.

Finally the First of the Twelve spoke. "We have decided to help you." Loriscus blew out his pent-up breath. "We did not come to this decision lightly and it is not only your words which have convinced us. Long ago it was written of this time when strangers from across the Universes and a dragon who had turned to good would come and save us at a time of crisis. The crisis has come and we must play our part in delivering our race and planet from destruction." The Drock sat pensively for a few more moments.

"However …" ("Oh no! Not another condition," Loriscus thought desperately), "we do not wish to leave this to chance or to others upon whom we have had no reason to depend. So it is our command that Drock the Outcast accompany you on your journey back to the Dragon King, and that he report to us when the danger has passed. He may not return until such time. If he survives he will be renamed Drock the Reunited." Drock the Outcast nodded his head in supplication. Loriscus did too. Another warrior, particularly one who had proven himself in battle, was always welcome.

"Thank you," Loriscus replied simply. "We need to obtain the salt crystals that I spoke of earlier. Can you help us to bypass the Guardians?"

The chamber echoed with a weird hissing.

"I did not mean to offend," Loriscus called hastily.

"They are not offended, they are laughing," Gremlic realised. "But why?"

The First of the Twelve lifted his hand and instantly regained order. "Stranger, we *are* the Guardians."

"Oh," Loriscus said blankly. Why, By the Many Stars, had Taerg not told them of this? That question would have to wait until later.

"Proceed Drock the Outcast. Take the incomers and show them the salt crystals. They are not permitted to touch any other treasure, particularly that which we honour and guard so well." They began to turn to leave. "May the luck of the Three Suns go with you." The Councillor said gently.

Drock the Outcast and the Drock soldiers led them out. This time the mood was very different as the quietly offered messages of support and hope accompanied them on their mission. Drock the Outcast walked tall.

"Well, that went better than expected," the Drock soldier to Loriscus's right whispered cheerily.

"Camelion, you are a wonder of the universes!" The Elverine was delighted.

"Thank you," Camelion said modestly. "I think I'll stay like this until we are out of here though. You never know."

Drock the Outcast glanced over his shoulder curiously. It was unusual for a soldier to talk without permission. Camelion straightened up and fell back into the rhythm of the other guards.

Without hesitation the newly-appointed member of the companions guided them through the labyrinth of passageways. It became clear that they were walking both in and up. Finally a superbly carved and engraved entrance soared before them. The Place of Treasures was within.

The soldiers, as one, stepped back. Well, not quite as one. Camelion could look like a Drock, but he didn't know their rules. He was left standing by Loriscus. Drock the Lieutenant spoke angrily, telling his troop to place the miscreant under arrest.

"What now?" Poldant urged telepathically.

"I do not know," Loriscus was thrown into a panic.

Drock the Outcast stepped forward unexpectedly. "The First Councillor requested that this soldier accompany us into the Place of Treasure."

"I did not hear this," the Lieutenant objected, still angry.

"We shall wait here whilst you despatch a messenger to the Council Chamber."

There was a pregnant pause.

"That will not be necessary. Proceed."

Drock the Outcast nodded and walked sedately through the archway hastily followed by his newfound friends.

Once out of sight the cavalcade stopped. "How did you know?" Loriscus asked.

"I am not sure of what I know. Only that this Drock was not behaving like the others. Is he outcast like myself? Why was he speaking with you?"

Loriscus signed to Camelion who transformed back into his original form. The Drock became immobile with shock.

"Please, do not fear. This is Camelion, he is one of us. He was left behind in the first attack. We had thought him dead." Gremlic explained. Camelion bowed briefly and then turned to receive the joyful welcome of the others. Crysgar, who had seemed to feel responsible for the changeling's loss, was foremost amongst them.

The composure of the little Drock was shaken, but he still had his wits about him. "Quietly now, or the guard will enter to see what has happened." The reaction was instant and sober. Deanna gave Camelion one last hug as the outcast pointed them into an antechamber.

Eyes wide with wonder the travellers took in an unexpected sight. The cave was packed from floor to ceiling with scrolls.

"Where is the treasure?" Douglas asked disappointed.

"This is the main treasure," Drock the Outcast said proudly.

The twins looked at each other in confusion. Where were the gold and jewels?

"The treasure is knowledge?" Loriscus looked at the Drock.

"Of course, there is no greater honour than to guard the knowledge of the ages."

"You are right," Gremlic said. "But perhaps part of that honour is to share the knowledge?" The lizard did not answer but became thoughtful.

Douglas didn't care about great philosophies, he was desperately disappointed. It would have been much more fun to see the place stacked with glistening chests of booty. He said as much to Er'nest.

"But why would you want to guard boxes of dragon food?" Er'nest was amazed. "You know, in the stories of the dragon who were attacked and killed on your world, the human's always took away their food store. It is one thing that has never made sense to us. We know you eat differently." Douglas was bereft of speech.

"Come," Drock the Outcast took them to a smaller cave, which whispered with a familiar sound. Water. At the far end of the cave the water had pooled. Around this the rocks were covered with a fragile shiny white substance. At last, the salt crystals!

Reverently the Drock knelt and broke off a tiny crumb. With a prayer of thanks he placed it in his mouth and shut his eyes in ecstasy. No one moved for a second, and then with great insight Loriscus went and knelt beside him. The others quickly joined them. Even the unicorns bowed in obeisance. Douglas had the inkling of a thought. Perhaps a healing crystal was a greater treasure than a piece of gold?

"May we take some of the crystals?" Loriscus asked formally. Drock the Outcast nodded, in too much of a beatific state to do anything else.

Gremlic pulled out a pouch and carefully filled it with the treasure. Deanna, hoping no one would notice, sneaked some into her own mouth. Instantly her body coursed with swiftly moving energy that she had never experienced before. It was incredible! She felt strong enough to fight a dozen bathawks! She nudged her brother and signalled that he do the same. He lifted a quizzical brow and then did so, more to humour her than anything. Douglas's eyes grew wide. Indeed he could now see why this ordinary rock pool was worth beyond a King's ransom. The crystals could heal the world ...

" ... or fuel an army." Gremlic's voice intruded into their minds. "The Drock are fully aware of the value of the crystals. They have to be kept secret. The Igrimig only see what it brings to their community, they have no larger vision of what this could do for those who seek power."

"What happens if the Dragon King finds out, or worse – Allamang?" Deanna asked.

"At present the Race of Dragon consider anything the lower species do to be nothing more than superstition. It will not yet have occurred to them that these crystals will hold any true benefit. If they did it would be a disaster."

"But isn't Allamang on his way to procure them?"

"Yes, but only as a means to an end."

"Won't he find out when he gets here?"

"He will not reach the crystals. The Drock are now aware of his approach. They will close all entrances to this place and will increase the magical magnetic force. Allamang will face a battle he is not expecting and I am not sure he will consider it worth his while."

"I hope you are right." Deanna felt dreadful about the awful possibilities this find could initiate. Why was it not simple, why not bring them into universal attention for the good of all? It was a hopeless thought. She knew, even within the recent limited experience of the quest, that it would take a miracle for the multiversal races to behave in such a way. Then she was struck by another thought, "What about Er'nest? It's a bit much to expect him to keep this to himself."

"Er'nest has not listened to this conversation," Gremlic assured the girl.

"But aren't we all in on this telepathy thing?"

"Yes, however you have only learnt the rudiments of such. It is possible to direct and protect your thoughts." Gremlic explained.

"Oh – but I haven't been!"

"I have."

The unicorns lifted their heads, ears twitching, nostrils flaring. The others instantly stiffened. "Someone comes, and he is in a hurry," Starlight warned. Drock the Outcast, Loriscus and Gremlic stepped toward the cave entrance, the latter tucking the pouch into his belt. Crysgar hissed urgently at Camelion who managed to transform back into the shape of the Drock soldier just as Drock the Sergeant rushed into view.

"The sentries from the peak warn of a troop of fighting dragons approaching fast. They are with the evil creatures that attacked us. The invaders are following down through the dark breath of Aidem; if they manage to endure the heat of Aidem's fiery blast, they may yet overcome the magic force field."

"Oh by the Gods!" Poldant groaned through clenched teeth.

"We must leave here and draw them off," Joalla spoke from behind them. All heads swung in her direction. "The bathawks are after us and the dragons who are in their thrall will follow."

"You are right," Loriscus agreed.

"What on earth for!" Douglas couldn't believe what he was hearing. "Surely we could slip away whilst they try to find a way in?"

"Douglas! What are you saying!" Deanna was shocked. "How can we leave these people to face our fight? Anyway, if they do get in – and find their way to the crystals - there will be an even bigger mess to sort out." Douglas reddened as everyone glared at him.

"Sorry, wasn't thinking," he said.

"The thing is," Er'nest interrupted, "what I mean is, somehow we have to be far enough away before they spot us. I could outfly them but you couldn't outrun them, not even on the swift backs of your unicorn friends." Everyone wracked their brains.

"I know!" Joalla clapped her hands. "We were not able to transport into this place because we may have ended inside a rock, but we do have the co-ordinates to transport out. We can go straight to the Seven Sentries. We should be far enough away to outfly the bathawks, but close enough for them to consider it worth the chase."

Loriscus ran his hand through his hair thoughtfully. "It may work, but it is an enormous risk." He gazed beyond them. "I have the most to lose, yet I am not sure it is right to ask this of you." He focused back on the gathering. "Perhaps it would be better if I follow Joalla's plan and draw them off, and you leave unobtrusively when the coast is clear." He was shouted down by vociferous objections, Douglas's voice being the loudest.

"We need a decision now," Drock the Sergeant urged.

Loriscus grinned. "Tell the Council that the outcast will return the victor!" And before the Drock's bemused gaze the travellers pressed some magical object on their belts and disappeared.

Their sudden manifestation in the midst of the waiting dragons caused complete consternation and chaos. This of course became very different in the telling of the tale through time. Eventually the dragons would speak of the incredible moment when the magical strangers appeared from thin air clutching a bewildered Drock. The story would paint the picture of how the warrior dragons took their allies onto their backs and swept swiftly into the sky, purposely bringing themselves to the notice of Allamang and the bathawks. No one ever mentioned the swearing or the unco-ordinated running around in circles.

The reality, the noise, the confusion were another matter. But Loriscus's hoarsely yelled explanation galvanised the dragons into action and within minutes they were mounted and airborne. They were barely up before they were spotted. The shrill cry of a bathawk carried through the air. The race was on.

Crysgar looked over his shoulder several times as the valiant dragons flew with all their might. He could see that despite their efforts they were severely hindered by the weight of their passengers. "They are gaining on us," he transmitted. Deanna turned around briefly and then lay as flat as she was able against her dragon's back, trying to help him all she could.

Despite their enormous strength, the dragons were not used to being hindered, and before many minutes had passed the strain began to show. Dragons don't sweat because they don't drink, so the heat builds up in their bodies until it literally becomes red hot. The Elverine were the first to sense the problem, mainly because it was becoming too difficult to hold on. Initially each thought it unique to him or herself, but quite quickly the whole group realised they were in trouble.

"We'll have to do something!" Poldant yelled to Loriscus telepathically.

"Ow! You don't have to shout!" Loriscus winced. "Yes I know but what? They are out of range so we cannot stun them, and if we allow them to come into range then we will not be able to fire fast enough to keep them all off!"

"I will slow them down," Gremlic said unexpectedly. "Camelion – I will require your help please." the little being spoke politely, ("For all the world as if there is no hurry!" Joalla marvelled) "Although I can fly, I do not have the speed to outmanoeuvre the evil ones, are you able to conjure up the shape of a dragon and assist me?" Camelion did not bother to answer, but instead transformed swiftly into shape. Gremlic leapt onto his back, leaving Douglas who felt a lot less safe without him.

"Do not hesitate or wait for us, we will catch you up," he said reassuringly.

"Gremlic, we should stand and fight together," Loriscus shouted, forgetting to speak normally.

"I am not going to fight – nor give myself up," Gremlic added as he heard their fears. "Camelion will be unable to keep up this form and fly at speed for long, his energy will be used up; therefore we shall act and flee. Now go and stop wasting time!"

"Be careful!" Crysgar called worriedly.

"I intend to," Camelion's grim voice was already becoming distant.

Douglas tried to crane his neck without shifting his position. He couldn't see much, but was just aware of a huge white flash of light and the vague commotion that came after. There was no time to observe more, because the frantic movements of the unicorns distracted him. Without Gremlic's magic, they had begun to become unstuck!

"Help them in the Name of the Many Universes!" Joalla screamed despairingly. The Elverine held onto their friends with all their might, but the scalding scales of the dragons were becoming unbearable. Sweat was now pouring off them all adding to the slipperiness.

Er'nest and the green dragon were the only ones not in trouble. Er'nest, because he had not been carrying anyone on his back, and the green dragon because he had been carrying the changeling and now only bore the light Drock, who clung on for dear life, daring look neither right or left.

"Siralicus! Go and fetch aid!" Er'nest ordered. "I am going back to Gremlic and Camelion." With that he swooped away. Siralicus sped up and left them behind.

"We are going to have to slow down, or we will lose the strangers," the yellow dragon groaned. His troop was too exhausted to reply, but obeyed gratefully.

"God, I hope Gremlic's plan has worked!" Douglas muttered out loud. He could not tell if his sister was crying or had perspiration running down her cheeks. He saw her turn her head anxiously and then start as she spotted something. Deanna pointed enthusiastically to the rear. Douglas saw Er'nest catching them up rapidly. Gremlic and Camelion were riding him! The bathawks were still there, but much further away than they had been. True to his word the Amorga's servant had bought them a little time.

The twins' excitement drew everyone else's attention. There was a breathless cheer as they saw Er'nest with Gremlic and Camelion, who were grinning exultantly. Gremlic instantaneously realised what had been happening in his absence, and threw a quick spell at the unicorns, which miraculously regained their balance.

"Right!" the yellow dragon bayed gleefully. "Follow me!" With renewed vigour they surged ahead. Even so, despite their mighty efforts, it was clear that the bathawks and Allamang were gaining again.

They flew on, refusing to despair, and their steadfastness was rewarded.

"Seralicus," one of the sentries panted. This time it was the dragon's turn to cheer. The others stared into the distance until their eyes watered, but it was several moments before they could see what their comrades had spotted.

"My Father!" Er'nest rang out. And then they saw it. A dark cloud. The cloud billowed nearer as if blown by the winds of a storm - and became a magnificent battalion of fighting dragons. At their head, roaring ferociously was Rialstus the King. Within moments the battalion was upon them and the grateful sentries wearily acknowledged their saviours as they charged past and clashed noisily with the bathawks beyond. The bathawks were too late to avoid the onslaught, but Allamang and his troops swerved and flew in the opposite direction. Neither cowards nor stupid, but hugely outnumbered, they left the evil ones to their fate, and lived. The bathawks, unable to escape cursed and fought viciously, spitting poisonous darts and cleaving through scales with equally poisonous talons. The fight was bitter but short.

Deanna covered her face with her hands as the screams of the injured and dying reached her, and only removed them when she heard Rialstus shout the order to halt. Two remaining bathawks limped away in the direction of the distant speck that was Allamang and his followers. "Let them go," Rialstus ordered as several of his dragons began an eager chase. As the heat of the kill left them, they became aware of the bodies of dragon and bathawk alike on the dry ground below them.

The King spoke again, quietly this time, and four dragons descended and reverently picked up their dead. The bathawks were left to shrivel and bleach in the sun. Sombrely they turned for home.

Er'nest led the way back into the now familiar caves. The travellers walked in his wake, each deep in his or her own thoughts. No one had communicated for the entire journey. There was nothing to say. The price of their escape had been high.

Eventually they sat in a circle passing and sharing a precious goblet of nectar. Er'nest, now used to this tradition, took no notice but sat with his head bowed. Drock the Outcast was glued to the casual procedure, an expression of fascination on his face.

Deanna eventually broke the silence. "Why is it that everyone seems to fight instead of talk?" No response. She tried again. "I mean, surely they don't *want* to fight?" Everyone stared at her and saw that she was trying to blink away tears.

Joalla sighed and put her arm around the girl's shoulders. "Who knows little one. Perhaps it comes from fear or a desire for power ..." she shrugged an elegant shoulder as words failed her.

"All I know is that our intent is not war but the rescue of an innocent maiden." Loriscus's voice seemed to come from a long way off, his despair over the loss of Silbeamia patent for all to see.

"The Zorgians can only manipulate evil where they find it. We all have the choice to resist." Gremlic was almost brusque. "Now I suggest we rest awhile, tomorrow we take the crystals to The Boss." Sleep overtook them within seconds. Gremlic watched his friends fondly for a while and then silently made his way to the chambers of the King.

Chapter 11

"*W*ake up ugly strangers!" a familiar voice yelled.

"Rackap!" Douglas felt surprisingly delighted to see the funny little creature, albeit through the one bleary eye that he had managed to open. "What are you doing here?"

"Come back to help. Are you not happy?"

Starlight groaned. They all knew it would not be from the goodness of the igrul's heart. This meant more leaves.

"I see," Loriscus said cautiously. "What did you have in mind exactly?"

"Will lead you to The Boss. Keep strangers safe," Rackap said rather ludicrously.

"We know the way to The Boss," Loriscus pointed out, but relented as the igrul's face fell. "Oh very well," he sighed.

"What!" Uraj spluttered. "We will starve at this rate!"

"Only a couple of leaves," Loriscus persuaded gently. "It may be useful to have him with us after all. The Boss is more comfortable negotiating through him I think."

Rackap's eyes swivelled back and forward as he followed the conversation. At Loriscus's decision he gave a little whoop and then hastily straightened his battered hat, slightly embarrassed. "Shall we go now?" He looked around at the group. "Where is furry creature with long tongue?"

"Rufus," Deanna realised with a giggle.

"Joining us later," Loriscus replied slightly absently, as if he had other thoughts on his mind. He became more assertive. "I do not think that we all need to go down to the

Igrimig. Er'nest can't come anyway because he does not fit, the unicorns struggle with the narrow ledges, and the humans are tired. It would make more sense if only a few of us went with Rackap to deliver the crystals."

Rackap's eyes gleamed. "Travellers have the crystals?" Loriscus nodded, and then seeing the expression on the igrul's face made a mental note to Gremlic to hold the precious load safe.

"I am not a thief," Rackap's head lifted with injured pride. Loriscus was startled, he had not voiced his concerns out loud, and yet the igrul appeared to have heard him! Joalla had once again to soothe the irascible one.

There was only a nominal protest over Loriscus's suggestion. It made sense, and besides there was certain advantage to having some of them rested for whatever was to come next. Eventually it was decided that Loriscus, Poldant and Gremlic would meet with The Boss. Everyone waved them off with the slightly jolly air of those on an unexpected holiday.

"Why don't they just transport down there and avoid the journey?" Douglas asked no one in particular.

"Well they could," Crysgar answered. "The problem is that they could appear in the wrong place at the wrong time and frighten the Igrimig. Frightened creatures become aggressive. That is the last thing we need." Douglas nodded at the explanation and wandered off to quiz Drock the Outcast about anything and everything.

Meanwhile the depleted force travelled swiftly into the depths of Igrimig territory. Rackap proved to be completely tireless, underlining the fact that he rode on the backs of others through sheer laziness. In a surprisingly short time they found themselves at the edge of the pool which contained the fearsome pets of the Igrimig. They paused to formulate a plan.

"I suggest that Rackap and I approach The Boss with one small crystal to prove that we have been successful. Once he has seen it we will bring him here to negotiate fully. You must hold the other crystals and keep them safe. We will only hand them over when the demands of King Rialstus have been met." Relieved at not having to risk slipping in the perilous waters, the two Elverine waited willingly in the dark whilst Gremlic flew away just above the head of the agile igrul.

"Perhaps we had better get ready in case we are attacked." Poldant watched the water anxiously as a line of bubbles moved towards them. Hastily they stood back to back, clutching their ray-shooters.

"I'm sure Gremlic would not have left us to face danger alone," Loriscus tried to sound reassuring, but his voice shook slightly.

"No of course not," Poldant agreed, adjusting his protection in a damp palm.

They both jumped out of their skins as the water boiled suddenly, weapons instantly at the ready, but were stopped in their tracks as the grinning face of The Boss popped up from the depths. He was joined by several more Igrimig, who continued to point vicious little spears at the Elverine despite smiling happily all the while.

Gremlic appeared out of the gloom and landed comfortingly on Loriscus's shoulder. Rackap splashed up noisily and stood beside them, chest swelled importantly. Loriscus felt he almost wanted to hug them both in his relief, but didn't.

"Welcome Ugly Foreigners," The Boss began politely. "igrul will lead you to the Talking Place where we will listen to words of King of Dragons." The Elverine turned and followed in Rackap's wake.

The Talking Place consisted of an island reached by one very thin strip of rock. The light-footed Elverine made easy work of this task, but realised how fortunate the decision to leave the others behind had been. Loriscus and Poldant sat cross-legged on the damp outcrop so that they could talk to The Boss at a more comfortable level.

Gremlic carefully dislodged his pouch from his belt and shook several glistening crystals into Loriscus's palm. All attention became riveted on them. Poldant continued to casually hold his ray-shooter, aware that the Igrimig did not know that it was a weapon. Wisely Loriscus let The Boss feast his eyes on the objects which could bring him such power. He could see the effect they were having on all present. There was a murmur of excitement from the audience of Igrimig who had come to hear for themselves the outcome of the negotiations. Was it to be war or peace?

The discussions continued for several hours, for although The Boss wanted the crystals, he took his position of protector of the people seriously.

"How do we truly know that the King will keep his word and treat us with respect?" The Boss demanded reasonably.

"We have faced many dangers to bring the crystals as requested," Poldant said. "Surely this is a sign of the King's high regard for you."

"It could be a trick."

"Well it is not," Poldant said clearly.

"We only have your word that Rialstus is offering peace."

"No, that is not true," Gremlic interrupted unexpectedly. Poldant, who had been nominated as an experienced negotiator to do all the talking, lifted an enquiring brow. "Rialstus gave me this to give to you with his high regards," Gremlic pulled a small thin slice of stone from his pocket.

"What's that?" Loriscus whispered out of the side of his mouth.

Gremlic held the piece of stone above his head for all to see. "This is engraved with the promise of equality and freedom and signed by the King himself."

The Boss signalled for one of his cohorts to take it from Gremlic. This was done and then brought to the leader's hand. Loriscus and Poldant watched him reading and deliberating, looking very wise, despite the fact that the stone was upside down. Obviously none of the Igrimig could read because they all hovered, somewhat awe-struck, deferentially awaiting his declaration.

"The Race of Igrimig accept the word of the King of Dragons and the gift of the salt crystals. It is peace." The high ceilings rang as the Igrimig erupted and yelled their approval.

Poldant waited a minute, relief shining from every pore. "It only remains, my friend, to ask you what is your intention when the representative of Allamang approaches you?" he asked when order was regained.

"Shall meet messenger with pets," The Boss smiled sinisterly.

Poldant, Loriscus and Gremlic stopped feeling cheerful instantly. The two Elverine looked at one another with horror and shuddered. Gremlic signalled caution. There was nothing more they could do here.

Rackap trotted in front of the delegation, chatting happily. As with all his kind he was sublimely unconcerned at the prospective fate of Allamang's messenger. The others were unable to enjoy the success of their mission because they felt so dreadful about it. They followed on in rueful silence.

"The furry one with the long tongue," Rackap suddenly shouted and shot off in the direction of Rufus's ecstatic barking. The sombre mood lifted as they sped up in a slightly panicky effort to keep up with him. So it was a laughing group that burst into the cave to be greeted by the sight of the twins rolling exuberantly on the floor with their beloved dog. Looming above them was the benign figure of Taerg.

The old Dragon glanced up at their noisy entrance. "Ah, success?" he rumbled.

Everyone turned at his question and as one converged on their friends. Rackap actually leapt onto a high rock with fright, thinking momentarily that the strangers had gone mad and were attacking them. It was only after several minutes of careful observation that he became convinced that this was probably a peculiar greeting ceremony. He jumped back down and joined Drock the Outcast who nodded serenely and continued to watch the spectacle.

"We did it! We did it!" the twins whooped, punching their arms in the air. Joalla laughed hysterically as Poldant swung her around. Crysgar and Camelion clapped Loriscus heartily on the back asking how things had gone of both the Elverine and Gremlic, and the unicorns trumpeted their delight. Er'nest and Taerg commented and pointed out particularly funny behaviour to one another, Er'nest trying to look casual at receiving the revered dragon's attention.

Loriscus, the quest ever in his mind, was the first to sober up. "Er'nest could you present us to your father. If all is well are you ready to join us and leave this place, for now is the time of reckoning?"

The young dragon became very still at these words, the enormity of them hitting him like a powerful blow. He did not respond for a few seconds and then shook himself, knowing he would always regret it if he didn't take this opportunity. After all it had been in his dreams ever since he could remember. "Come, we shall meet with him immediately," was all he said. They took leave of Rackap for the last time, giving the little igrul a further bundle of leaves wrapped with another unicorn hair (Crest's).

The mood in King Rialstus's chamber was somewhat different to when they had previously been escorted in. This time they were greeted as old friends. The presence of Taerg who had tagged along (not that anyone had the courage to tell him otherwise) delighted King Rialstus enormously and there were several minutes of the sort of chat that comes when old friends catch up. Then the King turned his attention to the others who were standing respectfully watching the interchange. There was another short interlude as he noted the Drock in amongst them. Even at his great age this was a first for him. The Drock were a very elusive race. At last he was ready to hear Loriscus's report.

"Well, well, so you did it," the King remarked, shaking his head in wonder. "Indeed you have kept your side of the bargain and we shall keep ours. Er'nest may go with you if he still wishes. We shall clear up the rest of the mess ourselves."

"Thank you father," Er'nest bowed his head, his eyes dancing with excitement. "Um … what mess exactly?" he asked as an afterthought.

"Even as we speak Allamang and his followers are forming up for battle." It was only then that the realisation hit them - the atmosphere was full of brooding anticipation. Against the walls of the chamber were honed, gleaming weapons.

"Father! I can't go now! I must stay and fight!"

"No! One more dragon will make little difference either here or there." Rialstus was adamant.

"Are the bathawks with them?" Loriscus took the opportunity to ask as Er'nest struggled to come to terms with his father's decree.

"Yes, despite casualties from the skirmish yesterday there are still at least six of the horrors present."

"When we leave the bathawks will follow, they have no loyalty to Allamang."

"I suspected as much. However the blood of the young dragons is up, it will be almost impossible to avoid a fight without great loss of face."

"Better than a great loss of life!" Deanna murmured out of the side of her mouth to Joalla. The Elveriness sighed in agreement. Douglas tried not to fidget as an overwhelming desire to go and examine the interesting looking weapons came into his head. Crysgar growled a warning and the boy subsided. *It's not as if I was really going to wander over there* he grumbled to himself, glancing regretfully at the forbidden fruit.

"Wait!" Gremlic interjected. Despite his tiny size even the huge Dragon King waited with due deference for his next words. "First I do not believe that Allamang's army can all be happy about the presence of the bathawks. These young dragons are fighting for a freedom they do not believe they have. They do not see themselves as either evil or in the wrong, therefore the dark aura surrounding the Zorgians will be making many uncomfortable, whatever power they offer. Also those others who truly believe the bathawks will make the difference in battle will have come to depend on them. So ... if we ensure that the bathawks know their prey has escaped before the battle they will instantly disappear. Perhaps this will cause enough consternation (and relief) to give an equerry time to go forward under a flag of truce to discuss terms. Allamang will know by then that the ploy of undermining the system using the Igrimig has not worked. You could offer enough to avoid that loss of face that seems to matter so much. It is worth a try do you not think?"

The King sat with his head resting in his claw as he considered Gremlic's idea. "There is certainly nothing to lose by trying it," he said at last, "but you will have to move fast or it will be too late. I am preparing to join the army immediately, you have an hour at most!"

"Our problem is that we have to seek an unmarked rainbow as there are bound to be guards on the main portals. This may take time." Loriscus explained anxiously.

"Time is one luxury you do not have," the King pointed out as he prepared to sweep from his chambers.

"How about if we create a rainbow? Will it have enough force to enable you to open a doorway?" Taerg suddenly enquired.

"There is very little water available to do such a thing, but yes if it were possible we will be able to do the rest," Loriscus stared at the old sage wondering what he had in mind.

"The water cannon," Taerg looked almost smug.

"Yes! Yes!" Loriscus's face lit up. It could work. The Elverine who were very practised in their art became animated as they discussed the possibilities. The King brought them back to the present.

"Perhaps you had better get on then," Rialstus said dryly. Then he turned with surprising tenderness to Er'nest, "Good luck my son, come back safe to Jalmar." Er'nest gave his father a wavering smile. Their eyes met with unspoken words, and then Rialstus was gone. There was a brief commotion as his courtiers and guards followed him. Within moments the companions found themselves alone.

"We could not possibly get back to my dwelling so quickly," Taerg said with dismay, as the flaw in his own plan glared at him.

"What about transporting? We have the co-ordinates, but will our devices cope with two dragons?" Poldant was clearly worried by the thought.

"Aha! The Amorga has prepared us for just such a possibility." Gremlic smiled as Poldant's head whipped around in his direction. "Do you think the All-Seeing would not know that there may be a need? Indeed, she entrusted me with two extra devices. Our problem is solved."

Taerg obviously had no idea what they were talking about and had to have the transporters explained in brief. He became engrossed and began to go into quite some scientific delving.

"Another time my friend," Gremlic urged gently.

"Of course! Of course!" Taerg responded remorsefully.

"We must get to the surface, it is too dangerous to attempt from here," Loriscus became brusque. Er'nest, who was beginning to show the ability to respond to any given situation, led them speedily up into the sunlight.

The Three Suns were dropping low in their orbit as the companions attained their goal, but even so a heat haze drifted lazily up from the scorched ground. Just visible on the horizon were the forces of Allamang. In the foreground were King Rialstus and his army. Despite the dread seriousness of the situation Douglas felt his heart quicken at the magnificent sight. Multi-coloured dragons had formed up in flanks behind flag bearers, terrifying yet noble, flames and steam ejecting in threatening spouts from their mouths and nostrils. Rialstus roared his supremacy and his followers swelled the sound until it reverberated from the hills opposite. Allamang's army responded vociferously. The ground began to tremble with the stamp of many feet marching on the spot. The dragons would take to the air to fight, this was a display of strength, each force intending to unnerve the other.

"This will go on for a little longer, but I'm afraid we may already be too late!" Taerg panted. It was many a century since he had had to run!

Gremlic hastily clipped the extra devices to the wrists of the dragons, with Crysgar and Camelion helping to tap in the co-ordinates. Douglas grabbed Drock the Outcast and

Deanna swept Rufus into her arms. The Elverine clasped the necks of the unicorns.

"Now!" Gremlic gave the order and the air rushed in to fill the place where they had stood only moments before.

"By the Great Heavens!" Taerg's excited voice was the first thing to hit them as they materialised at the entrance of the old scientist's cave. Shocked and traumatised igrul who had been contentedly sunning their wings scattered and ran for their holes. Taerg pulled himself together and quickly brought order as the cave rang with his instructions. The little creatures popped back out and then scattered again, this time to prepare the water cannon.

Deanna and Douglas were having a last gulp of water and checking that their kit was ready to go when a creeping sense of dread came over the girl. She tried to shake it off but her arms suddenly came up in goose bumps despite the heat. "Gremlic there's something wrong," she called, not sure if she was being silly. Gremlic flitted over to her immediately and tuned in to what she was feeling. The four unicorns, already restless, were drawn towards the intent group. Douglas was not into intuition, but he did have the odd connection that comes with being a twin. Whatever Deanna was sensing made his skin crawl.

"Bathawks!" Gremlic shouted suddenly. "There are two of them lifting off from that cliff face! We should have realised that Gordagn would have left lookouts!" Everyone else came running, the Elverine drawing their weapons at the same time. Taerg remained calm but grim. He flicked his device at Crysgar and pointed urgently to where the rainbow would probably form. Now they could hear the shrill cries of the Zorgians as they flew swiftly to intercept their prey. The igrul worked like mad to pump the water into the cannon, three actually stood on the lever ready to jump and release it with all the force in their little bodies.

"They are calling for help!" Loriscus yelled.

"Hurry! Hurry!" Joalla shrieked. Crest fled to her side ready to protect her friend to the death. Rufus had a very different reaction, leaping out of Deanna's grasp to run behind a rock formation.

"Rufus! Rufus! Come here now or you will be left behind!" Deanna screamed hysterically, but the instinct of the dog was to hide. "Please Rufus! We need you!" Tears were tumbling unheeded as she begged despairingly. Rufus barked incessantly, yelling things like "Keep off!" and "Hide!"

Taerg gave the command to be ready and the Elverine began the magic incantation.

"Deanna! Forget him or *you* will be left behind!" Douglas shouted.

Deanna looked over her shoulder pleadingly. Her eyes widened as they took in the two bathawks that were descending like arrows. Behind them closing fast were four more of the demons summoned by the lookouts. Taerg's claw came down decisively and the water shot skyward. The leading bathawk was close enough to be blasted and knocked off course, the second swerved but kept coming. The magic incantation became louder and more powerful as Gremlic added his energy to it. Crysgar stepped back and fired rapidly at the bathawk, trying to hold it off. Then disaster – one of the poisonous darts that the creature was spitting grazed the Elverine across his shoulder. Crysgar staggered as the poison caused him to go numb almost instantly. Douglas and Deanna leapt to his aid, catching the old Elverine as he crumpled.

"The portal opens," Poldant gritted, perspiration soaking his long blond hair. Before them a rainbow shone in all its beauty, incongruous in the aura of fear and despair. The strip of violet widened and moved towards the desperate group, and within it a doorway began to emerge. Douglas squared his jaw and scooped up Crysgar's weapon, and then shifting the weight of the Elverine, shot it furiously at the bathawk. His unpractised aim caught one of the huge featherless wings, more by luck than judgement, but it was just enough to do its work. The Zorgian lost its balance and, disorientated, smacked straight into the rock face.

"Good shot human!" Taerg yelled encouragement. "Now go – the others are upon us."

"And you?" Loriscus called worriedly.

"I shall be fine. Just go!" As he spoke the original bathawk struggled to an upright position, lending even further urgency to the situation. Taerg exploded from the cave mouth and blasted it with all the force of his gigantic body.

The violet doorway swung open fully and a strange white light beckoned from beyond. "Go!" Gremlic ordered, and as one they ran. Er'nest managed to back through lending Taerg all the help he could until the last moment. He saw Taerg withdraw into his fortress and the boulder roll across the entrance - the old dragon was safe! He turned and surged through the portal as it closed behind them. It was as if someone had flicked a switch, instead of the rage of battle all was complete silence.

Even in their present state of desperation the companions were stopped in their tracks. They were in a world of nothingness, just a radiating white light. There was no form - no sky, no ground, nothing recognisable, it was simply empty!

Chapter 12
Violet Zone - Chjimmer

The twins numbly lowered Crysgar in the direction of what should be the ground although it did not appear solid. Everyone drew closer as they tried to take in the situation. In its way this was scarier than the bathawks!

"I know none of us have ever been here before, but surely you must have known something of this planet from your magical training and historical lore," Camelion said pointedly to the Elverine.

"Yes, but knowing and experiencing are two different things." Poldant stared around at the nothingness with something between awe and dread.

"You could have warned us – tried to prepare us in some way," Douglas accused.

"Sorry, we just did not have the time. Anyway what difference would it make to the situation? *We* knew but are just as lost as to what to do as you are, so the information would have made no difference whatsoever," Loriscus said, an edge of irritation to his voice.

Deanna had something else on her mind. She tugged at her brother's sleeve, her face stricken. "Rufus!" Deanna whispered despondently.

"Yes," came the dog's gruff voice. She swung around in disbelief and squawked with surprise. There stood Rufus – and Drock the Outcast who stood a little nervously with his claw on the dog's collar.

"Ahem," the Drock cleared his throat. "Er … I thought you would be sad to lose your friend, so … I … er … brought him here for you." Drock the Outcast looked around somewhat nonplussed. "Wherever here is." Deanna gurgled somewhere between tears and joy and then flung her arms around both of them, much to the Drock's consternation. Douglas was not far behind, although he contented himself with pumping their new friend's claw.

"Cheers mate," was all he could manage because he was afraid he was going to cry as well.

"Sorry about my momentary lapse," Rufus said gruffly "lost it for a while there."

"Stupid dog," Deanna murmured with her face buried in his neck fur. Rufus wagged his tail to show he understood this was an expression of affection. Meanwhile Loriscus, Joalla and Poldant walked over to the Drock who was still trying to take in his surroundings with a baffled expression on his face.

"Welcome to the quest," Loriscus said grinning widely. This was wiped away by Camelion calling them urgently, he was kneeling together with Gremlic by the stricken Crysgar. Er'nest stood watching over them, he kept glancing around nervously and his huge body shook, mostly because of the sudden loss of heat. He looked as if he was afraid to speak in case he let himself down. The ferocious fighting dragon of only moments before had disappeared.

"Douglas, give me your magic water vial," Camelion demanded tersely. Douglas dropped his pack and rummaged through hastily, mortified that he had momentarily forgotten the Elverine. He handed it to the changeling who poured the liquid over the blackening wound, there was no blood but a strange blue tinged liquid leaked out of it. "Thankfully it is only a scratch," Camelion saw as the dirt washed away. "Hopefully he will recover fully, although I suspect there may be a day or two of sickness."

Gremlic gently moved the changeling's blue hand away and replaced it with his own tiny claw. A greenish white glow emitted from the palm, and to their amazement the strange gash began to heal before their transfixed gaze. Crysgar opened his blue eyes, which despite everything still held a vague twinkle. His face lost the twisted pained expression and became peaceful, his eyelids drooped and he slept.

Douglas heaved a sigh of relief that came from the heart. "OK," he said more cheerfully, "what now?"

"Maybe I could assist you there," a disembodied voice came from above them, Douglas ducked automatically. "There is no need to panic or become violent," it added "put down your weapons, they will be of no use here anyway."

"Here we go again," Douglas groaned irrepressibly. He searched for the source of the voice, but all he could see was a slight sparkle hovering above them, rather as if a child had thrown up a handful of glitter dust. "Er … hello?" he said.

"Ah, let me see. Two humans, some Elverine, representatives of the Tribe of Changelings, unicorns, a dragon, a dog and a Drock. You must be the party I have been expecting," the voice sounded as if it were reading from a list.

"You cannot have been expecting me because even I did not know I was coming," Drock the Outcast pointed out politely.

"I did."

"Oh," a pause, "are you sure?"

"Completely. Come along now please, an Honoured One is waiting for you." Everyone looked at each other. Not even Gremlic knew what was going on this time.

"Um … may we ask why?" Loriscus asked.

"How should I know. I'm just the Collector. Do not worry, you will be told soon enough."

"Right! Well!" Loriscus tried to sound decisive. "We had better go along with it for now. It's not as if we can go anywhere else – there doesn't seem to *be* an anywhere else anyway."

"Why did the … er … thing say *representatives* of the Tribe of Changelings?" Deanna realised what had been tickling the back of her mind for the last few seconds.

"Dunno!" Douglas was much struck by the question.

It didn't take long to clear up. As they turned to pick up the sleeping Crysgar they were faced with not his familiar form, but the same pulsing blue energy wave as Camelion. Camelion was still kneeling attentively beside him, a wry expression on his face.

"He was unable to retain his shape as an Elverine," Camelion said, pointing out the obvious. Everyone was too dumbstruck to respond. "He is my father," the changeling stated and then hesitated unsure as to how to go on.

"Blimey!" said Douglas weakly.

"What is going on? Has this whole quest been a trick? Are we truly headed for the rescue of Silbeamia," anguished questions suddenly poured out of Loriscus as the possibilities hit him.

Camelion looked aghast. "No, no! I told you from the first moment that I had my own reason for joining you, but that was not to hinder your undertaking. I promise you. I gave my word!"

Gremlic took over. "This was no plot Loriscus." The Elverine whipped around and glared at him, lips white with anger. Gremlic lifted a placatory claw. "I assure you that the Amorga knew of this, as did I, but I cannot tell you why just yet. Neither Crysgar nor Camelion have ever given you reason to distrust them. Quite the opposite in fact." Loriscus subsided slightly at this.

Starlight, Crest and Uraj looked at Glore with unspoken condemnation. "I am a real unicorn!" he protested hastily. "You know that my first loyalty is to the one I have sworn to defend and serve. I was not permitted to tell you of this, but I promise you that no harm was intended." This was a long speech from the normally taciturn Glore. Starlight opened his mouth to berate him, but was distracted by an irritated sigh from somewhere above his head.

"If you don't mind," the disembodied voice interrupted sarcastically, "I would like to get on. There are other parties to collect besides you. Of course, most of them come without their bodies. You are my most unusual case for a very long time."

Loriscus pulled himself together. "We will sort this out later," he promised. "Right, where are we going Collector?"

"Follow me," it said.

"We can't *see* you," Loriscus was now really exasperated.

"Right-oh. Forgot about that. Just a second." The glitter cloud billowed and enlarged until it became a kind of see-through outline of a person. "How's that?" it exclaimed smugly. "Haven't lost the touch you know. Believe I was a human once ... or was it a Mantanean ... close anyway. Come on then." As it floated away a vague path materialised before them. Thunderstruck they had no choice but to follow. Camelion picked up the sleeping Crysgar effortlessly and trod in their wake.

"Remind me - what are we doing here?" Douglas enquired of Joalla.

"The magical ingredient to put in the gum," she said briefly. The Elveriness was too busy trying to sense whether the rolling white energy billowing around them was friendly or not to pay him much attention. There was of course no sound or smell, even their footfall was silent, nothing in fact that gave a feeling of reality.

"Oh yes," Douglas whittered on nervously, and then after a moment's thought, "why?"

Joalla really looked him full in the face this time. "You really have very little idea of what is going on most of the time do you?" Douglas flushed and Deanna rolled her eyes and tutted. "Shut it!" he growled.

The Collector stopped and turned to address them. "Right-oh, here we are," it sounded much more cheerful now that the mission was accomplished.

"Thank you," Gremlic responded gravely. "Would it be possible for you to explain *where* exactly 'here' is?"

"Ah, good question. Well we are in the high vibration quarter of the seventh level of Chjimmer."

"I see, we are very grateful," Gremlic bowed at the outline.

"What for!" Camelion was recovering his normal good spirits despite the fact that everyone seemed to be ignoring him. Joalla's lips twitched.

"May I ask what is going to happen now?" Loriscus employed Gremlic's tactics at winning the Collector over and bowed also. It had the desired effect as the outline took on a tinge of pink.

"Does that mean it's feeling a bit more friendly?" Deanna whispered to Douglas, who shrugged and pulled a face.

"Another good question," the Collector sounded pleasantly surprised. "Well, two main events are going to enfold," it went on grandly, "and the second will depend on the outcome of the first."

"Right," said Loriscus patiently. "And ..." he prompted after an overlong pause.

"Trying to remember," it said apologetically. "I usually leave at this point you see. Now what is it? Well I know that the second thing is that if the first thing doesn't work out then you are chucked out – back whence you came – but if it does, work out that is, then a Developer helps you to manage while you are in this world." Another pause. "Or you might die anyway," it added cheerfully.

Loriscus and Poldant looked at each other perplexedly. "Did you get that?" Poldant asked out of the side of his mouth. Loriscus shook his head in exasperation.

"We are very grateful," Gremlic said and then managed to step back on Douglas's foot just as he was about to make one of his less than helpful comments.

"Right-oh. Pleasure actually," the Collector said happily. "I'll be off then. Good luck." And the bizarre outline disappeared in a small fizz of sparks.

"Now what?" Loriscus demanded of Gremlic.

"We wait," he answered unperturbed.

Camelion gently laid down Crysgar who was now snoring contentedly. He took the opportunity to re-examine the wound, but all that remained was a faint line.

"Is the changeling injured?" a deep booming voice enquired over his shoulder. He leapt into the air with fright.

"Oh bloody hell!" Douglas gasped as his stomach hit the back of his throat. Deanna hastily grabbed Rufus's collar as he began to bark frantically.

"It's a dog isn't it?" the voice enquired interestedly, this time it hovered just by her ear. Deanna nodded trying not to scream.

"Thought so. I've read about them in the Records you know. Interesting. I wonder what it's like to be one," it boomed even more loudly with enthusiasm. "Now, down to business. Let me have a look. Ah yes, yes I see." As it spoke a cooling sensation literally passed through Deanna's mind. She saw from the general reaction that the same was happening to everyone. There were a few moments of what felt like a loud silence. "Let me make this easier for you. I realise that you are not vibrating at a high enough level to see me, or indeed any of my world. I will slow the energy surrounding us. Ah that should do it." And all around the bewildered companions a room blossomed, complete with chairs. There was a concerted yelp of astonishment, even Gremlic blinked twice. "Is this more comfortable for you?" The voice had become embodied. Before them stood another person-shaped outline, but this one had a face. They all stared. "Is this not right? I am reasonably sure that this is a face I used millennia ago, on the planet Earth I think."

"Were you in a place called Africa?" Deanna asked timidly.

The face smiled at her approvingly. "That's it. Will it do?"

"Oh yes, it's a very nice face. We just weren't expecting it that's all," Deanna said hastily.

"Good. Now let us get on with the business in hand. Come on, take a seat, that's it." Everyone took a chair except obviously Er'nest and the unicorns, who simply found a space and sat in it. Er'nest had recovered his composure but had still not spoken since their arrival in Chjimmer. "Refreshments?" As soon as the question was asked a small table appeared by each of them filled with food, not just any food, but the absolute favourite dish that each craved.

"Wow! This is more like it!" Douglas tucked into a plate of bangers and mash. Deanna nodded, her mouth too full of fish and chips to risk an answer. Even the presence of the strange being couldn't put any of them off their meals. It was too wonderful to be enjoying a complete change from travelling biscuits to bother with polite chat. Only Er'nest and Drock the Outcast ate slowly and remained wary as they had not yet been deprived of interesting sustenance.

"Can I ask a question?" Poldant looked up satisfied at last.

"You just did," the face laughed heartily at its own joke. "No, no of course, what is it?"

"How did you know without asking? I mean what each individual wanted to eat?"

"I read your minds," it replied simply. Everyone's eyes became as wide as saucers. The energy being didn't notice but went on, "I must say I had forgotten what it's like to try to think in solid form. Everything is so slow isn't it?"

"I don't get it," Poldant looked lost. The others shook their heads equally nonplussed.

"Oh! Well it's very easy really. You can't see our world or us because we vibrate at a much faster rate than your eyes are capable of deciphering. In the same way we find you incredibly slow and easy to read, so solid and ... er ... lugubrious that it is almost like entertaining – a rock let us say. Because your brains creep along at that rate it is very straightforward to whiz our energy along your thought waves and read them."

"Does that mean you already know why we are here?" Loriscus asked cautiously.

"Yes precisely, well done." Loriscus felt like a child who was being encouraged by an enthusiastic adult, one who might clap in delight any minute.

"Your ... um ... Controller mentioned that there was a two-part process that we have to follow. Is that right?" Loriscus asked.

"Correct."

Douglas was dying to tell the being that they weren't *that* slow, but he didn't have to, it was already flowing along his thought waves. "Oh sorry," it addressed itself to the startled boy. "I'll speed up a bit." To everyone's dismay any further sound became like crackling white noise from an out of tune radio, while the face began to blur as if someone had pressed the fast forward button.

"Too fast, too fast," Loriscus called out.

"Oops, sorry again, takes a bit of adjusting to get onto your frequency."

"Before we get into this process you mentioned, can you explain something else to me?" Douglas interrupted. Loriscus looked annoyed, he was desperate to get on with things, but Douglas's scientific mind was buzzing with questions.

"Happy to! Happy to!" The ever-genial face continued to grin madly.

"I was just wondering whether this world is full of stuff like on the planet Earth or if it's just moving energy?"

"Oh yes. This is a very beautiful place. Shame you aren't developed enough to enjoy it really. The main difference is that we, the life forms of Chjimmer, create our surroundings as we go. The sky's the limit as I believe the saying goes amongst humans."

"So are there other ... er ... life-forms all around us now?" Douglas was fascinated.

"Of course. They have been having a little fun since you arrived, seeing how many of them you could walk through without noticing and that sort of thing."

"Did we hurt them?" Deanna was aghast.

"No! Bit of a funny sensation that's all. Anyway you move so slowly that some of us were laying bets on how long it would take you to reach my quarters, so you certainly couldn't interfere with our energy patterns. I suspect the two shapeshifters can detect us slightly more easily because they work with energy patterns all the time. Am I right about that?" He looked enquiringly at Camelion who merely nodded.

"Thanks," Douglas said, his eyes shifting from side to side as he tried to catch sight of something.

"Can we get back to business, time is of the essence after all, particularly as we move so slowly," Loriscus said sarcastically. Joalla groaned inwardly at his rudeness and then remembered that the Chjimmerian could literally read her like a book and so tried to force her mind into pleasant thoughts. Poldant was also aware of his friend's growing anxiety. "What should we call you?" he asked politely, more as a distraction technique than because he actually wanted to know.

"Let me see. Yes – I've got it – you can call me Akraj that will do."

"Isn't that your name then?" Douglas asked incorrigibly. Deanna kicked him as she watched Loriscus from under her eyelashes. "Ow! What!"

"It is the nearest you can get to it." Akraj turned to Loriscus, "I feel the rage building in this Elverine, let us put him out of his misery." It became clear that he wasn't talking either to himself or to them when an enormous circular table appeared in the middle of the room encircled on the far side by six other Chjimmerians who had also made themselves visible. "These are Honoured Ones in our world, they have earned the right to stay here and forgo further experiences in other dimensions." Douglas opened his mouth but his sister kicked him again and he shut it hastily. "We are here to help judge your case and to ascertain whether you continue to reside in your present bodies and go on your quest, or if it is time to die and start again." The words were said in such a pleasant tone of voice that it took several moments to take in their import.

"Do you mean that as a result of this trial we may be put to death?" Loriscus could barely believe his ears. His companions stiffened as their situation sank in.

"No, of course not." Akraj looked pained. Loriscus's shoulders slumped with relief, but only momentarily. "We only separate your spirit from your bodies and discard them, *you* don't die."

"And then?" Loriscus asked very quietly, his hand moved surreptitiously to his ray shooter even though he knew it was useless.

"Now don't be upset," Akraj begged. "It is a very easy matter. Either you leave here as you are because you haven't finished the work of this lifetime, or you get to remain here and prepare to enter another dimension where you will start again. It isn't as if none of you have ever done this before, you just don't remember. You are not supposed to, bit confusing otherwise." Everyone was too stunned to argue. Then Deanna was struck by an incredible thought, it was so amazing that she automatically clutched at Douglas's hand. Before she could communicate with Douglas Akraj smiled kindly and said, "Yes they are here." Her eyes swam with incredulous tears. They had never got to say goodbye, it had been the worst part. Douglas suddenly caught on and he just stared in disbelief at the Chjimmerian.

"Can we see them?" Deanna choked out.

"Probably not," Akraj shook his head gently. "Not unless you remain here."

"Oh please, you couldn't be so cruel," Deanna was sobbing openly now, Douglas fiercely wiped the corner of his eye on the back of his hand, but for once could think of nothing to say. Poldant and Camelion who were sitting each side of the twins tried to comfort them with awkward pats on their shoulders, but Loriscus had been overwhelmed with a notion of his own.

"Silbeamia?" He hardly dared to ask. His friends sat very still at this, even Deanna stopped crying although her breath juddered in her throat. All eyes were on Akraj.

"Not here yet," Akraj responded, Silbeamia and her plight were plainly already known to him. Loriscus expelled a huge breath and literally wilted with relief, it was not too late. The fear had chased him from dimension to dimension. "Thank the Universes!" he murmured gratefully, but the word 'yet' was not lost on him.

"Is there really nothing we can do about seeing our parents?" Douglas asked, sounding extraordinarily calm. The Honoured Ones blurred briefly as they consulted each other and then slowed to the speed of their audience.

"It is most unusual. In fact it has never happened before. We shall have to consult your records to ascertain whether this will have a beneficial effect on your life path," one of the Honoured Ones said.

"Our records?" Deanna's brow wrinkled.

"Any living being in every dimension and Universes has a record. This record is of each life they have ever lived, and the lessons gained from such. We will check and find out if your request will aid or hinder this life mission."

"Thank you, it would mean a great deal to both of us," Deanna said quietly. Douglas nodded, still unable to speak.

"What now?" Gremlic said.

"If you just sit for what I believe will be your concept of a short time, then we will consult, check with our higher source, and then share in each verdict." As he spoke the beings opposite smiled kindly and vanished followed instantly by Akraj.

Everyone sat immersed in his or her own thoughts. This situation was more perilous than all the battles they had fought to reach this point, because nothing they might say or do now would make any difference. Everything depended on how they had performed mentally and physically and on how true each had been, not just whilst on the quest, but even before that. It was a sobering reflection, every one of them had had moments they were ashamed of. Who hasn't?

The Honoured Ones reappeared. Loriscus straightened his back and squared his shoulders, ready to receive their verdict. Deanna grasped her shaking hands together under the table and glanced at her brother who was blinking rapidly as if hoping that the judges before them might disappear. Douglas felt Rufus gently lick his hand which he moved comfortingly to the dog's head. Er'nest who sat next to the Drock actually curled his tail around the little creature, the two races finally unified. Poldant and Joalla both looked amazingly serene, their history and beliefs made this experience slightly less frightening. Camelion kept turning to check the still motionless form of Crysgar who lay behind him. Gremlic, as ever, was unruffled and unafraid. The unicorns however behaved in the most unexpected way. They actually seemed delighted and completely relaxed, a unicorn's view on life is completely different from most life forms in the universes.

"We apologise for taking so long, but all is now reviewed and understood on our part," Akraj said. "It is time for each of you to give judgement on his or her self." This last comment was so unexpected that no one responded at all. The cooling sensation came again at the Chjimmerians probed their minds. "Ah, I see. You thought that the last judgement would be according to our own assessment? No indeed, it is for you to decide."

"Why do you sit before us then?" Loriscus burst out.

"We are here, with full knowledge of the lives you have led, to help you to review your own performance. Sometimes a being can be a little too hard on itself you know. The one thing you will be unable to do is avoid something you would rather not address." At that Akraj and the other six blurred and then slowed down, this time standing in a circle. "Each will take it in turn to join us, the rest of you will go and rest." Loriscus realised that his friends had all dematerialised, and that he stood alone in the centre of the circle. He suspected that this was going to be similar to the experience he had had just before meeting with the Amorga, but this time he had so much more on his conscience. All conscious thought ended as he became obliterated in a white light.

Chapter 13

L oriscus found himself lying on a huge comfortable bed. He stretched luxuriously, feeling refreshed, rested and completely at peace. It took a moment to remember the recent events, but when they came back to him he shot up in consternation. All around him lay the companions he had fought alongside and come to love, and not one of them was missing. His heart leapt in gratitude and silent celebration.

One by one they came into wakefulness. One by one they saw that each had passed the test. Then everything erupted as they all started talking and laughing at once, although strangely no one actually discussed the experience they had just been through. Douglas hugged Rufus who had been lying next to his feet and babbled nonsense to him in the way that people tend to do with their dogs. Rufus panted contentedly and said, "Well I knew I had nothing to worry about, the worst I have ever done is nick a pound of sausages from the kitchen table!" Deanna couldn't stop giggling at this. Crysgar was amazingly restored to full health, although the others were still finding his normal appearance quite an adjustment. Camelion was unashamedly affectionate to his father, no longer having to keep up the old pretence. Starlight and the other unicorns were stamping and neighing excitedly. Uraj kept exclaiming, "What an experience!" to all and sundry. Er'nest and Drock the Outcast were deep in discussion as their unlikely friendship developed. Crysgar began to try to explain himself to Loriscus, but was interrupted by the next turn of events.

Douglas nudged Deanna and jerked his head in the direction of several glittering energy clouds. "Thank you!" Deanna shouted happily, opening her arms wide as if to embrace them.

One of the clouds billowed and took on a shape. Everyone stopped mid-sentence and stared. "It's ... you're ..." Deanna stuttered, "you're a ... an angel!" she finally managed.

"Blimey!" Douglas swore, and then wondered anxiously whether he should have, but the angel obviously didn't mind.

"I believe that is our given title on your planet," the angel's voice floated to them like glorious music. "In this dimension we are called Developers. I am here to help you survive within this vibration and to guide you into the next world."

"How is it that we would find it difficult to survive here? It seems safe enough to me." Poldant said.

"Your energy moves too slowly, if you stay for any length of time your bodies will disintegrate and you will have no choice but to stay and wait for a new opportunity to be reborn."

"Blimey!" Douglas swore again.

"How soon may we move on into Kephlopodia?" Gremlic asked, a new sense of urgency making the question more abrupt than he meant.

"Very soon," the angel assured him, "but there are still a small number of things to sort out."

"Sort out?" Er'nest repeated.

The angel turned to him. "You and the one called Drock the Outcast, for instance, need to be prepared for the experience of a world consisting entirely of water. To most of those who exist on Jalmar this would be so terrifying that madness might ensue." Drock the Outcast bowed his head in his quaint way to acknowledge the point.

"And the magical ingredient to enable us to breathe in that world?" Loriscus asked, although somewhere in the back of his mind he vaguely remembered that this question had already been answered in the recent testing.

"You all still remain in your present physical form because each of you has displayed a complete belief in your quest. Of course the ingredient will be provided," the light-being smiled, "come now." Everyone gathered ready to move off, the beds vanished.

"Can I just ask another quick question?" Douglas was unable to resist. Although the angel clearly already knew what the boy was going to ask, he nodded his head agreeably. "Well, it's just that … I was wondering what happened to the bathawks who were following us?"

"Ah!" The angel sighed softly. "I think it is easier to understand if I show you." Instantly they found themselves dropping rapidly, rather as if someone had pressed the down button on a particularly fast lift. The further they fell the more real the sensations became around them. Bursts of sparkling firework like energy became visible, movement and feelings whizzed past them, but strangely the feelings were not their own. It was all completely bewildering. Then just as suddenly as they had dropped, they came to a standstill, and this time they were faced with a horrible reality.

Here was not a strangely beautiful light-filled place. Instead a ghastly heavy force hit them with such power that it caused several to step back. The angel lifted its hands and it was as if a screen had swept back revealing a vision of hell. As far as the eye could see were hundreds of beings in all shapes and sizes, the only thing that each had in common was that every one of them was screaming and shouting in either terror or fury. Deanna's eyes were like saucers and her body shook with fright. Crysgar put his hand on her shoulder, although it was shaking almost as badly. Joalla hid her face in Poldant's shoulder, but the others stood resolute, even Rufus only whined softly in the back of his throat.

"Why are they screaming when there is nothing there?" Douglas croaked.

"Because they *believe* there is something there," the angel said simply. Everyone stared at him in astonishment. "Each of these beings has lived the gift of life either evilly or wastefully. When they came to review their actions as you all have just done, they were plunged into their own version of hell."

"Will they remain here forever?" Joalla was very distressed.

"No, each will move up to the next level when they are able to forgive themselves and to start afresh."

"Let me get this straight. They are keeping themselves here?" Douglas was incredulous. "And it is up to them to leave, but they don't?" The angel nodded sadly. "But why? I don't get it?"

"The regret and sorrow of a wasted life is terrible to bear. When the spirit comes back to Chjimmer and recognises how they have behaved ..." the angel trailed off and shrugged his shoulders. A tiny tear trembled on Deanna's lashes. "Most move on in time you know," he said to her reassuringly.

Gremlic had been completely engrossed in the scene before them. He pointed to his left and everyone looked. There were two bathawks circling and tearing at each other in an eternal vicious fight, their black eyes burning with hate.

"They cannot see you, or any of the other beings, they think they are alone in this place," the angel said.

"Oh, how terrible!" Joalla cried. Er'nest tried to feel as compassionate as the Elveriness, but his world had been left in turmoil because of these creatures, and even now he did not know whether his father had avoided war. Guiltily he tried to push down a rather satisfied reaction to the ghastly sight. He glanced around and was transfixed with guilt as he found the angel looking directly at him.

"How do you know when they are ready to move up a level?" Poldant asked.

"The change is instantaneous. The moment a spirit understands the lesson it will find itself transported to another place."

"And then?"

"Then it will go to The Place of Healing where it will be fully healed, after which it continues through the system including returning to education at the Place of Learning. From here it earns back its happiness either by having a go at another existence or by working within one of the levels of Chjimmer ... and so the dance of life goes on."

"I have seen enough thank you," Douglas said quietly. No one could think of anything else to say, so they didn't. Once again, as if in response to an unspoken command, the swiftly moving lift jerked under their feet and shot them upwards. All motion stopped just as suddenly. Er'nest lost his balance and Loriscus leapt out of his way fearing he was about to be squashed. The angel laughed.

"Where are we now?" Loriscus asked. "I'm sorry, but Silbeamia is running out of time, we must get on."

Gremlic flew onto the Elverine's shoulder. "Do not despair Loriscus, we will make it, I am certain of this," he said. Loriscus blew out his cheeks in exasperation, if only he could be as sure himself!

"The one called Er'nest and the other from Jalmar – Drock the Outcast – will be taken from here to prepare for Kephlopodia. The changelings and Gremlic have their own private place that has been prepared for them. The Elverine and their unicorn friends are to go with my colleague here," a glorious golden angel materialised. "You two humans and the dog are to come with me." The twins just had time to grab each other and hold on as they were swept into another experience.

"Phew! It's like travelling on a roller coaster!" Douglas gasped as they jerked and floated gently into their destination. "Ouch!" he yelped as Deanna's fingers gripped his arm convulsively, "let go you idiot, you're hurting me!" Then he saw what she was looking at.

In front of the twins was a house with a thatched roof. It stood in a meadow full of wild flowers and to one side ran a clear bubbling brook. On closer inspection the house needed a little repair work, but the overall picture was delightful.

"Our old cottage," Deanna gulped and put her hand to her mouth in astonishment. Douglas slowly lowered Rufus to the ground, feeling that this had to be a surreal dream and soon it would all vanish. Rufus being of a simpler nature happily sniffed at the grass and found a good spot to cock his leg.

"What's this all about?" Douglas sounded as bewildered as he felt. Deanna began to walk towards the cottage, slowly, as if she was afraid that any sudden move might banish the illusion. Douglas went to call her back but thought better of it; after a brief hesitation he joined her. They had not been back to the family home from the time of their parent's death, it had disappeared as suddenly from their lives as had mum and dad. One day they had been a happy normal family, the next everything had gone, and some well-meaning person had put the twins in a car and driven them to their grandmother. They had not even been back to collect their personal belongings, someone had done that for them. Douglas felt overwhelmed and knew that Deanna felt the same. Until this moment neither had realised how dreadful the impact of the loss of their home had been.

Deanna interrupted his train of thought. "Do you think it's possible ... you know ... with the house being here that ... ?" She couldn't bring herself to finish the sentence.

"Everything is possible." It was the angel who answered. They had both forgotten about him, but at these words Deanna broke into a jog and Douglas rushed to catch up, more concerned for her potential disappointment than because he truly believed that a miracle was about to happen. The angel floated alongside effortlessly.

By the time Deanna reached the door she was running at full pelt, but as soon as her hand reached to push it open she paused and closed her eyes. "Please let it be true. Please let it be true. Please be there." The words revolved around her brain in a desperate wish.

"Deanna ..." Douglas searched hopelessly for the right thing to say. Deanna looked him full in the face.

"Anything is possible, you have to *believe* that," she was almost begging now. Douglas rubbed his forehead not sure how to handle this.

"OK, come on, we'll give it a go." Deanna lit up with a beam. "Just don't ... well you know," he tried to prepare her for disappointment. Deanna inclined her head momentarily and reached for his hand, just as she used to do when they were small. He didn't shake her off.

"Let's do it the old way." Now that Douglas was co-operating, it was Deanna who became unsure. Douglas rolled his eyes but didn't stop her. "Close your eyes then," she demanded. "Right. Izzy Whizzy magic spell keep us safe and make things well," she chanted childishly. "Now!" And they both stepped over the threshold in unison.

"Blimey! everything really is just the same. Look there's my old tennis racquet, it never did find it's way to gran's," Douglas said. Deanna ignored him.

"Someone's cooking in the kitchen," she whispered. Douglas's stomach swooped and he fought the desire to turn and run. They both crept forward cautiously and stopped again. Now that it came to it neither wanted to be the first to risk a peep. "You go," Deanna gave him a little shove.

"No way! This was your idea, you go," and he shoved her back.

"Is that you children?" They both froze and Douglas went white with shock. It was their mother's voice! Deanna's brown eyes were huge and swam with tears.

"Mum?" she said tremulously. Their mother appeared at the kitchen door, her familiar old smile just as they remembered it.

"Hello," she said. "We have been waiting for you." We! That could only mean … !

"Mum?" Deanna seemed, after all her professed belief in fairy tales, unable to accept the evidence of her own eyes. It was Douglas who pushed past her and threw himself at their mother.

"MUM!" he yelled incredulously and she held her arms out to welcome him. The next second he found that he had passed straight through her and had fallen onto the floor.

Mum looked mortified. "Dougie, I am so sorry, I forgot. You can't touch us."

"So you *are* an illusion," he said bitterly. Deanna blinked hard and tentatively poked her finger at their mother, only to have the same thing happen. A figure joined them and Douglas clutched his head feeling that he might go mad.

"Hello kids," their father said quietly. Everyone looked at each other nonplussed. Then Douglas got angry. He got really, really angry. Deanna could see that he was about to blow and tried to pre-empt it, but the storm hit anyway. Douglas glared at the angel and started to shout.

"HOW DARE YOU DO THIS. YOU KNEW HOW MUCH THIS MEANT TO US AND THEY ARE NOT EVEN REAL. CAN'T YOU SEE THAT THIS IS WORSE. WHAT ARE YOU PLAYING AT?" Deanna winced and waited for the beautiful dream to disintegrate, but it didn't.

"Douglas stop it," their father said firmly. Douglas halted mid-flow, more out of habit than anything else. His fury abated and grief flowed in to take its place. Douglas scrubbed at his wet eyes with the back of his hand, feeling bereft.

"It's just not fair," he muttered truculently. Deanna could not bring herself to say anything, a massive lump making it hard to swallow blocked her throat. Their parents looked distressed and sad, the angel started to vibrate with a calming energy cloud that helped to alleviate the twins' pain. Their mother, always the negotiator, tried again.

"Listen children, we *are* real. Honestly. It is just that you can only see our spirits, we left our bodies behind when we came here and so of course we are not solid enough to touch. Please believe this is not some cruel trick," she begged.

"We have had to have a few quick lessons in slowing down our vibrations just to make ourselves visible, it would take more time than you have for us to master the skill of becoming solid again," their father continued the explanation.

"The Honoured Ones have given you all a great opportunity, don't waste it," the angel said. "I will return for you shortly."

The twins relaxed slightly, but were still very wary. Their parents stood quietly waiting for them to come to terms with the situation. Suddenly Rufus burst joyfully into the room. "This place is amazing!" he said excitedly, "doesn't quite smell the same, but it's ..." They were never destined to hear the rest of the sentence as Rufus trailed off at the sight of their parents. With a yelp he leapt behind the children and swore loudly. Deanna giggled and the atmosphere changed.

"He swore!" Their mother couldn't believe her ears, and it was this more than anything that convinced Deanna that she was really standing in front of her. At some level anyway. Douglas who was always the more suspicious continued to watch cautiously.

"Hello old boy!" Dad knelt down and gently extended his hand to Rufus. Rufus sniffed and swore again, but his tail wagged slightly.

"He doesn't like being called old boy," Douglas said, a grin tugging at the corners of his mouth. Dad grinned back and winked just as he used to. "Oops," he said. Douglas gave in. If this was an illusion then it was a lovely one.

"Come and sit down," their mother invited. "I've been trying to get the hang of making tea, but it keeps dissipating, sorry."

"Oh mum! Who cares about the old tea anyway. Don't let's waste time with stuff like that. There is so much to say!" But as soon as they were sitting across the table from one another Deanna dried up completely. She just kept staring at her parents with wide eyes, as if she were trying to absorb them right into her heart.

"We are sorry that we died and left you so suddenly," dad began. Douglas's grin faded, Rufus pressed himself against Douglas's leg comfortingly.

"It's OK," Deanna muttered, not sure what else to say.

"No it isn't OK," mum said gently. "It was a terrible thing to have happened, we were both really cross when we got here and realised what was going on."

Deanna was astonished. Such a thought had never occurred to her. "Couldn't you have told them it was a mistake or something?" She asked.

"Actually we did try. Very hard in fact. But the Honoured Ones made us see that we had done our job and that you both would be better off with your gran for this part of your life."

"WHAT! You're *joking!*" Douglas was livid again. He jumped to his feet and began to pace in an attempt to control his rage.

"Douglas, come back and listen," their mother said firmly, "you are wasting time." Douglas threw himself back into the chair and glared at the wall beyond his parents. Deanna wanted to throttle him.

"Stop it," she gritted at him, but he shrugged one shoulder and ignored her. "How could it possibly be true, how could anyone think that we were better off without you. That's rubbish," Deanna wobbled.

"The thing is ..." dad searched for the right words, " ... apparently you two are fore-runners for a new species of human who will travel the dimensions and help to bring universal peace." Douglas's attention snapped back to his father.

"What a load of ..." he began. His father held up his hand peremptorily, clearly beginning to lose patience with his son's tantrum.

"I realise that this is almost beyond belief, but you and your friends will be filled in on the enormity of your mission very shortly. There is much more to it than you could possibly have imagined."

"Well, first I don't believe that we are here to help save the world or the Universes or anything else because we are just ordinary kids; and second, even if this were true then why did we have to do it without you two?"

"Because in our human form we would never have understood. We would not have let you go. Your gran however is a very different kettle of fish, she kind of 'gets' the Universes and all that stuff," dad said.

"Gran hasn't let us go, she doesn't know we are here," Deanna pointed out.

"No, but she will give you the space to be different, as she is herself. Also this is only the very beginning, there will come a day when you travel with her blessing." Mum tried to pat Deanna's hand but her own passed through it. However there was some sensation of presence and it soothed her aching heart just a little.

"We would have preferred to stay with you but it has become easier with time to understand that it wasn't possible. That doesn't mean that we didn't love you," dad said. Douglas was surprised because dad was not the emotional sort, he had never mentioned the 'love' word before.

The angel reappeared. "Oh no, just a few more minutes," Deanna pleaded, knowing what this meant. Douglas was frantic, he had wasted so much time being angry!

"I am afraid there is no more time," the angel said.

"Listen," mum said urgently, "we are always here, and the Honoured Ones keep us informed of all that you do. If you are in trouble, call on us. Although you may not see us, we will come to help." Douglas and Deanna tried to thank her, but she continued, "Close your eyes and *feel*." Obediently they both obeyed her request. Each felt the pressure of her lips upon their foreheads. "Goodbye my darlings."

"Good luck," dad said. When they opened their eyes their parents had gone. So had the house, the meadow, and even the chairs, they both found themselves floating once again in an energy cloud. It was too difficult to talk initially, even Rufus kept completely silent, but eventually Deanna pulled herself together.

"Come on moron!" she teased. Douglas saw to his relief that she wasn't upset at all, in fact her eyes were sparkling with a new-found happiness. He felt different too. It took a moment but he realised that the bubbling anger that he had lived with for the past year had gone and had been replaced by an inner calm, and a sense of - destiny.

"Thank you," Douglas turned to the angel. "That was wonderful, and the most fantastic bit of luck." It was Deanna's turn to be surprised. Douglas sounded and looked different, more grown-up somehow.

"There is no such thing as luck. You earned this experience through your own hard work and the willingness to take a risk. You could have stayed on Earth and bypassed this whole adventure you know, but you didn't." The angel smiled beatifically. "Take up your dog Douglas, the others are waiting for you." Rufus jumped into Douglas's arms and they were off again.

Chapter 14

*E*veryone found themselves back in Akraj's chamber. Initially the noise was incredible as they all excitedly tried to tell their own story, each experience unique to that being. Er'nest and Drock the Outcast, who had become firm friends, could barely get over the enormity of what had happened to them. They had been taken into a replica of Kephlopodia. The Drock in particular had so little perception of a mass of water, that the sudden complete immersion within it had been almost overwhelming. After the initial panic (both of them), Er'nest found that his bulk actually moved with great ease through the water and he had begun to enjoy the sensation. Drock the Outcast was of the opinion that the sooner they got in and then out of Kephlopodia, the better, - despite the terrors waiting at the other end. He said that he would rather fight the Hordes of Darkness than be encompassed in water! In amongst the excitement, only Joalla noticed a new yet deep power emanating from the dragon.

The twins were ecstatically relating their own experience to Joalla and Poldant when Akraj materialised and called for their attention.

"How are we all?" he asked jovially, his black face beaming. They all nodded and called out their thanks enthusiastically. The atmosphere was relaxed yet crackling with an underlying awareness that the next stage was about to begin. Douglas and Deanna in particular knew from the discussion with their parents that everyone was about to be told more than they had bargained for, and they were right.

Akraj invited his guests to make themselves comfortable. This time the chairs materialised in a large circle with no table in the centre. Akraj moved into the space and his face became grave. They all knew then that they were not likely to enjoy what they were about to hear. Akraj began to talk, and as he did so little figures and scenes materialised around him illustrating the information that he was imparting.

The Honoured One told the story to the present day, and Loriscus jumped out of his skin when a miniature but lifelike Silbeamia appeared before them. Joalla hid her eyes when they witnessed her manipulated attack on the innocent Elveriness. Douglas tried hard not to stare at Joalla as she was exposed to them all in the worst light possible. Those who had joined the quest later regarded with awe the incredible omnipotence of the Amorga, experiencing some of her powerful vibrations even in this distant form. Each saw their own thread of the story as they came one by one to join the quest, until eventually the very speeded-up version of the events that followed held no surprises for anyone.

"Now I come to the most difficult part." Akraj held them enthralled. "We in Chjimmer know that most of you think you are on a simple quest to rescue a beautiful and vulnerable Elveriness." Everyone looked at each other. Poldant raised his eyebrows at Loriscus and then returned his attention to Akraj. "That is of course true. However – I am afraid it is not the whole story." There were several surprised gasps. "Have you never wondered why Gordagn stole Silbeamia into his dimension? Beautiful as she is, do you not think that it was a great deal of effort to take one from the heart of Elver? No indeed, there is a great deal more to this than meets the eye." Douglas shifted in his chair and wished Akraj would get to the point, forgetting that the light being was aware of his every thought. "I *am* getting to the point Douglas," Akraj said much to his embarrassment. "Where was I? Oh yes. The plot. Well it is all about Gordagn's ambition. The Lord of Zorgia has a great deal of ambition, most of it to do with becoming the most powerful being throughout the Universes. Now that may sound laughable, but all that stands in the way of success is a small band of beings thrown together to form a rescue party. In effect – you lot."

Loriscus coughed politely and raised a hand. "Um, sorry, but what does our situation have to do with Gordagn taking over the Universes?"

"It is a devious but simple plan, you have to give him that. You see, as an Elveriness Silbeamia holds the incantations to six of the Seven Doorways of the Rainbow. Although Gordagn has managed to slip the odd bathawk through, an army is a different matter. Besides, the energy of the bathawks is such that it enables inter-dimensional transportation, but the work and power involved in just getting one small platoon to pursue you all is phenomenal, and not very practical on the larger scale of things. So unfortunately the Evil One will be working on forcing Silbeamia to take to the dark side. Once she is co-operating he has access to complete domination. Few worlds are prepared enough to repel the Dark Hordes, especially if taken by surprise."

There was a horrified silence, broken once again by Loriscus. "Why Silbeamia?" His voice shook. "Surely someone like my father would be a more powerful tool?"

"Powerful, but too knowledgeable to bend to Gordagn's will. Silbeamia was chosen for her very innocence and purity. However she has proven to be unexpectedly strong and resistant, and this is what has given you the opportunity to reach her in time. She still completely believes you will come, but Gordagn is too strong a force for her to hold out much longer." Loriscus became even paler, if that were possible. His blue eyes sparked with anger as he crashed his fist onto his own knee.

"But the Elverine would never allow this to happen. My father, Nasturtia and many others would fight the Zorgians to the end despite our ethos of peace. Some things are worth fighting for."

"Ah, but would they? Now we come to the really clever part. Yes, Silbeamia is an ideal tool within herself, but what if Gordagn held another ace up his sleeve?" Akraj looked straight at Loriscus and pointed. "You." Loriscus's jaw dropped. "Not only will he force Silbeamia to acquiesce to his scheme, but he will hold a valuable hostage – the King's son. Peolis will be in a quandary, and it is in those circumstances that Gordagn will act, the hesitation will be fatal for all."

"But Gordagn has been fighting me every centimetre of the way," Loriscus protested.

"Not you, your companions," Akraj said. "What Gordagn did not and could not see was the intervention of the Amorga. The Amorga foresaw the dreadful events just in time. She sent her servant Crysgar," Loriscus turned to stare at the changeling whose colour deepened to purple, "to prevent the plot from unfolding, but Crysgar was too late. All he could do was lead you to the Amorga in the hope that she would know what to do. Of course she did. Whilst you travelled to her lair she devised a plan to enable you to rescue Silbeamia and to escape yourself. She called Camelion, son of Crysgar, from the dimension of the Tribe of Changelings, and she searched the universes for the companions who would each hold some special quality. The All Knowing One recognised that you would have to risk the little known doorways to attain your goal, but on top of all that, each of you would be tested constantly as to whether you were able to complete the mission. The truth of the heart within cannot be faked."

231

This time it was Deanna who interrupted. "Our parents said that this is our destiny and that is why they had to leave us. But they died last year. It doesn't make sense to me that this Amorga placed us in Loriscus's pathway and anyway, what if we had not asked to come?"

"Firstly, time on Earth is very different to that on Elver. Secondly, the Amorga could only give each companion the opportunity to join the quest and fulfil his or her destiny. The whole point of freedom is free will."

"Oh. Right," said Deanna, hardly able to believe that she was involved in some dastardly plot to take over the universes.

"Any other questions?" Akraj gazed around at his audience. "No? Then I will give you a chance to discuss this turn of events. After that I suggest you prepare to enter into Kephlopodia." He smiled and dematerialised.

"Blimey!" said Douglas. "That's a bit heavy isn't it?" Deanna laughed hollowly, but the rest sat very quietly, trying to come to terms with the horrific plot that had just been revealed.

"Did you know of this too?" Joalla said accusingly. She was glaring at Gremlic, her face reflecting a huge sense of betrayal. The little creature looked sad and nodded. "Why did you not tell us this from the beginning. How could you keep it from us?" she burst out with disbelief. Loriscus jumped to his feet and began to pace, Poldant had his head in his hands, and the unicorns ostracised Glore. The twins looked from one to the other anxiously, unsure of what they could do to help, and Rufus whose only concern in life was them kept licking first Deanna's hand then Douglas's. The changelings quietly moved to stand behind Gremlic. Er'nest and Drock the Outcast seemed completely bewildered. At this crucial moment the unity within the group was close to falling apart.

Gremlic drew a deep breath and then paused a moment as if searching for the right words. "Would you not have come if you had known the true enormity of this task?" He addressed the question to the whole group. Several shook their heads, of course they would have still done exactly the same thing. "Knowing the peril into which you entered, would it have helped you to know that the pressure was so great?" Once again some shook their heads. Gremlic sighed, "Rightly or wrongly, the Amorga felt that you should become a true unit before you took on the full extent of what rested on your shoulders. She knew that you would become fully informed at this point, and that you would go into battle completely aware. This is soon enough to bear such a burden."

"Um, could I just point out something?" Deanna flushed at becoming the centre of attention. "Well, it's just … It occurred to me that actually Gremlic, Crysgar and Camelion joined the quest already aware of what we all face. So doesn't that kind of make them more on our side rather than anything?"

Loriscus seemed much struck by Deanna's words, and his face lightened considerably. "The young human is right!" he exclaimed and then everyone began to talk at once as friendships were reaffirmed. Poldant winked and bowed teasingly at Joalla, aware that she was still struggling with the cruel way in which Gordagn had used her.

"Well done Deanna," Gremlic spoke straight into her head. Several golden dust clouds billowed and swirled around her, a clear sign of approval. "Mum and dad," she thought delightedly, as a warm feeling kindled in the centre of her stomach.

Er'nest sat quietly and watched his friends as they came to terms with everything they had learned, a reflective expression played across his scaly face. Akraj had shown him in a few brief, terrifying seconds how much of the mission ahead depended on him. It had been made very clear that without his huge presence the group of beings in front of him would be unlikely to survive. It was time for the erstwhile dreamy and erratic dragon to grow up.

Two angels materialised, followed a brief second later by Akraj. The contrasting absence of sound was instant and intense. For once Akraj was not smiling. "Are you ready to continue?" he asked gently.

"Yes," Loriscus answered for all of them.

"Give the gum to these developers so that they can take it to their laboratories and invest it with the magical ingredient needed."

Poldant pulled the golden cup from a pouch in his belt. Before he could hand the precious object over, it vanished, reforming instantly in the glowing hands of one of the angels.

Everyone looked at Akraj. "Now please be very clear about what I am about to tell you," he said. "First these are for you." As he spoke he pointed to the ground. A fine shimmering chain of some indescribable metal lay before each of them apart from Er'nest. The dragon looked down at an intricately woven mesh jacket of the same material. "These fine chains will help to protect you whilst in Zorgia, but only when attached to this armour which Er'nest will be wearing. The strength of his energy will be enough to create a force field around all those connected with him. Your task is not only to rescue Silbeamia, but to shield Er'nest from the hordes who will assuredly attempt to kill him." Deanna put her hand over her mouth to smother a gasp. Douglas patted her shoulder reassuringly, but his own hand shook badly. The only one who didn't look shocked was Er'nest himself, who had already been made aware of his full role in the final battle. Loriscus stood very straight and still, his eyes looking straight into those of the huge dragon.

"You would do this for me?" he questioned wonderingly, his voice barely audible. Er'nest nodded calmly, but did not speak. Finally Joalla broke the stillness to step close to Er'nest. She gently put her forehead against his mighty neck and sighed deeply. "Thank you," she said simply.

The rest of the companions shifted closer to their friend, as if to protect him now. Drock the Outcast somersaulted lightly onto Er'nest's back and took on the stance of guardian. Somehow it did not strike as incongruous.

Gremlic fluttered onto Starlight's back. "My friends, you have truly become the Warriors of the Rainbow and I am proud to face battle with you." As the tiny creature spoke, the companions became aware that their disparate group had become exactly that, a band of warriors.

"This is very well done," but Akraj looked sad rather than pleased. The angels reappeared in a further shower of glistening sparks, and gave the golden cup to Akraj. He in turn floated it across the space between him and Poldant. They all watched mesmerised as it landed in the Elverine's outstretched hands. "I have just one last thing to tell you," Akraj said. Loriscus blew out a deep breath as was his habit, and squared his shoulders. "We fear that Gordagn will sacrifice a troop of bathawks in order to defeat you before the doorway to Kephlopodia is reached. They do not have the means to enter that place and to survive. This is their last opportunity to capture you before they have to face you in their own land, and that is a little too close for comfort."

"I thought they could not survive here either!" Joalla exclaimed in astonishment.

"They cannot," Akraj answered, "but if prepared properly, the bathawks will live long enough to wreak the necessary damage." Everyone looked at each other wide-eyed.

"Could I just point out that neither Dee nor I have any sort of weapon yet," Douglas said anxiously.

"You will not need a weapon to defeat the bathawks, only yourselves," Akraj said mysteriously.

"Great," Rufus grumbled

"Keep your heads clear and concentrate on the power within," Akraj started, but whatever he had been going to explain was lost as with a tremendous bang the sky suddenly exploded into visible activity. Terrifying, shrieking bathawks, each cocooned in a rippling dark energy field, cascaded upon them from an ugly rent in the ether. The companions froze, even Akraj was momentarily overwhelmed. Only momentarily though. The Chjimmerian shot upward in a dazzling blur and the heavens became filled with a firework display of sparks as others quickly joined him. Beautiful light beings were outlined briefly against the dark cocoons of their attackers as they fought to create a barrier between the bathawks and their intended prey.

Unexpectedly it was Er'nest who regained his equilibrium first. "Help me get this jacket on and link yourselves to me quickly," he shouted. The others leapt into action. Deanna's hands shook so badly that she realised she was being more hindrance than help and so stood back and tried instead to clasp the chain around her waist. She glanced fearfully at the battle raging above them and saw with a dawning clarity that the bathawks were sacrificing themselves willingly to protect one huge creature that was gradually working its way toward them. Black eyes gleamed evilly as it glared at them, but everyone was too frantically busy to spot the danger. Poldant, Loriscus and the changelings were struggling to fit the metal armour, but with no one to explain its intricacies it was absorbing all their attention. The bathawk was loading a poisonous dart carefully into its blowpipe and Deanna realised instantly that the target was Er'nest.

"Look out Er'nest!" she screamed desperately. Rufus barked an added warning so hysterically that even the translator struggled to keep up. It was enough to be heard above the fighting. Gremlic spun and threw an energy barrier around the dragon. At the same moment Drock the Outcast somersaulted swiftly onto his friend's head, drawing his sword in mid-air. With the true speed and grace of the Elverine, Loriscus began to attach the unicorns to the armoured jacket. Joalla managed to clip the main clasp across Er'nest's mighty chest and leap aside as the dragon transformed into the fighting machine they had glimpsed once before. Flame spouted from his mouth and nostrils. The bathawk veered out of range, but continued to prepare his deadly weapon.

A dart from elsewhere skimmed Deanna's hair and with a jolt she realised that she was not inside Gremlic's protective barrier. Golden brightness encompassed her and she heard her father's calm voice. "Move, attach yourself to the dragon. NOW. We can only protect you for a few moments." Douglas reached out his hand and grabbed his sister helping her to cover the last few paces, noting the mad grin on her face as she ran. Poldant snatched her chain and clipped it to the jacket. As soon as they were all attached Er'nest began to emanate the power that Joalla had noticed earlier. The changelings transformed into replica bathawks causing a moment of consternation from the oncoming terrors, but despite their abilities neither could create the cruel darts so the ploy only created a momentary diversion. The Elverine and the unicorns were now able to turn and help. Loriscus aimed carefully and shot at full power, but the beam glanced off the protective cocoon. Instantaneously Starlight triggered a magical laser beam from his horn which although not successful clearly diminished the dark energy field. The bathawk reloaded and came on. Other bathawks were now firing darts at the companions, the sheer density of which began to penetrate Gremlic's energy field, forcing them back closer to Er'nest's scaly hide.

Akraj materialised. "Remember what you were taught." He spoke into Er'nest's head, but they all heard him.

Drock the Outcast hastily sheathed his sword and yelled "Hold tight everyone!" just as a huge blast of power surged and exploded from Er'nest's entire body. The shock wave knocked the nearest attackers out of the sky including the main assassin. Chjimmerians closed in and quickly removed the souls of the prostrate bodies, their screaming dark shadows borne remorselessly away. This seemed to terrify the other bathawks more than anything else as the ordered ranks fell into confusion, and Douglas, whose ears were still ringing, didn't blame them.

"Well done!" Akraj whooped. "The Developer will lead you to a rainbow. Many blessings my friends, luck be with you." And he was gone, back into the mêlée.

An angel formed in front of them. "Come," it said, smiling sweetly as if the world around them had not gone mad. The strange hooking sensation projected them forward at speed, the battle disappeared in a blur. Then the only thing they could possibly see was the incredible, vivid rainbow that filled their entire vision. "The incantation," Joalla thought shakily. "No need," the angel reassured her kindly as he almost threw them at a silently opening orange door. "Goodbye," it sang into their heads as they shot through it.

Chapter 15
Orange Zone -
Kephlopodia

*D*eanna knew that she was drowning. She fought to release her chain from Er'nest but could not get a grip on it as the dragon, in paroxysms of panic, tumbled around and around taking them all with him. In their haste they had forgotten the magical elixir! Gremlic tried to gather himself in order to cast a calming spell but was thrown about like a twig in a storm. They all shouted telepathically, trying to pierce the fog of terror. Nothing worked and they were running out of time, the seconds felt like hours.

Poldant, with the clear mind of desperation, ripped the golden cup from his belt and within moments had inserted some gum into his own mouth. Instantly a strange bubbling sensation began in his nose and throat, and then strangely his lungs filled with water and yet, thank the Universes, he could breathe! Quickly, hand over hand, Poldant worked his way up the metal links to Er'nest's head, aware that the struggle had taken its toll and despite his enormous strength a frightening lethargy seeped into his straining muscles. With power borne from despair he forced himself along Er'nest's neck and risking the loss of a limb in the huge snapping jaws he thrust the gum in. The dragon became calm almost instantly, holding himself still so that the Elverine could help the others. By the time a gasping Deanna had managed to force some into Rufus's mouth he hung frighteningly limp in her arms. She and Douglas watched with anxious eyes as thankfully the dog began to revive. All the while in the background of their minds they could hear a sheepish litany from a very embarrassed Er'nest, "Sorry about that everyone. Got taken a bit unawares. Sorry! Sorry!"

"You did really well not to let go of him under the circumstances," Douglas gave his sister a rare compliment.

"Thanks," she grinned as Rufus weakly blew a bubble at her face. The twins looked at each other and giggled at the sight of Rufus's floppy ears floating comically above his face.

It was only then that the humans were able to take in their surroundings. They all hung suspended in the most beautiful clear turquoise sea. There was no sight of the sky above, so they must be pretty deep, yet everything was bathed in a mellow light. The long fair hair of the Elverine floated around their faces, giving them an ethereal appearance. The unicorns gently trod water, their magnificent hides glowing eerily white. Gremlic bobbed blissfully, managing at the same time to pat a reassuring claw on the shoulder of Drock the Outcast who was still holding grimly onto Er'nest's head. The funniest sight was that of Camelion and Crysgar who appeared to be happily allowing the water to wash through rather than around them. It looked most peculiar.

"My friends, we had better continue our journey," Gremlic spoke into their heads simultaneously. Everyone looked at him.

"Okaay," Douglas said cautiously. "But which way? There's nothing here but water."

"Mmm. good point." Loriscus stroked his chin. There was a thoughtful silence. Gremlic watched them all keenly.

Joalla gently kicked in their direction and flowed to a halt in front of them. She pushed her golden hair, which was developing a life of its own, from her eyes. "Perhaps it is the same as the Amorga's lair. Perhaps whichever direction we take will be the right one."

Loriscus grinned delightedly and started to clap his hand to his head, except the water slowed the movement down to an elegant balletic gesture. Everyone just knew instantly that Joalla was right. Gremlic smiled enigmatically, glancing conspiratorially at Crysgar who winked back.

"From memory there is little danger in this world," Poldant said, drawing on sketchy ancient knowledge of Kephlopodia, "but I suggest we re-attach ourselves to Er'nest to prevent separation. We might find it quite hard to find our way back to one another as there are no navigational points." The others obediently connected their chains to the dragon, apart from Drock the Outcast who had never disconnected in the first place. The little creature's knuckles were only a little less white, his grip still firmly clutching the tall spike between Er'nest's ears. His red eyes were tightly squeezed shut and his lips moved in a silent prayer of delivery.

"Funny," Deanna thought, "this is the safest I have felt since we left Earth, and yet the poor Drock is terrified." Joalla had also noticed the situation and allowed herself to float closer to the little warrior. She began a light telepathic conversation, knowing that he would be very affronted if she put her arm around him. The Drock relaxed visibly and opened first one eye and then the other. An amazed expression lit his face as he finally took in the wonder of the limitless sea of turquoise blue.

Er'nest meanwhile was thoroughly enjoying his first experience of weightlessness. He discovered to his joy that the tiniest flick of his mighty tail propelled him strongly in whichever direction he chose. His glorious red scales, washed clean of the multi-coloured dust of Jalmar, gleamed and shone with an iridescent beauty of their own. His huge dark eyes sparkled with the excitement of new adventure. His wings opened and spread luxuriously.

"Ow! Watch out!" Starlight yelled indignantly as a wing tip brushed the unicorn, somersaulting him to the full extent of his safety chain.

"Oops! Sorry!" Er'nest came to with a bump. Camelion started to laugh, but this was cut short as Er'nest enthusiastically shot forward, jerking his cargo from standstill to full flight in a split second.

"Blimey!" Douglas gasped as he belatedly kicked his legs in a feeble attempt to stay the right way up.

"No need to rush," Loriscus yelled frantically feeling as if the chain might snap him in two.

"Oops! Sorry!" Er'nest said again, stopping so suddenly that they all bumped into each other. Only the water cushioned them from a more painful collision.

Loriscus took a calming breath, untangled his waist-length plait from around his neck, and patted the various pieces of equipment on his belt to ensure their presence. "Right ..." he began.

"Wow, that was amazing!" Douglas exclaimed happily.

"Just like a brilliant roller coaster ride!" Deanna agreed, equally ecstatic.

Er'nest grinned and puffed a little jet of water from his nostrils. "Bloody idiot," Rufus grumbled under his breath. Er'nest chose not to hear him.

Gremlic bobbed aimlessly, unusually disconcerted. Drock the Outcast was back to a full death-like grip

"Right …" Loriscus tried again. "Slowly if you please my friend." And finally the dragon got the hang of it and they all slid comfortably through the water at a more sedate pace.

The companions had been swimming or floating (Drock the Outcast) for quite a time when Loriscus called a halt. "We do not seem to be getting anywhere with this. There must be a civilisation somewhere or surely the Amorga would not have sent us to this place."

"Well, if you remember, the Amorga said this was the best way through to Zorgia. She did not mention the need to interact with the inhabitants of Kephlopodia," Poldant pointed out.

"In fact I do not remember her mentioning the inhabitants at all," Joalla joined the discussion.

"Well, this place does have several species of life within it. We know that from lessons in The Place of Education," Loriscus said. "Anyway, how are we supposed to connect with a rainbow in the water?"

"Good point!" Poldant exclaimed. All three Elverine looked at Gremlic, hoping he knew the answer, but he wasn't paying attention. Instead his gaze passed beyond them. Silently he pointed his claw. With a feeling of dread the group turned. A barrage of dolphin-like fish surrounding a particularly large whale faced them. This was not however what held them riveted. It was the sight of what could only be described as an army of cuttlefish riding on the backs of their aquatic steeds that transfixed them. No one moved. Loriscus considered lifting his hand in the universal gesture of peace, but could not be sure that this would be received as such. In his experience it was just as likely to be regarded as a sign of attack! Still nothing moved, apart from the tails of the dolphins, which undulated gently.

"Where in the name of the Universes did they come from?" Joalla gasped.

Poldant took over, drawing on his experience as a Peace Warrior. He did lift his hand in the universal sign of peace, hoping fervently that he had remembered correctly. The foremost dolphin swam a little ahead of the cavalcade, guided there by one of the brown cuttle-like creatures. Poldant took in the six arms sprouting from an armour-plate back. Beady eyes in a round head stared warily back at the Elverine, whilst two antennae which grew from its forehead flicked constantly. The mouth was an inexpressive straight line. The creature was so unlike anything Poldant had ever dealt with that he had no way of gauging its mood, but he noted with relief that the pincers on the end of the arms held no weapon. This was a small comfort as they looked sharp enough to render such a thing unnecessary.

"How do we communicate with them?" Loriscus murmured.

"I am trying to remember."

"It will speak first," Gremlic said reassuringly, causing the Elverine to glance at him curiously. Once again they all waited.

Then, just as Poldant was thinking of trying telepathy, the most astonishing thing yet happened. The chest of the cuttleman lit up with a flashing display of fluorescent lights.

"Ooh! What does that mean?" Deanna whispered to her brother. Douglas shrugged without shifting his fascinated gaze.

"Adjust your translators," Gremlic gave the familiar order.

"You mean it's *talking* to us?" Joalla gasped. "How, by the many Stars, are we going to work without sound?" As she spoke the earpieces crackled and to their utter amazement a robotic voice spoke directly into their ears.

"What are you?" It seemed to hesitate momentarily. "We have never seen your like before. Why are you here?"

Poldant blinked twice, trying to think how he was going to communicate back. "We come from another place," he said lamely. To everyone's disbelief the translator emitted a series of flashes straight from the Elverine's ear.

"Just like Morse code," Douglas breathed.

"Drylanders!" it exclaimed with disbelief. "How do you exist here?" Poldant tried to think of an explanation that would make sense to the inquisitor. Before he could frame a reply there was an unexpected rumpus followed by a surge of movement from the dolphins. Loriscus looked around anxiously to see what had disturbed them. "By the Stars! No wonder!" he muttered as the two changelings, now transformed into mirror image cuttlemen, swam to the fore. "What are you doing?" he whispered into the head of the nearest. It turned out to be Camelion.

"We thought it would be easier to communicate with the full light range rather than a single flash just coming from the ear. It is quicker this way."

Initially the reaction from the Kephlopodians didn't appear to bode well. Pincers snapped threateningly and all antennae became fixed on the intruders. The dolphins began to emit high-pitched sonar signals to one another. Loriscus gulped anxiously and the two changelings imperceptibly shifted back a pace. Joalla drifted protectively a little closer to the twins. "Get ready to run," she suggested telepathically, looking pointedly into Er'nest's eyes. The twins gritted their teeth and held on to their chains tightly. Starlight, who had been remarkably quiet, groaned feelingly. He was already suffering with whiplash from the dragon's earlier gleeful aquatic antics. But Uraj had found himself in sticky situations with Poldant before and held himself ready for anything, his attention intensely fixed, watching for the smallest signal from his chosen rider.

Poldant remained calm. "We only wish to pass through your world in peace. Our friends here meant no harm but simply use the magic of their own kind to communicate with greater ease." The earpiece flashed the information laboriously. He held his breath as a flurry of flashes indicated a heated discussion. Too fast for their translators to keep up he only heard snippets, none of which told him anything.

Finally the cuttlefish spoke. "How long does your magic allow you to stay within our world?"

Poldant was completely disconcerted. No one had thought to ask that one!

The companions looked at one another in horror as the full implication of the question dawned on them all. They had not the slightest idea as to whether they had hours or days to find the door to Zorgia. "Also," Douglas's scientific mind worked overtime, "the bigger the body the shorter time the gum will have."

"Er, so I could be in danger of drowning at any moment?" Er'nest sounded oddly calm. He was certainly no coward.

The cuttle creature drew their attention back to him. "How long?" it repeated slowly.

Crysgar decided to risk full communication and started to tell their aggressors of their problem. As he spoke the lights on his chest flashed rapidly, keeping up with his thought process as he had hoped. All eyes and antennae became fixed on the changeling. There was a scary pause during which anything might happen, and then the tension visibly eased as the dolphins took on a relaxed pose along with their riders. Douglas thought that they almost appeared to be enjoying themselves although he couldn't have quite said why.

"Let us start again," the cuttle creature suggested. "I am Kroll and these are my friends. We are not a war-like race, it is only that some strange things have been happening lately which has put us on our guard so we have been patrolling our territory. Please explain why you are here and we will see if we can help."

Loriscus blew out his cheek with relief creating a bubble that drifted away lazily. Crysgar and Camelion introduced each by name before once again telling the story of the quest. The audience began to lean forward as their interest was further caught. By the time the explanation reached the present moment the two shapeshifters held them completely transfixed.

"These bathawks that you mention, are they able to bear themselves in the nothingness above our world, seemingly suspended in the empty space?" one cuttleman asked.

Camelion and Crysgar groaned at the implications of the question. "Yes," Crysgar answered wearily whilst his son told the others of the presence of their enemies.

"So all the while we are in the water they cannot attack us, but we have limited time down here and they are waiting for us to surface to find a rainbow," Poldant stated their case.

"That's about it," Camelion replied grimly. "They must have some strong magic working for them, even Akraj thought they couldn't follow us here."

"First let us find our portal, and then we can worry about the bathawks later," Gremlic was unfazed.

"Are we not even going to take time to rest for a while?" Deanna was suddenly immensely weary.

"No little human," Loriscus said gently. "Our only hope is to arrive quickly and suddenly, before they are fully ready for us."

"Oh," Deanna squeaked, feeling her stomach clench nervously.

Rufus nuzzled his nose into her shoulder, grumbling all the while. "Stupid quest! Should never have come. I'll give those bathawk thingummys something to worry about." For some reason it made her giggle.

"We would like to offer you our hospitality, but clearly that will have to wait for another day," Kroll said. "Let us lead you in the direction of the nothingness, it is the least we can do."

"Thank you," Loriscus replied gratefully. The companions gripped their chains as Er'nest readied himself to follow the whale. To everyone's astonishment the pod turned in an easterly direction, not upwards!

"Is the nothingness not above us?" Loriscus called anxiously. One of Kroll's antennae had remained fixed on them although the rest of his body was facing forward. It took a moment for the translator to signal the question. The cuttle creature's response played around the perimeter of his armoured back displaying how they spoke when not facing one another.

"Not everywhere above contains nothingness. There are only pockets, some large some small."

"So we could find a pocket with no bathawks in it?"

"Indeed."

Loriscus had just started to smile when Joalla pointed out, "Wherever there is a chance of a rainbow there will be bathawks."

"Well, we will just have to get there first then, hold tight," Er'nest rumbled. With a powerful flick of his tail he surged after the pod which was now on the move.

Chapter 16

D espite the urgency that gripped them, the strange beauty of this water world seeped into the consciousness of the travellers. Their new friends flashed easily through the water and yet managed to convey a jaunty cheerful presence. Clearly they were enjoying themselves hugely and their mood began to affect everyone else. Even Rufus stopped grumbling and looked around eager-eyed.

A peculiar kind of octopus drifted by, twinkling a curious question to the cavalcade at the sight of the Drylanders. One of the cuttle people flashed a reply and to the twins amusement the octopus turned and tagged on behind.

This happened several times. Before they knew it there was a whole procession of unusual creatures (large, small, odd shapes) pursuing them, creating quite a festival air.

"I don't think much happens around here," Douglas grinned to Gremlic who laughed out loud. It was so surreal that Loriscus felt he had to keep reminding them to prepare themselves for battle. But the warning seemed no more real than anything else. They gave themselves up to delighting in the moment. After all, how often were they going to follow the magnificent tail of a whale whilst riding on the back of a dragon?

After quite some time Kroll shouted out (in very bright flashes), "There's a pocket above." They rose rapidly. The water became brighter as they ascended. Just below the surface the whole troop came to a halt as each cautiously perused the sky for bathawks.

"We will have to show ourselves in order to look for a portal," Loriscus warned. "The water is so clear that the bathawks will spot us long before we are ready for them. If they are there, they will be waiting to pick us off." Deanna felt the hair lift on the back of her neck at his words and the jolly mood evaporated as reality struck. Starlight signalled goodbye to the octopus with whom he had been having an interesting if slow conversation.

"We cannot surface for more than a few moments otherwise we will drown," Kroll explained, "but if there is anything we can do to help then we will." Douglas was struck by the fact that these dolphins and whale could not breathe the air as could the like-species on Earth.

"Thank you my friend," Loriscus was grateful but doubted that the Kephlopodians could do very much. "All clear so far, I think it is time to risk the mind-link."

"Won't the magic alert them?" Douglas asked.

"Yes."

"Blimey!"

Cautiously the Elverine broke the surface, only to duck under almost immediately.

"What?" Starlight shouted, anxiously scanning the skies.

"Um, we have a problem," Joalla gasped. "We cannot breathe out of the water!"

There was a brief stunned silence. "What a cock up!" Douglas began to get angry.

"Doug, you're not helping," Deanna shook his arm,

"Well what would you call it? First we don't know how long we can stay *in* the water, and then we don't know when we can get *out* of the water! I ask you!"

"The human does have a point," Drock the Outcast said regretfully. The Drock had spoken so rarely that it immediately caught everyone's attention. Thankfully Douglas drew a calming breath and recovered himself. "Also we may not be ready to leave at the same time.

Er'nest's large body will use up the magic elixir much faster than, say, mine for instance."

"Hell!" Douglas muttered, more worried than cross now.

"I could not agree more," Joalla twisted a long skein of hair anxiously around her finger. Everyone went quiet again. The Kephlopodians had not even the slightest idea of a plan, this was all too new to them.

"We hold our breath?" Camelion suggested tentatively.

"How long for?" Starlight responded tersely. Another silence ensued.

"What about ..." Deanna spoke slowly as the idea formed in her head. "What about if we wait until Er'nest gets a bit short of breath and then each of us swims about fast until the magic is used up?" Everyone stared at her. "Just a thought," she said defensively, turning a bit red.

Loriscus swept her up in his arms for a delighted hug. "Brilliant!" he yelled. Douglas looked at his sister in wonder before his face split into a proud grin.

"We will have to plan this to the finest degree," Gremlic brought them up short. "We have to co-ordinate finding the rainbow, which may not be in this pocket, with expending our oxygen supply, and on top of that getting through the portal before the bathawks are upon us."

"Blimey!" Douglas muttered not for the first time.

"Hold on." Loriscus drew a huge breath and popped his head above the surface again. In a split second he had opened his third eye and quickly scanned the area before ducking down again. "Nothing here I'm afraid, and no sign of one to come. Hopefully that was such a short burst of magic that even Gordagn himself would not spot it." He was wrong. Instantly a split was rent in the sky and two ghastly bathawks shot like bullets down towards their prey, their claws held ready to scoop the Elverine from the water.

Kroll and his friends froze in fascination, unaware of the danger. "Down, down!" Poldant screamed. Er'nest desperately plunged deeper dragging them all with him. The poisonous claws skimmed the water a fraction from where Loriscus's head had been. Galvanised into action the Kephlopodians rushed after them. It was several minutes before the panic subsided and they drew to a gasping stop.

"So much for the element of surprise," Starlight said dryly looking at Loriscus in disbelief.

"Gordagn must have his entire magical forces working on finding me," Loriscus grated. "To have scented me in that moment is nigh impossible."

"Well obviously not," Starlight replied worriedly.

"We do not understand," Kroll interrupted, "what was the other Drylander trying to do?"

"Either capture or kill me depending on Gordagn's latest plan," Loriscus explained ruefully.

Kroll looked at the Elverine in amazement and then relayed the information to the other Kephlopodians. There were literal flashes of disbelief all round. Douglas noted that the colour of the flashes seemed to indicate the mood, these were red.

"So this is not just a battle game?" a cuttleman showed his bewilderment and lack of understanding. The Kephlopodians did not seem able to grasp the enormity of the situation.

"This is completely unacceptable!" Kroll shifted from disbelief to anger. "We do not allow this … *this* … *evil* in our world. Such a thing must not be allowed to happen."

"The bathawks will leave when we leave," Gremlic said. "They hold no interest in your world once we are no longer in it."

"But this terror, it will follow you wherever you go. Nowhere is safe?"

"Not until we have defeated Gordagn's plan."

"Then we shall lose no more time. The next place of nothingness is not far, let us go."

This time there was no carnival mood, although there was a suspicion of the young cuttlemen guiltily enjoying the adventure. Determined to help, no one wanted to be left out, so the entire motley cavalcade took off after them.

As they sped through the water Douglas tried to control the thoughts running amok in his mind. They were going into battle! They were actually going to face the bathawks and other unimagined monsters – in their own lair! There would be no escape until the quest was completed successfully! If it was. At this he stopped thinking at all because there was no point, all he was achieving was a state of personal terror.

Joalla on the other hand felt amazingly calm. At last, at long last, soon she would be able to rectify her wrong. One way or another soon there would be peace for her. She carried on a deep conversation with Kroll and his friends throughout the flight and came to see that much of their ethos was similar to that of Elver. A short time ago she would have been as stunned as they at the display of violence they had just witnessed.

"We are almost there," Kroll commented. He appeared to come to a decision and reached to his neck to lift off a coral necklace with a luminescent pearl suspended on it. "This has been valued within my family for generations. I would be honoured if you would wear it." Joalla tried to protest, but he held up his pincer to silence her. "There are ancient stories of power connected with the necklace, but I do not know if they are true. If nothing else it is a pretty thing to remind you of me." Joalla was deeply touched and smiled her thanks as he placed the gift over her head.

A sonar signal from the lead dolphin interrupted them. Above, light played a dappled tune on the calm waters, another pocket had been reached. As they began to rise

Crysgar suggested that the entire entourage be left behind. They were going to create a big enough target as it was. After a heated discussion it was agreed, so a rather disappointed group called a wistful, slightly despondent goodbye whilst only a smug Kroll and his dolphin accompanied the Drylanders. Everyone kept turning and waving madly at the Kephlopodians until Deanna realised with a subdued giggle that none of the watchers understood what they were doing. Eventually they found themselves suspended a metre or so from the surface.

"Describe this doorway to me again," Kroll said. "It would make much more sense if I look for it. Your enemy will not be seeking me."

"Mmm a good idea … yet …" Loriscus was grateful but reluctant. What if their new companion was endangered because of them, too many had suffered already.

"I am not a young sproutling in the care of his mother," Kroll pointed out. "I wish to do this."

"Let him go," Gremlic said eventually.

"Actually I rather think he is going to have to," Er'nest panted. "I hope there is a rainbow here because I'm running out of time. I'll have to go up very soon." Loriscus tried not to panic. Their choices were reducing by the second!

Kroll waited no longer and took the decision into his own pincers by gliding gracefully towards the light. Within minutes he was back shaking his head as he approached. "Your doorway is not there but neither is your enemy." Everyone thought desperately for a solution.

Douglas suddenly saw the flaw in the plan. "Er … don't we have to wait for rain before there can be a rainbow?"

Loriscus literally clutched his golden plait in despair. "How stupid could we be?"

"Um … so are we going to have to hang around for a storm as well as waiting for the elixir to run its course?"

Deanna asked tentatively. Even Gremlic rubbed his face worriedly at that.

"This isn't going very well is it?" Er'nest gasped. "Sorry, but I have to get some air." With that he flicked his tail and swept upwards taking everyone with him as their chains dragged them along in his wake. Despite his urgency Er'nest managed to break the surface gently and quietly, with only his nostrils fully exposed. Water spouted from him just like a whale until finally pure clear air filled his lungs. Better still, no dreaded bathawk swept from the skies.

The companions held a conference as they bobbed about as far down as their chains would allow. "Well we are not under attack," Gremlic said, "so I suspect that Gordagn's magical beam is set on Loriscus and not the rest of us."

"So if I surface last then it may give us the necessary time?"

"Yes, but you may not be able to do that," Joalla pointed out. "You're likely to run out of elixir before Drock the Outcast or any of the other small beings."

"She means us," Douglas thought indignantly.

"Oh don't be such a … *boy!*" Deanna thought back irritably. "It wouldn't matter if you were a full grown-up because you would still be small to them, so stop being an idiot."

"Who are you calling an idiot?"

"This is not the time to quarrel," Gremlic rebuked them much to their embarrassment. "I do not consider it an insult to be small."

"Sorry," Deanna mumbled.

All of this had been lost on Kroll who was still thinking through their plight. "Do you mean that you need to wait for the time of replenishment?"

"Replenishment?" Gremlic brought his attention back to the discussion.

"Yes, you know, the point of the day at which our world replenishes."

"Replenishes?" Gremlic the wise felt rather stupid.

"When the nothingness briefly fills with particles of our world," Kroll was at a loss. Everyone studied him closely in the hope that it would make his meaning clear.

"Particles of my world would be dust," Er'nest thought out loud. "So particles of your world would be ..."

"WATER!" Camelion and Crysgar shouted at once.

Loriscus whirled back to Kroll. "Yes, yes! Water in the nothingness! Rain! When is the time of replenishment?"

"As the light dims," Kroll said.

"Now we are getting somewhere," Starlight whinnied. "When will that happen?"

Kroll thought for a moment. "In a few cycles of the coral cave." Loriscus's face fell.

"The what?" They were getting nowhere.

"Is it a long wait?" Douglas asked in typical straightforward fashion.

"No." Everyone heaved a sigh of relief, particularly Kroll.

Joalla and Crest did a funny little jig of delight together, which unexpectedly used up the last of Crest's elixir. She too cautiously lifted her nose out of the water and spouted the water from her lungs. The other three unicorns followed suit almost immediately. Delight turned to concern. They did not want to all be exposed whilst waiting for the rain. Once Loriscus came up the attack would be on. The bathawks would pick them off easily.

Chapter 17

*A*s the light dimmed Loriscus knew he could hold on no longer. He had used as little energy as possible for the past while, but now there was nothing to do but to come up and breathe.

"It begins," he warned the others.

The twins, Drock the Outcast, Gremlic and Rufus were, as predicted, still breathing liquid. Everyone else were gently treading water and trying to keep their main bulk submerged. Poldant and Joalla cautiously lifted their ray shooters. The unicorns encircled the place where Loriscus would come up and Er'nest prepared for the fight of his life. Little gouts of steam drifted from his nostrils. The shapeshifters watched and waited.

"Goodbye Kroll and thank you," Loriscus managed before he was forced upwards.

The second his face emerged the terror began. Bathawks poured from the ether spiralling down screeching hatred at their prey.

"Steady," Poldant said calmly as his friend blew the last of the water from his lungs. He and Joalla pointed their weapons at the approaching onslaught knowing themselves to be far outnumbered. Joalla discovered that she was completely unafraid as she focused her intent. Then the enemy was upon them.

"NOW!" Poldant shouted as the first bathawks came into range. He and Joalla took aim and fired. They had both gone for the same target and the double stun caused it to plummet straight into the sea. Swiftly they shifted their sight to the next attacker and were only just in time to hit it with a glancing blow that knocked it off balance but didn't stupefy it. The bathawk already in the water floundered around trying to lift itself back into the air. Suddenly long tentacles closed around it and pulled it under. The octopus hadn't been able to resist hanging around to see what was going to happen.

A third bathawk plunged unseen towards Poldant's head. The evil eyes glowed darkly as it prepared to spit a dart. A shot knocked him back and into the churning waves. Poldant knew that Loriscus had joined the fray.

Camelion became a dolphin and Crysgar shifted into the form of an octopus. As a huge dark bathawk swept down, the dolphin leapt from the water and turned a graceful somersault flicking the unprepared creature into the path of the reaching tentacles of Crysgar. The creature was sucked down. Starlight directed the immobilising pink beam from his horn, freezing another in mid-air. The other unicorns could do nothing except lash out at anything that came within reach.

Er'nest roared his battle cry and projected a searing spout of flame at the oncoming attackers. It was enough to cause them to veer off and hold back momentarily to reform.

"We cannot keep this up," Starlight called out as they gratefully took advantage of this brief respite and caught their breath.

The heavens rumbled again. "Oh no!" Joalla screamed in despair. "They are sending more!" But the rumble was followed by the blessed feel of rain upon their faces. Douglas and Deanna popped up, but Rufus didn't. Deanna held him below the water whilst attempting to keep herself above it.

"Thank the Universes!" Loriscus exclaimed. "Joalla find a rainbow, we will hold the bathawks off." A squadron of terror was plunging towards them as he spoke.

Joalla opened her third eye and Crest ranged herself loyally alongside. Loriscus and Poldant began a series of rapid fire while Er'nest threw flames to an amazing height. Starlight created arcs of sparkling magic above their heads that appeared to give electric shocks to the unfortunates who touched them. Even so the converging force began to overwhelm them.

"Hurry Joalla," Starlight gritted as he felt his magic diminish.

Joalla tried not to panic as she eagerly scanned the skies. At last "I have one," she yelled with relief. It is to the west Er'nest but you'll have to swim because some are not ready." Er'nest sent a mental warning to those beneath him as he turned and sped in the direction that Joalla was pointing. As he surged forward the Elverine lost their concentration and spun helplessly leaving them open to the eagle-eyed bathawks. With triumphant piercing cries three flew low and poised to strike.

The Elverine struggled frantically to right themselves grasping the connecting chains with desperate hands. Suddenly just when all looked completely lost the water beside them exploded as the whale jumped clear into the air his great jaws gaping. The hindmost bathawk was crunched in one bite. The other unfortunates came around instantly to face this new attack, but were caught with the full force of the enormous tail as the whale plunged back into the sea. Their screams became gurgles as they were sucked into a turquoise blue grave.

"The Kephlopodians! They are still with us!" Joalla shouted exultantly. The remaining bathawks spiralled up high and hung there as if awaiting further instructions. The companions gave a ragged cheer.

"We are not safe yet," Poldant kept his head. "The portal is in sight and still three of us are unable to leave this place."

"There will be a way, there is always a way," Uraj soothed him. "We have been in danger before my friend."

Gremlic emerged abruptly and began to bob and skim over the surf rolling in the great dragon's wake. Breathlessly he summoned a spell to hold himself upright in an energy bubble. Rufus wiggled in Deanna's arms and she gratefully lifted him to her shoulder where he choked and spluttered. But Drock the Outcast was still beneath.

"What are we going to do? The portal is above us and will not last forever." Loriscus felt helpless.

"They are coming back," Deanna screamed. As one they turned and faced the enemy. There were only four bathawks left, but that was enough. Wearily the Elverine lifted their weapons and waited for them to come into range.

"My turn I think," Gremlic was as casual as someone taking part in a party game. He held up his claw. In it's palm was a tiny spark that rapidly blossomed into a white ball of energy. Gremlic drew back his arm and threw the ball with the speed and force of a colossus. As the ball spun through the air it expanded until it reached its target. The white energy wrapped around the bewildered bathawks holding them within, then without pause continued on its journey to the distant horizon where it disappeared. The distant cries of the captives faded away. Just as suddenly as the onslaught had begun, peace reigned.

The sea around them boiled. Dolphins with excited cuttlemen on their backs leapt high into the air before plunging back into the turquoise depths. Kroll waved delightedly as he whizzed past. Douglas and Deanna grinned and waved back. They had introduced a new tradition to this world.

Loriscus took a breath and stuck his head under the water. "Thank you," he flashed to the whale and the octopus. The octopus was looking rather proud and telling an ever-expanding tale of his heroics to all and sundry. The whale however was definitely looking green around the gills. Although he had had the sense to spit the bathawk out there was still a ghastly taste in his mouth.

Drock the Outcast was clinging to the underside of Er'nest's metal jacket and he was holding forth a conversation with a crowd of fascinated Kephlopodians. No one had ever witnessed a battle before.

Each of the companions ducked his or her head down to say a proper goodbye.

"We have to go, the portal will fade soon," Crysgar murmured to Gremlic. "The Drock has still not surfaced, what can we do?"

They switched to telepathy. "How close are you to joining us?" Gremlic asked the Drock.

"My breathing is certainly becoming shallow, I think it will not be long."

"My friend I ask you now to take a grave risk. If we miss this portal Gordagn will have time to send more troops. None of the attackers returned to him but he will gather quite soon that the battle is lost, at least it will give us a slight advantage if we travel now. Our only hope is this unknown doorway that he cannot monitor."

"I understand and am willing to try," Drock the Outcast was strangely serene.

"Think about this. I can give you the energy to survive for a few minutes, but after that …"

"I understand," Drock the Outcast repeated.

By now everyone had become aware of the conversation and were quietly listening. Nothing else was said because there was no point.

Drock the Outcast climbed up the chain mail on Er'nest's chest until his head was just below the water line. Gremlic positioned himself just above it, clinging to the metal links with one claw and placing the other on the

Drock's head. The others climbed onto the dragons mighty back, apart from the two changelings who became small dragons themselves.

"Ready?" Gremlic asked

"Ready," Drock the Outcast replied.

The Elverine began their ancient incantation. The rainbow sparkled innocently in a rapidly clearing sky. As the magical spell was cast the indigo energy billowed towards them. Er'nest bunched his muscles knowing it was going to take every ounce of strength to lift them all out of the water.

A door appeared.

"NOW!" Loriscus and Poldant both yelled.

With a mighty roar Er'nest exploded from the sea, water cascading off him like a waterfall. Crysgar and Camelion flew to the full length of their chains and pulled with all their might, lending the whole of their great power to the dragon.

The door swung open like a dark maw.

As they passed into the world from which none had returned, Douglas glanced back and saw the cuttlemen leaping to wave goodbye from the backs of their dolphins.

Chapter 18
Indigo Zone - Zorgia

Z oriscus now fully understood the Amorga's plan. They had crawled from stinking, cloying water, to fall exhausted onto the muddy shores of a lake. In the twilight it was only just possible to make out the gnarled trees leaning over them, groaning fearfully in the whistling wind.

They had flown from light to dark. From beauty to unutterable ugliness. But he would have found it hard to explain why. Zorgia *looked* normal, unexpectedly ordinary. It was how it *felt*. His skin crawled and prickled. The air around him hung heavy with a disquieting threat of constant danger. With each breath he choked on evil.

"Move closer to me," Er'nest rumbled. The newly gained power gifted to him in Chjimmer emanated from every scale creating a safe haven. Thus he began to fulfil the Amorga's plan. Although entering Zorgia by the Chjimmerian doorway had not been as unexpected as hoped, nothing Gordagn had tried to do had taken the power and support of the dragon and the rest of his friends from Loriscus.

As Loriscus stumbled back he became aware of Gremlic working desperately on Drock the Outcast. The little warrior lay prostrate between the mighty claws of the dragon. Gremlic was forcing the water from his lungs. Deanna watched wide-eyed whilst the others warily kept vigil, weapons poised. Douglas stood looking out from his position by Er'nest's tail with the stance of a warrior, his boyhood left behind.

"Can you not magic his lungs?" Loriscus asked.

"No, no magic," Gremlic did not even look up.

"I do not understand why Gordagn is not immediately aware of our presence," as Crysgar spoke he continued to scan the shadows.

"Perhaps he focused all his magical power on tracking Loriscus in other worlds. He did not expect us to get this far." Joalla had tucked her long hair into the back of her cloak so that it did not obscure her vision.

"He will realise soon enough and then all his resources will be turned on us," Glore whinnied quietly. The taciturn unicorn had seen magic of every type in his service of the Amorga.

Drock the Outcast began to choke as the water bubbled from his mouth and nostrils. Deanna clapped her hands with relief. Some of the tension left the group. The Drock dragged himself up to sitting position wheezing and gasping for air, then he smiled.

"Well this is a miserable place to which you have brought me," he grinned. "Still, better here than dead!" Er'nest nuzzled his friend delightedly.

"Lift him onto Er'nest's back," Loriscus ordered, looking at Deanna as he spoke. The Drock stiffened with outrage and, waving away Deanna's proffered hand, climbed shakily to his favourite place on Er'nest's head.

"Ready? Let's move into a more covered area for the night. At least the seer will not be able to find us in the dark. Tonight we rest, tomorrow we fight." No one flinched at his words. They were ready.

Chapter 19

*S*leep eluded all except Rufus who curled up with his head on Deanna's lap and was soon snoring. Deanna automatically stroked and soothed his head and ears, finding his presence comforting. They had discovered a dense thicket of trees that gave some shelter from the whistling wind. Douglas shivered miserably as his damp clothes dried on him. All their supplies were still wet so there was no respite from the chill night air.

"Lean against me," Starlight offered. Douglas did so gratefully, immediately feeling the unicorn's warmth seeping into his cold skin.

Er'nest was the most miserable. He had never been cold in his life and his huge body shook with every breeze that found him. Drock the Outcast, on the other hand, seemed unaffected and almost jolly.

"Couldn't we light a fire?" Douglas asked hopefully.

"Douglas we have no idea where we are or whether a fire is normal here. It could alert the Zorgians to our presence." Loriscus explained. Douglas sighed and snuggled closer to Starlight. Joalla handed around damp biscuits that were barely edible and some nectar, which was.

"I'm not all that hungry anyway," Deanna murmured to no one in particular. A crunching sound caught her attention. She nudged Douglas and they both gaped at the sight of Er'nest eating a king's ransom in diamonds and rubies which Poldant had pulled from a sack on Uraj's back. Drock the Outcast was chiselling and then sucking on a pebble he had produced from his pouch.

"Make the most of the nectar, only a few sips each, that is the last of it," Joalla warned. Crysgar had been about to take his turn, but at this held the flagon out to Camelion. Camelion handed it back and insisted his father have some. Crysgar lifted the flagon obediently to his lips, but Deanna suspected that he was only pretending in order to please his son.

"By the Three Suns, I would rather face Gordagn himself than spend another night in this miserable place," Er'nest grumbled as another tremor shook him.

The nectar worked its wonder and, although still wakeful, muscles eased and bodies relaxed. Each sat quietly for a while, lost in his or her own thoughts.

Douglas broke the silence. "Drock the Outcast, I was just wondering ... I mean, I've been wanting to ask you ..."

"Yes?"

"Why are you called 'outcast'?" Douglas asked in a rush. Everyone pretended not to be listening whilst managing to casually lean a little closer.

The Drock paused reflectively and for a moment Douglas thought he would not answer. "The way of the Drock does not allow an individual to truly exist. There is no place for dreams. A young Drock may not go to the surface to catch sight of the moon. A young Drock may not wish to be anything different to that which is planned for him by his position of birth. A young Drock may not learn of the things that interest him ..." The bitterness in their friend's voice told more than his words possibly could of the unhappy world in which he lived.

"So you decided to be different," Douglas said softly.

"Yes. I explored our world until it was no longer enough, then I went to the surface and saw the huge space out there. On return I asked my father why it was not permitted to do such things. He was very angry. He ... he ..." the Drock's voice became a whisper, " ... turned me over to the

Council." There was a concerted gasp. No one pretended they weren't listening any more.

"That's awful," Deanna sounded like she might cry.

Drock the Outcast lifted his head and, to their amazement, smiled. "Yes but outcast is also free. I could never have lived within their rules. It would have happened one day."

"Weren't you lonely?" Douglas tried to get his head around the solitary life his brave friend had led.

"Yes at times," it was clear that Drock the Outcast was finished with the conversation.

"Drock the Outcast is the title of a hero," Er'nest stated emphatically. The two, enemies by birth, grinned at one another. Silence reigned once more.

The moment the sickly light of dawn filtered through the leaves the entire camp galvanised, moving with practised speed to pack up and ready themselves for the road.

"Gremlic, could we use the water flagon Taerg gave me?" Douglas didn't sound very hopeful.

"It is a magical artefact Douglas."

"I know, but we're all pretty thirsty. It's hard to concentrate on anything else."

"Then you must use your energy to create a force field around it," Gremlic said calmly.

"We're not on the Starship Enterprise!" Douglas exclaimed crossly.

"I am afraid I do not understand you," Gremlic remained patient.

Douglas flushed. "Sorry, it's an Earth thing. We don't *do* force fields."

"Then I will show you," Gremlic made the statement as if it were the most normal thing in the world, any world.

Deanna rushed over. "Me too!"

Gremlic shut his eyes and held his hand out for the flagon. Douglas placed it there and watched with fascinated eyes. "Look inside yourself. Seek calmness. Feel the energy within. Now feed the energy until it is so great that it becomes impossible to hold within. Let it pulse from your centre and flow in and around you. You will find yourself in a force field."

The twins could see wisps of what looked like smoke curling around Gremlic. The huge red eyes snapped open. "Your turn," he handed the flagon back.

Douglas closed his eyes and tried to concentrate, but his mind kept wandering off. "Let me try," Deanna said impatiently.

"Its not easy," Douglas warned, secretly hoping that she couldn't do it.

Deanna closed her eyes and searched her memory for something that had made her feel calm and happy. She thought of the moment she had tasted the leaf of the magical tree, but she couldn't hold the feeling in her head. She went back further and suddenly remembered her seventh birthday when her parents had presented a longed-for doll's house. Instantly there was a warmth in her stomach. She imagined the feeling turning into a white energy that expanded until it enveloped her entire body.

"Blimey! You're doing it!" Douglas was torn between irritation and pride. As soon as he spoke Deanna lost concentration and her new found power evaporated.

"Well done," Gremlic was impressed. "Keep practising, when you can maintain the force field you may have a drink." Because they were all linked to Er'nest the twins had no choice but to keep trying under the amused eyes of their audience. Eventually everyone experimented, even Er'nest. Instantly they were all thrown to the full extent of their chains.

"Gently, more gently," Gremlic laughed as he picked himself up. Finally Deanna could hold the protective field around herself long enough to have a precious drink. It took

Douglas several determined minutes more, but finally he managed to slake his thirst.

"Wow, now that really is a trick worth knowing," he grinned smugly.

"It's no trick," Gremlic said. "Time to go," his voice changed, "I suggest only telepathy from now on."

"What about me?" Rufus said aloud. Telepathy wasn't his thing.

"I'm afraid you'll just have to stay quiet Rufus," Deanna said.

"I was talking about safety," Rufus replied.

"Oh!" Deanna glanced helplessly at Gremlic. Rufus had no chain.

"Jump up on my back and twist some links around your paws," Er'nest suggested. Even his best leap wasn't high enough, so eventually Poldant scooped the dog up and threw him onto the centre of the dragon's back. Rufus sat and looked down on them all, his tongue hanging out happily.

"Now we must focus," Gremlic brought their attention back by speaking into their heads simultaneously. He took from his pouch an object that looked a bit like a compass. He and Loriscus studied it intently.

"What is it?" Deanna whispered mentally to Douglas.

"It is a Dark Monitor," Crysgar answered. Both the twins looked up at the brightening sky in puzzlement. "I am speaking of evil. It will guide us to the fortress of Gordagn." Gremlic turned the object over and they could just see a gently flashing white light. Loriscus looked relieved and worried at the same time. Douglas raised his eyebrows at Crysgar. "That is the life force of Silbeamia, it will help us find her within the fortress."

"Why is Loriscus worried?"

"The signal is not strong." Crysgar's face clouded from light to dark purple-blue. "We are running out of time."

"This way," Loriscus pointed to their left, his jaw set. "We'll try to stick to the trees for as long as we can. Gordagn will be seeking us by now." He led the way with Gremlic perched on his shoulder. None of the Elverine mounted, the unicorns needed to be fresh for what was ahead.

At times it was difficult to slip between the trunks and branches because they were connected to Er'nest's vast bulk, but they managed to develop a technique which stopped them from constantly snagging. The Dark Monitor began to glow. Loriscus raised a hand to call a halt. He held the monitor up and turned in several directions before finally deciding that the strongest beam lay ahead.

"We must be getting closer, why has Gordagn not found us?" Camelion questioned.

"Perhaps he is waiting for us to come to him," Drock the Outcast's comment brought them to a standstill.

"By the Great Universes I think the Drock is right!" Loriscus slapped his hand to his forehead.

"What are we going to do?" Joalla gulped.

"The Amorga would not have sent us to certain death, there must be a way through, we just have to find it," Gremlic's belief in his mistress was unshaken. "We go on." No one moved, not even Loriscus. "We have no choice," he said gently.

Loriscus shook himself and squared his shoulders. "We go on," he repeated Gremlic's words.

They walked for quite some time, the Dark Monitor directing them. The trees began to thin out and it became more and more difficult to hide Er'nest's bulk. The air grew heavier. The hairs on the back of Douglas's neck began to stand on end. Suddenly he knew why.

"Bathawks!" Camelion shouted, forgetting to use telepathy. They were thrown into momentary confusion. The Elverine grappled to drag their weapons from their belts.

"They will try to drive us from Er'nest. Whatever happens do not release yourselves from him. He is their target. We must defend him at all costs if the quest is to succeed." Gremlic's voice, loud in their heads, only just seared through the panic in time, then the bathawks came.

A squadron of six flying terrors, their huge featherless wings creating grotesque shadows on the ground, shot towards them in the formation of an arrow. These did not shriek, they were already holding their blowpipes to beak-like mouths, ready to pierce the dragon's scales with poisonous darts. Douglas only just had time to think "Drock was right, they were waiting for us," before he was swept into the mêlée.

"Surround Er'nest," Loriscus ordered hastily as he shot randomly at the foremost attacker. Poldant and Joalla were rattling off shots with the speed of an earth machine gun. Drock the Outcast stood upright and calm on Er'nest's head, sword drawn. Gremlic hovered just above his back, an energy ball blossoming in his claw, while Rufus barked hysterical directions to him and anyone who would listen. Camelion and Crysgar shifted into large frightening animals that resembled lions and reared on their hind paws to leap at their prey. Starlight conjured his immobilising beam, but missed the swiftly moving onslaught. The other unicorns reared and pranced flashing lethal horns and hooves.

"What can we do? What can we do?" Douglas shouted to Deanna desperately. She shrugged helplessly.

"Use what you have learnt," Gremlic instructed them in his unruffled manner.

"What? What do you mean?" Douglas yelled as he watched the tiny Drock somersault into the air and cut the underside of a bathawk as he twisted.

Gremlic threw his energy ball, batting one opponent into the branches of a distant tree. "Use your force field and observe the energy it will help in the battle to come."

Er'nest was spurting flames, but Deanna saw that for some reason there seemed to be less power. And then she saw what Gremlic meant. She and Douglas had begun to understand energy. "Douglas come with me and stand at Er'nest chest." Douglas looked at her as if she was mad, but he came anyway. "Bring up our force field." Douglas glared at her again. "GO ON DOUGLAS!"

"Er'nest has his own force field," he pointed out.

"Yes but he's using it to keep us from absorbing evil energy. His force field is passing down the chains to keep our auras clear!"

Douglas's face cleared. They both shut their eyes and struggled to find the internal spark. A light expanded around them. A bathawk shot his dart at the helpless-looking humans. It bounced. Unable to halt it's flight the bathawk hit the force field with a sickening thud and slid to the ground. Drock the Outcast flipped down and finished it off.

"Well done!" he grinned.

"We did it!" Deanna was beside herself with excitement. Douglas punched the air jubilantly. As the twins refocused they saw one lonely bathawk flying away erratically, the rest were on the ground or in the sparse trees. The exhilaration of battle left them and the full enormity of the cost became clear. Five dead.

"Well we are still alive," Camelion said in a hesitant attempt to comfort everyone.

"More will come," Loriscus stated quietly. He pulled out the Dark Monitor and checked both sides. "Come," he sighed.

Loriscus was right. Twice in the next hour the enemy swept from the skies. Twice they were repulsed, each time death was left in their wake.

Now the companions walked with a weary sadness. The Elverine struggled to reconcile themselves with their in-built ethos which abhorred all violence. Joalla glanced back regretfully at the bodies from the last skirmish. They were gone! She stared perplexedly at where they should have been. A slight movement in the corner of her eye just caught sight of a squadron flying in the opposite direction. Everyone stopped and stared towards the horizon until their eyes watered. Only Er'nest and the unicorns could now see anything.

"That's odd," Starlight muttered.

"Well of course it's odd," Loriscus replied still craning anxiously.

"No, but there appear to be twice as many as attacked us originally."

"I agree," Er'nest's eyes followed the squadron until even he couldn't see it.

"We are missing something," Joalla played absently with the pearl necklace whilst she tried to think. "What does this mean?" At the moment the question left her lips the pearl was clasped in the palm of her hand. To her amazement it started to rotate giving off a subtle sonic vibration as it did so. The vibration travelled up her arm and expanded into the rest of her body. It happened so rapidly that Joalla didn't have a chance to let go of the pearl. She had barely registered the phenomenon when the vibrations reached her mind, probing it gently. It was as if a light had switched on! She laughed out loud and it was only then that the others realised something else was happening. Joalla's face shone exultantly, the weariness of a moment before had gone completely.

"Are you OK?" Douglas asked, wondering if she had gone mad.

"I am well if that is what you are asking Douglas," Joalla's eyes sparkled.

"And so?" Gremlic asked.

"It's the necklace, no wonder Kroll had never seen it's power, it is only triggered at times of danger." They all looked at the innocuous pearl resting in her hand.

"What does it *do*?" Poldant squinted closer.

"It does not *do* anything. It shares knowledge!" Joalla almost skipped with delight.

"Knowledge?" Douglas's brow wrinkled and he tried not to look disappointed.

"But it has given me the answer! The way through! Listen my friends, we must walk into Gordagn's fortress and take Silbeamia without a fight."

There was a pregnant pause. Then everyone started talking at once, mainly to tell Joalla that she was crazy. But Gremlic stroked his chin thoughtfully for a moment, "Ah, of course," he said speculatively.

"You see it don't you Gremlic?" Joalla beamed. Gremlic nodded. "They *want* us to fight. Don't you see? It feeds them. Here in their own world evil is the key. Every time we kill one of them they regenerate!"

"Do you mean to tell me that all those bathawks we killed have come back to life but now there are two of them?" Deanna was aghast.

"Yes exactly!"

"Oh, by the Greatest Universes! This *answer* you are giving us entails walking into Gordagn's lair without defending ourselves," Loriscus was pale.

"Yes"

"This is a joke right?" Douglas could not believe his ears. Joalla shook her head. "Let me get this straight. We are going to rescue Silbeamia from under Gordagn's nose, ignore all his soldiers (who are apparently going to let us do this), and then say thanks very much and goodbye?" His voice rose with incredulity. Deanna chewed her knuckles to hide her trembling lips.

"But Gordagn will annihilate us!" Camelion joined the discussion.

"That is the point Camelion. If we do this right then he cannot touch us." Joalla was almost pleading now, but the changeling just looked perplexed.

"Evil only begets evil if you let it. The Amorga's foresightedness has already protected us from a terrible fate," Gremlic took a breath as they all hung on his every word. "At the moment Er'nest's energy protects us from absorbing the dark power. Every time we react with the hatred and cruelty that Gordagn intends then that energy will be diminished. Gordagn must have worked it out."

"But surely he could still kill us?" Even Loriscus was doubtful.

"Not if we combine all our strength and ability. Er'nest will protect us and we will protect him."

"A force field?" Deanna suddenly got it.

"Exactly. If we focus completely on creating such a field the enemy will be unable to touch us, we will be beyond their reach." Gremlic patted Deanna approvingly.

"So we have to walk through the middle of them and trust that they are not able to penetrate the force field?" Douglas repeated stupidly.

"I do not know if I am brave enough to do that," Drock the Outcast said simply.

Chapter 20

"This is hopeless," Douglas grumbled.

"Again, try again," Gremlic ordered serenely.

Everyone straightened and closed their eyes. Er'nest sent a power surge along their chains which knocked all but the unicorns flat.

"Er'nest! You are supposed to protect us! At this rate the enemy's job will be done for them!" Poldant was not used to being thrown around.

"I just cannot do it," Er'nest grated in frustration.

"Why don't we do it the other way round. You know, us first and then Er'nest," Deanna had been watching the energy surges which appeared to her like silver and gold threads waving in the wind.

"Good idea Deanna," Joalla approved.

With a sigh they all closed their eyes once more and concentrated. Gremlic said, "Good, now you Er'nest." And then it happened. A mighty flash passed through each of them with the jolt of an electric current. When they opened their eyes they were standing within a visible clear white envelope of magic. For that moment they knew that no force could diminish them and were awestruck.

"Wow!" Douglas whistled.

"That is *so* amazing!" Deanna laughed.

Loriscus clapped Poldant on the back. Joalla hugged Er'nest around the neck. "Oh, I say," Er'nest would have blushed if he were not already red. Instantly the force field disintegrated, the euphoria went with it.

"Oh hell!" Douglas cursed.

"At least we know what we are aiming for now. The trick is to maintain it," Crysgar was not deflated at all. With new vigour they learnt to call on the protective power at will. With every success their confidence in Joalla's plan grew.

"We are ready," Gremlic said, his voice breaking into their jubilation.

Douglas and Deanna looked at each other and groaned. "Just as I was beginning to enjoy myself!" Douglas tried to smile at his sister.

Rufus, who was sitting back on the ground between them, licked first one hand then the other. "We will be OK," he said reassuringly, sounding more like a parent than their dog.

"Course we will," Deanna agreed hugging his warm body close.

Gremlic pulled out the Dark Monitor once again. It was buzzing frantically. "The forces gather, the monitor is almost off the scale. From this moment there will be no respite until it is over." There was nothing left to say. Silently Douglas handed around his water flagon. Silently each took his or her place spaced evenly around Er'nest, apart from Drock the Outcast who stood stalwartly on the dragon's head ("For I shall be Er'nest's ears and he shall be my eyes"). Deanna pushed Rufus into position onto Er'nest's back.

"Take a breath and focus," Loriscus ordered. The force field blossomed. They moved forward as one unit, each keeping pace with the other.

At first they walked on through the last of the stunted trees easily. Then a distant noise began to intrude. It was like the whistling of a ferocious wind, cutting but invisible. And it grew. It grew until it became clear that with every step they were forcing themselves through a barrage of unremitting evil. Deanna tried not to react as she saw dark tendrils weaving around their protective bubble, seeking a way in.

"Focus," Loriscus pulled back her wavering attention.

"There is a huge fortress ahead, built of boulders I think," Er'nest stared at a shape which appeared on the horizon, his great height and sharp eyes enabling him to see much more than the others. The Dark Monitor vibrated wildly and almost leapt from Gremlic's hand. As one they turned toward the shadowy edifice. "bathawks above," Er'nest sounded remarkably casual. Rufus began to bark, shouting rude comments as the bathawks hovered high above.

"Quiet Rufus, you must not react," Gremlic spoke softly but firmly. Rufus subsided sheepishly. One bathawk wheeled away and flew in the direction of the fortress.

"Why are they not attacking?" Deanna asked Joalla.

"They can see our light energy and do not know what to make of it. To them it is as unknown as their darkness is to us."

"There are creatures sliding over the ground towards us. Many of them," Er'nest warned. To her amazement Deanna found her mind to be extraordinarily clear. For once it wasn't shouting conflicting distracting thoughts. She realised that she was not afraid. And on they walked. "They are all around us now, but keeping their distance. I suspect they are closing off all retreat and await orders." Er'nest kept them informed, his voice unwavering.

"I can see them also." Uraj tossed his mane. Misshapen beings slithered everywhere bringing the ground to grotesque life. Poldant nodded at his friend and squared his broad shoulders.

"How kind, an escort!" Drock the Outcast grinned irrepressibly.

The sun reached its zenith, and yet there was no warmth. As they approached the fortress the earth under their feet was barren and dead. Not even grass could thrive here. Before them rose an enormous gateway criss-crossed with pulsating bars of black energy, more solid than any metal. Between the apertures they could see the main fortress creating shadows high into the sky.

"What now?" Loriscus thought to Gremlic. At that moment the Dark Army leapt to their feet with a triumphant roar, revealing their twisted, tortured bodies for the first time. Thousands of feet stamped as the soldiers marched on the spot and shrieked obscenities, the incredible noise battered at the minds of their prey.

"Sticks and stones may break my bones," Deanna thought to Douglas, swallowing bravely.

He glanced at her admiringly. "But names will never hurt me!" The playground chant came back to him.

The soldiers surged forward right to the perimeter of the force field increasing the volume to a crescendo.

"They are trying to break our concentration," Loriscus warned unnecessarily.

"Well, we cannot keep this up forever," Starlight pointed out. "How, by the Great Universes, do we get through that gate?"

Joalla felt a tiny pulse against her neck and reached to grasp the pearl. "Oh!" She was clearly puzzled.

"What?" Loriscus asked without turning.

"The pearl, it … er … it's saying that the bars are not there." Everyone stared at the bars, which looked very real at that moment. Even Gremlic was momentarily stumped. The Dark Army surged again and this time it seemed they were a little closer.

"Reinforce the field," Loriscus ordered hastily. The nearest grotesques were catapulted backwards. "Do you think we could teleport to the inner walls?" he suggested.

"We would be too vulnerable whilst re-energising," Gremlic dismissed the idea instantly.

"Perhaps it's a bit like Chjimmer," Douglas had a sudden thought. He tried to concentrate on the bubble and think things through at the same time. "You know how we vibrated more slowly than them, well suppose we were able to do the same thing."

"I am afraid you are not quite making sense, explain a little further," Gremlic encouraged.

Douglas tried again. "We couldn't see them because they vibrated faster than us, I mean we actually walked through them and other stuff without knowing it was there. It seems to me that this world is so heavy that we must be at a faster frequency, so …"

"But we can see everything here very clearly," Deanna didn't quite get it.

"It's not what we can see, it's what *they* can see. To them we are probably light beings."

"Whoa!" Deanna was rather taken with the idea. No wonder they had been able to fight off the bathawks so successfully, it must have been like attacking a fast moving smear.

"Even so, we are still visible to the Zorgians, our energy is not quite fast enough," Crysgar said. "We would have to speed up considerably to achieve what you suggest, and even then I am not sure we could keep it up."

"It would only have to be for a few moments."

"Douglas is right. I can aid us in this attempt, but it would take all my power, I will only be able hold on for a few seconds," Gremlic said. The Dark Army became irritated with their lack of attention or response and reinforced their clamour.

"Ready?" Gremlic murmured. A white pulse passed through them and the monstrous army slowed to a static freeze frame, appearing suspended in mid-air. To the stunned host, their prey, already almost too bright to look upon, became a misty blur that reformed in a split second on the other side of the gate. For now the bars protected instead of threatened the intruders.

"That was *beyond brilliant*," Douglas was beside himself with excitement.

"Quickly, focus, FOCUS!" Camelion spotted a heavy blast of power surging toward them. Only just in time the force field shone out deflecting it through the gate and into the slavering crowd, splattering the foremost into smithereens.

"Bloody hell!" Douglas swore, his mood swinging from excitement to shock.

"DOUGLAS, PULL YOURSELF TOGETHER!" Deanna yelled frantically. Squadrons of bathawks were plummeting from the sky, and riding the leader was a figure so frightening that she knew it could only be Gordagn.

Gordagn leapt from the back of the descending bathawk, his squat powerful body landing directly in front of their horrified eyes. The weight of evil had misshapen his body into ugly malformation. Huge, ape-like arms ended in knotted and twisted hands that gripped a spear as long as he was, from the tip of which curled wispy tendrils of dark magic. His broad chest was so out of proportion that his bandy legs seemed attached directly to it, appearing stuck to the bottom of the grey tunic that swathed the monster. A helmet covered the flattened head, its rim settling just above Gordagn's black smouldering eyes which glared from a yellow face. Bulbous lips gaped into a distorted sneer. The bathawks landed silently behind Gordagn, their featherless wings closing over the odd little arms and three-digit hands which held their blow pipes and darts. Close to, it could be seen that they had once been a beautiful race before joining allegiance to Gordagn. Now only the odd tuft of feathers sprouted on faces that had once been noble, revealing long straight mouths overhung by magnificent beaks. Claws tipped with poisoned talons dug into the dry soil.

"Do not waver," Gremlic was unflurried. "Remember, he cannot hurt us if we hold our courage."

Douglas tried not to become mesmerised by the powerful figure of Gordagn, but his shifting gaze fixed instead on the ghastly remains of the unfortunate Zorgians that smeared the gate. He could feel his legs shaking. Deanna was breathing fast and shallowly trying not to panic, and she wasn't the only one. But Er'nest stared straight through the Zorgian lord, his head unbowed. His fearlessness flowed along the chains to his friends feeding their courage. Shoulders straightened, eyes lifted and fixed calmly on the enemy.

Gordagn lifted his spear and the horde grew silent. "Son of Peolis, you have come far, but this is the end of your journey." There were guttural cries of delight at this. The spear was raised again and the obsequious ripples of laughter died out. Gordagn was used to reaction, but there was none from his victims. His face darkened with fury. Several bathawks actually looked puzzled. "You have come to meet your DEATHS at my hands," the monster screamed, showers of spittle spraying from his mouth.

"We have come to reclaim Silbeamia," Loriscus responded as if he had not heard the threat. "Give her to us and we shall not dishonour you before your warriors." His voice carried beyond Gordagn, and the ripples of whispers through the crowd at the gate ensured that the words spread to those who were out of range.

For a brief moment Gordagn appeared incredulous, and then he laughed, very loudly. His army joined in, even the bathawks shoulders shook.

Gremlic took the Dark Monitor from its pouch and turned it over. A faint beam flickered. "She is this way," he pointed to an enormous door which stood open at the side of the building. They turned and walked towards it. Briefly no one barred their way as their stunned audience watched their prey walk serenely away.

Gordagn shook himself and then with a roar pointed his spear. A black spark shot from the tip and sucked at the door, which slammed in their faces. Er'nest roared even more loudly catching the bathawks off guard. The sheer volume caused several to step back defensively. But the flame that spouted from the dragon's mouth was aimed at the heavy wood of the door, blasting it from its hinges. Drock the Outcast shook his head vigorously to get rid of the ringing in his ears, holding on tightly as Er'nest led the others inward.

They found themselves in a cavernous hallway, hung with remnants of victorious battles. Stone floors lay cold and unforgiving under their feet, sheer walls of rock rose to a vaulted ceiling. Flames flickered from torches ensconced in metal brackets creating a dim light. At the far end a stairway swept up into the shadows.

Gordagn and his servants ran after the intruders, the Dark Lord only pausing to magic away the bars of the gate, enabling the hordes to flood in. A bathawk loosed a dart at Loriscus. The deflected missile whizzed just over Gordagn's head. He ducked and killed the perpetrator on the spot without even looking at him.

"The signal comes from up there," Gremlic indicated the stairs. Once again they moved as one, traversing the long hall in moments. All the while Gordagn and his frustrated army bayed and struck at the force field. Deanna tried closing her eyes to blot out the slavering faces, but stumbled slightly on the uneven floor.

"All right?" Joalla caught her elbow. Deanna nodded. They slowly trod up the stairs, being careful not to allow the chains to entangle their bodies. Another narrower passageway confronted them, one wall dotted with tall thin windows, the other held a long line of arched doors. This time they did not need the Dark Monitor to signal Silbeamia's presence. A faint white beam flickered from beneath a wooden portal further along. They all felt Loriscus's surge of relief and elation.

"We have a problem," Er'nest spoke into their heads. His words halted Loriscus mid step. Before the dragon could explain manic shrieks of laughter rent the air.

"And what will you do now?" Gordagn shouted gleefully, at the same moment swooping over their heads on the back of a bathawk.

"I can go no further," Er'nest explained glumly. "The passageway is too narrow for me." The force field shivered slightly as uncertainty took hold. Another bathawk flew above and landed beside Gordagn who stood legs astride with the air of one who knew he had won.

"Focus and increase the energy," Gremlic remained aware of the surrounding danger. The white bubble reinforced and stretched instantaneously filling the hall to the ceiling, preventing any others from joining the three that blocked their path.

Starlight, who stood behind Er'nest, glanced back at the wall of terror which pushed just a metre or so from his tail. "Well, we cannot remain here," he said sounding more irritable than scared.

"This isn't good," Douglas whispered to Deanna, who giggled shakily. She had always got into trouble at school for giggling when she was told off, even though it was just a nervous reaction.

"What if …" Crysgar's voice entered their minds. They listened in awe as he outlined a plan that was more risky than wise.

"How will you survive that. It is too dangerous." Loriscus was appalled.

"Do you have a better idea?"

"No, but …"

"Are you in agreement?" Crysgar looked at Camelion who nodded grimly. They both turned questioningly to Gremlic who flitted onto Loriscus's shoulder in answer

Gordagn shifted slightly from his relaxed stance. What were the mad intruders up to?

"Ready?" Everyone took a deep breath waiting for Crysgar's command. "NOW!" With every fibre of their combined being they flooded the hall with a wave of white light which took on the power of a tsunami, sweeping the enemy from their feet. Howling creatures tumbled down the stairs behind, whilst Gordagn and the two bathawks were flung against the stone wall and lay stupefied. Even as the blast left them Loriscus, Gremlic and the changelings released their safety chains and raced for the door beyond which Silbeamia was held.

Loriscus ran full pelt into the centre of the large room, his heart in his mouth. He was brought short by a bizarre sight. There at last was Silbeamia. She lay unmoving on a low couch and for one terrible moment he thought she was dead. The once porcelain loveliness of her skin was now a dull grey. Next to her a remarkably beautiful fountain cascaded with a deep blue liquid. She had been lain so close that tendrils of her fair hair floated upon the bubbling water. As he stared her eyelids fluttered slightly as if watching a dream. Or nightmare. She was alive!

He was galvanised back into action and in a few bounds was at her side, reaching eagerly to lift her. "Be careful Loriscus," Gremlic warned anxiously. Loriscus didn't seem to hear him. "LORISCUS! NO!" There was a note in the normally calm voice that caught the Elverine's attention. "You must not allow any of the water to touch you. This is the Fountain of Dreams, once in it's clutch you will be drawn into a living nightmare. You will no longer know what is real." Loriscus shut his eyes momentarily, trying not to imagine the horrors that his betrothed had suffered.

Gently they drew the couch away from the fountain's edge, allowing no drop to splash on their skin.

"WATCH OUT!" Douglas, not knowing what was happening within, but able to see what was going on from his position at the top of the stairs, tried to warn them telepathically. Loriscus and Gremlic swung around.

"It is too late to save her," Gordagn spoke from the doorway. The two bathawks flanked him. The Dark Lord's smile was strangely sad as he looked into the face of his inert captive. Then he raised his eyes, the hardness returning. His jaw dropped. The bathawks hesitated, shocked and uncertain.

Before them stood two Loriscuses, both holding an unconscious Silbeamia. Gremlic hovered above. Gordagn pointed his spear.

"If you kill the wrong Loriscus, Peolis will feel the death of his son and all your plans will be for naught," Gremlic spoke almost conversationally. A low growl of fury rumbled from Gordagn.

The duplicate Loriscuses walked quickly towards the door, taking advantage of Gordagn's brief indecision. As they pushed past the fulminating bathawks, Gordagn came to a decision. "Kill them, kill them all. If they escape we will have lost anyway."

"Run! Run!" Gremlic shouted, as the bathawks whipped out their blowpipes. The little creature threw an energy ball at Gordagn's spear knocking it from his hand. Both Loriscuses ran wildly back into the sight of their friends who began yelling delighted encouragement, which switched to screams of warning as the bathawks came rushing after them.

Suddenly only one Loriscus ran to the safety of the dragon, the other toppled in dreadful slow-motion to the hard floor, a dart protruding from his back. Silbeamia tumbled from his grasp. The first Loriscus alerted by the cries of horror from the helpless onlookers began to turn back. "KEEP GOING," Gremlic ordered.

Gasping and exhausted Loriscus entered the force field and a trembling Joalla clasped the safety chain around his waist. Panting deeply he watched in despair as the fallen Silbeamia transformed into a bathawk and charged the attackers. The motionless Loriscus became Crysgar. Camelion's unexpected onslaught threw the bathawks into momentary chaos that was increased when a blast from Gordagn, who had retrieved his spear, killed one of his own servants.

"Not me Lord!" one bathawk screamed as the point swung towards him

"Not me Lord," The other begged as the lethal spear turned in his direction.

Gordagn shrugged and took a chance, exploding the nearest bathawk into nothingness. The remaining bathawk grasped Camelion in his claws and flew out of the nearest window. A white missile thrown by Gremlic forced Gordagn to dodge. It was just long enough to aid the changelings escape.

Gordagn whirled and, incandescent with rage, threw a spell of dark magic full at Loriscus who automatically ducked despite the force field. Er'nest, desperate to fry the monster on the spot, managed to stand his ground and stare back at their attacker with eyes that held many promises for another time. The spell bounced and ricocheted off the wall straight back at Gordagn who threw himself backwards just in time. He rolled into the chamber that had held Silbeamia prisoner, then they heard a splash followed by a grisly screaming.

Douglas punched the air and only just managed to stop himself from cheering when he caught Joalla's reproachful eye. "We didn't do that to him you know, he did it to himself," he pointed out to the Elveriness. The terrible cries became louder. "I bet he has some scary dreams to deal with," Douglas felt a bit more subdued. Silently Poldant lifted Silbeamia from Loriscus's arms and looked to Gremlic for orders.

Starlight had missed most of the action owing to his position behind Er'nest, and was trying to keep up through the telepathic conversations. "What's happening now?" he kept asking. Rufus turned and began to relate the series of events, but in doing so spotted the bathawk leader taking command of the Zorgian soldiers. One bathawk nodded and flew out of the door whilst the others formed into fighting units ready to take advantage of any weakness in the intruders' protection. He barked out his observations. Even as those stuck in front of Er'nest listened, the bathawk who had flown out of the door swooped in through a window before them and into the chamber which held Gordagn. The cries had become low moans of terror.

"It will be a short enough time before Gordagn is back in full control," Gremlic said anxiously. "Er'nest, can you walk backwards down the stairs if Rufus guides you?"

"Certainly," Er'nest flicked his tail experimentally causing Starlight to jump out of his skin. "Sorry!" Cautiously he lowered himself step by step. Rufus barked directions plus everything else he could see going on. Starlight skittered and kept his feet with great dexterity until finally the dragon's great bulk reached the wider point of the stairs, allowing his chain to run freely. Instantly Starlight turned and now able to see and move properly aided Er'nest in his awkward descent. Once on the straight bit Drock the Outcast added his voice to the instructions, until finally a bewildered Er'nest begged them to stop because they were only confusing him. As he spoke he became dangerously distracted and the magical bubble shivered then popped.

It took everyone a few seconds to realise what had happened, soldiers and rescuers alike. Then all hell broke loose.

"FOCUS, BRING THE SHIELD BACK UP!" Loriscus yelled.

"Easy for you to say!" Starlight panted as he reared and fought off the charging troops with his horn and flailing hooves. Drock the Outcast somersaulted from Er'nest's head releasing his chain and snapping it back on in one fluid movement as he landed on the dragon's tail. He sprung onto Starlight's back and swung lethally at the nearest monster who tumbled back into the mêlée.

"You are not supposed to fight!" Joalla protested.

"Well our choices are limited right now!" Drock the Outcast gritted as he and Starlight despatched three more soldiers. The wounded fell into those still pushing forwards, who suddenly realised they did not want to be in the front any more and tried to jump away. In that moment of disorder one of Gremlic's white projectiles fizzed over Er'nest's head and landed in the middle of the attackers. It blossomed into a huge sparkling tornado that swept everything from its path. The main hall was reduced to a shambles.

Er'nest slithered down the remaining steps and everyone ran to take their places at his sides. "Now," said Gremlic, "the force field I think?" Within seconds the white magic formed around them,

"Blimey!" Douglas looked at the groaning heaps of soldiers with wide eyes.

"They will regenerate soon, let us get out of here," Loriscus said, one anxious eye on the supine form of Silbeamia who Poldant was now holding on Uraj's back.

"What about Crysgar and Camelion?" Glore asked quietly. He appeared stunned by the loss of his lifelong companion.

"I do not know my friend," Loriscus replied gently. "We can only hope that Camelion will find us outside." No one broached the subject of Crysgar.

As they walked from the great hall into the daylight, the commander of the bathawks sat high on a rampart, unseen but watching. He signalled wordlessly and another bathawk wheeled silently away towards the distant forest.

Er'nest had managed to walk them safely to the other side of the gate before the Zorgian soldiers got their wits back and began to reform.

"We need to find a rainbow in this forsaken place," Loriscus kept his conversation telepathic, yet they could hear the mix of elation and urgency in his voice. In the dull daylight Silbeamia looked frail to the point of death. Her eyes remained shut and continued to twitch as if she looked around herself in constant terror, observing a nightmare world upon which they knew not how to intrude.

Gremlic placed a claw upon her forehead, closing his own eyes as he did so. After a few moments he sighed and opened them again. "I cannot reach her, the dark magic has sunk deep." The first soldier threw his truncheon at them, followed by a cascade of other equally pointless missiles. "Loriscus is right, we have to locate a portal. First let us make it difficult for these pitiful beings to surround us so easily." He pointed towards the trees and everyone turned, accompanied by a jeering crowd. Rufus couldn't resist barking rude words from his lofty standpoint on Er'nest's back.

The trees made no difference at all. In fact Poldant realised immediately that they had made a mistake. Now although their enemy could not crowd them in the same way, neither could they be seen as easily. Grotesque shapes hovered in every shadow, slithering and hanging from the trunks and branches. Poldant and Joalla opened their purple seeking eyes and began their desperate search whilst Loriscus lifted Silbeamia onto the ground. The unicorns tirelessly watched the waiting hordes, their deep blue eyes piercing the dimness. Drock the Outcast slipped down to join Rufus, wiping his grisly sword on the edge of his tunic as they sat together companionably.

Douglas and Deanna slipped exhausted to their haunches, leaning their backs against Er'nest's side. Douglas handed Deanna the water flagon. She gulped thirstily before handing it back with a grateful smile. The cool liquid revived her slightly. Something began to tickle at her newly developed senses. Initially her tired, fuzzy brain tried to avoid it, then slowly a realisation took shape. "Gremlic," she whispered into the little creature's head. Gremlic who was hovering at the highest point of the force field, looked down briefly but was almost immediately distracted by the sight of an enterprising monster stealthily sliding along a branch directly above Er'nest's head. A vicious knife gleamed between its clenched teeth.

"Gremlic!" Deanna insisted.

"Yes?"

"It's Er'nest, he is falling asleep!" Everyone heard and snapped to attention. Drock the Outcast clambered back up Er'nest's neck and shook at the dragon's ear. The twins began prodding the scaly flank although it was unlikely that Er'nest could feel them at all. Gremlic attempted a re-energising spell, but realised to his horror that he was too exhausted to summon it.

"Mmmm?" Er'nest responded to Drock the Outcast's vigorous pulling which was now accompanied by frantic shouting. With a shudder Er'nest pulled himself together, forcing his eyes wide open. "Sorry my friends, but I have used up almost every ounce of power. If we do not find a portal soon then I will be unable to protect you."

Throughout the brief episode the Elverine managed to remain focused and to continue their search. Deanna bit her lip and watched anxiously. Douglas helped Loriscus to lift Silbeamia onto Starlight's silken haunches. Drock the Outcast drew his newly cleaned sword, which he held pointed at the Zorgian perched on the branch above him.

Gremlic narrowed his eyes as he stared beyond the trees. "The situation is getting worse, the sun is beginning to sink. If we do not locate a rainbow soon then we will have to hold out all night."

"I can't," Er'nest was beyond pretending.

"I HAVE ONE!" Joalla was jubilant.

"Thank the Universes!" Poldant shifted his third eye to lock in with hers. "Ah, but it is a very great distance from here, we will only be in time if we teleport."

"I thought Gremlic said that we would be open to attack if we do that," Douglas said.

"We will be vulnerable anyway if we do not," Gremlic was clearly worried. "By now Gordagn will have his seer tracking our every move, wherever we go they will be ready for us."

"It is our only option, if we do not take the risk we will be finished anyway," Er'nest sounded unbearably tired. Deanna rubbed her face with both hands trying hard not to feel scared.

"Very well, give us the co-ordinates," Loriscus made the decision.

"And the changelings?" Glore questioned, a note of quiet despair in his voice. Loriscus looked at the unicorn and shook his head sadly. Glore's head drooped.

"Now!" Loriscus ordered. The Zorgian monster in the branches above found himself dropping a long way to the ground. His battle-cry turned to a yell of shock before he hit the earth. The other soldiers rushed forward to fill the space where their victims had been, trampling all over his indignant prostrate form.

Loriscus and his guardians reappeared a split second later within sight of the rainbow and hastily recharged an ever-weakening force field. For a moment he thought they had got away with it, but almost instantly a dark cloud billowed nearby. Gordagn and a squadron of grinning Zorgians stepped from it. They were not alone. Beside Gordagn stood a woman who stopped them in their tracks. Douglas and Deanna gasped, they had never seen anyone so beautiful.

"The Amorga!" Loriscus dropped to one knee in shock.

"No!" Gremlic's voice sounded strained. The woman turned and smiled at him, her smile lovely yet frightening. "She is Rorret, sister to the Amorga, her opposite in every way. I see you have become a puppet Gordagn." He called this last out for all to hear. The Dark Lord's grin disappeared. "Open the portal," he whispered into Poldant's head.

Rorret laughed cruelly. "Do you really think I am going to let you go?" There was something about her voice that sent shivers up Deanna's spine.

Poldant and Joalla began the magical chant. Immediately Rorret pointed one long finger and began an incantation of her own. Dark waves shot towards them weaving and encasing their force field. Er'nest groaned and shook slightly.

Silbeamia suddenly jerked and screamed, her blue eyes snapped open. She did not appear to see them, only Rorret. Her frail body suddenly became too powerful to hold. Loriscus fought to stop her from walking to the witch. Douglas grabbed one flailing arm, gritting his teeth and digging his heels into the dusty soil. The unicorns surged to help, but only Crest's chain was long enough. Bravely she placed her white body between Silbeamia and the enchantress. Deanna shouted anxiously, Gremlic desperately summoned the little power he had left and threw a spell. A faint whitish light formed around Silbeamia and held her still. "Do not let go," Gremlic gasped. "Rorret will overcome my magic very quickly." Even as he spoke, Silbeamia began to twitch again.

Joalla turned around, the incantation died on her lips. Poldant, aware she had ceased, struggled on alone. Joalla's green eyes fixed on Silbeamia. She withdrew a small golden knife from her belt. Deanna saw her release herself from her chain and walk calmly towards the other Elveriness and screamed a wordless warning. Loriscus whirled, saw the knife and with fury in his eyes struck Joalla full in the chest. She fell to her knees staring at him in disbelief. She tried to speak but the blow had taken her breath away. Loriscus lifted his fist again. Crest reared to protect her friend opening the way for Rorret's spell to draw Silbeamia towards her. The white bubble popped and dissipated, the dark magic rushed in to attack them.

Douglas found himself beating off an invisible enemy. Black strands of magic wove around him, seeking to crush the life force out of his body. He could see Deanna gritting her teeth and fighting with all her might, silent tears rolling down her face. Poldant was forced to stop his incantation to protect himself, a blue door hovered half formed nearby. All the while the Zorgians laughed with delight.

"Ah!" Gordagn crowed, "Here come my servants the bathawks to take part in this victory." A swiftly moving cloud became many bathawks. In their midst was a smaller paler bathawk, from his claws hung the body of Crysgar. "And they have captured your friends in time to watch the fun!"

Rorret did not even glance up. Silbeamia had lifted her hand towards the witch and in a trance had started to walk towards her again.

"Silbeamia," Loriscus tried to call her, increasing his desperate efforts to be free.

A hail of poisonous darts filled the air. One of them bounced off Gordagn's helmet, another found the outstretched arm of Rorret. Her spell broke as she shrieked and pulled at the wicked barb. Momentarily Gordagn and his soldiers stood frozen with disbelief, then a few more fell where they stood and pandemonium broke out. Some tried to attack the bathawks, others tried to run away. Gordagn tugged at Rorret roaring angrily, but the poison appeared to have dazed her.

Silbeamia swayed and became limp again. Loriscus clutched her to him thankfully. Joalla staggered to her feet, the knife still in her hand. Around her neck the pearl glowed luminescent white.

"It is Silbeamia's hair," she managed to gasp out. "It has absorbed the liquid of the Fountain of Dreams, it holds her linked to Rorret."

Loriscus paled. "Joalla … I am sorry … I … ." Joalla just shook her head and with a shaking hand cut at the offending locks.

The Commander of the bathawks landed lightly followed by the rest of his kind, forming a barrier between the rescuers and Gordagn's forces. The smaller bathawk transformed into Camelion who lifted the still inert body of his father into his arms. Glore trotted forwards neighing with delight and relief.

Poldant and Gremlic turned to the Commander. The black eyes that stared back at them now held an amber light, the hunched shoulders had become upright and proud.

"Why?" Poldant asked simply.

"Because your presence has reminded us of what we once were," the Commander answered equally simply. His eyes darkened again as he glared at Gordagn. "We reclaim our independence."

Douglas blew out his cheeks and pulled Deanna to her feet. Rufus leapt from Er'nest's back and rubbed himself against them. Drock the Outcast slid to sitting position and closed his eyes with relief. Er'nest finally allowed himself to relax and his knees gave way, causing him to land with a thump that made everyone jump out of their skin.

Meanwhile Joalla had cut away the affected golden strands, and Silbeamia's eyes fluttered open. She smiled faintly into Loriscus's overjoyed face and then fell asleep, this time her face held a healthier tinge. Starlight presented his back for Loriscus to rest her upon.

"Poldant, Loriscus, we must leave now. Rorret will not be affected by the poison for long," Gremlic brought them all back to their feet. Even as he spoke the enchantress raised her head and focused on them once again. Gordagn seeing her revive shouted at his chaotic troops to reform.

The two Elverine swiftly continued the incantation, but Joalla wearily leant her weight on Crest's haunch, too bruised and exhausted to help.

The Commander snapped out orders to his squadron who turned to face the unenthusiastic Zorgians, blowpipes at the ready.

The door began to swing open just as Rorret chanted a curse, her voice cutting through them with the horror of dark promises.

A new volley of darts rent the air, distracting Rorret just long enough to throw up her arm to disintegrate them in mid-flight.

"Hurry!" Sweat broke out on the Commander's forehead as his troops reloaded within a split second and spat another volley. Er'nest gathered his strength and threw a scorching flame at Gordagn and Rorret, causing even the enchantress to step back fearfully.

The door opened fully and with the terrible sound of battle echoing behind them, the exhausted adventurers limped through. The last thing they heard as the door swung shut was Rorret's shriek of pure rage.

Chapter 21

Blue Zone - Isomorph

*T*he peace of blue skies and lush green grass almost overwhelmed them. Douglas lifted his face wearily and breathed deeply. Drock the Outcast pulled his cowl to shade his red eyes, but nevertheless his whole demeanour was of pure delight. Deanna sat down abruptly and hugged Rufus to her, not knowing whether to laugh or cry. Poldant put his arms around Joalla and she gratefully dropped her head onto his broad shoulder, Crest nuzzled her anxiously. With a sigh Er'nest lay full-length on the green stuff he had never seen before and found it felt and smelt wonderful.

Loriscus lifted Silbeamia from Starlight's back to the ground and she murmured contentedly in her sleep. Gremlic fluttered down and lay a healing claw on her head.

Loriscus looked around at his guardians and companions. "Thank you," he began in a choked voice.

"Father," Camelion drew their attention to Crysgar who now lay pale and unmoving on the grass. Hastily Gremlic left Silbeamia and turned his healing abilities on the elderly changeling. Everyone watched anxiously, Glore occasionally pressing his nose against his old friend's face.

A cacophony of noise hit them, causing all but Gremlic to look up. A crowd of enchanted beings sped towards them. They had taken on all shapes and sizes depending on what they had thought would get them there the fastest. They flew and ran and slid calling in joyous welcome the whole time.

"Blimey!" Douglas said. Deanna giggled.

A tall woman swept to the front of the crowd.

"The Amorga!" Loriscus gasped for the second time. Only this time it was true.

Gremlic smiled gratefully as she came and knelt beside Crysgar. Gently she replaced her servant's tiny claw with her own elegant hand. Deanna could see the glow that flowed into the changeling's body. The blue and purple energy waves began to emanate and Crysgar opened his eyes. "My Lady," he murmured. Camelion yelled happily, enthusiastically clutching his weakly objecting father to his chest. Glore performed a little jig. The changelings all began cheering and transformed back into their original shape, apart from two who became living stretchers to lay Silbeamia and Crysgar upon. It was all so bizarre that Deanna found herself laughing hysterically which was so infectious that everyone joined in. Gouts of steam spouted from Er'nest's nostrils followed by flickers of flame. A changeling child was so fascinated that he became a tiny replica dragon and lay next to his new hero.

Several hours later the companions came together in an opulent room. They had been brought to a grand building to rest and recuperate. Refreshed, washed and fed they now gathered in a meeting presided over by the Amorga. Only Crysgar and Silbeamia were still in their beds.

The Amorga looked from one to the other. They all stared back at her. "Well done," she smiled. "What you have achieved was considered to be impossible. This is a tale to tell your children." She turned her gaze to the twins. Douglas found himself straightening his back and squaring his shoulders, grinning foolishly. "You young humans have surpassed all expectation. Thank you for all you have achieved." Everyone else clapped or stamped to show their approval. Douglas and Deanna blushed red. One by one the Amorga singled them out until each was thanked properly. Loriscus, glowing with happiness added his words to hers, ending by inviting them all to his wedding.

The Amorga became more serious. "Although you have beaten my sister Rorret this time, I suspect the war is not over." Their smiles faded. "There is predicted a time when all the doorways between the Universes will open, that time is almost upon us. Rorret does not wish that this should be in the spirit of harmony that is intended. She knows that if she can gain power before the races of the many Universes come together then it will be almost impossible to defeat her. Douglas and Deanna you are the first of your kind to travel the galaxies, but not the last. Earth is set to rejoin the Universal community." Her face lightened. "For now our task is done, it is time for us all to return to our homes." She lifted her goblet in a silent toast of congratulations. Everyone raised theirs in response. The twins grinned at one another. Gran's cottage beckoned, and it felt like home.

And I who tell this tale? I also returned to my homelands. Now I sit before the Council of Twelve and hold a position unique to my kind. I am re-named beyond all promise and expectation, no longer outcast, I am Drock the Storyteller.

302

The End
(15148 the next time)